FROM THE REALM OF TIME

RECOGNITION FOR
From the Realm of Time

Political turmoil and religious strife complicate a Roman general's plans for retirement in this sequel. . . . Prill's lucid and compelling prose style weaves together storylines involving the various players in this ambitious tale. Newcomers to the series may want to start with the first book; but new readers and fans should find references to Valerias' backstory and the full cast helpful. A rousing and captivating epic that should satisfy fans of historical fiction.

—Kirkus Review

This novel is a sequel to *Into the Realm of Time* and is fiction set against a background of historical facts. At times it reads more like a series of interlinked short stories as more characters are introduced and their backstories related. Each tale is individually engrossing, as is the novel as a whole. Maps and a glossary are included, together with a cast of characters. These are a useful reference for keeping track of characters and unfamiliar place names.

—Historical Novel Society

How far can friendship be trusted? How much can enemies be tolerated? This is a strong novel full of the strength of the Roman army, the strength of family, and, ultimately, the sacrifices made to preserve the strength of civilization. The strict organization and strategic intelligence that is a necessary backdrop in planning battles involving thousands is described. There is the last-minute suspense at the very edge of conflict, the beating of Roman swords on Roman shields just prior to engagement, and the crazed heroism that explodes in fighting scenes that inspire victory and, later, the aftermath of the muck of battle. The uncertain, harsh times are punctuated by striking bits of beauty as pictured by gently warming sunrises or hazardous sea crossings or the ever-changing seasons of nature. The vine of infant Christianity wends its way throughout, at times rotted by greed and power, at other times blooming with great, courageous belief. You will be thrust into this gritty, powerful, also loving and caring ancient universe in which to live by your strength and wit can be a deadly necessity.

—Arnold Gutkowski

From the Realm of Time—Savor the victory! Mr. Prill does a masterful job of weaving historical facts into this, his second historical fiction novel. The current event topics are seamlessly intertwined into the storyline. The reader is introduced to new characters while returning characters are further developed, showing their vivid complexity. A retired Roman general struggles to make sense of his new civilian life. His wife rises to her new role as head of the household while the General searches for a new purpose in life, looking, among other places, to a journey to his wife's homeland. At the end of the novel, I still hunger for more. Kudos to Mr. Prill on another seminal work!

—Christopher W. Barden

By chance I finished reading the delightful and well-paced *From the Realm of Time* the evening after I visited the Museum of Epigraphy in the Baths of Diocletian in Rome. One of the takeaway lessons from the museum is that written texts can last for millennia, be read by others than their target audience, and offer glimpses into past times. You will have to see why I could not have scripted a better ending for my day than to read the closing chapters of Scott Prill's book.

—Greg Buckle

Like *Into the Realm of Time*, Scott Prill's latest effort paints a vivid tale of epic proportion through well-developed characters who are not always what they appear to be. His crisp, well-paced writing entices you to keep turning the page, then toys with your passions and leaves you wanting more.

—Steven P. Bogart

Whenever I had to put this book down, I could not wait to get back to it. I loved (and hated) various characters and the different storylines that all ended up weaving together in the end. This book made the people, places, and issues of the fourth century Roman Empire seem real, and I felt a connection that made me want to read on to learn what would happen next. There is love and war, quiet scenes that made me think and suspenseful scenes that had me on the edge of my seat—an entertaining, easy-to-read book that has me hoping the author will write a third book!

—Shannon Davidson

Historical fiction intricately woven with strong characters and a great story. Formidable sequel to my favorite book.

—Jodi Fabis

Prill has done it again. He masterfully weaves a tale of suspense and adventure. *From the Realm of Time* is fun to read and hard to put down. The story draws you in and races toward the dramatic conclusion.

—Rev. Dee M. Anderson

From the Realm of Time reintroduces the readers to the aging but heroic Roman general Marcus Augustus Valerias and his equally brave wife, Claire, who are surrounded by other intriguing figures all swept up in a battle for power at a time of shifting fortunes. Once again, the author, Scott Prill, brings to life a time in history that one hears little about but infuses into the story richly developed characters—some with great capacity for good and others evil. I honestly did not want the story to end as it hurtled to a breathtaking conclusion.

—Mark Chelmowski

A magnificent story of valor and fidelity.

—Mark and Karen McClusky

FROM THE REALM OF TIME

A Novel of the Fourth Century Roman Empire

The Sequel

By

Scott Douglas Prill

ISBN: 978-0-9908604-3-3
U.S. Copyright Office Certificate of Registration Number: TX 8-736-545

To Marcie, my wife,

to Jeff, Emily, and Christy, my children,

to Mom,

and

to those who come after us

TABLE OF CONTENTS

CLOSING

ACKNOWLEDGEMENTS

Nicky Galliers—second edition editor and advisor

Lindsay (Dal Porto) Pietenpol—first edition proofreader and initial editor, second edition typist and proofreader

Drew Maxwell—cover designer

Kevin Rodgers—maps illustrator for Map of the Western Part of the Roman Empire Near the End of the Fourth Century and Map of Britannia, Fourth Century

Conor Ekstrom—map illustrator for Map of the Roman Empire Near the End of the Fourth Century

Christian Stoltman—map revisor

Carolyn Kott Washburne—editor

Paul Stockhausen—advisor

Jason Hattery—document production and map input

Jeff Djoum and **Cory DeGarmo**—IT information providers

Paula Haubrich—proofreader

Robyn Adair—cover photographer

Ashlee Mongoven, Chase Deda, and **Ashley Eklund**—document production

Dan Kattman—copyright advisor

I would like to thank my readers for their wise and thoughtful comments on drafts of the book. Thank you!

To Marcie, my wife, and Jeff, Emily, and Christy, my children—I am most appreciative of your invaluable assistance in the writing of this book. Your encouragement pushed me to finish *From the Realm of Time* and to make the book a better read.

CAST OF CHARACTERS

(By Group and in General Order of Appearance)

ROMANS

Marcus Augustus Valerias: Retired Roman army general

Bukarma: Former bodyguard for Valerias

Revious: Former chief scout for Valerias

Valens: Emperor of the Eastern Roman Empire

Olympia: Mistress of Emperor Valens

Claire: Wife of Valerias; former Briton queen

Alena: Oldest daughter of Claire; stepdaughter of Valerias

Elsha: Youngest daughter of Claire; stepdaughter of Valerias

Garzad: Roman soldier/officer

Octavio: Roman general to Garzad

Honorario: Aide to Garzad

Duvanous: Former Roman soldier

Joseph: Christian bishop

Wolf: Valerias' dog

Alexander: Head servant at Valerias' Villa

Diocles: Roman general, mentor to Garzad

Tiberian: Roman general

Penelope: Wife of Bukarma

Evaline: Daughter of Bukarma and Penelope

Lavonica: Daughter of Bukarma and Penelope

Olivertos: Former physician of Valerias' legions

Severus Gulic: A Roman tribune, formerly Sivas Gul the Goth

Victus: Roman governor-general of an Italia province

Flavius: Former Roman army officer; friend of Valerias and Claire

Marian: Daughter of Flavius

Luxcinious: General for Emperor Theodosius

Divinicus: General for Emperor Magnus Maximus

Tentrides: Former chief engineer for Valerias

Quintus: Roman general of the fort at Branodunum

BRITONS

Brother Silas: Monk at Branodunum hermitage

Brother Mark: Monk at Branodunum hermitage

Father Timothy: Abbot of the Branodunum hermitage

Drostan: Son of Claire

Ruth: A Briton, wife of Olivertos

Eustice: Brother of Claire; king of the Coritani Britons

Rega: Daughter of Maxwellium, wife of Eustice

Voltrex: Advisor to Rega

Amron: Cavalry captain to Eustice

Maxwellium: Father of Rega; king of the Cornovii Britons, the kingdom adjoining Eustice's kingdom to the west

Bilgio: Messenger for Father Timothy

Bradicus: Former accountant/administrator for Valerias; now living in Londinium

Leo: Son of Bradicus

Zircronic: Scout for Revious

Weylyn: Briton leader

Argus: Usurper to Claire's kingdom in Britannia; killed by Romans

Morguard: Former commander for Argus

Gerhard: Former king and husband to Claire; killed by Saxons

SAXONS

Staigrik: Son by marriage of Saxon King Alfredson; husband of Hildegarde; father of Guenter

Borgnar: Cousin of Staigrik

Guenter: Son of Staigrik and Hildegarde

Torberg: Friend of Guenter

Wulfric: Friend of Guenter

Alfredson: King of the Saxons

Hildegarde: Daughter of Alfredson; wife of Staigrik; mother of Guenter

Lathrin: Chieftain of the Jutes

Korken: Chieftain of the Angles

Kindrof: Saxon leader in Britannia

HUNS

Oxanos: Chieftain of the Huns

Arb: An Alan, advisor to Oxanos

ITALIA VILLAGERS

Antonio Felix: Elderman of Menze, a village near Mediolanum

Erasmus: Christian priest in Menze

Marcot: Church elder and aide to Erasmus

Leticus: Villager in Menze

Elderon: Aide to Joseph

Gerlok: Son of Elderman Felix

GLOSSARY

Certain terms are used in this book. Definitions of these terms are noted below. These definitions are from the resources included in the Addendum to a Note From the Author.

Arian Christians: Christians who believed God the Father was superior to Jesus the Son, and both superior to the Holy Spirit.

Augusta Treverorum: Trier.

Ballistae: Roman artillery; two-armed firing engines. Force was derived from the tightness of the coils of sinew rope holding the arms, which varied in size from small mobile units to massive instruments; the smallest was the "scorpion." The ballistae could be constructed to discharge stones, bolts, or darts.

Caletum: The current port of Calais.

Castrum (pl. castra): Roman forts and military encampments.

Comitatenses: Roman mobile field army forces; some placed centrally, others on major frontiers.

Fens (or Fenlands): Marshland area located around the coast of Metaris Aest (the Wash) in east Britannia.

Legate: Senior subordinate of a Roman general. Typically a senator.

Limitanei: Roman frontier garrison troops in permanent stations; paid less than the comitatenses.

Londinium: London.

Magister Militum: Master of soldiers; one of the most senior military commanders—second only to the emperors—from the fourth century onward.

Mediolanum: Milan.

Metaris Aest: Roman name for the large estuary in east Britannia; currently named the Wash.

Narrow Sea: Called Oceanus Britanicus by Romans; currently named the English Channel.

Nicene Christians: Christians who believed God the Father, Jesus the Son, and the Holy Spirit were of equal majesty; together they formed the Nicene Trinity. In January 381 AD, Emperor Theodosius issued a formal letter announcing that the only acceptable form of Christianity centered on the Nicene Trinity (the First Council of Constantinople).

Onager: Roman artillery; single upright throwing arm that could lob or shoot stones with considerable force; termed "wild ass" by the Romans.

Pagans: People who believed in the ancient gods of Greece and Rome and other religious movements that were not Christian or Jewish.

Sapor est victoria! Adhuc esurient! Savor the victory! Hunger for more! General Valerias' battle motto.

Sax or seax: A sword or dagger typical of Germanic people, especially the Saxons; generally had a large, single-edged blade.

Solidus (pl. solidi): From Constantine onward, the standard Roman gold coin, minted at seventy-two to the pound; half- and third-solidi were also minted.

Spatha: Longer Roman sword; used by cavalrymen and, in later years, infantrymen.

A Note From the Author

From the Realm of Time brings to closure the saga of General Marcus Augustus Valerias that began in *Into the Realm of Time*. I do not plan to write any more sequels or a prequel to the story.

When I finished writing the draft of *From the Realm of Time*, I took a moment for reflection. The story of General Valerias and his colleagues, friends, and adversaries has been a significant part of my life for several years. Creating the characters and storylines has been a joy to me. Now it is time to say good-bye.

From the Realm of Time takes place in 383 to 384 AD, roughly eight years after the end of *Into the Realm of Time*. Similar to *Into the Realm of Time*, this story is fiction set against a background of historical facts. For example, the emperors referenced in the story existed. Britannia was falling further out of the Roman orbit. The Saxons (among other tribes) were raiding Britannia on an ongoing basis. Finally, the Battle of Adrianople, a catastrophic Roman defeat, is believed by many writers to be a milestone event that led to the eventual fall of the western half of the Roman Empire.

I have taken liberties with certain events depicted in this book, which is why it is historical fiction. *From the Realm of Time* is simply a story and not intended to be a scholarly work.

As I noted in *Into the Realm of Time*, I also have used current American measurements in this book. Thus, you will see mention of distance, weight, and time as yards, pounds, and hours, respectively.

A Cast of Characters is included immediately after the Table of Contents, as well as a Glossary of Roman terms to assist the reader with the story, including names of locations.

In "A Note from the Author" in *Into the Realm of Time*, I referred to a cemetery and the stories residents of the cemetery could tell—stories that are now lost forever. Last week I drove by an old house that was for sale. The house, I'd guess, was about one hundred years old. I had a similar feeling with the house that I did with the cemetery: If the house was a person, what stories could it tell of all the residents and lives lived there? Now those stories are largely forgotten.

Finally, I want to say, enjoy your life *now*. The future becomes the past far too quickly. As Curtis Mayfield sang in 1971, "Keep On Keeping On."

Scott Douglas Prill

October 2017

ADDENDUM TO A NOTE FROM THE AUTHOR

When I completed the second edition of *Into the Realm of Time*, I knew I would need to prepare a second edition of *From the Realm of Time*. This is because the story is the sequel and flows from the original novel. To provide the consistency between the two books, I worked with Nicky Galliers as editor; Nicky was the editor for the second edition of *Into the Realm of Time*. I could not be more pleased with her historical background information, editing talents, and advice. I also appreciate the dedication of Lindsay Pietenpol in the completion of the second edition of both books.

I would like to add three notes to accompany the sequel:

1. I have continued to use king, queen, and kingdom in the second edition, even though it is debatable whether these terms were part of life in Britannia at the time the story takes place.

2. I have tried to use Roman names for geographical locations, such as cities (e.g., Mediolanum for Milan). These names are included in the Glossary.

3. If you would like to read more about the time in which *From the Realm of Time* takes place, I offer the following sources:

Barbero, Alessandro. Translated by John Cullen, 2007. *The Day of the Barbarians: The Battle That Led to the Fall of the Roman Empire*. Walker Publishing Company, Inc., New York, 2005.

Elton, Hugh. *Warfare in Roman Europe: A.D. 350-425*. Clarendon Press, Oxford, 1996.

Ferrill, Arther. *The Fall of the Roman Empire*. Thames and Hudson, New York, 1986.

Freeman, Charles. *AD 381: Heretics, Pagans and the Christian State*. Pimlico, Random House, London, 2008.

Goldsworthy, Adrian. *The Complete Roman Army*. Thames & Hudson Ltd., London, 2003.

Goldsworthy, Adrian. *How Rome Fell*. Yale University Press, New Haven, Connecticut, 2009.

Heather, Peter. *The Fall of the Roman Empire: A New History of Rome and the Barbarians*. Oxford University Press, 2006.

Jones, Michael E. *The End of Roman Britain*. Cornell University Press, Ithaca, New York, 1996.

Kelly, Christopher. *The End of Empire: Attila the Hun and the Fall of Rome*. W.W. Norton & Company, Ltd., London, 2009.

The Bible.

I also want to add that the chapter title "Comes the Time" is borrowed from Neil Young's 1978 song "Comes a Time."

Finally, the maps provided at the beginning of this book are sketches based on a compilation of information from multiple sources.

Scot Douglas Prill

June 2020

PREFACE
Into the Realm of Time—SUMMARY

To recap the events that transpired in Into the Realm of Time*, I have prepared a summary that will get you caught up to where* From the Realm of Time *begins. (Of course, I recommend that you read or reread* Into the Realm of Time*!)*

It is 372 AD and the Roman Empire roils on the cusp of its great decline. The formidable Roman General Marcus Augustus Valerias contemplates his future. He is the battle-hardened enforcer for the Roman emperors and has been highly effective at eliminating the empire's enemies.

However, the great General has grown weary of that role and desires another path outside of his legions and continual war. Where that path will lead is unknown. His men also have noticed changes in his behavior. When his army routs a band of Goths, he focuses on punishing the Goths and a Christian priest, named Joseph, who accompanied the Goths. Valerias believes Joseph's actions with the Goths are traitorous to Rome and to him. Initially, he plans to execute the priest and the Goths but stops when his close friend and chief administrator, Jacob, intervenes. Valerias grants Joseph and the Goth prisoners a stay of execution. Jacob warns Joseph that to stay alive, Joseph must acquiesce to Valerias by putting his Christianity aside.

Valerias is not a Christian because of events in his past, and because he previously served as a general to the pagan emperor, Emperor Julian. Joseph is terrified of Valerias, who seems to know everything about him. Joseph finds refuge from Valerias with Jacob, Valerias' chief physician, Olivertos, and Valerias' second in command, General Braxus.

The disheartened Valerias reaches the point where he wants to die in battle, so he leads a small force of Roman cavalry against a band of Suevi (Germanic barbarians) raiders with his third in command, a fiery general named Cratus. Valerias survives the battle and is despondent that he survived. However, Valerias rescues a small girl who survived the raid, Anastasis, and she changes his life.

When Valerias returns to his fort, he announces his retirement and decides to go to Britannia to seek a new life—alone. He grants Joseph his freedom, who also chooses to travel to Britannia in search of a Christian path. Once in Britannia, Valerias and Joseph go their separate ways.

At the same time in Britannia, Claire, a widowed queen, is held hostage by a usurper named Argus. Claire has three children, Drostan, Alena, and Elsha, with her husband, former King Gerhard. Argus is Gerhard's relative and arranged for Gerhard to be killed by Saxon raiders in eastern Britannia. With Gerhard dead, Argus plans to marry Claire by force—using her children as leverage.

Claire is wise to Argus and fakes Drostan's death. She then has her son transported to a hermitage in East Britannia for safekeeping. As her wedding to Argus approaches, Claire flees Argus' Black Fort with her daughters, Mary, her servant, and Belator, a guardsman, who is in love with Claire.

Argus is furious when he discovers Claire has escaped and sends a feared henchman, Flavius, after the fugitives. Flavius is a Roman army deserter. Unbeknownst to Claire, Belator, and Argus, Flavius is in love with Mary so he helps Claire's party avoid Argus' traps. Flavius takes Mary away, leaving Claire, Belator, and the girls. When Argus' men close in on Claire's group, Belator sacrifices himself to save Claire and her daughters.

Flavius secretly provides Claire with a horse and directions to a house in a nearby village. When Claire arrives at the house, she is reunited with Mary. After a restful time with Mary, Claire and her daughters embark on a journey to meet Claire's brother, Eustice, who has found refuge from Argus in the western wilds of Britannia. Flavius arranges a local guide, Solinus, to take Claire and her daughters to Eustice.

At first, Valerias' time in Britannia is a refreshing break from his life as a general. Then, life takes a turn and he finds that he is no longer able to live off the land. He encounters a Druid priestess, Edith, who tells him his destiny has not yet been fulfilled, so Valerias decides to rejoin civilization. He unwittingly becomes involved with Argus' mission to purge the countryside of rebels.

Argus suspects that Claire is still alive despite Flavius' efforts to prove otherwise. Argus also wants to stamp out any elements of rebellion against his rule. Argus questions Flavius' loyalty and retains a bloodthirsty officer, Morguard, to replace Flavius. Morguard punishes the countryside, causing villagers to flee. Solinus deserts Claire out of fear of Morguard. Claire and Valerias independently join a group of refugees fleeing Morguard led by a man Claire refers to as "Alpha." Alpha desires Claire; however, Valerias thwarts Alpha's efforts to take her at Alpha's refugee camp. When Morguard's men invade the camp, Claire chooses

Valerias over Alpha to lead her and her daughters to safety. Valerias accomplishes his goal, and Claire reaches Eustice.

Valerias is captured by Morguard, who takes him to the provincial city of Ratae. There, Morguard sets a trap for Flavius. When Argus arrives at Ratae, Morguard springs the trap and Flavius is taken prisoner.

Meanwhile, Joseph finds a village where he wants to become the priest. There, he encounters a young widow named Ruth. Joseph and Ruth become attracted to each other. Joseph is concerned he will fall in love with Ruth, which would go against his vows of celibacy. Ruth has fallen in love with Joseph. To delay a decision about choosing between Ruth and his religion, Joseph goes to Ratae to contemplate their futures. In Ratae, he comes face to face with Valerias, who, with Flavius, is being taken by Morguard to his likely execution in front of Argus. Joseph must make a choice: ignore the situation and let Valerias die, or try to save the man who previously tried to kill him.

Joseph chooses the latter and begins traveling to the nearest Roman garrison. On his way, he encounters men who try to kill him, but they are stymied by Roman cavalry. When brought before the Roman General Titus, the rescued Joseph explains Valerias' plight. Soon Titus, Joseph, and a large group of Roman cavalry set off for Ratae. There, a confrontation ensues and Argus is killed. Valerias is freed, although Flavius remains a prisoner. Valerias and Claire reunite and become lovers, much to the distaste of Eustice, who is now the king.

Flavius learns that Mary is in danger and escapes to search for her. He finds her after she has been attacked by Morguard's men. Flavius slays all those he can find and brings the wounded Mary back to the former Roman barracks in Ratae, where Joseph cares for her and she recovers. Flavius seeks forgiveness through Joseph for his actions conducted on behalf of Argus.

Meanwhile, in the great Eurasia steppes, twin Hun brothers, Uldric and Rao, are restless. They believe their father is a weak and unambitious old man. The brothers kill their father, take control of the village, and set out to conquer neighboring regions. Once they establish their power base, they are persuaded by another Hun leader, Zestras, to attack Rome or Constantinople. Uldric and Rao set out to do that, but Rao grows suspicious of Zestras' plan. Rao is killed by an act of betrayal. The enraged Uldric turns his fury to the Goths, who he believes assassinated his brother. Uldric attacks the Goths with his huge army of Huns and their allies, the Alans, the Sarmatians, and the Suevi.

Valerias reaches a point of contentment in his new life with Claire and her daughters, but he believes the feeling is only temporary. Titus brings word that the emperors have requested that Valerias take command again and campaign against the Huns, who are rampaging against the Goths. The emperors have heard rumors of a possible Hun attack on the empire. More important, the Huns have forced the Goths to the point where they are spilling across the Danube River into Roman territory to escape the Huns, creating a crisis in the empire. Valerias reluctantly agrees to resume command. He tells Claire of his mission and despite his many attempts to dissuade her, she demands to go with him. He eventually relents. He also persuades Joseph to accompany them. Soon, the group is off to Mediolanum. There, Claire says goodbye to her daughters as Flavius and Mary act as their temporary guardians.

Valerias, Claire, and Joseph travel to the Danube, where Valerias' former legions have come under the control of an unscrupulous general. Titus appears with soldiers provided by Emperor Valentinian, surprising Valerias. With Titus' help, Valerias regains control of his former legions. Once back in command, he locates the rest of his former officers, including Generals Braxus and Cratus; his primary bodyguard, Bukarma; and his chief spy, Revious. The reconstituted legions under Valerias' command cross the Danube River to meet the Huns.

As they travel east, a large group of Goths joins the Romans, forming odd allies against the Huns. Valerias sets a plan in motion that lures Uldric away from killing Goths to fight the Roman army alliance under his command. An epic battle is fought in which the Huns are defeated at great cost. Many lives are lost and Valerias loses his hand in a duel with the Hun leader. The survivors persevere and set courses for new destinies.

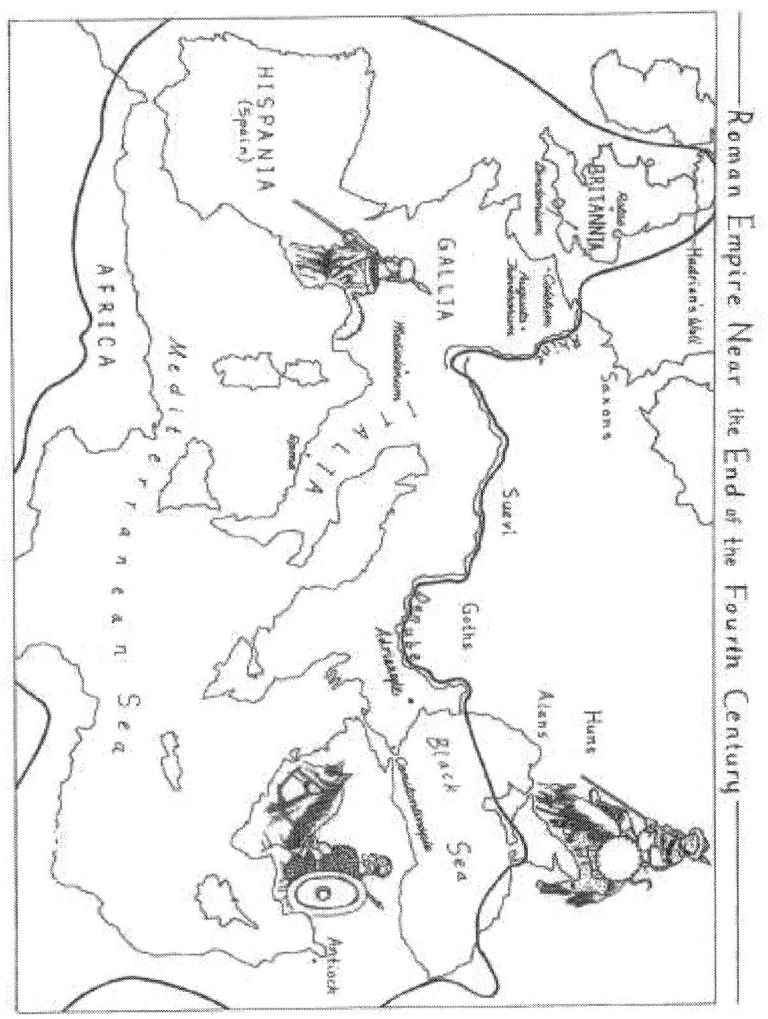
Roman Empire Near the End of the Fourth Century
Hadrian's Wall
BRITANNIA
Saxons
Suevi
Goths
Huns
Alans
GALLIA
HISPANIA
(Spain)
ITALIA
Black Sea
Mediterranean Sea
AFRICA
Antioch

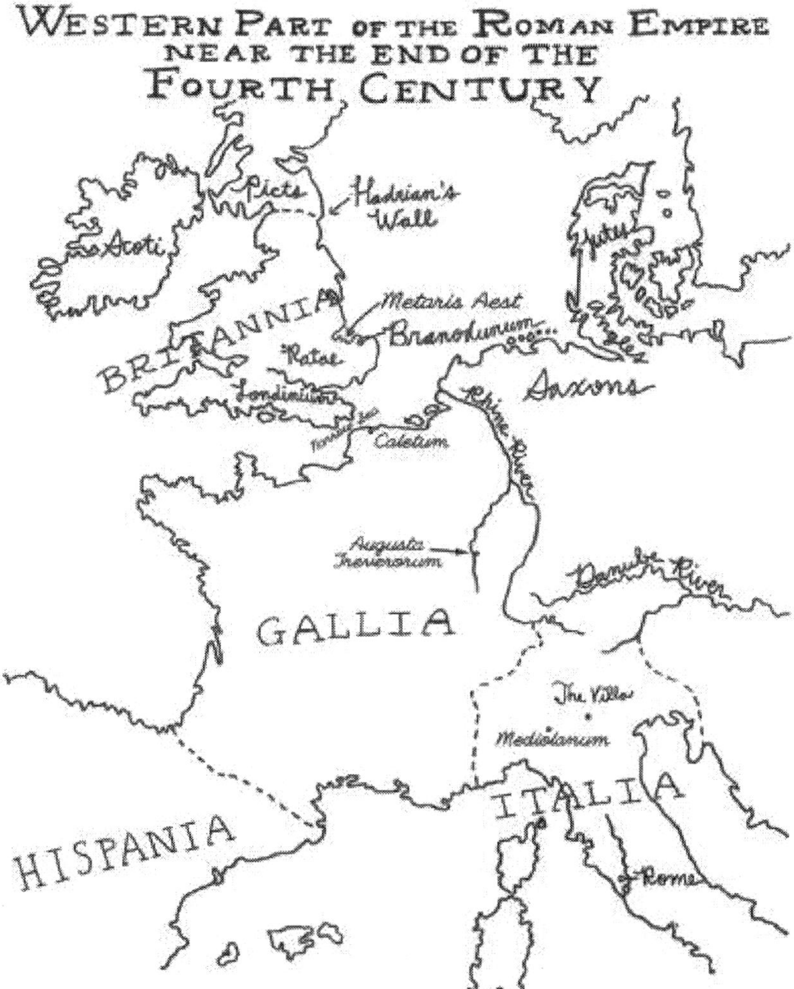
WESTERN PART OF THE ROMAN EMPIRE
NEAR THE END OF THE
FOURTH CENTURY
Picts
Hadrian's Wall
Scoti
Jutes
Metaris Aest
Branodunum
Angles
BRITANNIA
Ratae
Londinium
Saxons
Caletum
Rhine River
Augusta Treverorum
Danube River
GALLIA
The Villa
Mediolanum
ITALIA
HISPANIA
Rome

BRITANNIA
FOURTH CENTURY
Onnum
Cilurnum
Vindovala
Metaris Aest
(Saxons)
Corstopitum
Hadrian's Wall
Branodunum
(see detail)
Metaris Aest Estuary
Saxons
Ratae
Branodunum
Londinium
Narrow Sea

Opening

"Perhaps as many as two-thirds of the Roman Army perished (or were captured) in the fighting. Piles of fallen warriors and horses impeded Roman attempts at flight. Finally a moonless night engulfed the battlefield and brought an end to the bloody tragedy. Not since Cannae in the war against Hannibal had the Roman Army been so badly beaten."

—Arther Ferrill describing the aftermath of the Battle of Adrianople during August of 378 AD in *The Fall of the Roman Empire*

I

TURNING POINT 378 AD

It was difficult to tell who was breathing harder—the man or the horse. The man because of the overwhelming fear of his impending death; the horse because of the terror pulsing through the man, who pushed it to run even harder. Both were in full agreement to flee the area as quickly as possible.

The man was Flavius Julius Valens Augustus, the Eastern Roman emperor. He had just witnessed the destruction of his mighty army by the Goths at a place called Adrianople, located approximately one hundred and thirty miles northwest from his capital at Constantinople.

What started out as a great day for the empire was now a complete disaster. The Roman army had been crushed by the Goths, with the remnants in full flight. All the Roman soldiers who were wounded or could not escape were slaughtered unmercifully. Death watched with glee as blood washed over the countryside.

Emperor Valens believed that if he was captured, the Goths would parade him about as a spoil of their victory. The Goths would seal his fate in a manner similar to that of Roman Emperor Valerian, who had been captured by the Persian King Shapur I a century earlier. He accepted as truth the persistent rumors that the unfortunate late emperor had been flayed alive and his skin stuffed with straw.

Valens moved his thoughts away from that dreadful scenario and, in a brief moment of clarity, sensed a pain in his side. When he tried to rub the area, he felt a sharp, burning sensation. The arrow wedged inside his rib cage had penetrated his left lung. Blood oozed from the wound and soaked his clothes. His breaths became labored. *Perhaps I will die before the Goths capture me*, he thought, and said a quick prayer to God to save his soul.

In the chaos after the battle, Valens had been separated from his guard, his generals, and his loyal eunuchs. However, he was fortunate because it was twilight; darkness was about to envelop the landscape. The moonless night would provide cover for him. Unfortunately, Emperor Valens was not a man who could survive on his own.

A large man with dark skin in Roman battle dress rode up beside Valens on a black horse. At first, Valens did not know what to think of him. He was thankful, though—the large man was a Roman. But the pain took over his mind and before Valens could say anything, the large man easily pulled him onto his own horse.

"I am a loyal subject of Rome, Emperor," the large man said reassuringly. "I will take you to safety. I have friends in the woods across that ridge."

"What friends? And who are you?" Valens spoke meekly with eyes that could barely make out the shape of his rescuer.

"In time, Emperor. Now, just rest."

The two men rode by a barn where several Roman soldiers stood nearby. One solider recognized Valens and shouted for him and the large rider to join them in the barn.

"I am taking the emperor to safety in the woods," the large man shouted. "I would not stay in that barn, if I was you. The Goths will trap you in there. You will have better fortune in the woods."

The soldiers were barely visible in the growing darkness. They again urged Valens and his rider to join them, but the large man just waved. He continued to carry Valens by horseback into the woods.

The forest was abundant with vegetation; thickets of scrub dodged the dark shadows of the tall canopies. Even in the August heat, coolness permeated the woods.

Valens lost and regained consciousness several times as the large man wound his way over the forest floor. Once when he awoke, Valens inquired, "How can you know where we are going?"

The large man answered, "It is marked. Even at night I can follow the trail. We will be at our destination soon. Rest, Emperor."

About a half hour later, the two men slowly rode into a clearing. An old woodcutter's hut appeared to the south, illuminated by a torch. The hut had a poorly covered thatched roof with old wooden walls on three sides. The south side of the hut was partially exposed to the elements. It had been years since anyone had used it, as was evident from its dilapidated condition.

The man gently lifted Valens off his horse and carried him into the shelter. A large pile of leaves covered an area on the dirt floor at the back, serving as a rudimentary bed. The large man carefully laid Valens down, the dry leaves rustling as he settled. He opened Valens' tunic and stared at the wound. He straightened again and walked outside with a grimace.

The man surveyed the area around the hut. When he saw no sign of life, he gave the call of a night bird. He waited a short time before he repeated the call. He walked back into the hut and stood silently. He lit a second small torch and mounted it on the inside wall. Flickers of light from the torch broke the dark's hold. He could hear Valens' raspy cough, but could do nothing.

From the southwest, three figures emerged from the forest and rode slowly on their horses through the clearing. The man in front was thin and short with a mustache that smothered his upper lip and curved down on both sides of his mouth. He carried a lighted torch. Behind him came an older man with short, almost gray hair and a neatly cropped beard. The last to arrive was a woman in her mid-thirties. She had a pretty face with long, black hair that curled across the top of her cloak. Her face was starkly pale in the torchlight, which contrasted sharply with her crimson cloak and dark hair. She was someone who would be noticed in a crowd—and by an emperor. She had become Valens' mistress within days of their initial meeting.

The thin, mustachioed man dismounted first and walked quickly over to the woman to help her down from her horse. The large man assisted the older man as he dismounted.

The older man had a tired, worn face. He looked into the eyes of the large man and said, "Bukarma, tell me what has happened. I know it is not good."

"Marcus, it is worse than what you could ever imagine."

"Why?" Marcus Augustus Valerias appeared subdued.

"The army was soundly defeated and is in the final stage of being slaughtered. Only the impending darkness will prevent complete annihilation. I was fortunate to bring the emperor here. I never would have thought being his bodyguard would be such a harrowing experience. You should know, the emperor has taken a deep wound from an arrow. I fear there is nothing we can do for him. This day is a complete catastrophe."

The woman interjected, "I feared this would happen! When I last spoke to the emperor, he was confident of a great victory. Thank you, Marcus, for bringing me to this place. Where is he?"

"In the hut." Bukarma pointed to the wooden structure behind him. "You must not tell him about the battle. It is better that he not know."

The woman rushed into the hut and bent down by Valens.

Valerias' eyes followed her into the shelter. Bukarma returned to Valerias and the mustachioed man. Valerias raised the stump of his left hand, which was covered by a forged metal cylinder, and said, clearly frustrated, "Tell me more."

"Emperor Valens was foolish," Bukarma answered in a hushed voice. "He should have waited for Emperor Gratian before attacking, and he should have had a better battle plan. He wanted for himself all the glory such a victory could bring. Instead, he achieved disaster, and now he lies on a shit bed dying in some unknown forest."

"Revious, what do you think?" Valerias focused his attention on the thin man.

Revious spoke quietly. "That does not matter now. What does matter is that we leave this place soon, with or without the emperor and his woman. It will not be long before the Goth war parties find us."

"It is amazing," Valerias said softly. "Four short years ago the Goths were our allies in fighting the Huns, and now we hide like scared children from them. Four years!"

Valerias scowled; silence followed. He was thinking long term while Revious focused on the short term.

Bukarma broke the silence. "Who is this woman, Marcus?"

"Her name is Olympia. General Hyperion, who adopted me after my parents were killed, had a daughter late in life with a woman I never met. I knew of Olympia, but had never seen her until recently.

“She appeared unexpectedly at my home and begged that I look after her lover, Emperor Valens. She had a premonition that something very bad was going to happen to him. I agreed, and that was when I reached out for you two. Fortunately, Bukarma, you were nearby and not in Africa; and you, Revious, are always easy to locate.”

Valerias continued, “Bukarma, you are the ultimate bodyguard, and that is why I wanted you near the emperor during the battle. At great risk, you performed your task to perfection. I know placing you in the battlefield was precarious, and I am deeply grateful to you. Revious, you are a superb scout, even with a mouth that sometimes needs to be stitched shut. I knew you would get us safely near the emperor in case of either victory or defeat. Now I am counting on you to get us out of this place.”

Valerias spoke quietly to ensure that Valens and Olympia did not overhear him. He did not need to worry; Valens coughed blood and Olympia called for Valerias. Valerias, Bukarma, and Revious entered the hut and knelt by Valens. When Valens saw Valerias, his face brightened ever so slightly.

“My General, I was foolish today. I should have had you at my side leading us to victory. I don’t know why I didn’t ask for you. Damn hindsight!”

“I retired, Emperor. But do not worry; we can come back from this. Soon you will be well. I will join you, and we shall deal severe retribution to our enemies!”

“I can always count on you and trust you, General. I wish you were right, but there will not be a next time.”

Valens started coughing again and reached for Olympia’s hand. “My love, if I could do things differently . . .”

Valens’ voice trailed off. After one more soft cough, the rasping breathing quietened and his wounded chest was still.

Valerias looked at Revious, who bent over and placed his ear near Valens' mouth. He signaled that Emperor Valens was dead.

Valerias spoke to Olympia. "I am sorry, my sister. The emperor is with his Christian God now."

Olympia let out a cry. "My love, don't go! Not yet." She placed her head on Valens' chest. After a few moments of sobbing, she looked up at Valerias, tears freely flowing down her pale cheeks.

"Marcus, please give me a few moments with our emperor, and then we can leave this place."

Valerias nodded and waved to Bukarma and Revious to follow him outside. They stood several steps away from the ramshackle little building to give Olympia her privacy.

"Does Claire know about Olympia and why you are here?" Revious gave Valerias and Bukarma a quizzical look.

"Of course," Valerias answered. "We have no secrets." His tone belied the certainty of his words.

"She is not happy, though, I will wager," Bukarma speculated before Valerias could continue.

Valerias started to respond, but was interrupted by the sound of something hitting the ground inside. Revious reached the hut first, followed by Bukarma and Valerias. They saw Olympia slumped over Valens' chest. Revious gently pulled her up and saw a small thin knife pushed deep into her chest. She had died instantly and quietly. Blood from the emperor and his mistress mingled and flowed together into the earthen floor.

"They are together now, wherever that may be." Valerias spoke to no one in particular. He appeared unfazed by what had just happened.

Turning to Bukarma and Revious, he said, "We cannot take them with us, so we must build a pyre with the materials available to us. The Goths will surely come this way soon. I want no evidence of who was here or what transpired."

The men quickly gathered as much dry wood as possible and put it inside and around the hut. Valerias asked Bukarma to retrieve the emperor's ring and give it to him.

"Do either of them have other jewelry that could give away their status?"

Revious said both Valens and Olympia had necklaces, and Olympia also wore a jeweled ring indicative of royalty. The jewelry was removed and given to Valerias, who buried it deep in the woods.

Valerias returned to the shed and nodded to Revious. Revious and Bukarma started a fire using the torches mounted to the hut.

As the little wooden building began to burn, Valerias gazed at it and said, "May their God look after them in eternity. May it be a pleasant rest. For those of us left on this earth, there will be no such rest."

The fire in the hut swelled into an inferno. The burning wood crackled and sparks flew in every direction. The air quickly filled with smoke. The ground around the hut started burning and soon some of the surrounding trees were afire.

"That will alert the Goths," Bukarma noted calmly.

Off in the distance, a barely visible plume of smoke rose into the night sky, covering the stars.

"That is the barn where some soldiers decided to make a stand. I urged them to join me, but no one chose to do so," Bukarma recounted. "Now they burn. That is one way I do not want to die!"

Valerias watched the fire consume the hut as he also kept an eye on the outline of the smoke plume in the distance.

After a few moments of quiet, Valerias turned to Revious. “Get us out of here! The barbarians are many, we are few, and time is short!”

PART I

"It is Our will that all peoples ruled by the administration of Our Clemency shall practice that religion which the divine Peter the Apostle transmitted to the Romans . . . this is the religion followed by Bishop Damasus of Rome and by Bishop Peter of Alexandria, a man of apostolic sanctity: that is, according to the apostolic discipline of the evangelical doctrine, we shall believe in the single deity of the Father, the Son and the Holy Ghost under the concept of equal majesty and of the Holy Trinity.

"We command that persons who follow this rule shall embrace the name of catholic Christians. The rest, however, whom we judge demented and insane, shall carry the infamy of heretical dogmas. Their meeting places shall not receive the name of churches, and they shall be smitten first by Divine Vengeance, and secondly by the retribution of hostility which We shall assume in accordance with Divine Judgment."

—Edict issued from Thessalonica in January 380 AD by Emperor Theodosius to the people of Constantinople, taken from *AD 381 Heretics, Pagans and the Christian State,* by Charles Freeman

II

THE VILLA

Five years had passed since the Roman disaster at Adrianople in August 378 AD. The Roman Empire managed to survive one of its greatest defeats; however, its foundation had been severely weakened. The Goths roamed wild through a large portion of the empire, terrorizing the countryside. The possibility of such an occurrence would have been doubted by the average Roman even a few short years before Adrianople.

During that time, Valerias combined his extensive assets consisting of those inherited from his deceased parents and his deceased adopted father, as well as his own wealth. He purchased a vast estate located approximately fifty miles east of Mediolanum. In the center of the estate was a cluster of buildings known as the Villa. Valerias called the largest building the Grand House because of its importance to him; it had been built by a Roman senator several decades earlier.

The Grand House was a quadrangle, with an open atrium occupying the center. The building was one story with a small basement area that housed the furnace. A hypocaust conveyed heat from the furnace throughout the building, keeping it warm in the cool winters. The white outer walls were constructed of bricks and cement, and the smooth inside walls were decorated with frescoes. The roof was covered in red tiles.

The main entrance to the Grand House was on the south side. Upon entering, a visitor first admired the atrium, which had a garden and reflection pond, and was used for receptions during favorable weather. Busts of Emperors Julian and Valentinian on marble bases were prominently displayed on pedestals. An eclectic group of frescoes adorned the walls, conveying famous battles, landscapes, and scenes portraying the gods. Valerias mused to himself that the fiasco of Adrianople would never be painted as a fresco.

The floors of the building were primarily tile. In the atrium, the floor was covered with elaborate mosaics of animals, both mythological and real. Valerias' favorite image showed a scene of wolves chasing Suevi barbarians.

The Grand House served as the residence for Valerias' family, high-ranking attendants, and guests. Living quarters and Valerias' study were located on the eastern side of the Grand House. The Great Room occupied the west wing, where Valerias hosted many functions, such as banquets and large meetings. The northern portion of the Grand House was where the kitchen and senior attendant quarters were located.

A number of smaller buildings surrounded the main structure. Lower-ranked attendants and slaves were quartered in several of them and in the stables. Other buildings were used for storing grain, other foodstuffs, tools, equipment, and weapons.

The rest of the estate stretched for miles in all directions from the Villa. Freeborn people occupied the estate and farmed the arable land. Portions of the proceeds from the tenant farms were given to Valerias as tributum or tax. Valerias also owned tracts of land farther east and not contiguous with the central estate.

The Villa was perfectly situated for Valerias—close to Mediolanum and the emperor's court, but not too close. The Western Roman emperor was a younger man named Gratian, the son of Emperor Valentinian. In Constantinople, the Eastern Roman emperor was Theodosius, who had succeeded Valens. Valerias knew each emperor personally.

Valerias lived at the Villa with his wife Claire, a former queen of Britannia, and her two daughters from her first marriage, Alena and Elsha, adopted by Valerias when he married Claire. Even though Valerias was not their father by blood, the bonds among the four were strong.

Claire spent most of her time tending to the needs of the Villa, including overseeing crop production. When Claire was a child and young woman in Britannia, she learned farming techniques from her father. Having been a soldier almost his entire life, Valerias knew virtually nothing about farming and was grateful for Claire's knowledge of running the estate. Claire's position at the Villa became so important that she was soon called "Domina," or mistress of the house.

Claire's father wisely had her educated in both the content of books and physical activities. She was taught to use a bow and to defend herself. Being able to read, write, and fight was rare for a girl. Claire was grateful for the unusual education, and wanted the same for her daughters. Valerias—never one to shy away from military matters—agreed.

With Claire's insistence and Valerias' encouragement, Alena and Elsha became experts in the worlds of words and combat. Valerias was fully aware that neither daughter could defeat a trained Roman soldier, but they would fare well against a common thief or criminal.

In the year 383 AD, Alena and Elsha were approaching seventeen and fifteen years of age, respectively, and would need the lessons taught to them by their parents. The threat of barbarians to the empire had dramatically increased after Adrianople.

Valerias was now fifty-five years old, and the constant warfare he had experienced in his earlier years had aged him. Marrying Claire and retiring to the Villa had saved his life, and Valerias appreciated his good fortune. He had a loving wife, beautiful daughters, and a magnificent estate.

Yet, the feeling of contentment he craved still evaded him. He experienced restless and troubled periods that gnawed at his mind. These episodes increased in frequency and duration as he aged. They were not violent occurrences, but were times when he wanted to be alone. In those periods, he cursed his inability to be happy with his near-perfect life.

He dreaded old age and the feebleness that came with it. He wondered, *If I become too aged or fall ill, what will Claire do? Would my age and infirmity turn her away? Would she leave me for another man? Would my daughters think less of me?*

Valerias' dour outlook was not aided by his injury. He felt less of a man whenever he looked at the stump at the end of his left arm, his savage fight with the Hun king, Uldric, at the Battle of Three Tongues having cost him his left hand.

The crumbling state of the empire as a result of Adrianople also skewed his views negatively and drove him further into the dark. Fortunately for him and those around him, Valerias never stayed in a state of despair for long. He always returned to his normal self, shepherding the staff through their tasks, teasing Alena and Elsha, holding Claire's hand, and telling stories.

Claire was worried about her husband, yet she did not want to show her concern; she believed that would drive Valerias away. Instead, she kept her feelings inside.

She also worried about her son, Drostan, who lived in a hermitage along Britannia's remote eastern coast. The two exchanged letters occasionally, but communications were always in secret under the strict control of the abbot of the hermitage, Father Timothy. In her letters, Claire identified herself as Clarinda, an old family friend, not as his mother. Besides Father Timothy, only Valerias, Claire, and their friend Joseph knew Drostan's true identity—that he was the son of a king and queen.

Drostan remembered little of his boyhood except that he had lived in an old fort. His father had been a leader who had died. He had no idea that he was heir to a throne or that his mother and sisters were alive.

Claire had not seen her son in ten years, and she fiercely yearned to be with him. Unfortunately, she could not risk a visit. Her brother, Eustice, had claimed the throne after Claire abdicated it to him. Eustice would view Drostan as a rival. Also, rogues loyal to the dead usurper and her enemy, Argus, still roamed her old kingdom. Then there were the Saxons, who frequently appeared and terrorized the Britons. If taken prisoner by the Saxons and his identity compromised, Drostan would command a sizable ransom. A further complication: Claire could not bring Drostan to the Villa because he did not want to leave Father Timothy's religious order.

Claire's frustrations led to infrequent but harsh bursts of temper. She wisely avoided Valerias when she was in such a state, as it would only add to his despondency. Valerias, too, did not confront Claire when she was upset to avoid further turmoil.

Yet, Valerias and Claire's love for each other remained strong. They learned to live through each other's stormy times.

III

ZANTAR

During one particularly gloomy period when the weather matched Valerias' mood, Claire had an idea. A violent spring storm had swept through the region, damaging many of the houses and community structures in a nearby village. Valerias allowed the villagers to stay in temporary structures on his land until their homes were repaired.

The displaced children of the nearby village need someone who can tell a great story, she thought. *That person is Marcus.* By cheering up the children of the village, Claire hoped Valerias might also mend his soul.

Valerias was sitting on the porch outside the Grand House watching the turmoil in the dark clouds, contemplating the ills of old age. He was comparing his state in life to the decaying empire when Claire walked out to him.

"Marcus, I have an idea about how we can help the children of the village," she began. "We can invite them to our Great Room, where you can tell them one of your stories."

"Sorry?" Valerias was lost in his thoughts and only partially heard her.

"I said, the village—especially the children—needs your help," she repeated.

"Oh, I can't do that. I doubt little children would want to listen to an old man with one hand."

"Do not use that as an excuse, husband." Claire was firm. "The children are fond of you. I have seen them follow you around the village, and you talk to them. Sometimes you have more than ten children around you. Besides, you are a fine storyteller. For as long as I have known you, children have attached themselves to you and listened to you speak. I remember a story you told me of a little girl named Anastasis. Alena and Elsha adore you, and that started the day they met you. And telling a story may cure you of your disinterest in life."

"You are always seeking ways to cheer me up," Valerias gently chided Claire for intruding into his thoughts. "But I don't see how telling a fable will help me or the children."

"Trust me, it will," Claire said decisively. "You and the children need something else to think about besides misery."

The next day, Claire brought an anxious Valerias to the Great Room. Not only were the children present, but also their parents. The children were fidgety because they had been away from their homes for so long and were over-awed at the ornate room they were in. They knew Valerias as the friendly old man who appeared in the village from time to time. Their parents, however, were well aware of the great general in their company. They tended to remain still, only moving to reprimand a child.

After the room quieted down, Claire announced that in addition to being her husband, father to Alena and Elsha, and a retired Roman general, Valerias also was a marvelous storyteller.

Valerias felt apprehensive at first. *How can I, a man who stood before emperors, legions, and barbarian kings, be nervous in front of children?*

As he gazed around the room, it appeared to Valerias that many in the audience were focused on the metal cap over the stump where his left hand should have been. Valerias knew his stump was a welcome distraction, and that relaxed him. He looked again at his audience, took a deep breath, and, in a husky voice, began speaking.

"In a time long ago, yet not long enough ago for people to have forgotten, there was a village like yours that was perched by the sea. The inhabitants of the village were not people like us, though. Instead, they were a strange people who, under most circumstances, were invisible. They were peaceful and had no desire to do harm. When life was good, they could not be seen, except for a small flame in their hearts."

Valerias pointed to his heart with his right hand and continued.

"However, when they became stressed or if danger approached, their physical forms showed, like ours here, right now. I know that seems odd, because whenever danger is near us, we want to become invisible and not be seen. But I did say they were a strange people. They were called the Unseen Ones. Fortunately for them, they rarely experienced worry or fear.

"That is, until the great Rock Monster appeared. When he awoke from a long sleep, he rose up and shook the Earth." Valerias stomped his feet for effect.

"He was a monstrous being that spent his time far up in the mountains, terrorizing that part of the land. For whatever reason, he came near the village of the Unseen Ones. On his way, he did his worst—smashing everything in his path. Because the danger was so great and near, the Unseen Ones glowed and became the Seen Ones."

The crowd of people in the large room was silent—everyone was fully focused on Valerias' story and anxiously awaited what came next.

"Now, the Unseen Ones could be invisible, as I told you. But they could not be quiet, which was their biggest fault. Maybe they should have been called the Unseen Noisy Ones. After they became visible, they were the Seen Noisy Ones."

That brought a chuckle of amusement from the audience. Valerias continued the story.

"The Seen Ones panicked and wailed. The noise made the Rock Monster very angry—so angry that he wanted to destroy their village with one blow from his great fist."

Valerias showed the crowd his silver-capped stump and brought it down into his right hand with a sharp slap.

"But the crying caused something else to stir. There, somewhere in the heavens, lived the mighty dragon, Zantar. Zantar was immense, fearless, and could breathe fire—a fire so hot it could melt anything you can think of. He could boil a small lake with one strong breath.

"Many, many years before, the village people had taken care of Zantar when he was a little orphaned dragon. No one knew what had happened to his parents. The Unseen Ones found him in a cave at the outskirts of their village. They could have killed him or banished him from the area—after all, he was a dragon and dragons were not normally friends of the Unseen Ones.

"Zantar grew to adulthood. When he was twenty years old, he left the village and went where only dragons go, but said he would come back to the village someday. Fifty years later, he returned and was pleased to see the villagers waiting for him. He told the Unseen Ones he would be their guardian, on one condition: On the summer solstice, Zantar would return to his cave. On that date, a villager would enter Zantar's cave and place a gold coin just under his lower jaw. If they failed to do so, Zantar would no longer guard the village and the villagers could no longer call on him for help."

"Did the Unseen Ones always do what they were supposed to do?" an anxious child spoke up, impatient for an answer.

"What do you think?" Valerias asked softly.

"I don't know. I hope so. Tell us." The child's eyes expressed great anticipation for Valerias' next words.

"Yes, they did. You see, it took much courage to go into the cave and place gold under the dragon's jaw. No one knew what the dragon ate, and it could be Unseen Ones, for all they knew. His mouth was filled with one hundred sharp teeth. But you see, it came down to trust. The Unseen Ones had to trust that Zantar would return to the cave on the solstice and not eat them, and further, that when called upon, he would defend the village. Zantar trusted the Unseen Ones to always bring the coins he requested.

"But some of the younger Unseen Ones grew tired of the yearly ritual. 'We don't need to do this,' they told the older Unseen Ones. 'There is no threat to us. The dragon just wants the gold.' However, the older Unseen Ones were wise. They scolded the younger generation and insisted the ritual must be carried out annually. And being good and obedient, the younger Unseen Ones listened to the older Unseen Ones for over one hundred years! The older Unseen Ones knew that when Zantar was needed, he would come to help them.

"Now Zantar heard the Unseen Ones call for him—remember, they were now the Seen Ones because of the fear and stress caused by the Rock Monster. Before you could blink, Zantar came from the heavens and flew over the village. It did not take long for Zantar to determine the source of the villagers' despair. He saw the fearsome Rock Monster, intent on destroying the village.

"He flew directly at the Rock Monster and, with his sharp talons, tore off a chunk of the monster's shoulder. To Zantar's amazement, the Rock Monster was undeterred; he reached down, grabbed a boulder, and put it back in the hole of his shoulder. Rock Monsters heal quickly. He picked up another boulder and hurled it at Zantar. The Rock Monster had good aim, and despite quick maneuvering, Zantar was clipped on the left wing." Valerias slapped his left shoulder.

"Zantar flew high in the sky as the Rock Monster hurled boulder after boulder at him. They all missed, which was good for Zantar. Once the Rock Monster believed Zantar would not be a problem any further, he turned his attention back to the village. The Seen Ones started wailing even louder as their chances for survival diminished by the moment."

Valerias' eyes grew as wide as the children's that surrounded him. They watched every move Valerias made and listened to every word.

"The Rock Monster thought he would wipe out the village by smashing and pushing it into the sea. The Seen Ones would become food for the monsters of the sea."

Valerias was not fond of the sea, and he, too, imagined visions of sea monsters.

"The Rock Monster reached the outskirts of the village in gigantic steps. All the Seen Ones were frozen with fear and stood crying outside their huts. The great arm of the Rock Monster would quash and sweep them into the sea, and they would be lost forever. The Rock Monster laughed at the plight of the villagers." Valerias gave his audience his best hearty laugh.

The small children in the audience pressed their heads against their parents' chests and shoulders, fearing the worst for the poor villagers. Valerias noticed and waited to continue to increase the atmosphere of great uncertainty.

After a long pause, he said, "The village appeared doomed. Suddenly, something dove through the Rock Monster's enormous legs. Ripples of wind almost blew the villagers off balance. It happened so fast no one saw what had caused the wind. Then it happened again. The second time caught the Rock Monster's attention and he looked down. And what do you think he saw? A ring of fire encircled his legs. Another swoop and the fire burned hotter. It was white hot! Zantar was flying so fast no one could spot him. But he was there, and with every swoop he breathed more fire into the ring that surrounded the Rock Monster. The Rock Monster could not move; the fire was just too hot. What do you think happened next?"

A child in the crowd yelled out, "He melted!"

"No, not quite. You see, this Rock Monster could not melt—at least not completely. But the Rock Monster did not know that. So he stood inside the ring of fire thinking about how to escape the trap. Just then, there was a great collision. Zantar, with all the power he could muster, flew right onto the Rock Monster's back. The Rock Monster lost his balance and fell into the sea, along with Zantar, and they both disappeared. The Seen Ones held their breaths, worried that Zantar, their guardian, had died.

"After several long moments, Zantar suddenly emerged from the sea, showering the village with the water that fell from his great wings. The dragon turned and belched a burst of fire at the sun. The sun responded by shooting out a giant flare of light. Then it was over.

"Zantar flew down to the village and landed on a giant flat rock. The Seen Ones rushed toward him, thanking him profusely for his bravery. Zantar told the villagers he had finished what he came to do for them so long ago. He had fulfilled his destiny; it was time for him to leave. He told the villagers to be wise and not to be afraid. A small child came up to the dragon with a shiny gold piece and said it was for him. Zantar took the coin, and in a great salute to the villagers, flew off, his wings creating thunder, fire blasting from his mouth. He was gone forever.

"The villagers had experienced fear—real fear—for the first time. They would always keep some part of that fear in their hearts. They forever became the Seen Ones, and over time became people like you and me. And that is the story of Zantar and the Rock Monster. The morals of my story are to have faith in those you trust, like your parents, and always be true to yourselves and stand up for what you believe in. The Seen Ones believed in Zantar, and Zantar believed in the Seen Ones."

"What about the Rock Monster?" several children wanted to know. "Did he die?"

Valerias answered, "Of course not. Rock Monsters do not die. However, he did not threaten the village again. And do you know why? Rocks are heavier than water and they sink. The Rock Monster sank to the bottom of the sea. He still roams the sea floor looking for other Rock Monsters. Maybe he will find one and be happy, but that is a tale for another time."

Valerias finished his story and the children and adults cheered. The children clamored around him and asked a multitude of questions. Valerias patiently answered all of them while Claire passed out treats.

When the children and their parents had all left the Great Room to return to their temporary homes, Valerias walked outside and looked at the horizon. Claire joined him.

"You told a good story, Marcus. You had the young and old hanging on your every word. And you added humor. Perhaps the spirit of Titus resides up there." Claire pointed at Valerias' head.

"He could spin a tale. I couldn't help but learn from him when I was with him. I miss him. He would have told a better story today."

Valerias warmly recalled his old friend. Titus could concoct an interesting tale about any subject, at any time. He often picked Valerias to spin tales about. Titus had been a Roman general in Britannia, and after formally retiring from the army, he voluntarily joined Valerias' campaign against the Huns. He later died from the vicious injuries he suffered during the Battle of Three Tongues. To Valerias, Titus was a man and soldier well worth remembering.

Claire ignored the comment. "There are many people I miss, too. Yes, Titus was a good man." Claire paused, looked deeply at Valerias' weary face and asked, "Are you any relation to Zantar, Marcus?"

Without looking at Claire, Valerias smiled and quietly said, "It is only a story, Claire. Only a story."

Claire pressed Valerias on his answer. "Would a younger Zantar have slayed the Rock Monster instead of letting him live in the ocean?"

"Yes, I believe he would have. Time provided Zantar with the experience needed to make a wise decision. Sometimes to kill the enemy is not the best choice."

Claire glanced at Valerias. He stared stoically at the horizon. *I wonder what will happen to Zantar in the future. What will our future be?* Claire thought. She put her hand in his.

IV

CAMEL SPIDER

Twilight edged the brightness of day into darkness. The desert slowly shed its brutal blanket of heat and welcomed the coolness of night.

The camel spider slowly emerged from its daytime resting place. The spider sought a meal as the night provided cover from hungry predators. At over six inches in length, the camel spider was a king in its world. Small birds, lizards, and rodents avoided the creature if possible.

The spider moved slowly and carefully around rocks to avoid startling potential prey. Once it encountered prey, however, the camel spider could move with remarkable speed. The arachnid would plunge its fangs into its helpless victim, immobilize it, and devour it from the inside out.

This camel spider had located a potential meal on the other side of a piece of wood. It shifted into attack mode. Suddenly it reared up, reaching back as far as it could to try and remove a sharp object that had been plunged through its abdomen. The predator became the prey.

Garzad had a thick dark beard that mirrored the deepening night. He lifted the camel spider from the ground and brought it within a few inches of his face. The spider twisted violently back and forth, trying desperately to free itself from the thin spike Garzad had carefully driven through its body. There was just enough light for Garzad to see the spider, and plenty for the night hunting spider to see the man. If the camel spider could escape, it would give its attacker a very powerful bite that would not be forgotten.

Garzad was in control, though, and he laughed at the squirming creature.

"You would like to tear into me, wouldn't you?"

Garzad laughed again as he walked to an area where a fire had recently been lit. Two men were kneeling near it, their arms and legs in shackles. Garzad slowly took the spider over to one of the prisoners. He brought his face close and stared deep into the man's eyes. Garzad did not move for several heartbeats. To the prisoner, it seemed much longer. The captive's face was covered in grime, but through the dirt and sweat, Garzad could see apprehension in his eyes; the man knew something terrible was about to happen.

Garzad spoke slowly and clearly. "You will tell me what I want to know or you will soon be in great pain—pain like you have never felt before, or ever will again."

The prisoner just looked at Garzad. He knew "ever will again" meant his impending death. Still, he clenched his jaw in mock defiance.

"Where is your camp, you worthless shit?" Garzad spat impatiently. "You think you are brave, not telling me what I want to know. But we shall see just how brave you really are."

Without a moment's hesitation, Garzad thrust the furious camel spider and its churning fangs into the prisoner's right eye. The resulting shriek could be heard far out into the night.

Garzad pulled the spider from the prisoner's face. The man immediately dropped headfirst into the sandy, rocky soil. He was convulsing from the shock of the attack and the pain.

The second prisoner shook in terror. Garzad calmly walked over to him. The camel spider still twisted violently on its spike.

Garzad peered at the creature and thought the spider felt good about exacting revenge on humankind. The second prisoner urinated in fright as he begged for mercy.

"I will show you mercy when you tell me what I want to know," Garzad snarled from beneath his thick beard. "For starters, where is your camp? Is it north or west of here? How far? Who is your leader? What does he look like? How many men line up under his banner?"

Fear had struck the man dumb. Garzad grabbed the first prisoner by the hair and pulled him up onto his knees. He was barely conscious. In his other hand, Garzad still held the impaled spider. He shoved the mangled face of the first prisoner just in front of his companion.

"Speak now or both your eyes will be like his! And then the little beast shall have your tongue!" Garzad shouted.

The second prisoner regained his senses. He spoke in a ragged voice. "Yes, I will tell you anything. Ask me anything! Do not let that thing touch me!"

Garzad opened his fist and the man dropped back to the ground where he lay moaning incoherently. He yanked the second man to his feet, dragging him by the scruff of the neck over to a group of soldiers who were warming their hands by the fire. General Octavio, who stood with them, nodded in satisfaction.

"He will tell you anything you want to know, General," Garzad growled. "If he shows reluctance, call me back."

And the prisoner did talk. Once he started talking, he provided so much information that a scribe writing it all down had to ask the prisoner on several occasions to repeat his story. The interrogation took on the flavor of a confession at its end. When he had finished providing all the answers he could, the prisoner asked for and received water.

Garzad stood off to the side during the questioning. He was fascinated with how the camel spider tried to free itself and would not die, despite the spike almost bisecting its body. *What a tough little shit*, he thought.

General Octavio interrupted Garzad's musings. "Centurion Garzad, you have done well, as always. The prisoner told us everything we wanted to know—and much more. He was seeing a woman besides his wife."

"I am pleased you approve of my methods and the information the prisoner provided, General Octavio."

"I do approve. We leave in two hours for their camp. Our surprise will be the rebels' nightmare, as we rain terror on them!"

"I would like to ride point, General Octavio, when we attack. I want to be the first to draw blood," Garzad said.

"You shall have it, Centurion."

Garzad smiled broadly. *I cannot wait to kill rebels!*

"What would you like to do with the two prisoners, Centurion?"

"I do not care what happens to them, General. They are nothing to me but rebel scum whose value to the empire has ended. I will leave it for you, as commanding general, to decide."

"What about your partner?" General Octavio pointed to the camel spider.

"Oh, I will free our ally."

Using the broad side of his knife, Garzad gently pushed the spider off the spike onto the ground. The spider slowly moved away from the men.

"Do you think it will live?" Octavio asked.

"I hope so," Garzad remarked, watching the spider disappear into the dark. "But it is up to the will of the gods."

"Do you think the prisoner spoke the truth?" General Octavio sought reassurance from Garzad.

"Yes. You could tell by how fast he spoke. A lying man would have had to think first about what he said."

"Good," declared Octavio.

Both men smiled. Octavio turned to his men and slashed his arm downward through the air. Within moments, the two prisoners' heads rolled onto the sand.

A horse appeared out of the darkness and galloped up to Garzad and Octavio. The rider dismounted and removed a parchment from his satchel. He approached the two men and saluted the general. He turned to Garzad.

"I have a letter from the emperor that requires your immediate attention, Centurion."

Garzad carefully unrolled the scroll. He walked over to the fire and spent some time carefully reading the parchment in the poor light. When he finished, he walked back to General Octavio and the messenger.

"The emperor has commanded that I return to Rome and await further instructions. My orders are to leave now."

General Octavio was surprised, but he knew an order from the emperor could not be debated. Garzad disappeared and returned shortly with his horse and a small bag containing his possessions. He and the messenger mounted their horses. Garzad saluted General Octavio.

"My regret is that I could not serve you in the upcoming attack on the rebel camp. We will see each other again. Perhaps in Rome."

General Octavio nodded in agreement, and Garzad and the messenger rode off into the night.

When the two men were well away from camp, Garzad quietly said, "Well done, Honorario. The emperor and I are pleased with you."

Honorario chuckled. "Your reading has improved Centurion—I declare you literate!"

Garzad swore and tossed the letter to Honorario. "It consists of three sentences and it took me too long to read it. Your instruction is lacking. I hope, for your sake, I improve," he said with a sly smile.

The centurion gave his horse a sharp kick and the two riders picked up their pace to arrive at the port and take a ship to Italia as quickly as possible.

V

Companion

"We are here!" the voices of Alena and Elsha cried out together.

Valerias and Claire followed close behind the two girls as they made their way through the forest of tall trees that quickly gave way to a large meadow. With no trees to block the sun's comforting rays, the meadow was pleasantly warm.

The party of four took off their cloaks almost in unison as the heat from the sun swiftly penetrated their outer garments. The bright meadow was a favorite place for Claire and her daughters. A woodsman had told Claire about it, and they visited at least twice a year.

The meadow's flowering plants avoided the forest prison, but the forest was also the meadow's protector. Few people knew of the meadow, and Valerias and his family told no one of their secret place.

Valerias had contrasting opinions of the security of the meadow. On one hand, the meadow's isolation kept threats from an enemy at a low risk. Yet, the isolation could also allow an attacker free access to anyone in the meadow with an equally low risk of being caught. Thus, Valerias always carried his sword when they visited. He sometimes sheathed his blade on his back, as he had when he was an active general. However, his missing left hand prevented its easy removal and replacement. At other times, he kept it at his side. Claire tucked Valerias' dagger into her belt for added protection.

Valerias enjoyed the meadow for its solitude; the quiet allowed him to relax. He found his thoughts frequently wandered back to events in his past, and he gave little heed to the future. On this particular day, the meadow was a warm, old friend. He felt a distinct tranquility. *When I die, I want to be buried here.*

The four tied their horses to a gnarly tree branch that stuck out into the meadow. Alena and Elsha were well trained in caring for horses, and they removed the saddles for the horses' comfort. Alena then helped Valerias do the same. She carefully placed the saddle on the ground while Elsha aided Claire with her saddle.

"Thank you, Alena." Valerias smiled. Inside, he felt a now familiar upset that he could not manage the simple task of removing a saddle without help.

"Father, you are welcome," Alena replied sweetly.

Valerias was proud of his adopted daughters. Alena and Elsha had become fine young women. When he looked at them, he could see their mother.

Both Alena and Elsha had long, dark brown hair, though Elsha's was curlier. They were slender like their mother. Alena was taller than Elsha; however, Valerias attributed the height difference to Alena being two years older. Alena had hazel eyes; Elsha's were blue.

He viewed his daughters as pretty but not beautiful. This was a good thing, he thought. *They will need to depend on their intelligence and wit instead of their looks. And there will be fewer suitors to chase away!*

When Valerias and Claire were first married, Valerias insisted Alena and Elsha call him Marcus. He preferred not to be addressed as Father, and being called Marcus made Valerias feel younger. He thought the title of Father belonged to Gerhard, the girls' blood father, and Valerias did not wish to take Gerhard's title, even in death. Father was also a reference to Christian priests, and Valerias did not want to be aligned with Christianity.

Valerias would have been surprised to learn Alena and Elsha, even as young children, often referred to him as Father. As they grew older, it became the only term they used, even in his presence.

Once the horses were cared for, Alena went with Valerias as he wandered to a small hill near the edge of the meadow while Claire and Elsha stayed near the horses.

"Father, can we talk?" Alena asked once they were out of earshot of her mother.

"Certainly, Alena, what is on your mind?"

"I'm going to be seventeen."

"Yes. I know."

"There are suitors who desire my hand in marriage."

"I know that, too."

"Well, why won't you let them court me?"

"Because you are too young and they are unworthy of you—even if you were of age. I will wager that none of them is as educated as you, or can fight as well as you."

"You don't know all of them." Alena was frustrated.

"Yes, I do. I speak from experience."

"What experience?" Alena's tone was colored with sarcasm. "You know I'm approaching Mother's age when she married my father. But Mother has been your only wife, and you didn't marry her until you were older."

Valerias was patient with Alena, at least on the outside. "I will not have you go into an arranged marriage. Your mother and I agree on that point. And you are not yet the age she was when she married for the first time. When the time comes, we will see that you have the opportunity to select a husband."

"But how can I select a husband if I cannot meet potential suitors? Father, you make this so difficult."

Valerias grew tired of the subject and was looking forward to a nap. He preferred the time when Alena and Elsha were young girls and they studied nature or discussed military topics together. He did not like discussing marriage, or that his daughters were being pursued for marriage; the thought of Alena and Elsha married made him feel old.

"After we return to the Villa, I will talk with your mother and perhaps we can come to an agreement about possibly allowing some suitable young men to visit. But I must first approve of them. You will not become the wife of an old grandfather who lost his first two wives, or a younger man who has two wives!"

Valerias laughed at his outburst and Alena smiled. For a moment, he thought the subject was behind him. Alena felt differently.

She stared straight into Valerias' eyes and said, "I will hold you to your word, Father—when we return home."

She turned away to join Claire and Elsha.

Valerias was relieved that the conversation had been postponed. Yet, he was pleased with Alena. He and Claire had tried hard to teach the girls to be levelheaded and strong willed.

His daughters had matured fast, he thought, wandering on until he reached his favorite place at the meadow's edge underneath a squat leafy tree. He sat down and rested his head against the trunk, and fell fast asleep.

When he awoke, the soft air carried a bite of cold. The sun had turned away from the meadow. A large tree stood in front on him.

Valerias did not remember a tree in that spot. *My eyes deceive me. How did such a tree grow here so fast?*

The tree was ugly and resembled a bulky, hideous skeleton. It had a gnarled trunk with several twisted, leafless arms that reached outward. A giant knot six feet from its base was the circumference of the entire trunk. The tree was brown with black, claw-like marks carved into it. It would have frightened even a hardened woodsman.

Valerias did not fear a tree. Instead, he was angry that his nap had been disturbed. "What are you? What are you doing here in my meadow?" he asked arrogantly, getting to his feet.

"I am who you think I am, General." The tree spoke through the knot.

"You did not answer my questions." Valerias was unsure about the nature of the tree. "I don't know who you are."

"Who do you think I am, General?"

"You speak, but you are not a person. And trees do not talk." Valerias was trying to think his way logically through the perplexing circumstance. Standing before him was obviously not a tree or a person. *This thing must be a demon*, he thought.

The tree stood motionless and did not speak. It waited for Valerias to continue his questions.

"Are you a god or a demon?"

"I am neither, General."

Valerias became very frustrated and cursed.

The tree ignored him and asked, "What is not born and yet exists with a man?"

"You respond with a riddle. I would like to rid myself of you!" an agitated Valerias swore.

"I am at your side at all times; we are brothers."

"A tree demon is not my brother!"

"We are not today, but we have been brothers in the past and someday we will be again. Do you know who I am now?"

Valerias pondered the riddle for several moments and then the answer came to him. "You are Death."

"You are perceptive, my General, and you are correct."

"Have you come for me? Is it my time?" Valerias asked.

The tree spoke again. "Not yet, but in time, General. In time."

Valerias' seething anger surpassed all his other emotions. The obnoxious tree failed to give him answers to what he wanted to know. The tree was a loathsome tease. He reached for his sword to turn it into splinters.

"Marcus, wake up! Wake up!"

Valerias heard voices. He could feel his shoulders being pulled and women, like sirens, called to him. *I must slay this tree of Death,* he thought. Then a chilling thought occurred to him, *I cannot kill what is already dead!* Valerias' frustrations were at a boil. He flailed his arms at the tree like an untrained peasant, which vexed him even more.

Valerias suddenly awoke and sat straight up. He looked into the faces of Claire, Alena, and Elsha.

"You were having a terrible nightmare. You were yelling and arguing with someone." Claire was visibly shaken. "What were you dreaming about?"

Valerias slowly regained awareness. He pushed thoughts of Death out of his mind and turned to Claire.

"It was a bad dream, Claire. Nothing but a bad dream. I am happy again now that I see your faces. I am alive and with you, and that is all I want. The dream means nothing."

Valerias looked over at a patch of flowers where a butterfly hovered. He turned back to Alena and Elsha.

"Let us examine the type of flower that butterfly prefers."

VI

WILDERNESS

The ride back to the Villa from the meadow was slow and largely silent. Valerias was deeply disturbed by his dream encounter with Death. *Is Death going to be my constant companion?*

Valerias was also troubled by his relationship with Claire. He attributed the problem to his age and invalid condition. At times, he wished he had died in the Battle of Three Tongues against the Huns instead of having to live with only one useful arm. Claire was still vital and the center of life at the Villa. He was the old, infirm man in the corner watching life pass him by.

The specter of Death, combined with his increasing feelings of inadequacy, sent Valerias spiraling into bouts of misery.

Then there was the maturation of his daughters. Alena desired suitors and Elsha would soon follow. He was not ready for that, and their time in the meadow that afternoon confirmed his feelings.

What Valerias believed could not have been more incorrect. Although older and retired from the Roman army, he was well known at the Villa and in the region. He was the man who many times served as protector of the empire and who had always defeated its enemies.

His victory over the Huns solidified his legend. People from throughout the region constantly came to the Villa to seek his counsel. Even though he was not a magistrate, Valerias mediated numerous conflicts, and the vast majority of disputes were settled without violence.

Claire loved him deeply. She and the girls were his first priority. Valerias had brought peace to her life and safety for her daughters. Alena and Elsha were in awe of him. The fight in the cave where he slew six of Morguard's brigands to protect them was a memory they would never forget, even though they had been very young. Neither daughter would intentionally do anything that would cause him to be upset with them.

Valerias utilized dozens of freeborn citizens, indentured servants, and slaves at the Villa and in the nearby fields. He was a benevolent dominus who seldom issued punishment except in extreme situations. Although he was kind, everyone knew of his past and how he had treated enemies, prisoners, and soldiers who disobeyed him, which kept people on their best behavior. On several occasions, he freed worthy slaves, although most continued to work at the Villa as freemen.

Over time, Valerias stopped noticing the good in his life and focused only on the bad, and Claire grew increasingly concerned about her husband. One day, she was at the local market where she encountered Duvanous, a former army officer from Valerias' past and a periodic visitor at the Villa.

"Good morning, Domina," Duvanous opened the conversation. "Beautiful day."

"A pleasant day to you as well, Duvanous. Do you visit this market often?" Claire already knew the answer.

"Yes. I come almost daily. I get tired of being at home. The market gives me something to do. I have people to see and people to talk with. When you are in the legions for over twenty-five years and then end up at home with nothing much to do, you get a little lost. I thought I missed my wife, but I realized I miss the legions even more. But how are you? How is the General?"

"I am fine. Marcus is also doing well." Claire was reluctant to discuss her personal matters.

Duvanous, though, quickly saw through her lie.

"Domina, come with me." Duvanous pointed to the doorway of a nearby shop with no customers. The two headed toward it, Claire looking down at her feet the entire way.

When they were alone, Duvanous did not waste time. "I do not want to be presumptuous, Domina, but when I asked you about the General and your well-being, you would not meet my eye.

"You will recall that I was an interrogator in the legions for many years. I served with your husband during a good part of that time. As an interrogator, I learned to determine whether someone was telling the truth. My training tells me that you are suppressing something."

Duvanous was very careful not to offend Claire. He particularly did not want an ill-formed comment to reach Valerias.

Claire gave Duvanous a hard stare and looked away. She reconsidered and turned back to him with softer eyes.

"What I tell you is in complete confidence, between you and me. Understand?" Claire was not asking.

"Yes, I understand."

"Good." Claire sighed, thinking of the best way to explain the situation. "I am afraid Marcus is becoming lost to himself. He shows little energy to be the dominus of the Villa. There are periods when he goes off alone to some unknown place for hours, sometimes days. He used to be attentive to our daughters, but in the last several weeks he barely acknowledges them. I believe he wants to die. He is the most important person to me, along with my children. It is so difficult to see a man as dynamic as Marcus become what he is now. It is painful."

Tears spilled from Claire's eyes. She could never discuss this with anyone inside the household. It was a relief to speak now, yet it was difficult to admit.

Duvanous handed her a clean cloth to dry her eyes. He touched her hand and said quietly, "I know what you should do."

"What?" Claire immediately was skeptical that there was even the possibility of a solution to her problem. She had given up.

"He needs a friend, and with that friend he will find a purpose. That purpose will make him whole again. I do not wish to insult you, Domina. You are his mate. I speak as a former officer in the legions."

"What?" Claire repeated herself. "He has friends."

"No, he needs a friend from his time in the legions. He is missing that part of his life."

"Are you suggesting yourself as such a friend, Duvanous?" Claire was suspicious with the turn of the conversation.

"No, Claire. I am his friend, but not the friend he needs. Again, I'm not insulting you. This person would be someone who you both know well."

"But Braxus, Cratus, and Titus are dead. Joseph and Olivertos are in Britannia. And who knows where Revious is." She paused for a second and said, "Bukarma."

"Yes, Bukarma." Duvanous smiled. "He is the one I was thinking about."

"I do not know where he is, Duvanous."

"I can find out. He married my cousin, Penelope. I am going to visit my relatives within the month. I will convey a message to Bukarma that it is important for him to contact you."

Claire's mind raced through several scenarios, and she shared her thoughts with Duvanous. "I will not tell Marcus about this; however, I will have a feast at the Villa. You shall be my guest and Bukarma shall be your guest. Oh, and do bring your wife. Marcus will be so pleased and surprised. I hope this will turn him back into some semblance of his former self."

Claire paused to catch her breath and stared straight ahead. "I have not heard from Bukarma in several years. I, too, want to see him. I will send you details regarding the event. Thank you, Duvanous. You have made me happy and hopeful. Maybe this can save my Marcus."

***

The festivity would be held three weeks from the day Claire heard from Duvanous that Bukarma would attend. She debated whether the affair would be large or small, and eventually settled on a small banquet. The guest list would include Duvanous, his wife, several of Valerias' and her friends, and, of course, the guest of honor—Bukarma.

Meanwhile, Valerias slipped deeper into melancholy. When he talked, he spoke of Death stalking him. He spent most of his time in a barn carving wooden figures. He had taken a thick piece of wood with several short branches and whittled the wood into a small replica of the tree from his dream in the meadow. But he couldn't even do that right, not with only the one hand.

A week before the banquet, Claire had had enough of Valerias' behavior; it started to adversely affect her. With her jaw set tight, Claire strode into the barn. She found Valerias sitting in a chair carving a figure of something she did not recognize. He had placed several odd-looking objects on a table. In the center of the carved objects was the small, inexpertly carved tree. A scraggly looking dog sat off to his side, showing no interest in anything.

"Are you coming to supper tonight, Marcus?"

"It is not suppertime yet, Claire."

"It does not matter when it is, the question is: Are you going to join us tonight? Alena and Elsha would like to see their father."

"I am not their father." Valerias kept trying to carve the piece of wood held awkwardly between his knees, steadied as best he could with his stump.

His proclamation ignited Claire's wrath. "You are not their father?! Then who are you? A brother? A cousin? A nobody? A dead tree? You have become so thick in the brain that maybe you are a nobody. The great Roman general reduced to a barnyard animal!"

Valerias stopped carving and watched Claire intently. Her eyes and voice revealed true anguish.

Claire continued. "I fell in love with a great man. Not just a great general, but a great man. I love you. Your daughters love you. People here in the Villa and in the village have such respect for you. You were the general the emperors ordered to take the fight to the Huns, and you defeated them. The emperors respect you! That says so much. Yet look at you now, sitting alone in a barn with cows and their flies, and a dog that looks like a rug! What has caused the man I love to become a shadow hiding in a barn?"

Valerias turned his carving knife over from the hilt to the tip of blade several times with his right hand, not taking his eyes off Claire.

"I fear what I have become: an old man with gray hair and a withered body," Valerias pointed to the stump of his left arm. "And worst of all, a man without purpose. My final destiny is at hand. The specter of Death haunts me. But Death is nothing compared to what I am most afraid of—losing you. You are vibrant and can attract other men."

"That is absurd, Marcus!" Claire fiercely protested. "Yes, you are older, and so am I. My body is no longer firm and my breasts sag. I tire more easily. However, I am alive and I intend to make the most of the time I have left. I hope that time is spent with my husband, whom I truly love, and my children in this wonderful Villa. Won't you join me in this life, Marcus?"

Valerias continued to rhythmically spin his dagger, hilt over blade. "I had a dream when we were in the meadow recently."

"I remember you had a nightmare. What was it about?"

"It was so real, Claire. I saw Death. It took the form of a tree, a gnarled dead tree that could talk. *I felt like I was really there!*"

Claire's immediate reaction was to calmly tell Valerias that it could not be. She set that thought aside. She knew Valerias did not invent such stories; she would accept his belief.

"Did Death speak to you?"

"Yes. Death told me it was not my time."

"Did Death say whose time it was?"

"No, but I feel he is always with me. To know Death is at your side is unnerving. I have seen and been responsible for so much death that Death could be my brother. I believe Death is here beside me as we speak."

"Marcus, Death is standing with me, too. He stands with all of us, even Alena and Elsha. We all die and he is there for us. The best approach you can take is to become Marcus Augustus Valerias again. Know that Death is with you as he is with me, but forget him and accomplish good things. Please join us for supper. Bring Marcus Augustus Valerias to our table. But leave the dog here."

As Claire left the barn, she had no idea how Valerias would react. When suppertime came, she was nervous. She so wanted her husband to return to his true self, and joining them for supper would be the first step.

At the appropriate time, Valerias appeared in the doorway. He had washed and wore clean clothes. He sat down at the table and looked at Claire, then Alena, and finally Elsha. His eyes seemed alive and he flashed a quick smile.

"I'm hungry. Elsha, tell me what you did today. Alena, you are next."

VII

The Hermitage

"He has arrived!"

The cry came from outside the hermitage. The monk called out to no one in particular as he scurried through the gate of the Branodunum hermitage. The man was clearly overweight, which impeded his pace but aided his powerful voice. Another monk stopped him in the courtyard.

"Brother Silas, you must calm down. Father Timothy appreciates only those who can keep their heads about them."

"My head is fine right where it is, Brother Mark. I have important news for the abbot. Do you know where he is?"

"He is in the garden tending his flowers, as he usually does at this time of day."

"His flowers will be a second priority today. The bishop is in the village and he is coming directly to the hermitage."

Brother Mark looked at the earnestness in Brother Silas' face and became excited himself. "Yes, let's go find the abbot."

Brother Mark turned to go to the garden when he found himself being pushed aside by Brother Silas. The race to the garden was on. Both men moved as fast as they could down the path, each showing the other the sharp point of his elbow. It was Brother Silas' girth versus Brother Mark's quickness, and neither had the advantage.

When they reached the garden, both men were out of breath. They found Father Timothy by a rose bush with pruning shears in his hand. He had watched them stumble forward and shook his head in disbelief.

"Father Timothy!" both men shouted in unison.

Father Timothy, typically a patient man, was annoyed at the rowdy intrusion into his gardening time, which he also used for meditation. His glare froze both men where they stood.

"I don't know if I'm more upset with you," Father Timothy pointed his shears at both men, "for interrupting my private time, or the manner in which you barged in here. You should be ashamed. You are men of God and you act like peasants chasing a farm girl. Your behavior is sorely lacking control!"

Both Brother Silas and Brother Mark had been poor tenant farmers before turning to the cloth, and they looked down sheepishly at their feet as Father Timothy scolded them.

"Now tell me what has happened. You first, Brother Silas, because I believe it is you who has some news."

An odd noise started to come out of Brother Mark's mouth, only to be stopped by a look from Father Timothy that would have halted a wild steer in its tracks. Father Timothy nodded to Brother Silas.

"Father Timothy, he has arrived. The bishop is in Branodunum! He will be at our hermitage within the hour!"

"That is it? When within the hour? What do you have to add, Brother Mark?"

Brother Mark mumbled incoherently and fell silent.

"I know he is in the village. I invited him here to our hermitage. You two have provided me with no new information and have shown poor manners. So, I have decided you two shall perform a full week of kitchen duty as punishment for your un-

Christianlike behavior. You will also add extra time for prayer and meditation because you need it. You will pray to God to forgive your childish ways. And you will pray that I forgive you as well."

Father Timothy waved off Brother Silas and Brother Mark. When the two men were out of sight, he went back to his garden and gently pruned a few flowering plants. Then he stopped and put the shears into an old leather sheath, and patted the sweat from his bald head with a dry cloth. He gazed upon his garden with a smile and walked briskly to his private study at the back of the wooden hall. There he changed into his best woolen habit, knelt in front of a large wooden cross, and prayed.

A hard knock on his door aroused Father Timothy from his meditation. Brother Silas stood on the other side. "The bishop is in the courtyard, Father abbot."

Father Timothy looked at Brother Silas' face and noted he was calm. Behind him was Brother Mark, who appeared fidgety. Father Timothy took in a deep breath and said, "Shall we go and meet our bishop?"

Together they entered the main part of the hall and were joined by several monks. They walked to the courtyard where a tall, slender man faced them. The bishop had a short black beard and stood with his hands clasped in front of him. He watched expressionless as the small horde descended around him. Surprisingly, he wore civilian clothes, hose, and a knee-length tunic—except his cloak was that of a bishop.

Father Timothy was not a shy man, and he greeted the bishop first.

"Bishop, welcome to our hermitage. I am Father Timothy, abbot of this house of God. This is Brother Silas, over here is Brother Mark . . ." Father Timothy proceeded to introduce ten monks. When he finished his opening greeting, all eyes of the group turned to the bishop.

"Thank you, Father abbot. I greet you on behalf of the Church of Rome, the Church of God, his son Jesus Christ, and the Holy Spirit. I am Bishop Joseph. I am visiting the churches and orders in my bishopric, and you, Father Timothy, were kind enough to invite me. I am pleased to be here. Your hermitage is beautiful, here on the edge of the sea. I like to be by the sea; I grew up near it. I feel this place is God's sanctum."

Joseph walked over to a wall overlooking the sea. The blue sky and water merged in the hazy horizon. He took in a deep breath and exhaled slowly as he closed his eyes.

He turned and faced his crowd. "Let us pray."

Joseph gave a succinct prayer. Afterward, he told the assembled monks, "I want to speak to each of you separately and as a group over the next two days. First, I will talk to your abbot, Father Timothy."

Joseph looked at Father Timothy and then spoke to no one in particular, "Please stable my horse."

Father Timothy took Joseph to his study and closed the door.

Joseph was first to talk. "Father Timothy, I am here foremost to get to know you and your brothers in Christ, and this hermitage. I also want to talk to you about the man who is not a monk here—Drostan. I understand you know his situation. I would like to speak to Drostan first."

Drostan was found in the kitchen helping prepare a meal in honor of the bishop. The monk sent by the abbot to fetch Drostan interrupted him as he stoked the cooking hearth.

"Drostan, the bishop has come to visit us. He and the abbot would like to talk with you."

"Why?" Drostan asked, straightening up. "I'm not a brother here. I should be the last person he wants to meet."

The monk shrugged. "Neither Bishop Joseph nor Father Timothy gave me the reason. They just told me to summon you."

"I guess I have no choice. Give me a moment."

Drostan retrieved his cloak from a hook on the wall well away from the hearth, and walked briskly to Father Timothy's study. He tried to think of a reason for being called before the bishop but failed. Whatever it was, he didn't think it would be good.

When he arrived at the study, he found Bishop Joseph and Father Timothy sitting side by side in carved wooden chairs. Across from them stood a third, empty chair that was shorter than the other two. Father Timothy motioned for Drostan to sit.

The abbot spoke first. "Drostan, it is my privilege to introduce Bishop Joseph to you. The bishop was recently appointed to his position by Rome."

Drostan was unsure how to respond to a man of such stature. He stood up and extended his hand. He quickly realized that was improper etiquette and sat back down, frustrated by his mistake.

"Rest easy, Drostan. I may have the title of bishop, but I am a simple man of God—like you and the abbot. We all serve the same God."

Drostan was relieved to discover Joseph was calm and not pretentious. He relaxed slightly. As he did so, Drostan felt a sharp corner of the folded sheet of parchment that he had tucked into his tunic dig into his skin. He pulled it out and held it in his hand, ready to give it to the bishop should he have the opportunity.

"I am your humble servant, Bishop Joseph, and I apologize for my behavior."

"There is no need to apologize. What is in your hand, Drostan?"

"A petition I want to give to you."

"What is this?" Father Timothy interjected and rebuked Drostan. "Bishop Joseph summoned you, not the other way around."

Father Timothy tried to intercept the document, but Drostan had already placed it in Joseph's hands.

"I would like to read this petition, Father Timothy," Joseph said calmly.

Joseph unfolded the document and looked at it carefully for several moments. The petition was short and Joseph gave more time to considering it than reading it.

"Your petition asks the church to allow you to become a monk and join Father Timothy and the other brothers here at the hermitage." Joseph paused and looked thoughtfully at Drostan. "I cannot grant you your request."

Drostan half rose from his seat, such was his surprise at Joseph's response, and swore softly under his breath. Timothy frowned, but Joseph's expression never changed.

"Why can't I join the order as a brother? Am I not good enough for God?"

"That has nothing to do with it." Joseph moved within inches of Drostan's face. "You are a prince, Drostan, and thus, I cannot grant your request."

"What?" Drostan was shocked. He gazed at Father Timothy, who nodded in agreement with Joseph, a little shamefaced at the deception imposed on the young man.

"Yes, a prince," Joseph confirmed. "In the past, you have corresponded with a woman named Clarinda. Her true name is Claire, and she is your mother. Your father was Gerhard. Many years ago, they were king and queen of a kingdom located west of here. Your father was killed and your mother abandoned her crown to escape a usurper. She sent you here, to the hermitage, to save your life. You were seven or eight at the time. You may remember some of what happened, but you may not understand why your life ran this course."

Drostan was completely stunned. His mother was alive! His mind raced to recall past people and events.

Joseph added, "Father Timothy is the only person in Britannia, besides me, who knows you are alive and your whereabouts. Everyone else believes you are dead.

"Your mother and I have corresponded by letter and we have met in person over these past years. Anyway, the point, my dear Drostan, is that I promised your mother that I would not allow you to become a monk until you have had a chance to talk to her directly."

"I do not understand," Drostan responded. "You are the bishop. How could you know of my status?"

"I have always been aware of you, Drostan."

"You know my mother well?"

"Yes, I even served with her during the Battle of Three Tongues against the Hun horde in a land across the Narrow Sea and east of Roman Dalmatia. She saved my life."

"Clarinda—or Claire—said she was married. She mentioned little of her husband in her letters. Do you know him?"

"Oh, I know her husband, Marcus Augustus Valerias, quite well. He was a great Roman general. I was his administrator at one time. We became friends after he granted my freedom."

Drostan's head could not contain any more new information, and he was deeply confused.

Joseph gently put his hand on Drostan's shoulder and with his other hand lifted up Drostan's face so they were eye to eye. "Drostan, you must listen to me very carefully. You must not tell anyone about what we talked about. Here, only Father Timothy and I—and now you—know of your status.

"Tomorrow I am going to visit the nearby village at Branodunum. I want you to accompany me as my aide. We can talk more then. I will answer any questions you may have. But let me repeat myself: talk to no one about our conversations. If anyone should ask, tell them we discussed your time at the hermitage and your petition. Tell them that you have not yet fulfilled the requirements for what I believe is necessary for you to join the monks. Do you understand?"

"Yes, Bishop, I understand."

Father Timothy escorted Drostan to the door and gave him a stern look as he departed.

"Do you think he will talk to the brothers here?"

"If he is smart, he won't," Father Timothy replied.

"I admire what you have done with Claire's son, Father Timothy. Perhaps you should be the bishop."

***

Joseph conducted several meetings with other monks during the rest of the afternoon. Then, Joseph and the monks shared a meal and prayers. Afterward, he and Father Timothy discussed the day's events and the next day's schedule.

When it was time to retire, Father Timothy showed Joseph to his spartan quarters and the two exchanged good evening pleasantries. Joseph waited several moments after Father Timothy left and then sat on his mattress. He pulled a flask from his belongings and took several deep drafts. He gradually laid down and slept the pain away.

VIII

Return of a Friend

It was time for bed. Alena and Elsha were old enough to stay up with Claire and Valerias, and they frequently outlasted their parents. The girls usually spent the late evening time reading, studying, and talking. Valerias, before his latest and darkest period, usually read during the day. He grew tired in the evening. Claire typically accompanied her husband to their bedchambers, which was when and where they could talk in private, before Valerias fell asleep. This night was particularly important to them because each hoped the darkness was being lifted from his soul.

After a bath, Valerias put on a loose-fitting tunic. He then helped Claire with her nightgown. *After the years we have been together, she looks as good to me now as when we met,* he thought. He embraced her quickly but tightly, then they climbed into bed.

"Claire, you awoke me from the murky fog I was in. I felt normal tonight for the first time in many weeks. I worry, though, that I may return to that darkness," Valerias said quietly.

"But with you by my side, I hope that does not happen. I do not know what comes over me and drives me to solitude. I much prefer to be with you and the girls. When I have so many negative thoughts on my mind, I accomplish so little. I promise to be better. You are what I live for. Help me to that path."

"I would like that more than anything, Marcus," Claire responded.

As the night candle was about to be extinguished, a call came from outside their room.

"General and Domina, this animal wants to come into your room. We tried to make it leave, but it will not be told what to do. Should we beat it and use it as bait to attract wolves for killing?"

Valerias had long given up having people not call him the General, so he acquiesced and allowed it to be his title to the numerous servants, freeborns, and guests at the Villa.

As the servant was talking through the door, a furry head peered inside the room and let out a series of hoarse barks.

"Alexander!" Claire called to the head servant as she reacted swiftly to the sound.

"Yes, Domina. We shall remove the beast at once."

"Stop." Valerias said firmly.

His tone surprised Claire and she looked at him quizzically.

"The wolf-dog has been by my side in the barn and on my journeys into the hills. He sometimes disappears, but he always returns."

"I knew that thing was around here, but I did not know it was your pet." Claire narrowed her eyes. "It is not like you to possess such an animal. Was it your secret to having this wolf-dog live at the Villa?"

"There is no secret. I never had an animal companion before. I never needed one. I don't need one now. Still, the wolf-dog appears attached to me, and I do not want it harmed."

"What is its name?" Claire's curiosity had surpassed her initial irritation at the sight of the animal.

"I call him Wolf," Valerias said hesitantly, knowing Claire would tease him.

And she did. “I am not surprised.” Claire rolled her eyes. “Why not name the animal after one of your departed officers, such as Braxus, as a kind of a memorial?”

“Because, Claire, they are different. Wolf is here and they are not. Besides, he is an animal and they were men. You cannot compare them. I have too many colleagues who are now with the gods. I want the dog’s name limited to one syllable, and not after anyone I know.”

Valerias was pleased with his response, yet he feared Claire wasn’t convinced.

Claire, though, surprised him by saying to Alexander, “Have Wolf washed and groomed, and we can discuss the matter further in the morning.”

Valerias seconded Claire. “Yes, Alexander, have the servants clean him up. I, too, would like to see the real Wolf tomorrow morning before we discuss his future.”

For the first time in several weeks, Valerias felt genuinely happy. On the inside, he felt exuberance, but he wanted to temper that feeling with Claire. *I don’t want to get her hopes up if I slip back into the darkness,* he thought. *Or if Wolf wrecks our home.*

Alexander, the other servants, and Wolf departed the bedchamber. Claire and Valerias lay back down to sleep. Valerias reached for her, but her mind was elsewhere. She gazed at the ceiling.

“Marcus, I want to see my son again.”

Valerias was surprised by the change in topic and hesitated before answering. “Do you mean Drostan coming here to the Villa to live, or us traveling to Britannia?”

“Either is fine with me. It has been ten years since I took him to the hermitage. I have not seen him since. You know we have exchanged letters, but not as his mother. He thinks I am dead. I want to see him in person and talk to him. I want to tell him that I am his mother and explain what has happened during the past ten years. I miss him so. If he wants to come here, I would like to present him with that opportunity."

Valerias also peered at the ceiling. He wanted to make Claire happy, and he would do whatever she wanted. To Valerias, the goal was a simple one—see Drostan. However, attaining that goal would be difficult. He thought that going to Britannia would give him an adventure—something he would likely not find at the Villa.

"Yes. We will see Drostan soon. Let me think about the best way to accomplish it," Valerias concluded. "We can talk tomorrow morning." He pulled Claire close to him and they kissed.

Morning arrived in a blend of dew and sun. Valerias had slept hard for the first time in months. When he awoke, he found Claire sitting in a chair across from the bed, looking at him.

"Why are you not in bed?"

"I forgot to mention last night, husband, that we are having a small banquet in three days to honor a special guest. I want you to be here and not wandering around in the hills." Claire was only half joking.

"Who is the special guest?" Valerias' interest was piqued.

"Someone you know, and that is all I will say."

People's names flooded Valerias' mind. He knew he would get no more information from Claire on the subject. He just nodded and smiled. "I will be there. Is there anything I can do to help with the preparations?"

"Just be here." Claire repeated, "Just be here."

The three days passed quickly. Claire organized the preparations for the banquet while Valerias began training Wolf near the main house. Alena and Elsha divided their time between helping their mother and assisting Valerias with Wolf's training. Wolf posed an interesting project for Valerias—a wild animal, yet one that seemed to want to please him, and particularly his daughters.

When it came time for the festivities to begin, Valerias changed into his best welcoming attire, including a new tunic. Valerias normally did not look at his reflection, as it was just another reminder of his age. He also intensely hated his stump. *It is a useless, non-functioning appendage*, he thought. However, he did look at his image for this occasion. *I can still pass as a general. An old general, but still a general.*

Valerias presumed the honored guest was a current or former high-ranking officer in the army; he doubted it was an emperor. He stretched his mind in all directions trying to figure out who Claire had invited to their house. As the guests began to arrive, he stood in the reception line and greeted everyone. Always in the back of his mind was, *Who is this mystery guest?*

After everyone had apparently arrived at the Grand House, Valerias looked around and saw no one he considered unusual. He began to think Claire had tricked him into staying at home. He felt perturbed at being fooled, even if it involved good intentions.

Then a large, dark man rounded the corner into the Great Room and strode directly to Valerias. His long black hair was tied back in a knot, and he still possessed a physique that demanded attention. Bukarma had arrived.

IX

SAXONS

The war hammer hit the large, oval, metal plate with a resounding clang that startled the attendees, but did not bring the desired quiet.

"Silence!"

The word was followed by another loud clang from the hammer. This time, the Great Hall became silent. Borgnar, the man with the war hammer, stared across the hall with a deep frown etched in his face. The man was clean-shaven with long blond hair tied at the back of his head. He was strongly built and wasn't shy to show it. His arms were exposed at the shoulders even though it was cold outside the lodge. They appeared to be war hammers themselves.

"Welcome, my Saxon friends, to the hall of our great kings." Borgnar looked to his left. "And we extend our welcome and praise to the Angles and the Jutes, who have traveled many miles to be here. I am Borgnar, son of the mighty warrior Kinderk. But I am not here to speak to you. That is for Staigrik, son by marriage of our great King Alfredson and my cousin. He is here and now is his time!"

The war hammer again found plate, and this time the fully engaged crowd drowned the hall with the sound of their energetic roar. In response, a man even larger than Borgnar stepped forward and stood at his side. Staigrik viewed the crowd with the same fierce expression as Borgnar. Staigrik, a powerfully built man, possessed a bushy beard that extended down to the middle of his chest. His long, reddish hair with intermixed puffs of gray hung over his massive shoulders. He carried an enormous battleax with a sharp, two-sided head that gleamed in the firelight.

"Welcome, all who assemble here!" Staigrik growled, his voice gravelly and rough. "Over the next three days, we will eat and drink and toast the gods to our coming good fortune. We will have games, and our slaves will act as warriors. They will fight each other, and the winners . . . will fight again!

"Most importantly, I want to tell you of my vision, a vision sent by the gods to raid and plunder Britannia. I want to take its wealth. I want to enslave the cowardly Britons. I want to show their women what a real man is. I want all of that and more. I know the gods will be with us!

"I have a plan that I will tell you tomorrow. But tonight, I want you all to experience my hospitality. I have just one warning for you: Do not touch—in any way—my wife and daughters." Staigrik pointed them out to the crowd. "Otherwise . . ." Staigrik raised his mighty ax with one arm and brought it down on a small nearby wooden table. The blow splintered the table. Staigrik cursed and raised the ax above his head.

"The Britons shall feel my wrath!"

The men in the hall shouted, "Staigrik, Staigrik" in a pulsating chorus, and each man raised his weapon above his head. Battleaxes, war hammers, spears, and seaxes filled the air.

Staigrik was pleased. In the corner of the Great Hall, a young man watched the proceedings with amusement.

"Guenter, what do you think of your father now?"

"I think he is immense," Guenter responded nonchalantly to Torberg.

"Do you mean in stature or ideas?"

"You decide for yourself, Torberg. I say both."

"He is impressive," Torberg replied.

Both men laughed as a third man, Wulfric, joined them. All three were twenty-two years old. Because Guenter was Staigrik's son, his presence in the hall attracted other young warriors who wanted to be seen in his company.

"Do you know what your father's plans are for Britannia?" This time Wulfric asked the question.

"No. He does not confide in me. He talks to his other chiefs when they drink. I am not a chief. I am barely his son."

"Guenter, don't worry. You are heir to the throne," Torberg said. He made his remark partially in honesty to Guenter and partially to curry his friend's favor.

A call went out for Guenter and he dreaded what was to come. Borgnar suddenly appeared in front of him.

"Staigrik wants you to come to him, now."

Guenter walked at Borgnar's fast pace to where Staigrik stood. Staigrik held a very large drinking horn of beer in one hand and his great battleax in the other. He motioned for Guenter to join him. Staigrik had already consumed several drinking horns full of beer, but he was not drunk.

To a bystander who did not know Staigrik and Guenter, the scene in front of them was almost comical. Staigrik stood large, hairy, and slightly portly next to Guenter, who was slender and beardless. He kept his blond hair at his shoulders. Staigrik's battleax, with the handle resting on the ground, stood up to the middle of Guenter's chest. Guenter did not carry a weapon.

"This is my son, Guenter, second in line to be king." Staigrik shouted his son's name, with bravado melded to each word. The crowd voiced its concurrence.

"Come," Staigrik bellowed. "It is time to show our guests that you are a man, my son, and a warrior."

The crowd again shouted their approval. Guenter, however, was apprehensive.

"Bring them out!" commanded Staigrik.

Five men and three women emerged from the side room of the Great Hall. They were filthy, their clothes in tatters. Now Guenter was deeply worried. His right eye twitched with nervousness. Staigrik ordering of the slaves with their arms tied behind their backs meant only one thing—they were going to die soon. A Saxon cut the rope binding the arms of a slave, freeing his hands. Another Saxon placed a short, damaged sword on the ground in front of the slave.

"We caught these Alamanni trying to steal our horses. Now they must answer for their crime."

Guenter knew that statement was a lie. *I know the Alamanni were captured during a raid on their village. Those who were not killed became prisoners, and these prisoners are about to become fodder for Father's whims.*

"Guenter will fight this slave to the death. Because he is my son, I know he will inflict the deserved punishment and kill the bastard!"

Guenter looked at the Alamanni. He was about thirty and barely wore any clothes. Those he did wear were shredded. The slave had long, dark, greasy hair. He gave the impression of someone who had not eaten for days. He was weak, and his left hand shook from a disease. The man's eyes gave no sign of life as he looked hopelessly at Guenter.

A Saxon warrior handed Guenter a seax. The seax, like Staigrik's battleax, gleamed in the firelight. The blade had been sharpened and could easily sever a limb.

The crowd urged the slave to pick up the sword and fight for his life. Instead, the man fell to his knees and began sobbing. The crowd's mood immediately shifted and called for Guenter to execute him for refusing to fight.

Staigrik joined in shouting, "Kill! Kill! Kill!"

Guenter raised his seax and looked down at the man. The man in turn looked directly into Guenter's eyes, calling for mercy. Guenter knew he could not execute him. He stepped back and lowered his seax. He looked at the men gathered around them. They had stopped chanting and stared at him, puzzled. Guenter released the seax and it dropped to the floor.

"I am not an executioner! I do not kill slaves or those who cannot fight for themselves. We do not need to do this!"

"Coward!" A shout came from the crowd. Additional cries followed. Guenter's concern shifted from the Alamanni slave to himself. Because Guenter was the son of a chief, he at first was not worried about his life. Now not only was his reputation at stake, but, more importantly, so was Staigrik's.

For his part, Staigrik was not only furious that his son would not kill a pitiful slave, but that he could not follow an order. He did not debate with himself which of the two took priority for his wrath.

Staigrik needed to do something to show the assembled warriors that he deserved their respect. He threw down his drinking horn and strode over to Guenter with his battleax in his left hand.

Guenter's relaxed attitude from just moments earlier changed abruptly. He was concerned for his well-being. Staigrik's intense anger was evident, and Guenter was very afraid.

X

CATALYST

The ship dutifully arrived on the west side of Italia at Ostia, near Rome, after an unremarkable voyage from Africa. Garzad and Honorario disembarked and had their horses brought to them. They mounted and rode to a large army barracks on the north side of Rome. The two men entered the officers' quarters and announced themselves to the commanding officer, a general named Diocles. The general was pleased to see them and handed Garzad a satchel.

"This is from the emperor himself." Diocles smiled and continued, "You made good time reaching Rome. Timeliness pleases the emperor. A separate written order placed in the satchel states that you are promoted to the rank of tribune. You are now Tribune Garzad. You have risen quickly in the ranks, and you deserve this promotion. Congratulations, Tribune."

Diocles saluted Garzad, which Garzad enthusiastically returned.

"I am pleased to accept the emperor's promotion. Considering only a few years ago I was just a simple soldier and now I am a tribune, this is such a reward. Thank you, General Diocles."

Garzad paused and looked in Honorario's direction. He turned back to Diocles. "General, I have one special request that I hope you will hear."

"Yes, Tribune Garzad. I already know what you are going to ask."

Diocles looked at Garzad and Honorario in quick succession.

Diocles dryly announced, "I have granted your aide, Honorario, status of centurion."

Diocles reached out and handed Honorario a separate scroll, which Honorario read quickly. The words confirmed that Honorario had been promoted. Honorario was ecstatic about receiving his new rank. He tried to control his emotions, but his joy showed in his broad smile.

"Congratulations, Centurion Honorario." Diocles grinned slightly in response to Honorario's exhilaration.

"Thank you, General Diocles," Honorario replied robustly.

Diocles moved on to the real reason for their meeting.

"You two now have the titles of tribune and centurion; however, you will have no centuries, no legions, and no army to command in the short term. Instead, your tasks are to collect information and conduct certain actions that will benefit our emperor. So far, your results have been exemplary. Keep up the good work and you will continue to be rewarded.

"I have a room in the barracks that will serve as your temporary quarters. There you will review the contents in the satchel. Later, you will join me for supper. Tomorrow, you will be on your way to your next destination. The emperor demands fast, excellent results, which you two have a history of producing."

An aide to Diocles led Garzad and Honorario to their quarters. As General Diocles ordered, they read the papers, ate their evening meal with the general, and left the barracks before the sun rose.

Within days, Garzad and Honorario were in Mediolanum. After a brief rest, the two traveled northward to a large fort in south central Gallia. Emperor Gratian, his court, various generals and officers, and two legions were stationed there. Following

General Diocles' orders, Garzad reported to the general's aide. They were also ordered to avoid meeting with Gratian.

"Do you think General Diocles is a relative of the old Emperor Diocletian?" Honorario asked Garzad as they settled into their quarters.

"Who cares?" Garzad responded flatly, as he truly did not care. "Your role is not to be concerned about past emperors, but to think about Emperor Gratian."

Honorario was downcast after being chastised.

"Diocletian was a great emperor, but he felt he needed to share power with other emperors. In the end, that arrangement failed."

Garzad smiled at Honorario and continued, "A strong emperor does not share power. Magnus Maximus will be such an emperor. Once he is the true emperor of the Western Roman Empire, he will not share the throne with fools like this one." Garzad pointed in the direction of Emperor Gratian's encampment.

"Remember what we came for, Garzad—to sting and not to kill. Others will do that for us."

"I know the orders, Honorario. I am just a tribune and you a centurion. However, we must cause the havoc that will allow the generals to do what must be done."

The next two weeks proceeded quietly. Garzad and Honorario observed the emperor's fort, and specifically the generals who exerted the greatest power. They also focused on the individuals and groups with whom Gratian spent the most time. At night, they compared what they had seen and Honorario wrote it all down.

General Diocles joined the camp one week after Garzad and Honorario's arrival. To their surprise, they learned through other officers that Diocles was an early mentor of their former general in Africa, Octavio. As planned, Diocles initially ignored Garzad. Instead, an aide served as the intermediary between the two men.

On the fifteenth night after Garzad and Honorario had arrived at Emperor Gratian's fort, a number of generals and their aides convened a meeting in a large room at the back of the fort. The drink flowed freely, as did the talk.

"This is foolish. We should be out fighting barbarians; instead, we sit here drinking and getting fat. We talk like old women." A general unknown to Garzad offered his opinion in a slurred voice.

"You are right," Diocles added. "My men are becoming soft. Soon the Goth women will be able to defeat us."

"Yes, I agree as well," said Garzad. "The condition of the men in this camp is appalling."

The unidentified general replied, his voice low and hostile, "Is this a joke? Am I witnessing a tribune addressing us as equals? This is not correct. Who is this man's commander?" The general glared at Garzad and added, "You should be reduced in rank and flogged for impertinence."

"Let the man be! He is my new tribune and I have given him permission to speak when necessary!" Diocles snapped back.

"You have taught him well, Diocles." The general's sarcasm flowed through the room.

"I want to hear more from this tribune," Diocles remarked calmly. "He is new to the camp. I want to find out where he has been and what he has seen."

The eyes of powerful generals focused on Garzad.

"I am Tribune Garzad, and I have spent the past several years in Africa guarding the fields and grain storage that feed the empire. My commanding general was General Octavio, whom many of you know."

Several generals nodded at the mention of Octavio.

"We were constantly on alert for bandits, and we seemed to be at endless war with any number of tribes in the area. We were battle tested and hardened by our experiences. What I see here is not what I saw in Africa. You have become soft."

Garzad's last statement elicited another uproar from the room. Curses flew at him. Another general's tribune drew his sword.

"Let him finish!" shouted Diocles. "You can tie him to a post and whip him when he has concluded his remarks—*if* you still think he is arrogant and does not speak the truth."

The room calmed and swords were sheathed. Honorario relaxed slightly, but his heart still pounded, anticipating a rough ending for him and Garzad. However, he noted that nothing flustered Garzad.

"You have an emperor who avoids battle and indulges himself with pleasures like drink," Garzad added forcefully. "Meanwhile, the barbarians run free, murdering and pillaging while we stay entombed in this fort. Emperor Gratian is to blame for the state of affairs in the empire!"

Garzad took a drink from the cup of wine in his hand, turned, and smashed the cup against the wall behind him. He faced the room full of officers again. He had everyone's attention. Garzad's thick beard foamed with white, causing a striking contrast to his angry, dark facial features. *I cannot tell if the foam is from the drink or drool as a result of his passion*, thought Honorario. *Whatever the cause, I know it has had an effect on the officers.* No curses emanated from the crowd this time.

"Gratian, the emperor you serve, even has *Alan* guards, not Roman guards! And he wears barbarian clothes! Why?" Garzad was in full lather. "This is a farce! We need an emperor who leads, not one who plays! We need an emperor who is skilled at punishing barbarians and taking back our territories. We pat the backs of the barbarians when we should be crushing our enemies—Rome's enemies—under Roman boots! This includes their women and children. If they can't be slaves, then we eliminate them!"

"Many troops in our army hail from the barbarian tribes." Someone spoke up from the back of the room. "Do you suggest we remove them from the army? We may have our own revolt!"

"Is this a Roman army or a barbarian army?" Garzad looked at the crowd and saw at least four Roman officers with apparent barbarian origins. He swiftly recalculated his comments.

"All current officers and soldiers shall retain their posts. But everyone must retake their oath of loyalty to the empire and to the true emperor."

"And tell us, Tribune, who do you suggest as such a leader?" The speaker at the back stood up. He had a low, powerful voice that easily filled the room.

"The man I propose to replace Gratian as emperor is Magnus Maximus—the great general from Britannia," Garzad responded. "The soldiers of Britannia and Gallia are already in full support of his claim to the emperor's purple. I, too, support this man to become emperor and I'm from Roman posts in Africa."

A long pause followed Garzad's proposal. Finally, the man with the low voice walked forward with bodyguards in tow. He was clean-shaven with a chin that protruded out past his nose. There was no mistaking the man—it was General Tiberian, a key general in Emperor Gratian's army.

"What you say is treason. Suggesting to overthrow a sitting emperor will not be good for your military career. You seem to forget that I, along with everyone in this room, took an oath to Rome and Emperor Gratian. The proper course of action is your torture and execution. Your centurion will join you."

Tiberian motioned his guards forward. Honorario cringed, but Garzad stood motionless and made no attempt to draw his sword.

XI

BUKARMA

"It is very good to see you again, Marcus."

The baritone voice belonged to Bukarma, but Valerias could not believe what he was hearing and seeing in front of him. They shook hands as if they were still in the army. Bukarma's arms were huge compared to Valerias'.

Valerias remembered those arms as a distinguishing feature of his old friend, who did not appear to have changed.

"Bukarma, what are you doing here? After Adrianople I thought you went to Africa, away from the legions."

"I did, Marcus. I went looking for treasure, and I found it!"

"What treasure did you find? Gold? Land? Ships?"

"Ha! Ha!" Bukarma laughed so hard he bent over at the waist.

"I don't understand. Why do you laugh? If your treasure was not those things, what was it?"

Bukarma waved his hand behind his back. A woman and two small children appeared. Bukarma motioned for the trio to stand in front of Valerias.

"Marcus, this is my wife, Penelope, and my daughters, Evaline and Lavonica."

Valerias was speechless. He took a moment to compose himself as he gazed upon Penelope and the two young girls. Valerias finally spoke, but in the formal way of a general. "I am most pleased to have you in my presence."

Bukarma cast Valerias a pained look, and then turned to Penelope. "I must interpret for Marcus. He is glad to meet you and invites us into his home. He acknowledges your beauty, my dear, and thinks our children are adorable."

Bukarma bent down and effortlessly picked up Evaline and Lavonica. The three were face to face with Valerias. Evaline reached out and touched Valerias' beard.

Bukarma smiled and added a wink. Both men laughed heartily.

Valerias shook off his surprise at seeing his special guests. He relished the opportunity to see his friend again.

"Please come in! Claire will want to see you."

"Marcus, she already knows we are here. It was she who invited us."

Claire watched Bukarma and Valerias talking together and crossed the room to join them. She embraced Bukarma lightly and greeted his wife and daughters.

Once all the introductions had been made, Bukarma and his family were shown to their table in the Great Room. Valerias lingered and gently tugged on Claire's sleeve to join him.

"You invited Bukarma and his family here and did not let me know? I am so surprised!"

"Perhaps you were not paying attention. They are the special guests."

"How did you find them? I lost track of Bukarma some time ago."

"About a year ago, I sent out messengers to find Bukarma with no results. Then one day I encountered an old soldier of yours, Duvanous, who knew where to find him. Duvanous and his wife are here tonight, as you know. He contacted Bukarma. Bukarma had been retained by a cruel nobleman who beat those who worked for him. It was a bad situation and Bukarma feared for his wife and children, so I invited them to come and live with us at the Villa."

"Where was I when all this happened?" Valerias asked, his face screwed up with confusion.

"You were up in the hills, searching for something, and that something is here. You are certainly much more than a man lost in the country. I want the man I fell in love with to really return to me and stay with me. I will help you. Bukarma will help you. Marcus, you are too vital to be confined to a shed talking to Wolf."

Valerias was embarrassed. "I know that I have been distracted and feeling low. As I told you in our bedchamber the other night, I am restless, searching for something. Perhaps I am trying to outrun or hide from my past. I also question whether I have a future. When I was in the army, everything was always clear to me. Now it isn't, and I am struggling. However, I want you to know that I have returned to you, with or without Bukarma. Of course, having Bukarma here will help me focus better!"

Valerias stopped talking and squinted slightly at Claire. "How did you free Bukarma from that cruel nobleman, as you called him?"

"It was easy, husband. I said he was commissioned to work for General Marcus Augustus Valerias. That was it; he released Bukarma from his employment. You see, your past is not something to hide from!"

Valerias smiled at Claire and held her hand as they moved to their places at the center of the head table. Bukarma and his family sat to Valerias' right. Claire, Alena, and Elsha were seated to his left, followed by an empty setting and chair.

Bukarma immediately was curious and nodded toward the empty place. "Who is that for, Marcus?"

"Joseph," Valerias replied casually.

"What?" Bukarma's brow creased in puzzlement.

"Yes, it is Joseph's, whether he is here or not. It is his permanent place. I realize it may seem absurd to keep a place for someone who is rarely here, but when I think of Joseph, balance is added to my life.

"Joseph is a bishop in Britannia. We regularly correspond, and Claire does too. He has established a vital ministry in his diocese."

"Does that mean you . . .?"

"No." Valerias cut off Bukarma's question.

"Claire?"

"No again, Bukarma. We are good friends, not converts. We have interesting discussions in our correspondence and when he comes to visit. He has strong morals, something I see little of in his religion."

"How often does he venture away from Britannia?" Bukarma asked.

"Joseph has visited us twice. He is required to make periodic trips to Rome. When here, he stays out and away from the Grand House in a shed I use to store tools. He believes his superiors would disapprove if they discovered that he resided in comfort with wealthy non-Christians. Joseph dines with us, though. I have told him that if he does not try to convert me or my family, he is always welcome. Otherwise, he and Wolf can dine together."

Valerias pointed to the large dog and laughed.

"What about Joseph and . . .?"

Valerias again stopped him mid-question. "That is for another time, my friend. Not now."

Bukarma knew to drop the subject.

The banquet was typical of those hosted by Valerias and Claire. A select group of former soldiers and noblemen and their wives attended. For Valerias, however, the evening was anything but normal. The surprise appearance of Bukarma and his family rekindled nostalgic feelings from his past. When he looked at Bukarma's children, he thought of Alena and Elsha when they were young, and of little Anastasis from the poor village after the battle with the Suevi raiders many years ago.

He was most pleased with Claire, who made the evening possible. It was her efforts that brought him back from the dark abyss. He vowed that he would not let her down.

After the banquet, Valerias and Bukarma sat outside watching the stars. It was a new moon, so it was nearly black at the Villa. Torches had been lit, but the darkness seemed to steal the light. Wolf lay at Valerias' side, but it was Bukarma who reached over and rubbed the dog's head.

"I have recently been discussing something with Claire, and having you here has solidified my ideas. I would like to open a training facility in the empty parcel of land north of the Villa."

"Do you want to train gladiators?" Bukarma asked, unsure what Valerias meant.

"Of course not. Our forefathers can have that display of barbarism. No, this facility would train men, and I suppose women, to fight and defend themselves with various types of weapons and techniques. I also want to teach strategies that can be employed in different battle conditions. For example, one session would instruct how to defend a village. Basically, the sessions are for those who want to learn what I can teach them. They may benefit from my experiences. Now that you are here, you can be my partner. You have as much experience as I do in the ways of war."

"Who would take this training? How long would the sessions last? What would the nearby Roman governor-general think about you, and not him, training his men?" Bukarma asked his questions rapidly.

"Anyone, anytime, and I don't care. General Victus over there," Valerias pointed to the west, "is weak and indolent. He could pass for the village idiot. His forces are not ready for any kind of combat. Emperor Valentinian, if he was still alive, would have removed him long ago. Unfortunately, General Victus is the governor, for the time being."

"He may grow jealous, Marcus. Then you will have another enemy to contend with."

"And so I will. Maybe Emperor Gratian will remove him or transfer him to the lower Danube where he can learn what a real enemy is. Perhaps the Goths can teach him about warfare."

"Be careful, Marcus. Even the village idiot can carry a knife and have friends—dangerous friends."

"I understand, Bukarma. I will not underestimate the man."

***

The construction of the training facility was completed within one month, although its final location was farther north than where Valerias and Bukarma had initially wanted it. Claire liked the idea of the facility because it would keep Valerias centered and occupied. However, having too many men close to the Villa and her daughters made Claire uneasy. Valerias also felt uncomfortable with Alena and Elsha having potential suitors nearby. When Claire pushed for a more northerly location, Valerias agreed and the new site was selected an easy one-hour horse ride north of the Villa.

Word about the facility spread before it even opened. Valerias was approached by men of all types wanting to learn what he could teach them. They included former and current soldiers, villagers, and strangers. It was well-known throughout the land that General Valerias had never lost a battle, including several where he was outnumbered. And he had defeated the Huns at the famous Battle of Three Tongues. General Marcus Augustus Valerias was a legend.

The horrific defeat of the Roman army at Adrianople and the Goths' subsequent rampage of the countryside and attempt to storm Constantinople created a lack of confidence in the army. Thus, a desire arose from local citizens and army units to establish their own strong defenses against the barbarians' menacing presence.

Valerias' training camp was developed to address that need, and Valerias and Bukarma promoted the camp among the locals. Consequently, a number of groups and individuals told Valerias that they would come to his camp. Valerias and Bukarma anticipated the multitude of attendees and appointed a suitable number of instructors.

Activities at the training facility progressed well once it opened. Some men trained at the camp for one day and others stayed longer, depending on their profession. Current Roman soldiers stayed the least amount of time while soldiers out of the army generally stayed longer. Retired soldiers, including Duvanous, were the preferred instructors.

Valerias did not charge a fee to attend the camp. He was not interested in making money; instead, he wanted to field the next generation of Roman soldiers and officers who could defend the empire. Proper training would go a long way to meeting that goal, he believed.

After the end of a productive session at the training facility, Valerias said to Bukarma, "Our training camp is a success. We need to come up with a name for it."

"I agree. But I don't understand whether it is the facility, the trainers, or all your war stories that attract the most trainees."

"Well, if it is my war stories, then you must be failing at *your* job."

"Perhaps it is a little of all those, Marcus." Both men chuckled.

After a few moments of teasing each other, Marcus concluded, "Bukarma, you are doing a masterful job running all this. I know it is in good hands and I do not need to be here as much. I am going to return to the Villa for a few days."

"I understand. You have been away from the Villa for almost two weeks. Do you miss Claire?"

"Of course. However, I need to do something that I fear."

This piqued Bukarma's interest. "You, the great general, fear something?"

"Yes. I promised Alena that I would discuss potential suitors. I know Elsha will listen in as well. Alena is of a suitable age and Elsha is on the cusp. I also fear time. It doesn't seem that long ago when the girls were interested in what I could teach them. Now they are thinking of marriage. I will soon turn into just a memory."

Bukarma laughed enthusiastically as Valerias squirmed. The upcoming encounter with his oldest daughter was one Valerias did not relish.

"Someday you will be in my position, and then you won't laugh so hard," Valerias warned, grimacing at Bukarma.

Valerias slowly returned to the Villa. He entered the Grand House and walked to his study, a room oblong in shape and naturally dark except when the sun shone through a window in the afternoon. Valerias sometimes spent time hidden away in there to avoid people.

As expected, Valerias found Alena waiting for him. Claire and Elsha stationed themselves in the background.

"I see you knew I was coming, Alena."

"Yes, Father, I have my sources—as you do."

"Is everything going well for you?" Valerias was not sure what to say. He felt uneasy.

Claire noticed the state of her husband and interjected. "Marcus, when will Bukarma join us again? Penelope and the girls dine with us, but I think Penelope desires for her man to return."

"I will have him return the day after tomorrow. We are taking a break in the schedule anyway. We will resume in one week's time. The . . ."

"Father!" Alena politely cut off Valerias, as she knew he was stalling.

Valerias decided to meet the challenge, like all others, straight on. "Alena, I know perfectly well what you wish to discuss, and in the end, I know what you want. It is not that easy, though. There are men of all types out there who would like you for a wife. Most of them, though, are not worth Wolf's bedding. I see these men and know what motivates them and how they act when your back is turned. I will not have my daughters marry anyone who is unworthy of them."

Valerias tried to give both Alena and Elsha a stern look. Wolf cocked his head.

"What do you expect, Father? Shall Elsha and I end up lonely old women?" Alena's eyes flashed determination.

"Of course not. But tell me, who do you propose is an acceptable suitor for you?"

"What about Legathos? He is mature, and I heard you say he is a good soldier."

"He has a wife in another province."

Valerias replied so swiftly that Alena was caught off guard. She was flustered but quickly regained her composure.

"Antonio, then."

"He wants to get close to me through you. Instead of falling in love with you, he wants to gain my favor. He is a weakling."

"Cariso?"

"Too old."

"I guess you have an excuse for any name I provide, so it is hopeless."

"Not at all, Alena. It takes time. And as I have told you and Elsha, your mother and I will never allow you to become involved in an arranged marriage. We want you to fall in love, as we did. Love takes time. I promise you that there will be candidates who rise to the top."

Alena knew she wasn't going to move the conversation any further and gave Valerias a curt nod. She knew her mother and Valerias cared deeply for her and her happiness, so she decided to wait a little longer before pressing the issue more strenuously.

Valerias smiled and said, "Give it time." He was secretly relieved the topic had been shelved awhile longer. Yet he admired Alena's ability to stand up to him. He knew the day would come when he could no longer delay or deny what was inevitable—Alena would take a husband.

Supper that night was a pleasurable affair. Valerias spent part of the time demonstrating all the tricks he had taught Wolf. Claire noted none was taught well and she mused who was the better trainer, the man or the dog. Alena and Elsha debated between them who was the greatest Roman emperor. Valerias refused to become entangled in the debate. He grunted as he told himself that he would not declare most emperors "great."

After supper, Valerias returned to the study to review materials for the training facility. The room was dark when he entered and as he moved to light a candle, he was stunned to find a man resting comfortably in his chair.

XII

ROAD TO BERGEN

Drostan endured a restless night. He awoke several times, thinking about his past, present, and future. Over and over he contemplated a host of random thoughts. *Why did my mother desert me? Will I see her again? Will she want to see me? How could she marry a Roman? How are Joseph and the Romans connected? Was Bishop Joseph a Roman soldier?*

It disturbed him greatly that all he had were questions and no answers. His frustration became relentless. Additional thoughts arose. *Why do I feel such pressure? Is it from the weight of all my thoughts?* He abruptly opened his eyes and found the rotund Brother Silas rubbing his shoulder in a not-so-gentle manner.

"Wake up, Drostan. Father Timothy and Bishop Joseph want to see you now. You were having a bad dream. You were twitching all over your cot and mumbling nonsense. They were not Christian thoughts."

"It was closer to a nightmare, Brother Silas."

Drostan saw Brother Silas' jealousy of his unexpected favorable status with the bishop in his curled lip and narrowed eyes.

"Why do you rate so highly with a man of the bishop's position? You are not even good enough to be a monk." Brother Silas' sharp tone confirmed Drostan's thoughts.

"He knew my parents, Brother Silas. That is all," Drostan said quickly to limit Brother Silas' suspicion.

"At some point, I would like you to talk about your parents," Brother Silas responded, not giving up. "In the meantime, make haste to the study, where the bishop and the abbot are breaking their fast."

When Drostan arrived at the study, Joseph and Father Timothy were waiting for him.

"Drostan, are you ready to accompany me into the village?" Joseph spoke without hesitation. Father Timothy nodded in agreement.

"Don't worry what the others will say. Father Timothy will handle that. I must say that I approve of the Father's willingness to mix with the villagers. I think an order cloistered behind walls is a waste of human spirit when so many others outside the hermitage need our spiritual guidance."

Joseph and Drostan left Father Timothy and arrived at the gates of the hermitage on foot. Joseph looked forward to what was outside of the gates while Drostan glanced back at the buildings.

"Normally, we would travel by horse. However, Branodunum is nearby and I don't want the brothers to think I am giving you preferential treatment. We will walk."

Drostan was relieved at Joseph's decision, but for a different reason. He had no experience riding a horse and didn't care for the animals.

When they had traveled about five hundred yards from the hermitage, Joseph began a monologue. "What I am about to tell you is what I have learned from your mother in our letters and meetings. You and I briefly discussed this yesterday. Today I wish to be more specific.

"Your mother was a queen, Queen Claire, of a kingdom many miles west of the hermitage. Your father was King Gerhard. You have two sisters, Alena and Elsha. Your sisters live with your mother on an estate owned by your mother's husband, retired Roman General Marcus Augustus Valerias. The estate is located about fifty miles east of Mediolanum in Italia.

"When you were young, your father was killed by Saxons in a battle. His death was actually arranged by Argus, who was your father's uncle. After your father's death, Argus craved the throne. To get it, he tried to force your mother to marry him. Of course, you were the true heir to the kingdom and Argus wanted to have you killed. Your mother, though, was clever and quicker than Argus. She faked your death and sent you to the hermitage at Branodunum where Father Timothy accepted you.

"Your mother fled from Argus. She was very fortunate to have survived. One of the people who helped her was General Valerias. As you know, they married. Argus died at the hands of the Romans. Your mother's brother, your uncle Eustice, became king after Argus' death. For a number of reasons, your mother willingly ceded any claim to power to Eustice.

"Believe me, your mother wanted to send for you, but it was too risky. Argus, even in death, has many followers who want to kill you and your mother out of vengeance. Your mother still has a price on her head that tantalizes the groups of brigands that infest our country.

"You see, Drostan, we live in a lawless time. The Roman usurper, Magnus Maximus, has declared himself emperor of the western part of the Roman Empire. And Britannia is under his rule. The usurper's attention is not on Britannia, though; it lies to the south, to perhaps even Rome. The Romans are beginning to pull out of Britannia and soon the Britons will be on their own.

"Rome's void has drawn the attention of Britannia's enemies. The Picts are crossing Hadrian's Wall to the north, the Scoti are invading from Ireland in the west, and then there are the Saxons, who raid along the eastern coast.

"As a result, I have counseled your mother not to visit you. It is also too dangerous for you to try to leave the safety of the hermitage without a proper escort. And Father Timothy has informed me that you do not wish to leave Branodunum.

"Be that as it may, your mother has vowed to visit you this year. When she does, you can decide whether to stay and become a monk or leave for Italia with her. The choice will be yours *after* you speak with your mother. Until then, you are not to speak to anyone about our conversation today. Do you have any questions?"

He did have several questions, and Joseph tried his best to answer them. However, he refused to answer anything Drostan asked about the future. He would only say, "It is in God's hands."

Drostan liked Joseph and was drawn to him; he was calm and direct. Even though he had known the bishop only a short time, Drostan had no doubt Joseph was a religious and truthful man.

Drostan was also interested in Valerias. In particular, he queried, "Joseph, as a man of God, how could you be close friends with a Roman, who was a brutal military man and is a non-Christian?"

Joseph evaded answering by saying, "You will learn these things when you meet him. Know that Marcus Augustus Valerias is a man you cannot ignore or forget."

Drostan looked confused and Joseph added, "Marcus and your mother form a powerful, loving union. Your mother is very happy to be married to him and him to her. They are good for each other."

After a visit to the village of Branodunum, Joseph and Drostan returned to the hermitage. Joseph met privately with Father

Timothy, and then held meetings with several of the monks. When Drostan arose the next morning, Joseph and his horse were already gone.

Joseph stopped at the nearest village south of Branodunum and filled his flasks at a wine merchant. He knew he would need full flasks for the task ahead.

A group of Roman cavalry rode through the small village, and Joseph, who was not eager to travel alone in the rural, wild country, joined the riders. The trip to Bergen, in Joseph's mind, hurried by much too fast. Once in the village, he bid farewell to his escorts.

The villagers immediately recognized him—he was a luminary to them. He had been their priest when no one else wanted the position, and now he returned as a bishop. Joseph did not want all the attention he received, but in his position, he had to accept it. And Bergen no longer had a priest.

Several villagers wanted Joseph to perform various religious services for them. Joseph explained that he would conduct all such rites for those who requested them. But first, he had to make a stop.

Joseph gave his horse to a stablehand for feeding and grooming. The owner of the stable agreed to the task if Joseph would bless him, his family, and his stable. Joseph complied and then walked to the house at the end of a long street. The house was still as Joseph remembered it—two stories tall and well kept. He approached and said a prayer for guidance as he knocked on the door.

The door opened and out stepped a woman with the radiant beauty he recalled.

"Joseph!" the woman shouted and gave Joseph a warm embrace.

"Good day, Ruth." Inwardly, Joseph felt an unwanted longing as he returned the embrace.

"I am sorry, Joseph, I should address you as Bishop Joseph."

"For you, Ruth, Joseph is fine." Joseph saw that Ruth's face had not changed in the years since they had last seen each other. He looked up to Ruth's immediate right at a man clutching a baby.

"Joseph!" the man said in exactly the same tone as Ruth. He handed the baby to Ruth and embraced Joseph.

"It is grand to see you, Olivertos." Joseph returned Olivertos' embrace.

Joseph recalled many years ago when Valerias had spared his life in the Roman camp. It was Olivertos, the kind physician and skilled surgeon, who became one of his mentors. He had learned so much from Olivertos: the pursuit of knowledge, ways of healing body and spirit, and insight into understanding those around him—particularly the great General Valerias.

He further remembered the days after the bloodbath at the Battle of Three Tongues. Olivertos was overwhelmed with the futility of his efforts against the butchery and slaughter. The human devastation of the brutal war had broken him. The crushed shell of the healer was removed from the battlefields of war and taken to Britannia by Joseph. And yet, here Olivertos stood, rejuvenated in his new life.

"And who is this?" Joseph smiled at the baby.

Ruth and Olivertos hesitated briefly. Ruth looked at Olivertos and Olivertos said, "His name is Joseph."

Joseph was happy and pained at the same moment. Yet, he showed only happiness toward his two friends. Joseph took the baby and gently held him in his arms.

"I see the resemblance of you both in the child, but it is more than just a physical presence. He wears a look of kindness and serenity that both of you possess. I feel honored that he has the same name as me."

"He *is* named after you." Olivertos' eyes showed a softness that melted Joseph's apprehension.

Joseph gave the baby back to Ruth and looked down. A toddler looked up at him through Olivertos' legs.

"And who are you, young man?" Joseph smiled.

The child felt comfort in Joseph's face and voice. He said shyly, "Jacob."

Joseph was warmed by the mention of Jacob. Joseph's memory took him back to the man he knew as General Valerias' administrator. Jacob was a kind, intelligent man who had saved his life; a man who died before his time. Joseph said a silent prayer for Jacob's soul. *May he rest in peace.*

Joseph became so lost in his thoughts that Ruth had to speak his name twice to snap him back to reality.

"Please, come inside," she offered.

Joseph obeyed and walked into the house that he had first entered ten years earlier.

"Is Garth here?" Joseph inquired about Ruth's father. He noticed the house was in about the same condition as when he had first seen it.

"No, Joseph. My father died almost a year ago now. He fell ill. It was sudden. I am grateful, though, that he lived long enough to see his grandson, Jacob."

"I'm sorry to hear that he died. He was a man of God. I will add a blessing in his name tomorrow, and I will include him in my prayers tonight."

"Thank you, Joseph. Now I must make our evening meal. You *are* staying for supper." Ruth avoided meeting Josephs' eyes.

"Yes, I will share supper with you. I am hungry from my travels. First, though, I must walk to my former church and check its condition." Joseph continued to feel uneasy in Ruth's presence.

"Are you aware that we do not have a priest?" Ruth asked.

"Yes, I know. There is a monk at the hermitage of Saint James who has expressed an interest in transferring from the hermitage to Bergen. He would be a good fit here. We should know his decision soon."

Joseph craved a break in conversation with Ruth and eagerly left for the church. He was pleased to find it just as he left it. Several villagers stopped to talk to him as he walked there and during his time at the church. What they chatted about was so varied that Joseph felt a rekindled exuberance for his ministry. He knew the village deserved a good priest as soon as possible.

He lost track of time. After consoling a woman who had lost her garden to hares, he turned and was surprised to see Olivertos.

"I am pleased you are still at the church. Ruth sent me to escort you back for supper. I also want to talk to you alone," Olivertos said.

"That is fine, Olivertos. I am finished with church matters for the time being. Let me fetch a couple of things and then we can go to your house. I am hungry, and my stomach recalls that Ruth is a good cook."

Joseph collected a book, a small flask of water, and a cloak, and walked briskly to the entrance. Olivertos had gone outside to wait for him and ended up talking to fellow villagers. Joseph stared at his friend from the church door. He seemed younger than when they had left for Britannia after the battle with the Huns almost nine years earlier. *Married life away from the legions has served him well*, thought Joseph.

When Olivertos saw Joseph emerge from the church, he excused himself from the villagers. Seeing that no one else was nearby, Olivertos immediately started talking.

"I know how hard this trip is for you, Joseph."

"That is nonsense, Olivertos. I looked forward to coming back to my first church. I enjoy visiting my dear friends."

"You know what I mean." Olivertos peered deep into Joseph's eyes, trying to see if he could retrieve an honest response.

Joseph's eyes, though, did not betray his thoughts. "I do know what you mean. I am very happy for you and Ruth. And now you have two wonderful children who are named after my favorite people." Joseph laughed at his remark and continued, "I know little Joseph and Jacob will grow up to be like you two—extraordinary people."

"She still loves you, Joseph." Olivertos was serious.

"I love her too, as well as you. My first love, however, is Jesus Christ and the church that serves my Lord."

"Do you ever regret not marrying Ruth and becoming a less-committed disciple of Christ?"

"No. I choose Christ over all earthly matters. As a famous general once said, 'I have no regrets.'" Joseph replied, referring to Valerias, and he knew his quote was not entirely truthful for either him or Valerias.

Olivertos laughed at Joseph's comment and Joseph responded with more laughter, though more out of a hopeful relief that the line of questioning was to end.

"How is the General? I know you have seen him."

"Yes, twice. He lives with Claire on a large estate east of Mediolanum. He adopted Claire's two daughters, Alena and Elsha. Claire writes to me that she is concerned about him. He tends to wander off into the nearby hills and forests, sometimes for days at a time. I believe all the past warfare and his approaching status as an elder have taken a toll on his spirit. But Marcus still is, and always will be, the General. And he keeps a permanent place for me at his supper table, even when I'm not there."

Joseph and Olivertos laughed again—Joseph genuinely this time. Olivertos placed his arm around Joseph's shoulders as they walked back to the house.

Ruth's supper was everything Joseph thought it would be, and he ate ravenously. After supper, he pulled out his ritual book, cloak, and flask of water, which he said contained holy water. Joseph blessed each child in a formal ceremony. When the ceremony was over, Ruth and Olivertos felt they too were blessed.

Yet, Ruth was mildly concerned. "Joseph, why did you conduct the blessing at our home instead of at the church as part of tomorrow's mass blessing?"

"I want to perform a special blessing for you, whom I consider my closest friends—outside of Jesus, of course. And there is Marcus . . ."

Olivertos chuckled at the mention of Valerias. Ruth did not understand the remark.

When the children had been put to bed, Joseph said a prayer over each child as sleep washed over them. Joseph, Ruth, and Olivertos subsequently had a lively conversation late into the night. Joseph even imagined he saw Garth sitting in his customary chair, taking in the discussion. After bidding Ruth and Olivertos good night, he returned to the church.

The next day arrived warm and sunny. The entire village came for the service—after all, it was the prodigal son, the bishop, who would be leading the ceremony. Joseph gave a sermon on being true followers of Christ. When the service was over, he spent several hours chatting with the villagers and conducting a multitude of blessings and prayers. Ruth and Olivertos felt Joseph's private blessing for their children was indeed special. The village then held a banquet in Joseph's honor and Joseph was treated to another delicious meal.

At the end of the long day, Joseph said good evening to his remaining visitors, and lastly to Ruth and Olivertos.

Joseph told them, "I will visit Bergen again within the year. It will always be a home to me."

After they left, Joseph returned to the church and closed the door. He pulled a flask from his belongings and took several deep drafts. The pain, though, would not subside as it usually did when he took to the flask. So he drank another flask of wine. In a moment of self-pity, he told himself, *If events had played out differently, Jacob and Olivertos would be the names of my children.*

The next morning, Joseph awoke to a choir of tiny anvils hammering in his head. He still managed to leave the church, find his horse in the stable, and depart before the village stirred. He rode away from the rising sun, toward a new destination. This time he was alone, and that did not bother him.

XIII

REGA

Dawn muscled its way into the departing darkness as wild birdcalls echoed back and forth from the nearby forest. Eustice had always liked this time of day. A fresh start to life was how he referred to dawn. It wasn't so much that it was a new day, but a day to accomplish something new, and perhaps better than the day before.

Eustice was a happy man. He was the undisputed leader of a substantial kingdom in Britannia. He preferred to be addressed as king by his subjects. Only his closest friends or equals called him by his given name, and that name was only to be used in private. His kingdom was relatively quiet due, Eustice believed, to his leadership of the army that had recently repulsed a large group of raiders from the north.

Eustice was forty-two years old and had established himself as a well-respected ruler. He had brought his kingdom back to a prosperous state after the disastrous rule of the dead tyrant, Argus. He was clean shaven. When he was on the run from Argus, he had grown a long, unkempt beard. As king, he vowed never to grow a beard again.

As calm returned to the kingdom, Eustice married a beautiful woman, Rega, who was the daughter of another king, Maxwellium. Rega's beauty was renowned throughout the region. She was a tall, full-figured woman with raven black hair. A small beauty mark graced the left side of her chin. The color of her eyes mirrored her mood.

As a princess with striking physical attractiveness, Rega was a valuable commodity to Maxwellium. He had several suitors for her hand, but he had held out for the man he wanted most for his daughter—Eustice. Maxwellium's patience was rewarded when Eustice and Rega were wed as autumn turned into winter.

The marriage had been strategically arranged. Eustice belonged to the Coritani tribe and Maxwellium to the Cornovii tribe. The Cornoviis occupied the land west of Eustice's kingdom.

Eustice and Maxwellium agreed that Eustice bonding with Rega would allow the two kingdoms to form an alliance—an alliance that would better repel both internal enemies and foreign invaders. Further, there was the possibility of absorbing other provinces and kingdoms in the future. Rega was Maxwellium's only child, so on his death the two kingdoms would merge to form a large realm.

Rega had slept late that morning, as she was inclined to do. She had told Eustice that morning that sleep allowed beauty to last longer. Eustice loved her beauty, and so he let her rise at her choosing. On this particular morning, Eustice convened a small army of his trusted officers for a deer hunt. The sun eased its way into the forest as Eustice and his company set off to kill as many deer as they could.

After a couple of hours traipsing through the woods and nearby meadows, the group had killed only a small doe and a hare. Eustice, frustrated and hungry, decided to return to the old Roman castrum, called the Black Fort by the native Britons. His companions wisely chose to give him credit for killing the deer, although he had been relieving himself at the moment of the kill.

On his return to the fort, Eustice found Rega breaking her fast.

"Best of the day to you, my beautiful wife." The newness of marriage had not yet worn off. He always beamed when he saw her.

"Good morning, my great king. How was the hunt?"

"Slow. We only killed one deer. The deer population is down this year. I don't know why." Eustice did not want to give his wife even an inclination that the poor morning hunt was not a result of the deer population, but from a lack of passion from the hunters.

"Was it you who got the kill?"

"Yes," Eustice lied, hoping no one from his hunting party would reveal the truth.

Someone had, though. Voltrex, who had been with the hunting party, had returned ahead of the king and told Rega the truth about the hunt. Voltrex, Rega's loyal advisor from Maxwellium's court, was slightly taller than Eustice but much slimmer. He had a contrarian attitude that Eustice found annoying.

"Husband, why don't you ask your servants to bring a late meal for you? I am just finishing mine and would like your company."

Perfect, thought Eustice. *A poor hunt results in eating with my wife. I prefer to be with her than to hunt anyway. And it is comfortable in the fort.*

"That is a charming idea, Rega." Eustice ordered a servant, "Bring me a feast fit for a king. I am starved!"

As a rebel against Argus, Eustice had become a tough and skilled outdoorsman. Living off the land for years had turned him into a hardened warrior. To his men, he was known as Iron Eustice. Now, after almost ten years of living as king in the Black Fort, he had become soft. His every need was catered to by servants who pampered him. Claire would not recognize her brother.

"Rega, I would like to start a family. I need a male heir. Will you soon be ready to have children?" Eustice's food arrived as he posed the question. He started eating as soon as the food was placed before him, almost forgetting the question he had just asked.

"What?" Rega sputtered.

Rega's reaction sent Eustice reeling. "I'm sorry, my precious queen, for startling you." Eustice paused, not wanting to irritate his wife. "I was out on the hunt today and thought what a good thing it will be to hunt with my sons."

"What if your children are daughters?"

"Yes, they could come too." Eustice's response was lukewarm at best. He was far more interested in having sons.

"Forgive me, my king. I did not expect the subject of children to come up so soon. I understand your desire, though, and I will consider what you have asked. Unfortunately, my monthly courses have arrived so we cannot indulge. I hope you understand, my sweet Eustice. We can arrange to try for a later time."

Eustice was dejected, but he showed none of that emotion to Rega. As king, he had grown to expect quick actions in response to his commands. He also had recently become highly impulsive on the subject of children. He now knew he would have to temper his requests for heirs.

"I understand, my queen. We can wait."

"Do not worry, husband. You shall have heirs in no time. As I have told you before, it is good that your sister renounced all ties to the throne. And I understand her two daughters have no claim to your throne either." Rega's reference to Claire, Alena, and Elsha sought confirmation from Eustice.

"Yes, they live with the old Roman general, Valerias, somewhere in northern Italia. The letters that I have received from my sister give no indication that her mind has changed regarding the crown. Claire is happy with her life in Italia."

"Does Valerias have any thoughts of laying a claim in Britannia because of his marriage to Claire?"

"No, Rega. First, he is a Roman and not a Briton. Second, he has no desire to return to Britannia. He almost died here and would have except for the intervention of another Roman general, Titus."

"My father knew Titus," Rega recalled. "I even met him once. My father said he was a fair man—for a Roman."

"Claire will stay with Valerias in Italia. She has no ambition to return to Britannia. She has grown accustomed to Roman finery. Her daughters have as well. I will wager they are more Roman than Briton now."

"Yes, and Claire is without a living male heir, so I agree, you have no reason to be concerned. I will produce an heir for you. Give me time." Rega stood up and rubbed her husband's shoulders.

Eustice was pleased. His sister posed no threat to his crown, he had a wife who he loved, and she loved him. He was about to suggest that they return to bed and practice conceiving regardless of her cycle, but his thoughts were interrupted.

"My king," a man interrupted then paused.

"Amron, continue," Eustice said, waving his hand to confirm his words. Amron had been promoted to captain when Eustice became king. Despite Amron's origins being from western Britannia, Eustice trusted him implicitly.

"We have received word of a vicious squabble between two villages about a half day's ride west from the Black Fort."

"What is the nature of this squabble?" Eustice asked, unhappy that he had been interrupted for something so trivial. *I am king and should not have to deal with a petty problem like this,* he thought.

"It is a disagreement over water rights, my king."

Eustice had already made up his mind to dispatch one of his senior captains to address the situation and turn his attention back to his lovely wife.

Amron wasn't finished. "And there is a rumor that Morguard is in the area."

Nothing could have upset Eustice more than the mention of that name—Morguard. Morguard had formed a triumvirate of evil in Eustice's mind that included Argus and Flavius. Together they had killed Gerhard. They had forced Eustice out of the kingdom to live like an animal. And they had held his sister captive, and then tried to murder her when she escaped.

Eustice hated the vile trio and ten years on still thought of them daily. When Argus ruled the kingdom, he initiated a bloodbath that murdered a multitude of men and women, and turned the kingdom into a poverty-stricken land. Flavius and Morguard had been Argus' killing instruments.

Eustice gritted his teeth. *Argus was killed at the hands of Titus. Flavius, though, leads a comfortable life in Spain. I should have executed him long ago. That damned Valerias saved his life. Morguard has not been seen for many years. He may be dead, or he may be alive. Either way, Morguard escaped my justice.*

Eustice cursed all of them by name out loud. Thoughts of Rega melted; his focus was revenge.

"Captain Amron, assemble a cavalry unit of fifty good soldiers. We leave for those villages in one hour. I will settle this matter and be back here tomorrow afternoon." *Unless we encounter Morguard*, he thought. *Then I shall stay until I slay that monster. Hunting Morguard will not be like hunting does.*

Eustice turned to Rega. "My queen, I will return as soon as I have dealt with this problem. I must prepare for the journey."

He gave Rega a light kiss and left with Amron. Soon Eustice and a large company of cavalry rode out of the Black Fort. Rega watched them leave. She headed back to her room and dismissed her servants, saying she did not feel well and needed to rest.

Rega closed and carefully locked the door. She disrobed and climbed into bed—and into Voltrex's waiting arms.

"We have all afternoon for pleasure, my love, before anyone becomes suspicious," Rega purred softly.

"Maxwellium would highly disapprove of this behavior. And Eustice would kill me." Voltrex smiled broadly and kissed her warm neck.

Not only was Voltrex about to bed the queen, but he did not care for Maxwellium or Eustice. Part of what he was about to do with Rega was out of spite.

"Take me," Rega murmured. "Take me now and do not waste a moment."

"Yes," he responded softly. "I will do my best to serve the queen."

XIV

Unforeseen

It took time for Valerias' eyes to adjust to the dark and focus on the intruder sitting in his chair. Valerias was unarmed, and he knew a potential assassin sat directly in front of him.

"Who are you? What do you want?" Valerias said sternly.

"You are an old man. You can't see, and are unarmed. If I was a barbarian, you would no longer be standing!"

The man's voice gave him away. "Then it is good that you are not a barbarian. You would be a poor excuse for one," Valerias responded.

"I was a poor barbarian, but, alas, I am now a poor Roman citizen," the voice said.

"Who was the fool who helped you become a citizen of the empire?"

"That would be the former General Valerias—now a farmer lost somewhere in the hinterlands."

"Revious, you are here!" Valerias could not play any longer. He was too excited to see his old friend.

Revious and Bukarma—we are together again, Valerias thought.

The two men embraced.

"How long has it been since I last laid eyes on you, Revious?"

"Five years, General. Remember? It was at Adrianople." Revious pointed to his head, indicating Valerias' poor memory. "Emperor Valens and his mistress went up in flames. You buried their jewelry and I returned several times to find it, but never could."

"How do you know I actually buried it?"

Revious could not tell if Valerias was serious or just being coy.

"I want you to think about that, and maybe someday, when I'm old and infirm, I will tell you."

"You already are, General. So, tell me now."

"I forgot, Revious. When you get old like me, sometimes your memory fails."

"See, you admit you are old!"

The two men laughed. Soon they were catching up on the directions their lives had taken over the past five years until the talking left them thirsty.

"I will get wine and we can talk more."

Valerias called for a servant. As they drank, Valerias asked Revious, "Tell me, what brings you to my Villa? I am not fighting any wars, except with the wretches that inhabit these hills. I know your visit is not happenstance. So . . ."

"I have something for you to see, General. But I will not discuss the matter further until you see what I'm talking about."

"Is this a riddle, Revious? Because I can't talk about something I know nothing of. What am I to think?"

As much as Valerias was pleased that his old friend and former chief scout was again in his presence after so long, he suspected there was a serious purpose and it was not merely for pleasure.

"You can think about passing me more wine," Revious said, holding out his cup.

Valerias poured wine for each of them from the carafe the servant had left.

"Where have you been, my old friend?"

"I have been everywhere, General. I spent time east of Germania, in the company of the Alans."

"Aren't they your people?"

"Oh, yes. But one has to be careful with whom one associates and fights—even if those people are his people. This is especially true if one rode with an infamous Roman general and is now a Roman citizen."

"Interesting. More riddles from a poorly performing scout!" Valerias added, "When and where do we look for your mystery?"

"If the General approves, we can leave tomorrow. It is less than a quarter day's ride from here—to the east."

"We will leave at sunrise. I will inform Claire. Do I need a squad of cavalry to accompany us?"

"No, all you need is your poorly performing scout to protect you. You do not need to worry, though. As an old man with one hand, not even the wolves will want to feast on you!"

Both men laughed. Valerias finished his wine and showed Revious to his guest quarters. He then joined Claire in their bedchamber where he told her of Revious' surprise visit and their journey the next day. Claire was suspicious of Revious' motive, but she kept those suspicions to herself. Her husband was in high spirits, which she did not wish to deflate.

At sunrise, and in a drizzle, the two men set off to the east. The dampness turned into dry warmth as the morning sun perched above the clouds. Valerias and Revious took little notice of the weather or terrain as they continued to recall their pasts. They dissected the Battle of Three Tongues. Their interest was not so much on the results but why the battle took the course it did. It was a subject that Valerias had replayed over and over in his mind. Revious had a keen understanding of the battle and offered points of view, which Valerias eagerly absorbed.

Valerias informed Revious, "Bukarma has reemerged in my life, too, and is the manager of the training facility at the Villa. He has a wife and two children. What happened to you, old scout? No woman would take you with that hairy monstrosity covering your face?"

"I have had many women," Revious responded. "Too many to choose from. I am pleased for Bukarma, though; at least he found one woman who could put up with him!"

Valerias fixated on Revious' mustache. "Revious, I have never seen such a hairy eyesore. Can you sheath your dagger in that mustache?"

"The women love it, General. And I'm not in the army anymore, so what do you care?"

After approximately three hours of easy riding, Valerias and Revious faced a steep ridge. The short climb was arduous, and the horses had to navigate around jagged boulders and trees. Revious was first to reach the top. At the summit, they were greeted by an equally steep, obstacle-strewn slope down into a lush green valley. Valerias scanned the valley and his eyes focused on the scene at the bottom, where luxuriant vegetation and a quiet stream created a picturesque landscape.

But Valerias' attention was not on the scenery.

"Revious, what am I looking at?"

"Refugees. They come from lands far to the east," Revious answered, looking directly at Valerias.

"I see," responded Valerias as he continued to gaze at the wretched mass of people. "How long have they been here?"

"Two days. They are new to the area."

"Do you know on whose land they squat, Revious?" Valerias asked, his voice dripping with sarcasm.

"Yes. It is your land, General."

Valerias sat motionless on his horse. He stared at the people, unblinking. When he spoke, he barely opened his mouth. “And who are these people?”

Revious replied with one word: “Huns.”

XV

KING

Guenter cowered from his father. His weak action toward the Alamanni slave had spurred the assembled Saxons into a frenzy.

"Punish him!" voices in the crowd yelled. "A son must obey his father! Be a man! Coward! Punish him!"

Staigrik strode up to his son. That was the easy part. Now he had to act. That would be the hard part. He knew a show of disrespect from a son to a father could not be tolerated. He, Staigrik, was the heir to the throne, and he did not want to show weakness in front of his fellow warriors.

However, Staigrik was torn as to what to do about Guenter. *How severe a punishment shall I inflict on my son? I must do something, but I do not want to hurt him too badly.*

He had to appease the crowd, which was at the point of becoming unruly. On the other hand, his wife and Guenter's mother, Hildegarde, would never forgive him if he was too harsh. Most importantly, the king would not forgive him.

Staigrik decided he must be a forceful leader. A rash thought entered his head: He would cut off Guenter's little finger. *He can live without that finger,* he reasoned. *And I will not be criticized by my wife or the king.*

He grabbed Guenter's left hand and slammed it down on a table. He had already set aside his battleax and pulled out his seax.

Guenter did not say a word and did not resist. He turned his head away from his father.

Staigrik placed the seax a few inches above Guenter's hand, where his little finger and his palm met. Before he sliced off Guenter's finger, he glanced at his son. Guenter turned back and saw a father who appeared reluctant to take such an action. But Staigrik's words told him differently.

"Next time you will obey me!" Staigrik shouted to the room.

His words were quickly followed by another cry. "Halt!"

A figure moved forward slowly from the back of the hall, his arms draped around two large men. Several other burly men—bodyguards—trailed behind him. Guenter stared at Alfredson, the king of this Saxon clan, father of Hildegarde, and his grandfather.

The assembled warriors parted obediently for Alfredson as he moved to the front near Staigrik and Guenter. Most of the men yelled war cries; others shouted his name. Alfredson appeared unmoved by the mass until he reached the front.

The two men carrying Alfredson placed him gently on a large chair covered in furs. They then took positions holding spears on each side of their king. Alfredson's other bodyguards stood in front of him facing the crowd. A large wooden staff shaped like a serpent was presented to him by one of his bodyguards. The serpent had the head of a dragon and the tail of a snake that was tipped with a wooden sphere. Alfredson surveyed the crowd. After he was satisfied that everyone's attention was on him, he hammered the end of the staff onto the floor three times. The sound echoed throughout the Great Hall and quietened all within.

"I am the son of Gertoff, grandson of Hermson. I am Alfredson, your king! Do you pledge your loyalty to me?"

The crowd roared their support. Alfredson's powerful voice belied his frail physique. His wispy white hair revealed an old man, while his bright blue eyes and voice conveyed a warrior with absolute power.

"Does anyone here reject me as king?" Alfredson stared at the room with blazing eyes. For the first time, the Great Hall became totally silent.

"You will support Staigrik, the husband to my daughter, Hildegarde, and heir to my throne!"

The Saxons again voiced their agreement loudly and enthusiastically as Staigrik raised his great battleax in acknowledgement, despite his uncertainty of the meaning of Alfredson's intrusion.

"And you will support my grandson, Guenter! He is Staigrik's heir!"

The crowd's response was muted this time. Alfredson again hit the floor three times with his staff. The sharpness of the strikes vibrated like tidal waves of air. Alfredson's bodyguards stiffened, their large spears at the ready. This time the Saxon warriors responded more vigorously.

"I would like to speak to my daughter's husband and my grandson about an important matter. We will return shortly. In the meantime, help yourself to my beer."

Several servants appeared in the Great Hall carrying large wooden kegs of beer. Soon the hall was awash with drink. The issue between Staigrik and Guenter was pushed aside.

The two large men accompanying Alfredson carried him to a small, more private room off the main hall. Once comfortably seated, Alfredson ordered his bodyguards to stand outside. They took Staigrik's weapons with them. Alfredson motioned for the father and son to sit in front of him.

"Grandfather, thanks be to the gods for your timely appearance. I did not want to kill an Alamanni who did not want to fight," Guenter explained breathlessly about the odd situation the king had walked in on.

"I do not care about a worthless Alamanni prisoner, grandson. He means absolutely nothing to me. However, you, Guenter, are important to me."

Staigrik looked annoyed, but Alfredson gave him a quick flick of his wrist, telling him to be quiet.

Alfredson spoke sternly to Guenter. "You disrespected your father today. When your father gives you an order, carry it to fruition. He will soon be king and you are to follow his command. There is to be no question. Saxons follow their leaders' orders. A son must follow his father's orders!"

Alfredson turned to Staigrik and then back to Guenter as he spoke. "Your father is a great warrior and I have no doubt he will be a good and just king."

Staigrik felt a rush of satisfaction as he heard Alfredson's words. But he still felt a strong desire to punish his son. *I am the future king, and I cannot be shown disrespect from anyone, including my own son.*

Alfredson read Staigrik's thoughts as they flitted across his face. "Leave your son be. He will do as he is told from now on. This matter is concluded.

"I had a dream last night, which is why I came to the Great Hall today, the hall of our ancestors. I dreamed of a messenger sent by the gods in the form of a raven. He spoke to me in the old tongue, which only I understand. The raven said Guenter will be a great king."

Staigrik became agitated at Alfredson's story and started to protest. Alfredson waved his hand, and Staigrik immediately fell into a trance and sat motionless, staring unseeing like a statue at Alfredson.

“Guenter will someday be the king of our people. This is the will of the gods as they spoke to me, and so it is to be. You, Staigrik, must make sure this happens. To go against the gods will prove fatal. Do you understand?”

Staigrik nodded without expression.

XVI

UPHEAVAL

General Tiberian's guards flanked Garzad on his right and left. Honorario stood nervously behind him. The guards had not drawn their swords, but their hands rested on the hilts. Tiberian stood directly in front of Garzad and glared straight into his eyes for several long moments. Garzad did not flinch. It was not in his nature. Instead, he stared just as harshly back at Tiberian.

The general broke the silence. "Why should I not have you arrested, bound, and dragged in front of Gratian where he can proclaim your punishment, which would be death? Or I could be the instrument of the emperor and execute you myself as a traitor to Rome."

"Before you become the emperor's instrument of death, I have one question for you, General Tiberian. As an agent for Rome's greatness, do you condone Gratian's flirtations with the Alans? He dresses like those barbarians instead of a Roman emperor. I cannot respect such behavior from an emperor. Do you respect such behavior?"

"It is not my place to like or dislike the emperor's way of dress, with whom he associates, how he behaves, or even how he breathes. He is the emperor. He commands and I obey."

"Yes, it is your position to obey the emperor," Garzad responded with a touch of earnestness. "Years ago, I never would have made such a suggestion as I do now. Emperor Gratian of yesterday won battles and proved to be a good administrator. But that time is gone. Now he is more Alan than Roman. He is corruptible. That cannot be accepted."

From his peripheral vision, Garzad saw several officers in the room nodding.

"Tell me, General Tiberian—in his present state, do you think Emperor Gratian has the balls, the will, to fight our enemies? Or will he do nothing, or even join the barbarians?"

"Of course he would fight the enemies of Rome. It is not my place to say what the emperor would or wouldn't do. But you seem to know, Tribune. Have you ever met the emperor?"

Tiberian stepped back slightly from Garzad, but his eyes didn't stray.

"Perhaps we should attend the emperor's court together and see what he thinks of your idea," Tiberian continued. "I doubt he will treat you or your idea kindly. When was the last time you trimmed your beard to look like a Roman officer, Tribune?"

"His beard is irrelevant to this discussion, General Tiberian."

"Ah, General Diocles speaks. Your lackey needs his defender!"

Garzad stepped forward into Tiberian's space. "I am no lackey and I need no defender!" he shouted. "And I have a beard because it covers the many scars I received in conflicts with rebels and various African tribes. I proudly carry these wounds because of my sworn duty to the empire, but I don't need to share them with anyone."

"Where precisely did you serve in Africa, Tribune?" Tiberian's attitude changed slightly from his confrontational stance.

Garzad recounted the units he had served with, the officers he had served under, and the battles he had fought. He praised the leadership of General Octavio, his mentor. When he finished, Garzad noticed Tiberian had relaxed.

"I support everything said by Tribune Garzad. We all agree, Octavio is a great general and a personal friend of mine," General Diocles added.

Tiberian ignored Diocles and spoke to Garzad. "What you say may or may not be true, Tribune. And my colleagues here in this room may or may not agree with you. What is true is that you sponsor the removal of Gratian as emperor. And you want Magnus Maximus to take his place. Is that accurate?"

Without hesitation, Garzad agreed. "Yes, the great general of Britannia, Magnus Maximus! He should wear the purple!"

"Do you think he can defeat the sitting emperor, Tribune? From Britannia as well?" Tiberian fiddled with the gold chain around his neck.

"Yes, General. Even now his forces have crossed the Narrow Sea from Britannia and are marching through Gallia. I promise you that Maximus will not be wearing the clothes of the barbarian Alans when he triumphs over Gratian. He will restore the empire to its great glory! You and your officers can become part of his court!"

Several officers in the crowd nodded vigorously in agreement. A few men shouted their approval. Tiberian noted the responses but waved his hand for quiet.

"Should Maximus defeat Gratian and become emperor, will he then turn his attention to the boy emperor, Valentinian, in Italia? I do not much care to serve a child."

"General, I cannot tell you what Maximus will do when he takes the purple from Gratian. You can ask the true emperor yourself, if you join us."

Tiberian looked into Garzad's eyes before turning to face the officers, who pressed closely to him. He placed his hands behind his back and stood motionless before speaking.

"Tribune Garzad is a traitor," Tiberian said without emotion.

Honorario's heart sank, and he feared what was coming. He noticed Garzad did not move, not even to put his hand on his sword.

"He is a traitor . . . to this emperor—Emperor Gratian."

The officers in the room murmured to each other in confusion.

Tiberian continued, "I, too, have witnessed the actions by our emperor that Tribune Garzad has spoken about tonight. I also have seen evidence of his administration's ineptitude and the corruption of his officials. I have done nothing in response to that which I have seen. When I take an oath of loyalty, I take such an oath seriously and to my death. However, under these conditions, I can no longer support Emperor Gratian. We need a change. Tribune Garzad has opened my eyes to what I already knew, but I did nothing to remedy the problem."

Tiberian glanced briefly at Garzad before returning his attention back to the room. "All junior officers, leave now. That includes you, Tribune Garzad. I must consult with the generals about how we will proceed. Before you leave, I want all of you to take an oath that what has been said in this room, at this hour, on this day, is kept among us. Failure to keep this a secret will result in your death, either at my hand or Gratian's. We must take action or let the Alans be our commanders."

Tiberian pulled his spatha from its sheath and raised it over his head.

"Do you swear on the fate of our empire that your allegiance is to the empire that we serve and not the emperor in power, and that you shall not speak of what we are about to do in service of the empire and the new emperor?"

A hearty, "Yea," greeted Tiberian in response to the oath. All the officers lifted their spathas in the air above their heads three times.

After Garzad and Honorario left Tiberian and the generals, Honorario said proudly, "It is an honor to serve with you. You turned a great general from loyally supporting Emperor Gratian to supporting Maximus. There was a moment when I believed Tiberian would execute us for treason. Then he ended up agreeing with you!"

"I only pointed out to Tiberian what he already knew, but his passiveness was an obstacle to our plan. I simply planted the seed, Honorario. Now it is up to Diocles to bring in the harvest. I was the catalyst. I have no doubt our generals will convince the others that our way is best for Rome. I predict Gratian will be dead by the end of summer. I would personally like to be the one who removes his head; perhaps Maximus will allow me the honor."

XVII

Sanctuary

Valerias sat astride his horse like a statue unmoved by time. He stared down at the Hun camp with an occasional blink, the only evidence he was alive. Even Revious, a man known for his extreme patience, grew restless and swatted at a fly.

"Revious, tell me again what I am looking at," Valerias instructed, breaking the long silence. He still had not moved.

"Huns, Marcus. They are Huns."

More silence followed. Revious finally had enough. "This is not what you think, Marcus. These Huns are what is left of a tribe that revolted against their leaders."

"Did they fight against us at the Battle of Three Tongues?"

"They fought for Uldric, if that is what you mean."

"So, these Huns are our enemy—my enemy."

Valerias turned his head and gave Revious a scowl that would cause most men to recoil in fright. Revious, though, was not most men. He was used to Valerias and he stared back, unflinching.

"Yes, they fought for Uldric, who is dead. They chose not to fight for the new leaders and came here. They are not your enemy."

"Explain further, Revious." Valerias turned back to watch the Huns.

Revious knew that the future of the Hun camp depended on his answer.

"The Huns you defeated were from a group called the Northern Confederation, led by Uldric. When you defeated the Northern Confederation, you also decimated them, including their leadership. That left a vacuum that was filled by the Southern Confederation and a powerful leader named Zestras. Zestras unified the tribes, but he died. His son, Braga, took over as leader. He was weak and eventually assassinated. After that, the Huns splintered back into tribal groups. Groups that did not have strong affiliations were caught in shifting allegiances and targeted for attack.

"That is what happened to the group before you." Revious gestured to the crowd below. "They fought for Uldric, and when that failed, they declared loyalty to Zestras and Braga. That also ended in failure. After Braga's death, they became a tribe without support from any other Hun tribe—outliers, if you will. Consequently, their camp was constantly raided by other tribes to supply those tribes with slaves. In the interest of self-preservation, their leader brought them to where you see them now."

"How did they find their way to my land from a place so far east?" Valerias never averted his eyes from the people below.

"I brought them here, Marcus."

Before Revious could say more, Valerias snapped another question. "And how did an Alan from the Roman army end up riding with Huns, our enemy?"

"It is a long story, Marcus."

"Give me the short version." Valerias' patience was tried.

Revious nodded. "After our battle with the Huns, I became a Roman citizen—for which I am grateful to you. I then decided to return to my Alan homeland, where I quickly became bored. So, I left and traveled to the land of the Goths to seek employment as a scout and find a Goth wife. You know the Goth woman can be beautiful, good fighters and . . ."

"I was unaware of all those attributes. Continue."

"Instead of finding Goths, I ran into the Hun clan you see below. It didn't hurt that I knew their chief scout, a man named Arb."

"I recall him," Valerias said with a slight frown. "He rode with Uldric and was a translator for him during our parlay before Three Tongues."

"The Huns were on the run from tribes that wanted to kill or enslave them," Revious reiterated. "When Arb asked me to find them sanctuary, I knew where to take them."

"And you assumed I would let them trespass on my land." Valerias' face was twisted with open annoyance and he began waving his arms around in frustration.

"I knew you would be fair, Marcus, and hear what they ask." The request had turned into a plea.

"You have assumed wrong, Revious. I will not allow my enemies free range over my land!"

Revious opened his mouth to speak but was immediately cut off.

"You have a choice now, my friend. You can return with me to the Villa and its accommodating surroundings, or go and live with your poor friends in their squalor. In any event, I order them off my land within one week."

Valerias wheeled his horse around and rode back down the slope of the hill. Revious remained on the crest of the hill, torn between his past loyalty to Valerias and his new life as protector of the displaced Huns. After about a hundred yards, Valerias stopped and looked over his shoulder at a motionless Revious. Valerias sat on his horse remembering his experience with the Huns at the

Battle of Three Tongues. He then thought of his friend. Valerias sighed, turned his horse around and rode back to Revious.

"Revious, do you trust these Huns with your life?" Valerias asked as he reached Revious.

"Yes, I do, Marcus. I do."

"Can I trust them with my life?"

"Yes, you can. I place my own life in front of you as an affirmation to you that I speak the truth." He bit his lip as if considering whether to say more. "The Hun tribe on your land believes you are a god."

"Ha!" Valerias scoffed. "Does that make me a god?" Valerias held out the stump at the end of his left arm.

"With or without your hand, they think you are a god—with a little vulnerability. You are the warrior who defeated the Huns in battle. You killed Uldric. Many Huns considered him a god, and you slayed him. That makes you a god in their eyes."

Valerias could see that Revious was telling the truth. "A god?" After a few moments of thoughtful silence, Valerias said, "Take me to their camp, Revious. I have changed my mind and I want to put your faith to the test."

"Were you testing me now—whether I would come with you or stay with the Huns?" A quizzical look spread across Revious' face.

"Perhaps I was, my old scout."

The two men rode down toward the Hun encampment. About five hundred yards from the camp, a cry sprang from the group in the valley followed by several calls of warning. A man emerged from one of the ramshackle shelters. He mounted his horse and rode up to the two approaching men. Valerias watched several others run to their horses carrying bows and swords.

"Now we shall see your judgment of character in action, Revious."

Revious suspected Valerias actually looked forward to the impending encounter with the Huns. Doubts, on the other hand, had sprung into his head. Revious was now concerned that the meeting might not work out well for everyone, including himself.

The first rider came closer. He was a small man with Alan features and wore a large red head covering.

"Revious!" the man cried out. "We have been awaiting your return."

"I am back, as I promised I would be, Arb."

Arb glanced at Valerias, who was watching not only him, but a procession of riders coming up fast. Arb heard the approaching horses and put his arm up, signaling for them to stop.

"General, we anticipated your arrival. Revious said you would come!"

The excitement in Arb's voice surprised Valerias. Then, without taking his eyes from him, Arb held up a single finger. A rider emerged from the pack, an older man with abundant gray hair that was partially tied behind his head and flowed halfway down his back. He was slender but hard and sinewy. Valerias immediately knew he was their leader.

"General Valerias," Arb began. "This is our leader, Oxanos the Great."

Oxanos waved off Arb as he sauntered his horse up to Valerias. Oxanos stared intensely at Valerias, who stared back, unblinking.

Oxanos smiled. "My friend Arb jests, General Valerias. I am not 'great.' I am simply Oxanos, the elder here. If I was 'great,' I would not be here in front of you begging for mercy for my people."

"What mercy do you want, Oxanos? But first, you speak Latin intelligibly. How?"

"Our friend Arb and your General Revious are teaching us the language of the Romans. We are getting better, but we have much to learn. We want sanctuary from our Hun enemies. They seek to enslave or kill us if we stay in the lands of our ancestors."

Revious could not read Valerias' expression as he listened to Oxanos.

"Yes, my friend Revious is a good teacher and also a great storyteller. General Revious, translate Oxanos' last statement into Hun for me." Valerias spoke without a hint of sarcasm, which made Revious nervous.

Revious could only roughly speak the Hun language. He had to rely on Arb to translate accurately. Valerias noted that Arb, on the other hand, seemed fluent in all the languages needed to communicate between the parties.

After enough awkward chatter, Valerias said, "Oxanos, I would like to see your camp."

"General Valerias, I am ashamed to show you our settlement. It does not reflect well on us. We have barely arrived here and . . ."

Valerias stopped him. "I would like to see the state of things as they are. I will let you lead."

As they rode down to the Hun encampment, Revious glanced over to see if Valerias had any trepidation about entering the camp. After all, he and Valerias were descending alone into the den of what could be dozens of hostile Hun warriors.

Valerias showed no emotion, yet he spoke quietly to Revious without turning his head.

"I have put my trust in you. I hope your evaluation of this situation carries through to reality."

The living conditions in the village were even more squalid up close. Valerias' first impression was that the Huns were an unkempt lot of vagabonds. They were malnourished, and many exhibited signs of disease. Which diseases, Valerias could not tell. Yet as he passed by the people, they all stood silently with their heads bowed. No one brandished a weapon.

"Oxanos, why do your people bow to me? I am not the emperor."

"They bow out of respect for you, General. You are the great Hun killer. You are master over Uldric."

"That would make me their enemy. They should want to kill me."

"No, no, great General. You are above a man. You are a god in man's form."

Revious shot Valerias a look, pleading with him not to say anything to the contrary. Valerias understood and said nothing.

Oxanos added, "You also have provided a safe place for us. In return, we will do whatever you ask of us."

Valerias reached the center of the camp. He stopped, still atop his horse, and watched Oxanos, Arb, and Revious dismount. He started to climb down as well, only to find three Hun men waiting to help him. Another held his horse. Once back on his feet, Valerias was escorted to a fire pit. It looked robust and healthy, unlike its caretakers, with a ring of stones and logs around it to contain it and serve as seats. Valerias was offered the largest boulder, which had a flat surface, upon which to sit.

Revious sat to his right; Oxanos and Arb were to his left. Older men occupied the rest of the seats nearest the fire. Younger men, women, and children stood around them. They all seemed fascinated with Valerias' presence. Many pointed at the sturdy metal cover over the stump of his left forearm.

One woman brought him a drink. Another served him food. Despite his reticence to eat anything offered by an erstwhile enemy, it was polite to at least try the offerings. Valerias found they tasted better than he expected, particularly the beverage. He declined the Huns' offer for more food, but accepted more drink. He took a sip from his refilled cup and nodded at Oxanos. *It has an odd but good flavor. Yet, I do not want to know the contents*, he thought.

Revious interrupted his thoughts and whispered, "They want you to speak."

Valerias spoke hesitantly, "Oxanos, I welcome you and your people to my land. I understand you have had a harrowing journey here. What is it you want from me?"

Oxanos replied in broken Latin, but Valerias understood. "Great General, you see before you remnants of our once-bountiful tribe. At one time, we were five thousand strong with one thousand warriors. But war with the Romans and Goths reduced our population. My own Hun people tried to wipe us out. There would be none of us left if we had stayed. So, with the help of Arb and your General Revious, we came to your land. We ask your blessing to give us sanctuary here. Otherwise, we will die out."

"How many of you are here in this camp?"

Oxanos responded, "There are three hundred seventy-eight of our people. We have one hundred and eleven warriors. Four hundred of us died on our journey here. Most of our livestock perished as well. Fortunately, many horses survived. We are a very poor people who have come a long way from our homeland. We are also a proud people, so it hurts us to ask you for help."

"Oxanos, you realize you are in an area that has never seen a Hun before, and has very little knowledge of the Huns. What has been heard of your people is not good. Your reputation creates terror among the locals."

"That is why we need your help, great General."

Valerias looked into Oxanos' eyes and saw an earnestness he did not expect from a Hun. He looked at Arb and Revious, and saw the same look. He focused on those around him. He saw a wretched people, not a bloodthirsty, warlike horde of barbarians. Valerias reached a decision regarding their future.

"Oxanos, your people may stay here temporarily until I decide on a more permanent solution. However, I have two conditions that I expect to be obeyed without question and without exception. Those conditions are: You are to stay in this valley and not leave it, and you are not to conduct *any* raiding. You will live in peace. If you fail to meet these conditions, I will bring the might of the Roman army down on you, and your tribe will be expunged from this earth."

Oxanos and the tribal elders listened intently. After Valerias finished listing his conditions, they were translated for the Hun elders. In unison, the elders nodded their approval. One elder spoke softly to Oxanos, and Arb translated.

"The elder wants to know what will happen if outsiders come into the valley and cause trouble for our people."

"If you have any problem with outsiders, send Arb or Revious to me at once. I give you my word that I shall personally deal with any incursions into your area. This valley is quite remote. It is mine, though I rarely come here. Your concern should not be an issue, but it is noted."

Subsequently, more drinks were poured. The Huns discussed many subjects, including detailed aspects of the plight of Oxanos' tribe and the condition of the Hun tribes after Braga's death. One subject that fascinated Valerias was the Battle of Three Tongues from a Hun's point of view.

Valerias became thoroughly engrossed in stories of the Hun way of life and the weapons they used. Before he realized the time, dusk had settled into nighttime. Valerias and Revious decided to stay the night rather than pick their way back in the dark. At first light, the two bid goodbye to their hosts and left to return to the Villa.

The first words Valerias spoke when they left the camp revealed a reservation that Revious rarely witnessed in Valerias.

"Claire is going to be quite upset with me. She will be worried, and rightly so. She will think I have been harmed or returned to my wandering ways."

"Perhaps she will understand when you tell her why you did not come home last night."

"No, I deserve her wrath. She will be justly concerned." Valerias paused, gazed at Revious solemnly, and added, "Your immediate future with Claire will not be much better than mine."

Revious altered the topic. "Marcus, why did you change your mind about letting the Huns remain on your land?"

"I have empathy for their plight, Revious. That is all."

"What would a younger General Valerias have done? Would he have brought the army to the valley and wiped them out?"

"I do not have to make that decision. A younger general may have taken a different approach. Mark my words, though: If they conduct any raiding of innocent people, you shall see what a younger me would have done. I am counting on you to see that I do not have to be an enforcer again!"

XVIII

Renewal

Valerias and Revious arrived back at the Villa in the late morning. It was quiet; there was no sign of anyone, including attendants to take their horses. Valerias knew what it meant.

"You know I was worried." Claire strode out of the Grand House's main door and came straight to Valerias, Wolf walking briskly at her side.

Revious mumbled about having something to do, but Valerias grabbed his arm. "You are not going anywhere, my friend."

Claire continued. "For months you went off to who knows where for days at a time, and I worried. I thought something had happened and you weren't coming back. I had visions of your bones being picked over by scavengers. You finally returned to me as the man I love, and then you leave again. You tell me you are going somewhere to see something, but you don't know what. You do not come back at night. What am I to think, husband?"

"I am truly sorry, Claire. I did not mean to worry you. A very unusual thing happened to me yesterday. As you can see, I am all right. So is Revious."

Claire's anger toward Valerias faded slightly with the word "unusual."

"Tell me what was *unusual* that kept you away for the night."

"Revious wanted to show me something."

Claire's glare shifted from Valerias to Revious. It was a cold stare.

"Revious, it has been a long time since we have seen each other. Now you just appear and then Marcus is gone. You tell me what was so unusual to take my husband into the countryside overnight."

"Claire, I escorted refugees to your valley located two ridges east of here. They were being persecuted by other tribes. They would be dead if they hadn't come with me. I wanted Marcus to meet them. He did, and he offered them sanctuary."

Valerias scowled at Revious, and Revious added quickly, "He is *considering* their request for permanent sanctuary."

"Who are these people, Revious?" Claire was curious.

Revious hesitated. When he spoke, his voice was low and barely audible. "They are a tribe of Huns."

"What?! You took my husband to the camp of his enemy? What if they had wanted revenge?" Claire shouted.

Valerias interjected. "They are no longer my enemy, at least not this band of Huns."

"How do you know that?" Claire again glared at Valerias and then at Revious, trying to understand what the two meant.

Valerias said, "I know because I trust Revious. And I met these Huns. They are very poor, bordering on starvation, and many are ill. I took pity on them. They gave me their word they would stay in the valley, which will serve as their sanctuary in the short term. They will not raid. If they disobey, I will crush them."

Claire relaxed. She trusted her husband implicitly. He always had been an excellent judge of character and manager of difficult situations. She looked Valerias in the eye and said, "I want to go to the camp and see these Huns."

Valerias was not surprised. They were partners, and she wanted her part in this.

"I do think you should see the conditions of this group. Wc leave the day after tomorrow. Revious will take us there."

Turning to Revious, Valerias said, "Prepare for our return to the Hun camp. I want to take them supplies for shelters and food. And I want to talk more with them about Three Tongues."

Two days later, a small group consisting of Claire, Valerias, Revious, and a retired soldier from the training facility left in the early dawn as the sun began to crack the horizon. Bukarma was reluctantly left in charge of the Villa for the day. He, too, had wanted to see the Huns. The group brought four packhorses carrying supplies consisting of foodstuffs, tools, and a tent. Revious was surprised that Valerias had authorized even these limited supplies be provided.

"Marcus, you have grown soft. You provide aid to the barbarians instead of unleashing your sword." Revious gently teased.

"Perhaps it is your kindness that I want to emulate, Revious."

"No, I think the spirit of Joseph has affected you. Perhaps you are becoming a Christian."

Valerias shot a challenging glance at Revious. "You don't need to be a Christian to give some measure of comfort to those who need it."

Claire listened to the men's conversation and changed the subject. "I forgot to tell you, Marcus, that while you were away, a man came to visit you. His name is Gulic. He said he knew you."

"I do not recall such a name," Valerias said, his brow creasing as he thought about who it could be.

"The man anticipated that response. You may remember him as Sivas Gul the Goth. He has a Roman name now: Severus Gulic."

Valerias pulled back on his reins and drew his horse to a sharp halt. "Gul? Here? Why?"

"Gulic is a tribune in the Roman army. He is a highly decorated engineer. He said it was you who gave him a chance for rebirth."

"Sounds like another Joseph," Revious said.

Valerias stared at Revious. "Both men were enemies of Rome when I first encountered them. They would have deserved any punishment I doled out to them. Instead, I was merciful. And look how my mercy turned out—Joseph is a bishop and Gul, or Gulic, is a tribune."

"Jacob may have influenced your mercifulness. Claire also has been good for you." Revious winked at Claire.

This time, Valerias did not look at Revious. He focused straight ahead at something the others could not see. "You are correct, old friend. I wonder what I would be like today without my friends' and my wife's influences."

Claire added, "Many influences shape our being, not just one person or act. The fact that you did *not* execute Joseph or Gulic is indicative that you are not quite as hard a man as you thought you were."

"You are my optimist, Claire. I love you for that." Valerias continued to look straight ahead. "Please tell me more about Gulic."

"Gulic was humble, not arrogant like some Roman officers I have met. He is on loan to Emperor Gratian at Emperor Theodosius' behest to construct a bridge over a river not far from here. It will be a challenging project. I like Tribune Gulic, based on our conversation."

"Did he tell you about my first encounter with him?"

"No, but Bukarma did. Bukarma told me that you acted correctly. Gulic should have been executed for leading his men against your army."

"Yes, he should have been executed, yet he wasn't, and now he is here as a tribune in the Roman army. He also appears to be a favorite of the emperor, and he is a Goth."

"You made a powerful impression on him. Tribune Gulic speaks of you like a son does a father."

"Good. We shall invite him to the Villa after our return, assuming the Huns don't butcher us."

Valerias looked at Revious, who just shrugged and smiled back.

When the foursome reached the ridge before the Hun camp, a large Hun suddenly appeared from behind a thick pine tree, armed with a bow, the arrow poised. He was nervous and Valerias saw the slight twitching of the arm that held the bow.

Valerias motioned for his group to stop. He realized that he should have sent Revious ahead to announce their coming. *I have been away from the army for too long now, as I set us up for an ambush.*

Valerias decided the best course of action was to wait the Hun out. A call came from the other side of the ridge in the Hun tongue.

Arb rode up to the Hun with the bow and issued a short command. The Hun relaxed.

"We cannot be too careful." Arb spoke in Latin. "We have posted sentries on both sides of the valley; we do not want to be surprised."

Arb's attention turned from Valerias to Claire. "Domina, Revious has told me about you. You are most welcome to our camp, as poor as it is."

"Revious has told me about you as well, Arb."

Arb kept smiling, but he was unsure whether that was good or bad.

Those thoughts rolled around in Arb's mind until Revious brought him back to reality. "Arb, lead the way."

The group slowly rode into the Hun camp. The presence of the men in Valerias' group barely caused a stir. Claire drew all the attention. Several Huns pointed at her, and when she dismounted, women of the village crowded around her, some touching her clothes and her hair.

Claire's background as a former queen allowed her to remain stoic, although her mind churned. She could not help but remember that the last Huns she encountered had tried to kill her, her friends, and her husband at Three Tongues. And she had killed them. Now she was in a camp surrounded by her old enemy.

A sharp command was shouted above the din. The crowd backed away from Claire as Oxanos approached the group.

"Welcome, great General, as you return to our camp. Who have you brought with you today?" Oxanos said in Latin.

"This is my wife, Claire. Claire, this is the Hun's leader, Oxanos.

Oxanos was not shy. "I watched you riding side by side with the great General, not behind the men. Therefore, the wife of the great General must also be a great person. Please join us at our camp."

Oxanos spoke soothingly, and Claire relaxed.

"You will have to pardon my people, Domina. They have never seen a Roman woman before. You were not afraid to come here today. I admire that."

Oxanos spotted the packhorses that Valerias brought.

"Claire and I," Valerias looked over at Revious, "and Revious, brought supplies to help you—mostly food and a tent."

Valerias gazed at the shelters the Huns had erected in the valley. They were constructed of wooden boughs and branches, and were of such poor quality that he likened them to hovels.

"Revious will show you how to set up the tent. My soldier behind me will distribute the food. We also have tools for you. They should help."

Revious erected the tent, and the food was unloaded and given to the Huns. Valerias was pleasantly surprised that the Huns waited their turns for the provisions. There was no rioting that Valerias had previously witnessed even in civilized areas during food crises.

Afterward, the Huns prepared a meal for their guests. Valerias enjoyed the food. Claire sat beside Valerias during the meal and behind her stood what seemed like the entire population of women in the camp. Revious and Arb sat on the other side of Oxanos.

"You have made a great impression, Domina. Revious and Arb have told me that you were with the great General during our battle and that you killed several of Uldric's fighters."

Both Claire and Oxanos noticed Valerias' uneasiness at Oxanos' comment.

Still, Claire replied. "I did not want to kill anyone, Oxanos; however, I had to protect our physicians. The Huns were the attackers, and I defended my people from their attack."

Oxanos looked at Arb and Arb translated. "Romans use the term physicians; we call them healers."

Oxanos turned back to Claire. “I have heard you are a bow warrior, and that is how you killed the Huns.”

“Yes, I used a bow. My father taught me when I was young, and I have honed my skill over the years.”

“Domina, would you honor us by showing your skill with the bow?”

“I did not bring it with me.”

Oxanos was visibly disappointed. He issued a command and a Hun brought a bow to Oxanos, who presented it to Claire. She took it with her left hand and examined it carefully. The bow did not resemble one she had seen before. Oxanos noticed Claire’s puzzled look and explained that it was a recurve bow, shorter and heavier than a typical Roman bow. The stave was a composite of bone, sinew, and horn. Valerias also took a turn holding it.

“Not today, Oxanos,” Valerias said. “However, I would like your men to provide Claire and me with a demonstration.”

Oxanos gave an order and several Hun men appeared with bows. Each carried two arrows. The group left the fire pit area where they had eaten and moved to a clearing. A large log placed in the clearing approximately fifty yards away from the archers served as their target. Several smaller pieces of wood were added to the top of the log.

All the Hun men hit the log with their first arrows. The shafts penetrated deeply into the wood. The smaller targets were subsequently knocked off the log with the men’s second arrows. Valerias was impressed with their accuracy and force.

He had witnessed the skill of the Hun archers during the Battle of Three Tongues. He now observed up close how deadly the Huns could be with a bow. Valerias knew good Roman archers could be effective in battle, but the Huns’ skill was a notable notch above a Roman archer’s ability.

"Domina, would you like a turn?" Oxanos again gently prodded Claire to show her talent.

She thought to herself, *Why does he want me to use the bow? Does he really not believe that I, a foreign woman, can use a bow?*

"Oxanos, I appreciate the opportunity, but I will pass. The next time I return to your camp, I will bring my bow and demonstrate what I can do."

Valerias stared at Oxanos as Claire spoke, indicating that the discussion had ended. He stated he wanted to return to the Villa before dark, and the group prepared to leave. Valerias gave the four packhorses to the Huns as an additional gift.

Before they left, he took Oxanos aside and said Revious would return with more supplies.

"Also remember our agreement, Oxanos. If you keep your word and do not cause trouble, I will allow you to stay in the valley. I will reward your people for good behavior and punish you for any violation of our agreement."

Oxanos nodded, and Valerias smiled. The Roman group left the camp to return to the Villa.

When the group reached the ridgetop above the Hun camp, Valerias said to Revious, "So far, so good, my friend. I hope it continues."

Valerias was straight-faced as he spoke, and Revious understood his friend's gravity.

XIX

Soul Crusher

The knocks on the door came fast and heavy.

"Father Erasmus, it is done! It is done." Thc voices outside the door were high-pitched and not as forceful as the knocking.

"Good," Erasmus answered once he had opened the creaky wooden door. Three men stood before him, hoods covering their heads and concealing their faces.

"Come in."

The three men stepped into the building. Once the door was firmly closed behind them, the men removed their hoods.

"Did anyone see you?"

"Yes, Father Erasmus, several people witnessed our act. But I don't think they identified us."

"Good," answered Erasmus. "I want all to see the parchment you nailed on the announcement post in the village square. I want them to talk about what it says. I want them to comprehend its meaning."

"Why do you care if the villagers know who we are? We're all on the same side."

"I want to be the one responsible. If there is any negative reaction, I will take the brunt of it. Be thankful to God that you are not linked to me—at least for the time being. You can leave now. We will meet again at the church when I call for you. Bring all who side with us. Purging the village of blasphemers, heretics, pagans, and—worst of all—Arians, is what we must do. God is on our side, and God has called us to action!"

Erasmus offered a short prayer and showed the three men out. About an hour later, there was another deliberate and forceful knock at the door.

Erasmus hesitated to answer until the second round of knocking ended. He opened the door. "Good evening, Elderman Felix. I have been expecting you."

Antonio Felix of Menze was a short, thin man who made up for his small stature by dressing very well.

"What is the meaning of this parchment?" Felix demanded without exchanging any pleasantries. He held out the document that Erasmus had the three men post in the village square.

"It is exactly what it says it is. As you are aware, the Nicene Creed is the basis for our Christian religion. I have preached on this righteous fundamental Christian belief several times. Do you need me to conduct a private session to refresh your knowledge of this most relevant subject?"

Erasmus' condescending tone made Felix even angrier.

"Of course I know the Nicene Creed. The Father, his son Jesus Christ, and the Holy Spirit are equals."

"They are the Trinity and the cornerstone of our faith. Jesus is not subordinate to the Father, as some believe." Erasmus maintained his smugness. "I must remind you that Emperor Theodosius issued the edict that decrees the people will adopt the Nicene Creed. All who refuse to accept this foundation of the church are non-believers and will be punished."

"But . . ." Felix started to speak and was immediately interrupted.

"Emperor Theodosius issued his decree and the church adopted this position. If you do not accept the Nicene Creed as the absolute truth, you will be viewed as a non-believer—perhaps even a heretic. Is that what you want, Elderman?"

Felix grew concerned. *How could a country priest be so aggressive? I am the authority in the village, not him, and yet he is positioning himself to be the one who has control.*

"Are you going to answer me, Elderman Felix?"

Erasmus took advantage of Felix's stumbling. He knew he had the upper hand, as Felix lacked the fortitude to stand up to him. Erasmus noticed beads of sweat on Felix's forehead and pressed his verbal attack.

"If you don't support my position, I will report you to my superiors." Erasmus grew more intense as he spoke.

"I think it is wrong to blatantly persecute others who do not believe in what *you* believe," Felix responded.

"Then *you,* as the leader of our village, will be declared an infidel. That is what I will tell Bishop Ambrose in Mediolanum. The bishop concurs with Emperors Theodosius and Gratian on the edict. We will see what they think of you. I predict *you* will not be our leader for long."

"But I am a Christian, like you," Felix stammered. Sweat now stained his collar.

"Are you a true believer of the Christian faith? I know you have sympathy for the Arians. Arians have no place in the future of the church. Which are worse, Arians or pagans? I believe Arians are worse because Arians give Christ a subordinate position to God the Father. And we know that is a lie. Pagans don't know anything, but they can be taught. Arians are heretics."

"What is it you want, Erasmus?"

"I am simply a conveyor of the word of God. I only want what the church wants, what God wants, what Christ wants: the village to be purged of all non-believers. God approves of what we must do."

"This is very disturbing, Erasmus. I will go and think about what I must do."

"I am sure you will make the correct decision, for the village and for yourself."

Antonio Felix left Erasmus' church in haste. He had gone there to confront Erasmus. As Elderman of the village, Felix thought he had the power to dictate to a rebellious priest how he should act. Now, in just a few short moments, he had become more worried about his professional and personal futures. Erasmus took the power he thought he had. *I wonder how many people in the village support Erasmus' beliefs.*

Felix returned home and began writing a letter explaining the situation in Menze. When finished, he sent the letter to an old friend he knew from his earlier days in Rome. The friend was a bishop, Bishop Joseph. *He should be able to stop the mad priest, Erasmus.*

After Felix left, Erasmus sat alone. The only light was a small fire in the hearth that cried out for more fuel, but Erasmus ignored it.

When I was a child, they all hated me. I was more intelligent than them, and instead of embracing me, they resented and ostracized me. They were fools.

I came to this shithole of a village as a humble priest. The rich and those in power turned their backs on me and, most importantly, my message. God knows my message and I am his messenger. Why do they not understand? That is their mistake.

Today I am the leader—the true facilitator of God's Word. Anyone who crosses me and His Word shall pay dearly. God will allow me to carry out his will. The church hierarchy will hear me.

The false bishops and priests will learn who is the real Christian. It is I who will inherit their palaces and power.

In the end, those who fight me will grovel before me, asking for forgiveness and mercy. A change is in the air, and I am the instrument of that change. Menze is just the beginning. God expects great things of me, and I shall deliver for Him.

Erasmus stood and placed several logs on his meager fire. Soon the fire roared in response and Erasmus warmed his hands and smiled.

***

During the following months, Erasmus wasted no time in demonstrating his power. He was an influential orator and could sway even doubters to his cause. The more power Erasmus obtained, the more he craved. Many in the village joined him simply because they feared him. Felix tried to stand up to Erasmus, but it proved fruitless. The Elderman had been reduced to an impotent figurehead.

Some villagers did not share Erasmus' beliefs. Most decided it was best to leave the village and did so under the cover of night. Erasmus welcomed their exodus. Pockets of Arians, pagans, and even rebellious Nicene Christians refused to be intimidated by Erasmus and remained in the village. The community scorned those people, subjecting them to minor ill behavior such as spitting and the occasional shove.

At first, Erasmus himself did not rage against those he considered non-believers; instead, he met any resistance with a calm coolness. He had a plan, which he unveiled at a church meeting with several of his followers, whom he termed "elders." His plan would cause a sharp change in how he dealt with non-believers.

"My brothers," Erasmus began, "I can do only so much. I have tried to teach and gently persuade all disbelievers in our village to come into the light—the true light of our beloved church—to accept the Nicene Creed in the same way we accept the gospels. All I have received in return for my gentle persuasion is resistance from those infected with evil who deny God's holy truth. God has told me this is unacceptable to Him, as it is with me. Is this acceptable to you? Is it right to allow these heretics in our midst?"

A loud chorus of "No!" echoed around the wooden walls.

"Then what am I to do? You are my elders. What do you think I should do?"

Quiet fell over the church, as the elders did not know quite what to say. Finally, a man from the front spoke. "Ask God. He will tell you what to do."

"Good, Marcot," Erasmus said, pleased that the chief adherent of his teachings and fervor had played his part to perfection. "That is what I shall do. I will pray to God tonight, and tomorrow night we will meet back here at the same time."

The following night brought a storm. Violent cracks of thunder and flashes of bright lightning preceded a cold, heavy rain that soaked the elders as they made their way to the church. They were superstitious and believed God, through Erasmus, had brought the storm to Menze.

Erasmus sat in his usual chair. This time he had placed a table in front of him. On the table was a sword. Erasmus watched as several pairs of eyes focused on the sword.

"I prayed last night, as you recommended, Elder Marcot. God came to me in a dream. It was dark—dark as it can possibly be. Suddenly, there was a very bright light coming from a small speck of a hole. It was so bright that I had to cover my eyes and turn my head. Then the bright light was gone, replaced by a softer light. I turned back, and in front of me was an angel. The angel held a sword. When I blinked, the sword was gone, and the angel held her hands out to touch my face. Brothers in Christ, I have never felt such an overwhelming emotion.

"I cried out, 'What do you want me to do, Lord? How can I best serve my God?'

"I blinked again, and the sword was with the angel. I was frightened, as I thought the angel would slay me for not having faith in God. But the angel did not harm me.

"Instead, the angel spoke. 'You must do what must be done. That is the will of the Lord.' And then I knew what I had to do." Erasmus paused and folded his hands in prayer.

From the elders' perspective, the silence lasted forever.

Suddenly, Marcot exclaimed loudly, "What can we do to help carry out the will of God?"

Erasmus unfolded his hands and smiled. "There is much we can do—but really only one thing we must do. We must finally purge our village of the sinners and heretics. If we set an example, others will follow. Then we can have a true Christian kingdom. God will hold us accountable if we fail. We must not fail! Are you with me to carry out God's command?"

"Yes!" the elders, led by Marcot, shouted in unison.

Another elder who could not take his eyes off the sword asked, "Was that the sword of the angel in your dream?"

Erasmus was annoyed by the question. It interrupted the course procession of how he wanted his sermon to flow.

"Of course not. We on Earth cannot receive physical gifts from God or his angels. The angel told me where to find this sword, which I did, and now it is here for you to see."

The sword looked like it had been neglected for many years.

"Have the sword cleaned, as we must cleanse the evil from our midst," Erasmus exclaimed while giving the questioning elder a stern look and the sword. "I heard last night that a group of pagans sacrificed a calf to their false gods. Their leader is Leticus. Bring him to me."

The storm had ended, but clouds still covered the night sky. Several elders left the church. Within the hour, they found Leticus and brought the struggling man to the church. They rudely shoved him down on his knees before Erasmus.

"I understand, pagan, that you have violated the laws of our great emperors and the church. The emperors have forbidden such sacrifices and order you to completely and unconditionally accept the Nicene Trinity. So, pagan, will you convert and denounce all your pagan beliefs and name all the other pagans of your sect?"

Leticus replied strongly, "I have done no wrong, and I know of no others who have done wrong. I denounce your request. We are peaceful, and I reject your accusations!"

"On the contrary, pagan, you deserve everything you will receive. I ask again, do you recant your sins or not?" The redness in Erasmus' round face spread to the top of his bald head.

"I am not a sinner! *You* are the sinner! This is nothing but a sham. Elderman Felix will support us." Leticus' voice quavered.

"He supports nothing. He bows before the Lord and me, God's humble servant. God and I have had enough of your insolence and stupidity. You do not denounce your false religion, and now you shall suffer the consequences." Erasmus was very calm as he spoke to the agitated Leticus.

Erasmus turned to his elders. "He must be made an example for all the other pagans and heretics. Take him to the stake and burn him. If we are lucky, we will witness Satan rise up and grab his soul."

"You can't do this! You can't do this!" Leticus shouted hysterically over and over again as they took him to a wooden stake in the center of the village square. They chained him there and placed firewood and bundles of kindling around him. Leticus fought hard to free himself, twisting desperately to try and remove the stake from the ground. He called out for help, but no help came. A small crowd gathered around, mostly the elders of the church.

In the middle of the crowd, Erasmus stepped forward, grabbed Leticus' chin and said, "May God forgive you."

Leticus, reduced to weeping, quietly moaned, "I did nothing wrong. Why is this happening?"

Erasmus nodded to several men carrying torches. Marcot was the first to add fire to the brush; the others spread fire all around, the flames spreading and licking up the stake. Leticus was rapidly engulfed. His screams became muffled and stopped.

Erasmus' expression did not change. It was a face not of gladness or sadness, but of contentment—a contentment based on his new place as the undisputed leader of Menze. Erasmus was pleased. *Now that Menze is mine, I shall expand God's word to other communities.* He smiled to himself as the fire continued to burn brightly.

Erasmus called for Marcot. "Choose several elders and go to the house of our elderman. Arrest him for crimes against God. Place him in a stockade. If he does not repent, he, too, shall feel the fires of hell."

"Father Erasmus, he will not repent. Do you have a day set for his execution?" Marcot was excited; he desired more blood.

"Patience, my loyal Marcot," Erasmus answered. "I want him to think of his transgressions. Do not worry; he shall join Satan as well as any others who stand in my way—and God's, of course."

XX

GULIC

Valerias, Claire, Revious, and the soldier returned to the Villa from their visit to the Hun camp. It was a sultry evening at the end of a long day, and Valerias was tired and craved a bath and a large cup of wine. As they rode up to the front of the Villa, Valerias saw a horse he didn't recognize being taken to the stables. He dismounted and asked the attendant who owned it.

"A Roman officer has just arrived. He is inside with Bukarma."

"Did he give his name?"

"No."

Valerias was both irritated and intrigued. He did not like strangers admitted into the Grand House without his approval.

Valerias strode into the Grand House, Claire following behind, and spotted the soldier with his back to them talking to Bukarma, Alena, and Elsha. He wore formal Roman officer attire, and Valerias' head whirled with names, trying to identify his mysterious visitor. The officer heard Valerias approach and turned around to face him, and greeted him with a broad smile.

"General Valerias! It is good to see you after all these years."

"Yes?" Valerias wasn't sure what to say. He did not recognize the man.

Claire walked up and stood by Valerias, and the man bowed. "Domina, it is my honor to see you again." He took her hand and gently kissed her ring.

The man took a step back and addressed Valerias once more. "I am Severus Gulic. You may remember me as Gul, son of Mostar Gulivus, King of the Goths."

Valerias was taken aback. The man in front of him appeared more Roman than himself. Gulic spoke flawless Latin and was impeccably dressed—the ideal Roman officer.

Valerias stared hard at Gulic and gradually began to recognize his features. Could the Roman officer standing before him really be the same young Goth he had taken prisoner during a long-ago battle? The man who then became a Roman engineer's apprentice? Gulic was taller than Valerias remembered and had added muscle to fill out his frame. He had short-cropped, dark brown hair and no beard. A woman might consider him handsome.

"Tell me." Valerias wanted more information.

"As you know, after the battle with the Huns, you offered me a choice: I could return to the Goths and take my place as their king, or I could be a soldier in the Roman army—in the engineering division."

Valerias nodded. He remembered now.

"It was a difficult choice, but you were persuasive. I chose the latter. I was sent to Constantinople and underwent training. I learned quickly and caught the eye of Emperor Theodosius. He promoted me to the rank of tribune—master engineer. When Emperor Gratian requested an engineer to construct a bridge not far from here, Emperor Theodosius sent me here. Now I stand before you."

As Gulic finished speaking, Bukarma, Alena, and Elsha joined the group. Revious also entered the room and nodded to him.

"You have had a rapid rise through the ranks, Tribune," Valerias said, impressed.

"I am a quick lcarncr and I follow orders. I also avoided making enemies."

"Why did Emperor Theodosius send you here when Emperor Gratian has his own engineers?" Valerias asked skeptically.

Gulic started to sputter a response but was relieved when Claire intervened.

"You will be our guest for supper and stay the night, if you can." Claire turned to Alexander and requested preparations be made for Gulic.

Gulic inquired where the stables were located so he could retrieve a few items from his saddlebags. Before Claire could answer, Alena spoke up.

"I will take you to the stables."

Elsha announced that she too would accompany Gulic and Alena. Once they left, Claire turned to her husband.

"He is our guest. He came here to see you, and you start interrogating him. You can talk to him after supper, but be mindful to be a gracious host."

Valerias knew Claire was right. Still, he managed to say, "He is a Goth."

Claire countered, "He looks and acts more like a Roman soldier than you do."

Valerias gave her a wry smile and chuckled. Yet, troubling thoughts about his history with Gulic fermented in the back of his mind.

On the way to the stables, Alena and Elsha peppered Gulic with questions. What was Constantinople like? What did Emperor Theodosius look like? What was life like in the emperor's court? Is he, Gulic, a regular attendee at the court? During the great battle with the Huns, what did he do? What was it like to be a Goth? Did he have a wife?

Slipped in the flurry of questions was a query both girls wanted an answer to but did not want to make it obvious: "What was Father like when he was a general?"

Gulic did not look at Alena and Elsha when he answered. "Your father is everything that the legends say he is. His bravery and fighting skills are beyond reproach. He motivates men by setting an example and is intelligent—thoroughly planning a battle strategy beforehand. He is fair and can be generous. He does not stand for incompetence or corruption in the ranks. He is not kind to his enemies—and he has many. He could be brutal, but looking back, it was necessary."

Gulic knew he had said too much and stopped speaking. He was concerned that what he had said to Alena and Elsha would get back to Valerias, and he had not forgotten Valerias' temper. That would not be good for him or his career.

However, the girls would not relent. "When you fought with Father against the Huns, what was your role? Were you his aide?" Alena fired questions faster than Gulic could respond.

"I was not his aide. He assigned me as an apprentice to his field army engineer, a kind man named Tentrides. He was a tribune."

"How did you get to know Father? When was the first time you met him?"

Gulic wanted to avoid discussing this part of his past. He had to say something, though, and that something needed to be truthful. "I am the son of a dead Goth king. I was your father's enemy at one time. As you can see, that time has passed. If you want more details, ask your father."

The bluntness of Gulic's response stunned the girls. They stopped walking and stared after him until he reached the stables and disappeared inside.

"We need to ask Father about his relationship with Tribune Gulic," Alena said softly to Elsha after Gulic was gone.

The girls hurried back to the Grand House, where Valerias sat in the study, reading a document and petting Wolf. He had been expecting them.

"How is Tribune Gulic, daughters?" Valerias remarked nonchalantly.

"Was he your enemy, Father?" Elsha blurted out before Alena could ask.

Valerias, like Gulic, did not want to go over their past in detail, so he said briefly, "Yes. Our armies tangled and his lost. Gulic was given a choice to join the Roman army or go back to the Goths. He made the correct choice and is a Roman tribune. That is all there is to the story. What he does now and in the future is important to the empire."

Valerias did not want to tell his daughters that his army had slaughtered Gulic's warriors and took Gulic prisoner. If it hadn't been for the fortunate timely appearance of Joseph, and Jacob's persuasion, he would have executed Gulic. And Gulic would not be joining them for supper that night.

Valerias continued to act disinterested. He went back to reading his document and told the girls to take Wolf for a walk. As they left the house, Valerias sighed with relief. Outside, Alena and Elsha knew they had not been told the entire truth and vowed to find out more about the relationship between their father and Gulic.

At supper that night, Valerias gradually warmed up to Gulic, who was eager to please his former commander. Valerias enjoyed discussing events in the empire from an officer's point of view. He was particularly interested in Emperor Theodosius' strategies for dealing with the Persians and Goths. Valerias became so engrossed in his conversation with Gulic that when he glanced at Claire, he noticed she was scowling at him.

"I must apologize to my wife, Tribune. I have dominated the conversation and been a poor host."

Valerias sat back in his chair, hoping he had mollified Claire. But she appeared to relax very little, which made Valerias uneasy. He never liked to treat her poorly.

"No, it is I who must apologize." Gulic attempted to take the blame. "I was rude to my hostess. I should know better. I apologize, Domina."

Gulic shifted his focus to Alena and Elsha. "And I must apologize to you, as well. I see you girls get your beauty from your mother."

Gulic again faced Claire and bowed his head slightly. "Domina, I thank you for inviting me to share supper with you and your family."

Claire smiled and Valerias was pleased. He began to see Gulic as a Roman soldier and not as a Goth barbarian.

The remainder of the evening went smoothly. Valerias and Claire both knew that Gulic embellished some of his stories, but that was fine for the circumstances; he was trying to make a good impression.

When it was time for Gulic to go to his quarters, Alena boldly announced, "I will escort Tribune Gulic there." She glowered at Elsha, indicating that she should remain at the Grand House.

As they walked to his quarters, Alena asked Gulic, "Will you be returning to the Villa, Tribune? I would like that."

Gulic smiled and said, "Yes, I will return—and soon."

Alena awoke the next morning and found Gulic was well on his way to the bridge.

XXI

Assassin

Garzad and Honorario waited patiently by the tent pitched on the north side of a small brook. They were the only people in the area, which Honorario found eerie. It was a still day; the constant sound of water lapping against the rocks along the brook added to Honorario's apprehension. Garzad was occupied with sharpening his sword. *Nothing seems to bother him*, Honorario thought, watching him. *I wish I had his stoutness.*

Honorario stood up when he heard the faint sound of horses approaching.

"They are here," Garzad stated calmly. He finished cleaning his sword and placed it in the sheath he carried on his back.

Within moments, a large group of Roman cavalry arrived near the tent. Two men dismounted, one taking the reins of the other.

"We have been waiting for you, General Diocles." Garzad saluted Diocles.

"It is good you are here, Tribune." He paused and looked at Honorario. "And you too, Centurion. You have done well, as always. Emperor Maximus is pleased with you. It is largely through your efforts that the incompetent Gratian will be dethroned.

"Emperor Maximus gave me an order to pass on to you. You are to proceed to Augusta Treverorum and await your next orders. Should you successfully complete that assignment, you will be promoted to general and enter Emperor Maximus' inner circle. I know few soldiers who have risen through the ranks as fast as you, and you have earned it." Diocles strongly emphasized "earned it."

"We are to go directly to the emperor's fort in Augusta Treverorum?" Garzad asked.

"Of course," the general said, as if it were obvious. "You are my finest tribune," he added. "I will be pleased to hear of your next promotion."

Diocles smiled at Garzad and mounted his horse, taking back his reins. He remarked to Garzad, "Before going to Augusta Treverorum, the governor-general of Venetia would like to speak with you. His name is Victus. I do not know the reason, but you must see him. But beware, Tribune. The country is rife with intrigue, and Gratian has allies. Victus may be one of those them. Remember, we serve the emperor, Magnus Maximus."

Diocles and his men rode off to the north, leaving Garzad and Honorario alone again.

"I don't like the idea of visiting this man Victus. I prefer to go directly to Augusta Treverorum and obtain our orders." Honorario's concern was clear.

"Relax, Honorario. We need Diocles' support, and performing this task for him will help our situation. Besides, I am interested in what this governor-general wants from us."

***

Within the week, Garzad and Honorario stood outside the offices of Governor-General Victus. The fall day was warm, and both men basked in the sunshine. However, the good feeling melted away the longer they waited for Victus. In an attempt to hurry things along, Garzad began sharpening his sword in front of Victus' secretary. Garzad's point was made, and the secretary disappeared. He reappeared a few moments later and announced the governor-general would see them.

"Good afternoon, Tribune Garzad and Centurion Honorario. Welcome to my palace."

Garzad had already noted that Victus' quarters were elegant, but it wasn't a palace. Victus sat behind a large table full of parchments. He dressed as a civilian.

"You are asking yourselves why I ordered you here."

Garzad wanted to tell Victus that he came of his own volition, not because of an order from a pompous administrator. Instead, he held his tongue and just nodded.

"Your history is impressive, Tribune Garzad, for such a short time in the army. You have successfully led men into battle and shown unabashed courage. Your aide has done well, too." Victus glanced at Honorario.

Victus continued, "I particularly admire the manner in which you complete the tasks you are assigned. You do not allow principles to affect your performance."

Victus sat back in his chair and stared at Garzad. Garzad, with perfect composure, stared back, unflinching.

"What do you require, Governor-General? I serve the emperor."

"Yes, hail the emperor. I understand you are a man of few words, Tribune. What about your aide? Does he speak?"

"Less than I do, Governor-General."

"Good, because I have a special mission for you two. No one outside this room must know what I have ordered you to do. Is that clear?"

"Yes," Garzad and Honorario answered in unison. Garzad did not like the condescending attitude of this bureaucrat. He was again unsure how Victus could order him to do anything.

Victus nodded. "About forty miles west of here is the large estate of a man who is a traitor to the empire. In these unruly times, he wants our great emperor deposed so he himself can assume his throne. It is true. His arrogance knows no bounds. And he runs around with barbarians. As I said, he is a traitor."

Victus looked at Garzad and Honorario to gauge their reactions. Neither man showed any expression.

Victus felt comfortable that he had selected the right men to carry out his task. "I know that I can trust you to do as I ask."

Garzad nodded and Victus continued, "A traitor must pay for his betrayal. He must be executed or assassinated. Don't you agree?"

"An execution is more public than an assassination." Honorario chimed in.

"I thought your aide spoke less than you, Tribune?"

"He speaks when he must speak the truth, Governor-General. Let me carry Centurion Honorario's response even further. I understand that you want us to either assassinate this man or execute him."

"Execute or assassinate, they are the same to me." Victus noticed Garzad's hesitancy. He pulled out a bag from under a pile of documents and tossed it to Garzad. Garzad opened it and saw several gold coins glinting in the light.

"Fifty solidi, Tribune. Do we have a deal? The solidi for the man's life."

"Yes, we have an arrangement. Now tell me, specifically whom do you want me to kill?"

"His name is Marcus Augustus Valerias. He is an infirm retired army general. Valerias has caused me great harm. And he is a spy. He must be killed for treason."

Victus did not reveal the true reason for his hatred of Valerias—Victus was disturbingly jealous of him. When Victus thought of Valerias, his lips narrowed and he ground his teeth. *I am the governor-general, and he is retired and old. Yet it is he who is respected. I should have that respect! He is the bane of my position and leadership. My soldiers look up to that man, who is a step from death, instead of me. He should be subordinate to me, not I to him!*

"Who does he spy for, Governor-General?" Garzad interrupted Victus' invidious thoughts and wanted to know where Victus' loyalties lay. *Does he support Gratian or Magnus Maximus?* he wondered.

"A man with high status." Victus gave no further explanation, and Garzad did not press the issue.

"I am pleased that you trust me, Governor-General. Is there anything more that I should know about this man Valerias?"

"He is an old general, far past his prime. He has been disrespectful to me and my position as governor-general. You should have no difficulty killing him. I would do it, but someone might recognize me at his villa."

"His villa?" Garzad brushed off Victus' comment about Valerias' past as a general. "Tell me more about his villa."

"Valerias' estate is very large, no doubt inherited. The villa is a group of buildings on his estate. The main house lies in the central portion of the compound. Valerias calls it the Grand House. You should have easy access to it."

"Does Valerias have bodyguards that I should be aware of?"

"There is an old African. I forget his name. If he gets in the way, your aide could readily dispatch him."

Honorario coughed.

"Valerias' wife is a Briton barbarian. Kill her, if you like. They have two barbarian daughters—take them for your pleasure."

"This sounds so easy, Governor-General. Maybe I should pay you for this opportunity."

"When will you kill the old man, Tribune?"

"When it suits me, Governor-General."

"Your temperament tells me that you want to kill Valcrias during the day—not an ambush at night."

"I'll handle your request when and how I desire, Governor-General," Garzad repeated. "Honorario and I will take our leave. You should hear of our success shortly. Centurion, let's go."

As Garzad and Honorario rode away from Victus' quarters, Honorario asked, "Are we really going to kill a retired Roman general? That could be suicide! I do not trust Victus."

"Honorario, I take my orders from Emperor Maximus, and we must obey those commands."

"But Victus is not the emperor. We don't even know which emperor he serves. Are we conducting this assassination for the emperor, whoever that is, or for Victus?"

"Neither matters to me, Honorario. Victus is a lackey for Emperor Gratian. I will do it for me! That damned Valerias is mine!"

XXII

Doubts

Eustice was pleased. The latest hunt went well, and he had killed two stags. When he returned to the Black Fort, he was finally able to be intimate with his queen. The kingdom was peaceful. He thought back on his time of exile in western Britannia. Life had been hard then. Food was scarce and seldom good. Shelter was temporary. Most nights were spent without cover in the rain and snow.

The warmth from the fire in his council room at the fort made him appreciate his current situation even more. He had the best that could be provided to a man. He was a king and he lived like one. He no longer had to worry about shelter or food. He commanded an army and had a beautiful wife. The only thing he lacked was an heir to his throne.

He and Rega had tried multiple times to conceive a child, but the results were fruitless. He didn't know whether the issue was him or Rega. *I will just continue to give it more time. I know I'm good*, he thought. *I will have our spirit master place a spell on Rega, and then I will have an heir.*

Eustice became so lost in thought that he didn't see Rega approach. She handed him a parchment. Eustice read her face for a sign of what it said and noticed she looked worried; lines creased the skin around her eyes.

"Have you already read this?" he asked as he cast his eye over the parchment. Thoughts of an heir vanished from Eustice's mind.

"I skimmed it. I don't think you will like what it says. I do not like it."

After he read the document, Eustice swore violently and tossed the letter on the floor. His initial reaction was even better than Rega had expected.

"I'm not sure what to say, Rega." Eustice picked up the document, slowly read it again, and glanced at Rega. "I *am* pleased he is alive. Drostan is my nephew. However, he is not ready to assume the throne. A sheltered boy is not ready to walk into the Black Fort and rule. Are you sure Drostan is alive?"

"No, my king, I am not. But my source is usually accurate."

"Where did they see him?"

"To the south, between here and Londinium."

"How could anyone recognize him? Drostan was a boy the last time anyone saw him, and few people saw him then. Gerhard and Claire allowed their children to have only limited contact with the world outside of the Black Fort."

"He wore the necklace of office," Rega explained.

"How do you know that?"

"Read the letter again, husband."

Eustice read the letter for the third time and said, "I still do not see anything about a necklace."

Rega snatched the letter from Eustice, scouring it for that bit of information. "Oh, um, the author told me that."

"Where is this author now? Who is he?"

"He was an old servant for Gerhard and Claire. He has already left. Do you want me to send Captain Amron after him?"

"No, that is not necessary. Any evidence that Drostan is alive is very weak. I'm surprised, Rega, that you would even show me this. If I see real evidence that he is alive, I will address the matter at that time. This document is hearsay."

"How would you respond if the information was true, my king?"

"I would welcome him with open arms."

Rega noticed a slight waver in Eustice's voice.

"Even if he wanted to reclaim the throne on which you rightfully sit?" Rega questioned Eustice's shift in attitude toward Drostan.

"Yes," Eustice answered curtly and firmly this time. "But I will address that issue if and when it becomes necessary."

He wanted to change the subject, as talk of Drostan made him uneasy. Voltrex entered the room, and Eustice was thankful for the interruption. "Any more sightings of that murderous traitor, Morguard?"

"We have heard from several people who thought they saw him, but we have no definitive proof. For all we know, he could be dead, living in another country, or out in the wilds of Britannia," Voltrex said.

"Morguard came here at Argus' request. After Argus' death, he disappeared. I think he was a worse man than either Argus or his butcher, Flavius," Eustice spat.

Eustice turned pensive. "I'm not even sure I could identify the monster if he walked in this room. I know I could not identify Drostan, either. It has been too long."

"My king, we will scour the land for both men," Voltrex replied.

"Morguard can be brought back to me dead or alive, I don't care. I want Drostan, of course, alive. He is my sister's son."

"Do you wish to offer a reward for either person, my king?"

"There is already a bounty on Morguard. I'll double it—dead or alive. For Drostan, there shall be no bounty. Only a reward if he is brought to me alive."

"Yes, my king. If you will allow, I must attend to other business first and then I will focus on our two fugitives."

"Good. But remember, Drostan is *not* a fugitive, he is a casualty of war."

Voltrex took his leave.

"My queen, I, too, must leave for the rest of the day. I have another mediation I must attend in a nearby village. Captain Amron will accompany me. I am tired of resolving these petty jurisdictional disputes. They seem to have no end."

"That is what a good king must do, my husband."

"I know." Eustice looked longingly at his wife and left.

Rega watched Eustice leave the Black Fort with his bodyguards and attendants. She ordered her servants not to disturb her; she needed to rest. She maintained a sitting room off of Eustice's and her bedchamber. Once inside the sitting room, she closed the door and Voltrex emerged from the dark. He placed his hands on her shoulders and removed her cloak. Rega's remaining clothes were just as easily removed.

"Do you think he suspects us?" Voltrex asked as he shed his tunic.

"No. I watched him when he left. No matter what he says, he is worried about Drostan and the threat he poses. Morguard is also in the back of his mind. The seeds of suspicion have been planted. Now they must take root."

"Yes, my love." Voltrex was not thinking of Eustice, Drostan, or Morguard as he kissed the back of Rega's neck and slowly moved down her back.

"We must always be discreet, lover," Rega murmured. "Eustice has many allies. I do not want them to suspect us or our motives. We have one hour—do what you can."

XXIII

Beggar

Joseph returned to his office in the village of Oreton a weary man. The never-ending conflict between church matters and his personal life raged in his mind. It tore his soul apart. He loved Ruth and yearned for her; he desired for her to be the mother of his children.

Yet Joseph was a bishop. He was committed to the church—a church he loved. He devoted himself to helping people not only spiritually but physically. Joseph frequently traveled to the villages and countryside in his jurisdiction. He personally helped people construct houses and ancillary structures, provided food and medical care for the poor, and gave clothing to the needy. Joseph attended village meetings and settled disputes. His reputation spread, and he became known as Joseph the Good.

The demands on his time, though, were becoming too much. He contemplated retaining an aide, but no one met his standards. There were two monks at Father Timothy's hermitage who he thought might be a good fit, but he doubted they could be talked into leaving the hermitage. *Life outside the hermitage is difficult,* he thought. *Not everyone can practice the life led by Jesus. Such a life has rewards, but it has worn on me.*

Thus, he was relieved when he found a letter on his desk from Bishop Ambrose requesting that he attend a council meeting in Mediolanum. It would be a long trip; however, he believed it would be a good opportunity to renew his spirituality. And most importantly, he could visit his cherished friends, Marcus Augustus Valerias and Claire.

A week after receiving Bishop Ambrose's correspondence, Joseph was packed for the journey and headed south toward Mediolanum. He told local priests and village elders where he was going and the tasks they were to perform in his absence. When the time came to leave, he was pleased with the state of his diocese, and looking forward to a rest.

Joseph reached Gallia in less than two weeks. The weather was mild, and he prayed to God for his continued good fortune. Unfortunately, Joseph's luck took a turn for the worse in Gallia. A storm blew in that forced him to find shelter. He spotted a tavern just off the road he was traveling on. He tied his horse inside a nearby ramshackle barn and entered the tavern, where several men were gathered. Joseph could not tell if they were also seeking shelter or were there for the drink. He introduced himself to the men as Father Joseph, avoiding using his title as a bishop to strangers, as usual.

"Can I get you a drink, Father?" one of the men asked.

Joseph looked around him and saw that the place was dilapidated and in need of substantial repair.

"That would be kind of you. The weather is rough. I imagine we will be here for a while."

"I think some of us will be here longer than others," one of the men responded.

A scruffy-looking barman brought Joseph a beer. The barman had a deep scar above his left eye. As Joseph reached for his drink, he felt a sharp blow to the back of his head. There were bright sparkling lights behind his eyes.

"Father, Father." One of the lights was speaking to him. Then another light spoke. He opened his eyes, and several blurry figures poked their faces into his face.

"Father, can you hear me?"

Joseph mumbled incoherently as his vision went in and out of focus. He felt something cold on his face. A man's face appeared but disappeared when he began talking to someone else. Gradually his vision of the world returned. He saw four men standing nearby.

"He is coming around now. Praise the Lord."

"Where am I?" Joseph managed to ask.

"You are at Boar's Lake Inn outside the village of Obsetik." A man held a cold, damp cloth to Joseph's head.

"What happened?" Joseph rubbed his head.

"Thieves," answered one of the men.

Joseph realized what had happened. He sat up and looked for the pack that he had brought with him. It was gone. He reached to his belt where he had tucked his purse, but that was gone, too. All he had left were the clothes he was wearing.

"How did they get away with this?" Joseph became angry.

"There were five of them and four of us. What did you want us to do, Father? They were rough men. We are farmers and a barman."

Joseph was not listening. He thought of all his possessions he had lost: his Bible, his money, a clean set of clothes, food, and of course his flasks. The thieves had taken everything.

"We have sent for help. Maybe they can catch them. The robbers are not from around here. They came from a village many miles to the south."

The men helped Joseph to his feet and sat him in a nearby chair. Joseph welcomed its sturdiness.

"Do you have a local priest?" Joseph asked rubbing his head.

"Not in this village, but in the next village to the west there is a priest called Thaddeus."

The men exchanged wary glances before one spoke up again, "By the way, who are you really, Father? You seem too finely dressed to be a simple priest."

"I am Bishop Joseph, from Britannia," Joseph decided it was the appropriate time to reveal his title.

"You are a bishop?" The men exclaimed in surprise.

"Yes. I am on my way to Mediolanum to attend the Council of Bishops."

The four men acted as if they had never been in the presence of someone so lofty before, and they weren't sure how to act. Joseph saw their uneasiness; they were no longer sure where to look and shuffled their feet.

"Fear not. I don't hold you responsible for what happened here. Adversity is God's way of sharpening my focus to reach Mediolanum." Joseph turned to the men, curious. "Are you all believers in Christ?"

"Yes," they responded unanimously.

"Very good." Joseph had gained control of the room. He requested a beer, which he drank readily. Afterward, the men asked for a blessing, which Joseph performed. When he finished, a thought abruptly shot into his head, *Where is my horse? Did the thieves take it too?* Joseph bolted from his chair and hurried to the barn where he had tied up his horse, and found the animal where he had left it. He ran into the flimsy shelter and hugged his horse's head, thanking God.

The men from the inn followed him.

"We didn't think men of the cloth had horses. We thought you clerics walked everywhere. That is why the thieves didn't steal your horse, they didn't think you had one."

"I am an exception. I have always had a horse; it makes travel much faster. Sometimes God cannot wait. Fortunately, God saw that my horse was not taken."

Just then, there was a rustling of straw in the farthest area of the barn. Joseph felt a rush of cold fear that a robber had decided to remain near the tavern.

"Who is there?" Joseph cried out.

More commotion followed, as if someone was waking up.

"I said, who is there? Speak up! We won't harm you," Joseph called again.

Finally, a voice squeaked back, obviously drunk. "It is only me, Elderon. I am coming out!"

"Who is Elderon?" Joseph asked the men standing behind him.

"A drunk. I should have known he would be passed out in here. His wife threw him out years ago, and since then he has become the village drunk," one of the men said.

"He was a drunk before his wife cast him out. That is why she did it," a second man added.

"Yes, and the soldier who wooed her away also may be a cause for his drunkenness."

The four men laughed heartily. Elderon clambered to his feet and blinked in the light. Joseph couldn't help wrinkling his nose at the stench of the filthy beggar in his rags, but he turned to the men and chided them for teasing the unfortunate.

"Who are you, kind master?" Elderon pointed shakily at Joseph, slurring his words.

"I am Bishop Joseph of Britannia."

"Why are you here in Obsetik? To save us from us?" Elderon swayed as he spoke.

"You are imprudent, wretch. Address him as his Holiness the Bishop!" one of the men yelled at Elderon.

These men really dislike Elderon, thought Joseph. *If I was not here, I fear they would beat him, perhaps even kill him.* Joseph held up his hand for silence.

"I am on my way to Mediolanum to attend the Council of Bishops."

"Can I come with you, your Holiness?" Elderon's voice was more forceful, with a hint of fear.

The four men cursed at Elderon for his impertinence. Again, Joseph held up his hand.

"Are you a Christian, Elderon?" Joseph asked, looking directly at him.

"Yes, I believe in the Father, the Son, and the Holy Spirit. All of them."

"As equals? As defined by the Nicene Creed?"

"Yes?" Elderon answered hesitantly, not knowing the correct answer.

"How can this wretch of a man be a Christian? He is drunk all the time." A man hurled a curse at Elderon. "Drunks cannot be saved."

"I believe him," Joseph said looking intensely at Elderon. "Yes, you can ride with me to Mediolanum, Elderon. I have work you can help me with. I need an aide."

The four men behind Joseph burst into cries of dissent, arguing why he was making a mistake. They let Joseph know he was naïve and tried to persuade him that Elderon was useless, but Joseph ignored them. He told Elderon to retrieve his belongings, but Elderon said he had none. Outside of his horse and saddle, Joseph possessed nothing either.

Joseph and Elderon left the village without another word. The storm had passed, and the air's humid touch felt good to Elderon, who sat behind Joseph on Joseph's horse. Once they were well out of Obsetik, Joseph thought it was a good idea for Elderon to walk and sober up. He also couldn't tolerate the man's stale, sour breath any longer. In the late afternoon, Joseph gave his horse a rest. The two men talked by a stream while the horse drank and cropped the grass.

"You realize the four men back at Obsetik were the ones who robbed you," a newly sober Elderon told Joseph.

"Yes," Joseph said to a surprised Elderon. "That is why I did not spend the night."

"When they realized you were more than a common priest, they let you be. If you had not been a bishop, you would be dead now and your body thrown in a ravine."

"It was God's will, Elderon. I am alive, you are alive, and we have my horse. Let us pray and give thanks to God."

"Yes, let us give thanks," Elderon repeated.

"Before we go to Mediolanum," Joseph told his companion, "we will stop at the villa of Marcus Augustus Valerias. I would like to spend a couple of days there. He and his wife, Claire, are my cherished friends. You will refer to them as the General and Domina."

"General Valerias?" Elderon asked timidly.

"Yes. Have you heard of him?"

"Only in passing. He has a brutal reputation."

"He has changed. You will have nothing to fear."

XXIV

LOVE

A period of temperate weather descended upon the land, and Gulic made frequent visits to the Villa. Valerias and Claire knew that he wasn't coming to see just them. There was a spark of interest between him and Alena. Elsha, who happily took on the role of informant, confirmed this spark.

One day, Gulic rode into the Villa wearing his dress uniform as usual. He was met by Valerias and Wolf, and Bukarma joined them after Gulic dismounted. Seeing Valerias and Bukarma together brought back memories from his youth that Gulic had tried to forget. More than ten years had passed since he was lined up with the rest of the surviving Goths and interrogated by the fierce General Valerias, with the equally fearsome Bukarma beside him.

Fortunately, he had become a Roman officer and citizen since that time. *That should help my standing with General Valerias,* he thought.

"Welcome back to the Villa," Valerias said casually.

"I am pleased to be back," Gulic responded enthusiastically. He rubbed Wolf's ears; the dog was grateful for the attention.

"How is the bridge progressing?" Valerias held his dagger in his hand. The blade was normally sheathed to his left calf.

Valerias rarely carried his sword while he was at the Villa, but he always had the dagger with him. He also held in his hand an irregular piece of wood Gulic thought might be for carving. *I wonder how General Valerias could carve anything well with only one hand.*

Gulic ignored Valerias' question. "Can I help you with any tasks that need to be done at the Villa? I can work until supper."

"You were invited to supper, Tribune?"

"Yes, the Domina and Alena invited me."

Valerias placed the dagger back in its sheath and tossed the piece of wood for Wolf to fetch. Wolf just looked at the stick, then at Valerias. Valerias sighed. He tried to give Wolf a stern look, but the daft dog always seemed to make him smile. Wolf just sat at Valerias' side with his tongue hanging out slightly. *What a dog,* Valerias thought. *Panting for doing nothing!*

"Bukarma, could you please take Wolf inside to Elsha? Perhaps he will listen to her. I would like to have a word with Tribune Gulic."

"Of course, Marcus. Come, Wolf." Bukarma and the dog went inside.

"Have a seat, Tribune." Valerias pointed to a chair on the porch and the men sat.

"Your bridge construction must be proceeding well. You seem to find time to visit here regularly."

"Yes. We are ahead of schedule," Gulic said nervously.

"Do you know how much longer it will take to finish the project?"

"Not exactly, but I believe we are moving toward a timely finish."

Valerias had had enough small talk. He shifted closer to Gulic and spoke quietly.

"I want to tell you the story of a young man who had an inclination for a certain girl. The young man perceived that the girl's father was frail and weak. Thus, he thought he had a good opportunity to take advantage of the girl. He was wrong, as the father had the physical abilities of a younger man and the wisdom of an older man. It turned out to be an unfortunate day for the young man."

Valerias sat back in his chair without taking his eyes off of Gulic. "Do you understand what I'm trying to tell you, Tribune?"

Gulic understood completely but was lost for words; he knew he had to answer, but didn't know what to say.

"I understand why you told me this story, General Valerias. Alena and I are friends, and that is all."

"The same way you are friends with Elsha?"

"Ah," Gulic began and then stopped.

"Precisely," Valerias retorted. "Alena has had many suitors, but not one was worthy of her. I have my standards for a qualified suitor. To date, all have failed."

"I think I can see why."

"Alena is my adopted daughter, but I consider her to be of my own blood. I would readily die for her and Elsha, and, of course, Claire, if it would save their lives. Do you question that?"

"Ah," Gulic mumbled.

"Let me know when you can discuss this matter like a man, Tribune."

Valerias changed the subject abruptly. "Go see Revious by that shed over there." Valerias pointed with his stump. "I need you to help him repair the roof."

Valerias rose from his chair and went inside the Grand House. Claire waited for him.

"Were you hard on the boy, Marcus?" Claire asked with a note of curiosity.

"I have been harder on the rabble that comes calling for Alena's hand. Besides, Tribune Gulic is not a boy. No tribune is a boy."

"Alena favors him over the other 'rabble,'" Claire said firmly.

"She is so young, and she is my daughter. I believe Gulic is twenty-seven years old and Alena is barely seventeen. That is quite an age difference," Valerias replied.

"Marcus, the age difference between us is the same."

"He is a Goth!"

"He is a Roman!" Claire countered. "He fought for *you* at Three Tongues. The fortunes of the battle may have swung in our favor when he replaced his dead father on the battlefield. He serves Emperor Theodosius without question. His birth as a Goth has no relevance anymore."

Valerias paused and gazed outside. "I understand, Claire. You are right. Thank you for reminding me of that which I sometimes forget."

Valerias went to his study. He tried reading but lost interest. Instead, he turned and looked out his small window. Elsha was playing fetch with Wolf, and the dog responded to her commands. He shook his head and smiled.

Time continues on its course. There is the past, which has been lived, the present, which is now, and the future, which is unknown. Just like a river, time flows on and does not stop. It is hard for me to see my time pass by.

Alena and Elsha still have their destinies to fulfill. It is their time now. I must let them live their lives as I have lived mine. I cannot halt the inevitable or turn back time. They will get married, have children, and grow old, too. It is the natural order. I promise I will try to let my daughters experience life for themselves—within reason.

He wasn't quite sure what he meant by "within reason." *I like to be flexible.* He smiled at the thought.

Two hours had passed since Valerias talked with Gulic when there was a polite knock on his door.

"Come in, Alena," stated Valerias without turning around.

"Father, what did you say to Tribune Gulic? I went to see him and he was very quiet, like he didn't want to see me. Did you forbid him to see me?"

"No, I did not forbid him to see you. I just wanted to make clear the conditions between us. Besides, he said you two are just friends. Is that not true?"

"Yes . . . we are friends," Alena answered nervously.

"I need to remind you, Alena, that the men who have called on you in the past were not acceptable to me or your mother. You are my daughter."

"I love you, Father, but I am growing up. Please let me make my own decisions. You and Mother have always taught Elsha and me to be independent. Now is the time for me to prove to you and Mother that I deserve your trust."

"I understand, Alena. However, you must also understand that you will always be my daughter, and I will be protective of you. No matter your age."

Alena approached Valerias and embraced him, holding him close for a moment, and then stepped lightly out of his study. *I think I would rather be fighting Huns than dealing with this*, Valerias thought.

Supper that night went well. Claire, as usual, was a gracious hostess. She could always put visitors at ease. The fine meals she served had become the talk of the area.

Conversation was lively and light-hearted, with Gulic being the most talkative. He chatted about his bridge project and the challenges he had encountered. He carried an optimistic attitude, though, that all such challenges could be overcome. Gulic noted the project had gone so well that the people of the villages who would be served by the bridge treated him and his crew like heroes.

Valerias noticed Gulic had a knack for evading conflict. He refused to be involved in the rivalry between Gratian and Magnus Maximus. Gulic reported only to his emperor, Emperor Theodosius, without exception. He also avoided becoming entangled in the Christian controversies that swirled about.

At supper, Valerias abstained from any mention of the relationship between Alena and Gulic. Instead, he asked Gulic questions about Emperor Theodosius and the state of the Eastern Roman Empire's army and how it compared to the Western Roman Empire's army. Occasionally, when no one else was looking, he shot Gulic a look that said, *Behave as I expect you to behave with Alena.*

After supper, Alena volunteered to take Gulic for a walk around the Villa. Claire said yes, and Valerias gave a muffled approval. Elsha looked annoyed at the whole situation.

When Alena and Gulic were out of sight of the Grand House, Gulic took a leather pouch from his pocket and held it out to Alena.

"I want to give you this." Gulic tried to sound manly, but his nervousness showed.

"What is it, Tribune?" Alena was excited and eager.

Gulic partially opened the pouch and handed it to her. He remained apprehensive.

She reached in the pouch and gently pulled out a necklace. The chain was gold and narrow. A round, green stone about the size of a solidus was strung on the chain.

"It is a vesuvianite gemstone from southwest Italia," Gulic said. "A merchant had it for sale in one of the villages by the bridge we are constructing. The merchant said it was collected near Mount Vesuvius. He set it in the necklace especially for me."

"It's beautiful, Gulic! Thank you." Alena kissed Gulic on his cheek.

Gulic had desired that kiss since he first laid eyes on Alena. He felt a combination of warmth and excitement, and revealed, "The merchant told me the wearer will obtain strength and courage from the vesuvianite, and it will prevent thoughts of ill will."

"Perhaps we should give such a stone to Father so when he thinks of us, he will only have good thoughts!" Alena giggled.

Gulic placed the chain around her neck. "You look beautiful tonight, Alena." His nervousness had subsided.

Alena gazed warmly into his eyes.

"I want to show you everything," Alena said laughingly.

"This is such a beautiful setting. I can see why your mother and father are so attached to it," he responded.

They walked to the edge of the Villa's buildings and Alena spoke softly, "I want to take you to my special place."

Alena put her hand in Gulic's. In response, he clasped his fingers around her hand. They arrived at a meadow that seemed to glow from the full moon rising over the legion of trees surrounding it. A warm, steady breeze kept the insects at bay. Gulic felt relaxed for the first time since arriving at the Villa. He turned to face the forest and let go of Alena's hand. He raised his arms behind his head to stretch, closed his eyes, and took in a deep breath.

"I love this fresh air," he said quietly.

He heard no response and turned around. Alena stood naked in front of him. The necklace sparkled in the moonlight. In one second Gulic was flooded with sharply contrasting emotions. The first emotion was lust. A beautiful nude young woman he was especially fond of stood in front of him with the soft moonlight overhead. The thought of making love to her in such a beautiful place was almost too much.

He blinked to reassure himself he was awake and the Alena he had dreamed of so often was in front of him.

The second emotion, fear, took over. When he opened his eyes, he saw Valerias behind her, sword drawn. Fire burst forth from his bright red eyes. He raised his glowing sword. Gulic swallowed hard and blinked again. The General's image was thankfully gone.

"What is wrong, Gulic?" Alena asked sweetly. "I am ready for you."

"Put on your clothes, now!" Gulic felt flushed with fear.

"Why? Do you not feel well?"

"No, I don't. Please!" Gulic pointed to Alena's clothes. He turned his back while she dressed.

"It is Father isn't it? He can be gruff, I know."

"Have you seen your father at war?"

Alena was dressed again and Gulic turned back to face her. He was grim faced, an expression she had never seen before.

"Yes, I have seen him fight." Alena was transported back to the cave where Valerias had killed several men to protect her and her mother and sister.

"I have, too. You don't want to be his enemy."

"Go on."

"I want to tell you the true story of my first encounter with your father. Several years ago, when I was the naïve son of a Goth king, I led an ill-conceived war party against your father's legions. My men were young warriors and foolish. We were slaughtered. I was captured and brought forth before your father for sentencing. I believe I was to be executed, except that a Christian priest, who was also a prisoner, interfered in the sentencing. Somehow, I was spared. I live each day with the thought that I was the reason so many of our young men died while I survived. That day always haunts me. But now, so many years later, here I am with you. I am a man who genuinely wants you, but we must wait."

"I don't know what to say, Gulic."

"Your father is a very powerful man. If we had gone through tonight with what each of us wants, I would have betrayed his trust. I cannot do that. I hope you understand."

Alena shook her head affirmatively. "Will you continue to court me?"

"Of course, my sweet Alena, with your father's approval."

"And Mother's too?" she asked.

"Yes, of course. Can we return to the Villa now? I see your father behind every tree."

Alena laughed at Gulic and his desire to rush back to the Villa. Gulic felt greatly relieved to put this incident behind him, and he smiled. *Alena likes my necklace and we had a wonderful evening. She agrees with my decision, and I don't need to worry about explaining my time tonight with her to the General.*

The two walked back to the Villa holding hands. When they reached the Grand House, Gulic gave Alena a quick kiss and she went inside.

Gulic started to walk back to his quarters when a voice called to him from the dark porch.

"I trust all is well, Tribune?" Valerias walked up to Gulic and placed his face within inches of Gulic's. Valerias' eyes seemed to bore a hole into Gulic's soul.

"Yes, General. We had a pleasant evening together."

Gulic did not flinch as he spoke, knowing he had done nothing inappropriate with Alena. However, he prayed his churning gut would not betray his nerves.

Valerias stared at Gulic for another long, interminable, moment. He backed away and looked slowly at Gulic's body from head to toe. More time passed before Valerias spoke again.

"You have Claire's and my permission to court Alena. We expect you will always act with honor and treat her with respect."

"Yes, General. Thank you and the Domina for your approval. I promise to be a proper suitor."

"Good. I'm glad we understand each other."

Valerias smiled in a manner that did not comfort Gulic. He then disappeared into the dark.

For the second time in his life, Gulic was relieved to have survived an onerous encounter with the General.

XXV

Loss and Gain

The boredom evident on Staigrik's face was mirrored by his actions. He kept tapping his battleax into a stump while staring at the horizon. Borgnar, equally bored, had become mesmerized by the rhythmic sound of the ax.

"We have accomplished nothing for months. We wait here like children while Alfredson counsels with his shaman and oracles. I am not getting any younger. Are you, Borgnar?"

"He is the king, and there is little we can do until he decides what it is we should do."

"The king has become indifferent to our cause. I am the opposite! I am aggressive. If I was king, we would already be in Britannia. My battleax would be splitting heads, not this worn out stump. Now we sit here gathering moss on our backsides."

"Again, Staigrik, he is the king. We will hear word soon."

Staigrik knew he would get nowhere in this conversation with Borgnar, whose loyalty to Alfredson was unquestionable.

After he split the stump into several pieces, Staigrik thought it was time to sharpen his ax. He went to the blacksmith's hut to retrieve his whetstone. When he came out, Borgnar met him.

"King Alfredson has requested our presence at his court. Now!"

"Fine," answered Staigrik, who thought, *I suppose the old fool wants us to care for the children now. We are warriors, not women!*

Borgnar hurried to Alfredson's Great Hall with Staigrik exerting himself to keep up. Alfredson always held court in the large building constructed of stone and timber. The Great Hall could easily hold over two hundred men.

The hall was crowded when they arrived. Staigrik, out of breath, and Borgnar worked their way to the front. Several of the attendees patted Staigrik on his broad back as he walked by. A short while later, Alfredson entered the room. Alfredson enjoyed being king and liked a dramatic entrance. As usual, he was carried by two muscular men and surrounded by eight trusted bodyguards.

A roar erupted through the Great Hall and continued until Alfredson sat on his carved wooden chair lined with furs. Staigrik stood to Alfredson's right, Borgnar to his left. After absorbing the praise, Alfredson waved his serpent staff for silence.

"Saxon warriors," Alfredson began. "I have consulted my sources: the living, the dead, the magical, and the mysterious. They all agree that I should be patient, as I have been. This has not been easy for me or you."

Alfredson glanced toward Staigrik and continued. "But that is what had to be done. I cannot debate the spirits. They know more than me. Yet, last night they gave me a sign. It was twilight, just before the god of the night takes complete control. The raven came and sat in front of me. It had a white streak between its eyes. Soon there were two more ravens, then five, then a thousand. All the other ravens were totally black. They did not make a sound. Then, the very first one flew in front of my face, but it wasn't using its wings, and it spoke to me. The raven's voice was low and rumbled. It said, 'Wise king, you have been patient and listened to us. That is good. You will be rewarded. Now it is time. Build your ships, assemble your warriors, go to the Angles and Jutes and obtain allies, and set off to the west and conquer Britannia. It is the time of the Saxons!'

"When the raven finished speaking, all the ravens rose as one and silently flew west. Their message was clear. Now I know what must be done. As the raven spoke to me, it is time!

"Are you with me? Is the Saxon nation with me? It is time to take Britannia!" Alfredson's voice crescendoed as he spoke.

The men in the hall shouted their loyalty to Alfredson. Their voices were so loud that those who were outside the hall and couldn't clearly hear Alfredson's speech still banged their shields with their weapons.

"That is why we wait," Borgnar said to Staigrik as the adulation of Alfredson continued.

After the celebration ended, Alfredson requested counsel with Staigrik, his daughter Hildegarde, and Guenter.

"I will not be going to Britannia with you, my son and grandson." Alfredson frequently referred to Staigrik as his son. "Hildegarde will remain with me. As I speak, riders and ships are going to the villages and camps of other Saxon tribes, and to the Angles and Jutes. I am asking them to join us in our assault on Britannia. They will say yes. It is my vision."

Alfredson turned to Staigrik and said, "You will need hundreds of warships to carry our great warriors west to Britannia. Have the shipbuilders craft the greatest fleet the Saxon nation has ever seen. Prepare your armor and train the men. The time is ours, and yours, my son. It is time for the Saxon nation to rise. Go and see that it is done! Guenter, remain with me."

Staigrik was so aflame with passion for his mission that he did not see the signs as he left Alfredson.

Guenter, though, was well aware of the situation. He looked at his mother, who was weeping.

"Grandfather, are you feeling well?" Guenter asked.

"My well-being should not be your concern, grandson. You should only be concerned with remembering what I have taught you and what you have learned from your mother and father. Take that knowledge and do well for our people."

Alfredson appeared spent. He coughed weakly and continued, "I have used the last of my energy speaking my final thoughts to our nation. Your father is a great warrior and he will be king soon. But it is your fate that I have dreamed about. You will be king, but more importantly, a great leader. Be the leader who rules with wisdom and for the benefit of our people, and don't just grab spoils of war for yourself. Rule as I have ruled."

Hildegarde hugged Guenter and then sat close to her father. She gently stroked Alfredson's hair and continued weeping softly. Through tears, she hummed an old Saxon song of their ancestors. Guenter touched Alfredson's shoulder and bowed. He felt a great sadness as he left his grandfather and mother. From that moment forward, his life was to change. He soon would be one step from the throne.

Later that night, Alfredson died in his sleep. Guenter dreamed that the thousand ravens would come to his grandfather at the funeral to guide his passageway to an afterlife fit for a great king.

XXVI

Dark Encounter

Within days of their meeting with Victus, Garzad and Honorario arrived at the edge of Valerias' estate. Roman soldiers, both former and active, were everywhere. Garzad stopped a group of men to ask for directions to the Villa.

"It is over that hill." A man pointed to the rise in the land to the northeast. "Are you going to the training facility? We call it the Warriors' Palace. Hundreds of soldiers train there."

"Yes, of course." Garzad glanced at Honorario. "First, though, I must visit my old friend General Valerias."

Garzad and Honorario left the soldiers with a word of thanks and continued toward the Villa.

"This is not what I expected based on the governor-general's description," Honorario said. "It is not the quiet, pastoral picture painted by Victus. It is teeming with activity—military activity."

"Obviously," Garzad replied. "We may have to adjust our plan."

"Why are we here again, Garzad? We should be going to Augusta Treverorum and obtaining orders."

"In time, Honorario. A little detour won't slow us down. Besides, I want to meet this general. He is a legend."

The two wound their way through the estate in the direction given to the Villa. Both Garzad and Honorario wore their Roman uniforms, Garzad knowing proper military attire would draw less attention to them. He was correct. A few soldiers acknowledged their presence, but they were mostly ignored.

They drew to within one hundred feet of the Grand House and dismounted. Servants took the reins of their horses, leaving Garzad and Honorario to walk the rest of the way to the entrance.

A woman emerged from the house.

“Greetings, Tribune,” she began. “What brings you to the house of Valerias?”

“We seek the wise counsel of General Marcus Augustus Valerias.”

Garzad was unsure if the woman was a servant or somehow related to Valerias, so he asked respectfully, “Who are you?”

“I am the wife of General Valerias, the Domina of the Villa,” Claire said pointedly, which was not lost on Garzad. “And who are you?”

“My apologies, Domina.” Garzad bowed slightly. “I am Tribune Garzad and this is my aide, Centurion Honorario. We were stationed in Africa and are on our way to Augusta Treverorum for reassignment.”

At that moment, a strapping man came up behind them and startled Honorario. The man had long black hair that rested on his shoulders. His eyes were dark. He had a long knife sheathed in his belt.

“Tribune Garzad and Centurion Honorario, the man behind you is Bukarma, our friend and primary aide to General Valerias. Excuse me, I will see if the General is able to see you.”

Claire disappeared into the house and returned a short while later.

“He will see you now, Tribune Garzad. Centurion, you will wait outside with Bukarma.”

Honorario was edgy. Bukarma was large and fierce-looking, not feeble and old. *Victus has set us up*, he thought. *I will have to spend time with this man and not show any sign of nervousness. He is watching me take every breath.*

Garzad followed Claire into the Grand House. He saw two other men in the house, both of whom were armed.

"Marcus, Tribune Garzad is here to see you," Claire said as she showed Garzad into Valerias' study.

"Tribune, enter. Thank you, Domina."

Garzad entered the study and saw General Valerias standing behind a large table where numerous documents were laid out. What caught Garzad's attention was the hilt of Valerias' sword rising slightly beside his head. He also noticed the covered stump at the end of Valerias' left arm.

"I see, General, that the sheath for your sword is placed behind your back like mine. Do you think when you look at me you are looking in a mirror?"

"No. When I look at you, I only see you. I have always carried my sword this way. The sword gets in my way when it is at my side.

"I used to have it on my side and then switched it to my back." Garzad reached back and patted the hilt of his sword. "That makes us unique."

"There are other soldiers who use the back sheath, Tribune." Valerias changed the subject. "Where have you served? Perhaps we know some of the same generals."

"General, I served under Generals Octavio and Diocles. I was assigned to posts in Africa. We had great success there against traitors and rebellious tribesmen."

"Yes, I know General Diocles, and although I have never met him, I am aware of General Octavio. They are ambitious men, and your rise in rank tells me you are ambitious, too. I hear they are supporters of Magnus Maximus. Are you?"

"I serve my generals and the emperor."

"You avoided my question, Tribune. Whom do you think I support?"

"I believe you support Emperor Gratian, successor to Emperor Valentinian."

"Like you, I serve the emperor. I always have." Valerias fixed a hard stare on Garzad.

As tough as Garzad was, he felt pressure from Valerias, a feeling he seldom felt. *This is no feeble old man with rebellious loyalties,* thought Garzad.

"Tell me, Tribune, why have you come to my Villa? Do you have a message for me? Are you interested in the training facility—the Warrior's Palace? Do you want to become a trainer or a student?"

Garzad regrouped and stared into Valerias' eyes. "No, General Valerias, I am on my way to Augusta Treverorum under the orders of Emperor Magnus Maximus."

Garzad took a step closer to Valerias and lowered his voice. "I came here to kill you, General." The words did not come out as firmly as Garzad wanted, and he was upset with himself.

"I see." Valerias' expression never wavered.

Garzad was unnerved by Valerias' calmness. He blinked several times as Valerias stared at him.

"To kill me is much harder than contemplating such a task. Many have tried to do away with me, and yet here I am in front of you, and it is they who are dead. One of the last was the Hun warrior-king, Uldric. His head ended up on the blade of his own double scimitar. How do you think you would have fared against him, Tribune? It would be you one-on-one with the great Hun fighter, the fate of the battle in your hands. Would you have survived, or would it be your head impaled on a Roman spike?"

Although he was intimidated by Valerias, Garzad looked back at Valerias, this time not blinking. "I am not going kill you, General."

Valerias continued to glare. Garzad quickly backtracked from his statement and said, "I mean, I was given orders to come here to kill you, I did not come here to actually do it."

"Explain, Tribune."

Garzad was relieved the older man had not struck him down straight away and was happy to explain. "Governor-General Victus wants you dead. He described you as an old man with traitorous loyalties. He paid me to come here and kill you. If there is a traitor, it is Victus."

Garzad reached slowly into his cloak and pulled out a bag that jingled as he held it up.

"How much is my life worth to Victus?" Valerias asked.

"I don't know, I did not count it. I don't take blood money."

"And yet you have it with you." Valerias said, never taking his eyes from Garzad.

"If I had denied his request, he would have executed me. Take the money and apply it to whatever you want. I don't want it. Use it for the Warriors' Palace."

Valerias' eyes moved to the table, and Garzad placed the sack of solidi on the tabletop.

"I do not know if what you say is true, Tribune. I could give you a larger bag of solidi and have you kill Victus. But I do not do such things. I personally carry out my own punishments. Victus is a coward. He will not be with us much longer."

"I agree, General." Garzad said, happy to have made the right decision in revealing all to the General.

"Here is what I have decided." Valerias spoke sternly, and Garzad's feeling of relief disappeared.

"You can leave here now and ride to Augusta Treverorum as fast as your horse will take you. Or you can stay here and try to kill me. But I must warn you. Should you make such an attempt, I will raise up my left arm and Bukarma will snap your companion's neck as easily as a lion breaks the neck of a gazelle. You are familiar with lions, aren't you, from your time in Africa? And my friend, who is now behind you, will slit your throat while I disembowel you."

Garzad turned slightly and saw Revious standing behind him, knife in hand. When he looked back at Valerias, he saw he had unsheathed his dagger. Valerias held his left arm up with the iron cap at shoulder level. Bukarma could see Valerias through the window in the study. Wolf entered the room and stood menacingly at Valerias' side.

Garzad clearly had no choice. "I will take the first option, General."

"Wise decision, Tribune. Leave now. Revious and a company of my men will escort you to the edge of my estate. If you come back here or if I lay my eyes on you again, have no doubt—I will not hesitate to kill you. You are only alive at this instant because I know General Diocles. Do we understand each other?"

"Yes, General."

Revious and the other man in the house escorted Garzad to his horse. Honorario had already mounted his. Revious and a squad of ten cavalrymen took Garzad and Honorario well beyond the borders of Valerias' estate. Garzad and Honorario did not speak until Revious and his squad had turned back and were out of sight.

"That did not go well, Garzad," Honorario spoke first.

"No, it did not. Victus set us a trap and we fell into it. If I ever see either Victus or Valerias again, I will skin them before killing them. No one fools me or threatens me and gets away with it."

***

During the summer of 383 AD, Emperor Gratian moved his army north to confront the usurper, Magnus Maximus. Gradually, Emperor Gratian's command melted away. Fearing for his life, Gratian fled to Lugdunum, in southern Gallia. But it was to no avail. There, a Roman general loyal to Magnus Maximus executed Gratian.

Magnus Maximus had attained what he sought: the purple of the emperor.

Victus, Emperor Gratian's ally, disappeared shortly after Gratian's death and was never heard from again.

XXVII

JOSEPH

After Garzad and Honorario left the Villa under Revious' guard, Claire and Bukarma hurried to Valerias' study.

"I do not like that man. There was something not right about him." Claire spoke first.

"Yes, I agree. Something about him seemed so familiar, too," answered Valerias. "He thought we were mirror images of each other, but we are not."

"He came here today to kill you, Marcus," Bukarma said, concerned.

"He is arrogant, I'll give you that. But I doubt he was here to murder me. Curiosity lured him here. Besides, it is broad daylight with numerous soldiers, former soldiers, and attendants within a hundred feet or so of me. It would have been suicide on his part."

Valerias continued, "I believe Victus told Garzad how weak and vulnerable I was, and when he came to the Villa, he discovered that was not true. He knew Victus lied to him, so Garzad modified his plan. Any assassination attempt he had in his mind disappeared. Garzad already received his payment from Victus, so there was no need to push the matter. I doubt he'll come back."

Claire, however, wasn't so sure. "How do you know? There was another reason he came here, and it was not the solidi. Are you sure you do not know him?"

"No. I didn't recognize the man, and I can't think of another reason for his coming here. Garzad wants to impress Magnus Maximus, so he is under orders to go to Augusta Treverorum. Dealing with Victus and me was a distraction. I believe we have seen the last of him. Garzad is ambitious. He wants to accomplish great things, and killing me will hardly accomplish that."

Bukarma interjected. "Perhaps not, Marcus. Perhaps yes. He is motivated to achieve greatness for himself. I think he would like to kill you for the prestige, not the solidi—maybe just for the sport of it. I am a cautious man, Marcus. I will double the guard tonight, just in case he decides to return."

Valerias nodded in agreement. Bukarma excused himself to organize the guard, leaving Claire and Valerias alone.

"How are you feeling, husband, after your encounter with that man, Garzad?"

"Perfectly well. He is a mouse with a wolf's ambitions."

"Are you looking forward to Joseph's visit?" Claire changed the subject. "His last visit was a year ago."

"Absolutely!" A smile spread across Valerias' face.

Claire smiled back at him. "I, too, will be pleased to see him again. We will see if another year as bishop has changed him."

Wolf felt the happiness in his masters' voices and wagged his tail vigorously, brushing against Valerias' legs.

"Do you know his plans, Claire?"

"He should be here within the week. I'll arrange to have his quarters ready. I know he likes the shed furthest to the east. He calls it the Hut."

"Foolish man," answered Valerias, still smiling. "He could stay in the Grand House with us and enjoy a bit more luxury. He also would be here to talk to, as we have much to discuss. Yet, I appreciate him wanting to be alone with his God. Maybe he has a lonely God. In any event, I look forward to seeing him."

During the week that followed, Valerias helped prepare for Joseph's arrival. He gave Wolf a bath and assisted Claire and the servants with cleaning Joseph's quarters. The Hut, a simple, one-room building, was in disrepair when Joseph announced his visit. Some type of an animal had set up home in the building, making it uninhabitable. Valerias and Claire knew much work was required to make it hospitable for their guest. When the work was finished, Valerias hoped Joseph would be comfortable.

Most telling of Joseph's impending visit was that Valerias stored his sword out of sight. He wanted to convey to Joseph that a sword was no longer of primary importance in his life. Valerias did keep his dagger sheathed on his leg. With visions of Garzad active in his mind, Valerias wanted protection within arm's reach.

Joseph arrived a day after Valerias deemed the Hut acceptable. Revious had scouted Joseph's whereabouts and let Valerias know, who then told Claire. When Joseph approached the Villa, he saw Valerias, Claire, Bukarma, Revious, Alena, and Elsha, along with dozens of soldiers and attendants, awaiting his arrival.

"My, a welcome fit for an emperor—or maybe even a general!" Joseph exclaimed.

"I realize, though, that this is a small reception for a bishop!" Valerias replied.

Joseph dismounted and was embraced by Claire. "Welcome back to our Villa, Joseph," she said, smiling.

Joseph was engulfed by well-wishers and those requesting blessings. After some well-intentioned chaos, the crowd parted and Valerias and Joseph stood face to face.

"I am pleased you are here, Joseph. You had a safe journey?"

"The journey had its moments." Joseph knelt down next Wolf and rubbed his ears. "Who are you? I can tell that you are a good dog for such a master."

Wolf licked Joseph's face, making Valerias chuckle; the crowd joined in.

When the laughter subsided, Valerias said to Joseph, "Claire and I will take you to the Hut. I must warn you, though, that its previous occupant was a bit hairier than you. I realize it may not suffice for a bishop."

Joseph's eye widened and he turned abruptly and introduced Elderon, whom he had almost forgotten. "This is Elderon, my aide."

Elderon's appearance had drastically improved since he and Joseph first met. He had adopted Joseph's mannerisms, style of dress, and grooming.

"Elderon!" Valerias walked up and grasped Elderon's hand. "If you are with Joseph, then our hospitality is extended to you as well."

Valerias gave a quick glance to the head servant, Alexander.

"We will have your accommodation ready by nightfall," Alexander promised. He waved to a servant who took Joseph's horse to the stable.

Valerias and Claire moved to flank Joseph and began wandering away with him in the direction of the Hut. Elderon tried to join them, but Bukarma blocked his path.

"They want to be alone with Joseph," he said softly, but no less forcefully, to Elderon, who could only watch as Joseph walked away.

As the trio walked to the Hut, Marcus softened his voice. "Joseph, we received sad news several weeks ago." Valerias glanced at Claire, seeking reassurance, then turned again to Joseph. “Mary is dead.”

Joseph halted as his hand flew to his mouth. Mary was the woman whose life he had saved after she had been assaulted and left for dead by Morguard’s men all those years ago in Britannia. After her recovery, she married Flavius and they were exiled to Spain. Most importantly, Mary was one of his first converts. She was a warm and brave woman. Joseph struggled to control his sadness. He looked at Claire and saw tears in her eyes.

“You may remember that Mary was Claire’s servant when Claire was a queen in Britannia. Mary became Claire’s close friend. I didn’t know her well, but anything that hurts my wife hurts me.” Valerias put his arm around Claire.

“How did she die?” Joseph asked, stunned.

Valerias answered, “She never recovered from her brutal treatment at the hands of Morguard. She bore a child, a girl named Marian. I think she is four or five years old.”

“Why did she have to die, Joseph?” Claire’s voice quaked. Claire was a strong woman, yet to Joseph, she appeared so vulnerable in that moment.

“Mary was a servant of God, Claire—a very good servant. We never know when God will call us to serve in his kingdom. It was her time.” Joseph had regained his composure and spoke assuredly.

“But she has a child and husband who desperately need her.”

“Claire, I cannot tell you why God took her, but I trust Him to do what is right. Remember, God sent his son, Jesus Christ, to die for us so that we may live.”

“While your God did nothing, I took action.” Valerias signaled that he had had enough talk of God.

“What action did you take, Marcus?” Joseph was curious.

"I sent Emperor Theodosius a request to grant Flavius a full pardon. I received recent acknowledgment from the emperor that my request was approved. I have asked Flavius to come to the Villa and be coleader with Bukarma at my training camp. He has accepted the position. We can care for Marian better here than Flavius can alone. He should be here when you return from your Council of Bishops."

"Flavius is a man of God." Joseph stated that which Valerias and Claire already knew.

"I am sure Flavius' Christianity was a major factor in the emperor pardoning him," said Valerias.

"Flavius will want you to bless his child," Claire added.

"That would be my greatest pleasure. I look forward to renewing my spiritual bond with Flavius and meeting Marian."

Claire and Valerias showed Joseph to his quarters in the refurbished Hut. Joseph protested the luxury of his room, but Valerias and Claire were firm and Joseph relented.

That night, a special meal was prepared in Joseph's honor. Claire sat on Valerias' right and Joseph on his left. Bukarma, Penelope, and Revious were also seated at the table. The party was a festive affair. Bukarma and Revious amused the assembly with their stories—several at Valerias' expense—which made everyone laugh. For his part, Valerias enjoyed himself. It was clear to Joseph that Valerias had changed and become more tolerant. He was also pleased that Valerias wasn't carrying his sword. *My friend has made progress*, Joseph mused.

After the banquet, Valerias and two guards escorted Joseph to his Hut. Due to its isolated location, Valerias insisted the guards stay overnight at the building. Joseph protested, but eventually agreed. Elderon bunked in the building that housed the Villa's attendants.

Valerias left Joseph with a request. "When you return from the Council of Bishops, I want to discuss Emperor Theodosius' Edict."

"Yes, I look forward to our conversation," answered Joseph. As long as he had known Valerias, he had become used to hearing unusual requests involving Christianity. *Marcus has never accepted any religion, but he maintains a strong curiosity for it. I wonder why that is.*

Joseph settled in his quarters. When he felt secure in the quiet surroundings, he pulled out several flasks. A kind merchant at a nearby village had given Joseph flasks filled with wine. The pain of Ruth with someone other than himself, and especially the death of Mary, were too much for him to bear. He swigged at one of the flasks, seeking the oblivion that brought with it a little peace.

When Joseph awoke, it was completely dark inside his room except for a tiny flicker of light from an almost exhausted candle. Joseph fumbled in the dark trying to place his hands on a new candle before the old one burned out. He found one in a box on a shelf near the old candle.

Once the new candle was lit, he eased back onto his bed. The pain in his head from the drink equaled the pain in his heart for Mary and Ruth. He felt sick, and vomiting seemed to be the best option. He looked around for a night bucket and vomited the contents of his stomach into it. After he was finished, Joseph looked up and was startled to see a man sitting in a chair by his bed.

"Do not be alarmed, Joseph, I am your friend."

Joseph tried to compose himself, "I do not know you, so how could you be my friend?"

"I am Andrew. I have followed you for some time."

"Are you a man of the cloth, Andrew?"

"Yes, in a manner of speaking. You have accomplished many good things since you accepted Christ as your Lord and Savior. You have saved souls and lives. You are an inspiration to God's flock."

"I have tried to live my life as a true Christian," Joseph said warily.

"Then why do you punish yourself?"

"What do you mean?"

"You sacrificed your love for a woman so you could tend to the people. That is a worthy sacrifice."

The effects of the drink still lingered and Joseph's defenses were lowered. "It hurts so much," he admitted, releasing the pain he dared not speak aloud, "when I see Ruth and Olivertos, and know she could have been *my* wife, and *we* could have had children of *our* own."

"But think of the pain you have eased for so many people. You sacrificed your love for Ruth to save Olivertos."

"Yes, it worked out well for Olivertos." Joseph spoke with an air of sadness. He lowered his voice. "Mary . . . Mary taught me what good really meant. She was a true Christian; I am not."

"Not true, Joseph. Mary no longer suffers. Remember—it was you who saved her life and soul. Just like you did with Olivertos. God's blessing is with you."

"How do you know all these things, Andrew?"

Andrew did not answer. "You will have a decision to make shortly. That decision involves the strength of your faith. I have no doubt you will act wisely. Remember, Joseph, God is with you."

Andrew stood up and left. Joseph was unsure if he used the door. However, he was not interested in how Andrew had left the Hut; he was disturbed by Andrew's final comment. *What did he mean, I will have a decision to make? What decision? Who is this man?*

"Come back! Andrew, come back! I have more questions, many questions! You can't go now!"

Joseph tried to get out his bed, but he could not. He flew into full panic, arms and legs flailing wildly as he cried out for Andrew to return. He closed his eyes and prayed for it to end. He wanted to die. Finally, he fell back into a fitful sleep.

When Joseph opened his eyes again, he was looking into Valerias' concerned face.

"Wake up, Joseph. Wake up!" Valerias shouted at him.

Joseph tried to bring himself back to reality, pulling himself upright in the bed.

"Where is he?"

"Who?" Valerias asked.

"Andrew!"

"Who?" Valerias repeated, becoming alarmed.

"Andrew, the man who was here, sitting in that chair." Joseph pointed with a shaky hand.

"I can assure you that no one has been here tonight." Valerias turned his head to the two guards in the doorway who nodded in confirmation.

"I had guards standing outside your doorway all night. The only voice they heard was yours. I was walking nearby in the early morning and one of my guards came for me. He said you were ill or had a nightmare. That is why I'm here."

"It can't be. I know he was here," Joseph said quietly.

Valerias looked around the floor of the Hut and spotted several flasks strewn about. He also smelled vomit and saw a spill on the floor by the night bucket. He ordered the guards to return to their posts.

"I see the source of the problem." Valerias reached for an empty flask. "You use drink try to ease your suffering. Drinking won't solve your problems or make matters better." Valerias held up a second flask. "Your feelings for Ruth and Mary, and whatever else distresses you, are simply what they are, and you just have to deal with them."

Joseph sat in his bed with his head down. He looked like a beaten man.

"Get dressed," Valerias ordered.

"Why?" Joseph looked up at Valerias. "I'm a failure as a bishop and a Christian. I let my feelings interfere with my role as God's emissary."

"Nonsense," Valerias replied. "I know no man more moral than you. Wallowing here in self-pity says you are a weak man. I know you are not weak! Now prove it to the rest of the people out there that you deserve your title of bishop. Meet me outside in half an hour. I need to show you something. Be ready to ride."

Joseph decided it would be prudent to do as his friend told him.

Claire was waiting for Valerias just outside the Hut.

"Is he well?" she asked, her face creased with worry.

"He will be, in time. The news of Mary's death reignited his feelings for Ruth and what he may have lost with her. I will give him something to right his course."

When Joseph emerged from the Hut, he was met by Valerias, Revious, and several men on horses waiting for him. His own horse stood by Valerias.

Joseph mounted. "Where are we going?"

"To find your salvation."

They rode hard to the east; the fast pace prevented any conversation.

They crossed a steep ridge, halted, and looked down into the valley where the Huns were camped.

"What is this?" Joseph asked, confused.

"Huns!" Valerias said.

Apprehension spread rapidly across Joseph's face. Then he heard Valerias and Revious laughing at him.

"Why do you laugh? Aren't these the people who tried to kill you—to kill us?"

"Yes, they are." Valerias continued to laugh. "I had the same reaction when Revious first showed me their camp. Shall we go meet them? There may be some evangelizing work for you."

The sentries did not stop the group as they rode into the camp. Oxanos greeted the group, but was guarded when introduced to Joseph. He was a stranger who had to earn their trust.

"How long have the Huns been here?" Joseph asked Valerias.

"I'm not sure, exactly. Revious brought them here," Valerias explained, adding, "without my permission." Valerias feigned his disapproval, then smiled.

The Romans unloaded supplies while Valerias talked to Oxanos, with Arb translating when necessary. Valerias happily found that conditions in the camp had markedly improved since their first meeting.

Valerias and his group left the camp in the mid-afternoon, in time to reach the Villa by dusk. Valerias no longer liked to travel at night.

As they rode back, Valerias asked Joseph, "Are you surprised that I would allow my former enemies to occupy my land?"

"Nothing about you, Marcus, surprises me," replied Joseph.

Two days later, Joseph and Elderon left for the nearby Council of Bishops. Valerias gave Elderon a horse to ride. He believed Joseph's aide should have his own horse.

As they rode out of the courtyard, Joseph said, “We will return to the Villa after the council meeting. I want to see the Huns again.”

XXVIII

THE EDICT

"He returns!" The call swept through the Villa like a gentle breeze carrying its soothing comfort to those within. Joseph had been away at the Council of Bishops for six weeks.

Valerias watched Elsha throw a stick for Wolf to retrieve when he heard the message. *I cannot understand why Wolf obeys Elsha and not me!*

"Go and tell your mother that Joseph is here." Valerias held his hand out to Elsha, who gave him the stick. Valerias heaved it into the untamed area behind the grain store. Wolf just looked at him, and Valerias shook his head. He then strode into the courtyard to await Joseph's arrival, Wolf walking at his side.

"You have returned, my friend!" Valerias exclaimed as Joseph and Elderon drew their horses to a halt near him. The men dismounted and attendants took their horses away to the stables. Claire emerged from the Grand House and gave Joseph a hug.

"And welcome to you as well, Elderon," Claire added warmly.

"Thank you, Domina," Elderon replied. "It is good to be back at your Villa. Your hospitality is magnificent. I have never been treated so well."

"Come and refresh yourselves after your journey," Claire continued. "We will have supper in your honor two hours from now."

After the meal, Valerias excused himself and Joseph to have a private conversation in the study. Valerias did not say what he wanted to discuss, which made Joseph apprehensive. He expected Valerias to talk over the same subjects debated by the recent Council of Bishops, including full implementation of Emperor Theodosius' Edict.

"Joseph," Valerias began, "I understand that through the Edict of Thessalonica issued in 380, Emperors Theodosius and Gratian proclaimed that all Christians, and even non-Christians, must subscribe to the concept of an equal Trinity. In January 381, Theodosius issued his formal letter proclaiming the only acceptable form of Christianity is centered on the Trinity of equality between God the Father, Jesus the Son, and the Holy Spirit. Is that correct?"

"Yes," Joseph answered, unsure what direction Valerias was going. "God the Father, Jesus His son, and the Holy Spirit are of equal status. They form the Trinity, as you said."

"And Arians believe that is not the case. They believe that Jesus Christ is subordinate to God. Yes?"

"Yes. However, Emperor Theodosius has demanded a uniform Christianity throughout the empire centered on the belief of the Triune God. This concept is the basis of our Nicene faith."

"Of course, Joseph, pagans have no say in the matter. They must conform to the belief of the emperor."

"And also to the Council of Bishops," Joseph added.

"Certain bishops," Valerias countered. "I am well aware that not all bishops share the emperor's view."

"They will come around, Marcus. We must be patient. The evidence shows that we are on the right path."

"What evidence, Joseph?"

"It is what God has proclaimed through his messengers."

"I see men positioning themselves as centers of power, not as messengers of God. They use that power to force their beliefs on others. I see no proof that the Nicene Trinity takes precedence over other forms of religion. I think the Nicenes are no better than other religions, and may even be worse."

Valerias' forcefulness surprised Joseph. "It amazes me that you, a non-Christian, know so much about my religion."

"I am not, nor will I ever be. But I have had time to study your religion in detail. Perhaps in the beginning Jesus and his disciples thought, ideally, they could change the world and make it better. But others seeking power have seized those beliefs for their purposes. And with power comes greed. Power and greed feed on each other, and together create a synergy that is so intoxicating that the truth is lost. Those people have twisted the truth for their own gain."

"I understand what you are saying. There are those Christians, but there is so much more. The Christian faith was a beacon of hope to people during Rome's oppression."

Valerias swallowed hard so as not to respond.

Joseph continued, "Today, we continue to offer hope to the weak and suffering. We provide a pathway to enter our Father's kingdom—heaven. I must be honest with you. I believe there is more value showing people the promise of Christianity and not getting tangled up in doctrinaire arguments. That is what I want to do. That is what I have tried to do. But I must follow the teachings of the church. In the end, one true faith will unite all Christians!"

Joseph's passion convinced Valerias that his friend's faith was sincere.

"You are a good man, Joseph. I don't believe in the message you offer, but I believe in you. The example you set is a message of hope to those who accept *and* question the tenets of Christianity.

"I must confess, though, that I'm concerned for you. I see you as a tolerant Christian. There are those who are not as accepting as you. I have heard reports of Nicene Christians persecuting other faiths. Some of the reports even cite Arian and pagan fatalities. Your beliefs may clash with those who have no tolerance for people who fall outside the Nicene faith."

"That is true, and I look forward to that challenge," Joseph replied. "There is one thing I question, Marcus. You, yourself, seem to have no fear of Emperor Theodosius' Edict. Aren't you concerned about your status? Don't you worry about what may happen to your property if a purge comes?"

Smiling, Valerias responded, "Allow me to explain. I served with Emperor Theodosius' father, Count Theodosius; we were friends. The count was an outstanding military officer. He led a successful campaign against barbarians in Britannia. Unfortunately, he was caught in a power struggle in Emperor Gratian's court and was executed. It was a sad end to a great man. His life is a lesson to all of us. The direction of wind changes. One minute you are in favor, the next you're dead.

"I also mentored Emperor Theodosius during his training when he was younger. I know Theodosius personally. He will let me be regardless of my religious beliefs."

Joseph was surprised at what he had just heard. "Is there anyone in the Roman hierarchy who you do not know, Marcus?"

"Joseph, I have many friends and allies. At the same time, there are many who would like to see me beheaded."

Later that night, Valerias recounted to Claire what he and Joseph had discussed, including his concern for Joseph's safety.

The following day, Valerias and Joseph returned to the Hun camp. Having concluded that the Huns posed no risk to him, Valerias left Bukarma and Revious at the Villa. Elderon said he had a terrible headache and also remained behind. Wolf required exercise, so Valerias convinced Elsha to let the dog come with him.

Another addition to the party was Gulic, who had just ridden into the Villa. Valerias decided Gulic needed to spend less time with Alena, so he suggested the young man accompany him. Gulic was easily persuaded; he had not seen a Hun since the Battle of Three Tongues and was curious how Valerias would interact with them. He also wondered how he, himself, would react toward the people who killed his father, Mostar Gulivus.

At the camp, Gulic was surprised by how well Valerias treated the Huns and the respect they showed him. As usual, Valerias brought supplies with him, and it was clear their camp was becoming an active village. Winter had arrived in 383 AD, and the supplies were particularly welcome.

The Huns again acted tentatively around Joseph. They viewed him as a shaman eager to collect their souls. However, Joseph demonstrated his knowledge of medicine, learned from Olivertos, when he treated two Hun children with minor injuries. As Joseph helped the children, he thought, *Thank you, Olivertos, for being a great teacher and for sharing your knowledge as a healer with me. There is still much I could learn from you.*

He avoided an attempt at converting the Huns, but at the end of this second visit, Joseph was pleased that the barrier between him and the Huns appeared to be lifting.

Gulic found he did not hate the Huns. He was fascinated with their lifestyle and, in particular, their weapons. He favored the Hun bows and how they were constructed. Oxanos had seen Gulic's fascination with the Hun weaponry and gifted him a bow and quiver of arrows. Gulic in turn gave Oxanos his crossbow. After a couple of quick lessons from Gulic, the crossbow became one of Oxanos' favorite weapons.

Before they left the Hun village, Valerias invited Oxanos, Arb, and ten Hun warriors to the Villa for an archery tournament in one week's time—dependent on the winter weather. Valerias told Oxanos that it was the Domina's invitation as well. Oxanos gratefully accepted the privilege of being invited to the house of General Valerias and the Domina.

XXIX

Impatient Delay

"Alfredson's death could not have come at a worse time. There should be a limit to the mourning period!" Staigrik broke into a frenzy and smashed his war ax down hard on a feeble log, splintering it into shards.

"Careful, cousin," Borgnar replied. "You may be the king-in-waiting, but Alfredson was a god to many Saxons. They would not appreciate what you desire during this time of mourning. And remember, he was the father of your wife and grandfather of your son. You must exercise understanding and patience."

Alfredson's passing was marked with a combination of mourning and celebration. Leaders of the Saxons, Jutes, and Angles came from lands far away to pay their respects to the great king. His funeral took place in his home village of Harsgood. His carefully prepared body was placed in a Saxon warship with hundreds of weapons and gold relics that had been stolen during raids—goods to bring comfort to the king in his afterlife.

The ship was set adrift as dusk darkened into night. When the ship was fifty yards from the shore, Borgnar sent a flaming arrow through the night and onto the ship, setting it ablaze. At its crest, the flames reached high into the night sky, illuminating the shoreline around the bay. Guenter later swore he saw the thousand ravens that Alfredson had dreamed of descend on the ship to accompany Alfredson's spirit into the afterlife.

Staigrik was required to play multiple roles during the long mourning period: the grieving son, the consoling husband to Hildegarde, the calm advisor to the people, and the wise appointed heir to the throne. Staigrik did not perform any of these roles well. Instead, he was impatient and preoccupied with seizing the riches of Britannia. His obsession grew as Alfredson's mourning period stretched on for weeks.

Staigrik's actions caused consternation among several Saxon chiefs, who began to question his loyalty to Alfredson. Borgnar was aware of the subversive rumblings, and he continually reminded his cousin to be patient. Finally, Staigrik heeded Borgnar's advice that patience occasionally was necessary.

One month after the end of the mourning period, Staigrik summoned the Saxon chiefs, who served as a council of elders, for a meeting. Leaders and representatives from other Saxon tribes that were present at Harsgood were also invited.

Staigrik began the council meeting with a flourish. "The gods have taken the great King Alfredson to rest with his father and his father's father in immortality. The time for mourning our great king is over. Now, with your approval, it is my turn to carry the staff of the kings. Our forefathers are watching us, so we must proceed with what they asked me to do and what we must do!"

"What must we do?" a voice in the crowd shouted.

"We must go to Britannia and take all the riches we can seize, including their women, for ourselves. I have been told by Saxons who have been to Britannia that the land is ripe with wealth—and did I mention the women?" Staigrik proclaimed boldly.

The crowd loudly voiced their approval.

"When do we leave?" the same voice demanded.

"I want to depart within the month!" Staigrik responded energetically.

Borgnar strode to Staigrik's side and spoke into his ear for some time.

Staigrik took in a deep breath and softened his tone. "To strike now is what Staigrik the warrior would have wanted. But being your king-in-waiting has granted me wisdom. To leave in such a short time is foolish. We need to finish building our fleet and rallying our allies. Besides, winter is at the door, so we will wait until spring."

The council meeting carried on for several hours and became raucous as the beer flowed freely. Eventually, the council of elders took a vote, and Staigrik was endorsed as king, after which more drinking followed to celebrate. After the attendees dispersed, many on unsteady legs, a drunken Staigrik sat with a sober Borgnar.

"I did not like your advice before or during the council meeting, cousin. I want to go *now*. We can prepare the ships and attack. Why wait? We are Saxons! The weather is not a reason to wait!" Staigrik slurred his words. He could not stand, and his battleax, which he was using as a staff, kept him from falling face first on the ground.

"We have gone over the reasons for waiting many times, my king. It will go much more easily for us if the weather is warmer, the seas are calmer, and our fleet is larger. Besides, the Angles and Jutes are not ready."

Borgnar spoke in a measured, knowledgeable voice that appeased Staigrik. Borgnar knew the Saxon fleet would need more time to adequately prepare to raid Britannia. He did not share his thoughts with Staigrik, though. *The best way to deal with my cousin is to avoid saying anything that indicates the Saxon nation is not ready to follow his Britannian adventure. It is best to offer helpful suggestions.*

"Where is my son?" Staigrik continued to slur his words as he changed the subject.

Borgnar snapped his fingers at a guard. Half an hour passed before Guenter stood in front of Staigrik.

"Where were you? Out counting sea birds on the cliff?" Staigrik laughed at his own insult.

Borgnar glanced at Guenter and blinked his eyes quickly as a warning.

"I was reviewing the fleet, Father."

Remarkably, Staigrik regained a semblance of sobriety and pounced. "Were you now? I have never noticed your interest in warships. Since you have developed such an interest, I have a task for you."

"Yes?" answered Guenter, curious and alarmed.

"You are now responsible for providing me with a daily update on the condition of all warships in our fleet. I want to know their status and when they will be ready to leave our shores for Britannia. I want to know how many men each ship can carry. You are to do this daily and give me the results nightly."

Staigrik was pleased with himself. He managed to give Guenter a task that would require substantial time to complete. *This will keep him from reading his books and wandering about aimlessly looking at things, such as rocks and clouds, which have nothing to do with preparing for our raid against Britannia.*

"Yes," Guenter agreed. He added, "Father, have you given more thought to us establishing a Saxon kingdom in Britannia?"

"No!" Staigrik responded gruffly. "I have no interest in such things. Go!"

Guenter's shoulders fell as he left the hall.

"He will never be a man or a warrior," Staigrik said to Borgnar. "I think he belongs with the women more than men."

“I believe he will be a great leader,” countered Borgnar. “The prophecies have declared it so.”

“The prophets you refer to are dried up old men who can barely carry themselves about, let alone a weapon. They want to sit in their lodges smoking strange herbs instead of doing what men are supposed to do—crush enemies. Shaking a few bones about tells us little. A battleax speaks loudly!

“My men will follow me without question. They want a bold leader. Alfredson is dead, and my son is weaker than the prophets. In the spring, we will assemble one thousand warships and move against Britannia. That is my prophecy! I can only hope that the gods will turn my weak son into a fierce warrior, but I know that is against all odds.” Staigrik scoffed at his own remark.

XXX

TURMOIL

When Valerias and his company returned to the Villa after their visit to the Hun camp, Valerias spotted Bukarma standing at the entrance to the Grand House, his left hand behind his back. Valerias dismounted and told Joseph he had a business matter to address. He suggested it would be a good time for him and Claire to have the private conversation they wanted, so Joseph left to find Claire.

Gulic was also surprised to be encouraged by Valerias to enjoy Alena's company before supper. He did not object and left to look for her.

Valerias strode briskly into the house and headed directly for his study.

"What do we need to discuss, Bukarma?" Valerias felt tired from his visit with the Huns and was impatient.

"This," Bukarma replied. He pulled Elderon in front of him, a leather strap wrapped tightly around his neck.

Valerias glanced at Elderon and then fixed his eyes on the table. Several objects were placed there, including silver candlesticks and some of Claire's jewelry.

"Explain," Valerias said to the room.

Revious, who was standing in the corner, said, "Joseph's aide has a strong affinity for earthly things—more so than of the spiritual type."

"Approach, little man." Valerias immediately surmised the situation and was in charge of Elderon's future. He was angry but spoke calmly. Elderon walked hesitantly toward Valerias, with Bukarma close behind holding the leather strap.

"I want you to explain to me what you have done." Valerias gazed intently at Elderon. Elderon knew his time on Earth was about to end. Sweat beaded on his skin.

Elderon mumbled incoherently.

"Nothing to say? Not going to defend yourself? You are a weak man, Elderon. What Joseph sees in you, I cannot imagine, because I see nothing good."

Valerias unsheathed his dagger and pointed it at Elderon as he spoke. "There are many ways to handle your fate. I could have Bukarma garrote you with a wave of my hand. I could gut you myself, but that would leave a mess. I could have Revious take you into the woods, where you would disappear. We could explain to Joseph that you simply decided to return home. We could give you to the Huns as a slave. What they would do to you, I don't know. I think that would be my last choice, if I was you. So, thief, which option do you choose?"

"I am so sorry, General Valerias. I . . . I . . . I have done wrong, something evil. God forgive me." Elderon's voice was low and he stuttered from fear. He bowed his head. A bald spot capped its crown.

"Yes, you are a common thief. What is one of your Christian commandments—thou shalt not steal? And yet you steal from me." Valerias held Claire's jewelry in his hand. "And you have stolen from my wife. Lastly, and most importantly, you have taken Joseph's trust and discarded it like a pile of shit."

Elderon sobbed. Valerias looked at Bukarma and Revious, and then at Elderon.

"On your knees, thief," Valerias commanded. Bukarma shoved Elderon down onto his knees.

"Please forgive me." It was not clear to whom Elderon's pleas were directed. He continued, "Please forgive me! Forgive me!" Elderon repeated over and over again. "I am a sinner. I have abused the trust that was given to me. I am a thief. I am a criminal. I do not deserve your mercy. Forgive me!"

He stopped sobbing as his prayers became more intense. "Thank you, Lord, for giving me parents who provided me with a strong background on which I could have built a good life—a life from which I strayed. God, I thank you for my life. I pray that I will be accepted into heaven and not be sent to hell. I repent my evil ways, and I am ready to stand in front of You and face Your judgment!"

Elderon swayed back and forth on his knees, speaking in a volume that was just shy of a shout. He finally stopped and looked up at Valerias. His eyes were clear and showed no sign of tears.

"I am ready, General. Choose whatever means of execution you deem fit for my crime. I am truly sorry. I ask for your forgiveness before you punish me."

Valerias had interrogated hundreds of prisoners when he was in the army and had learned to tell an honest man from a liar. He glanced at Bukarma and motioned for him to pick Elderon up off his knees. Valerias moved within inches of Elderon's face and stared into his eyes. Elderon tried to look Valerias in the eyes, but it proved to be too difficult. Instead, he peered down at the floor.

Valerias stood back. "It is a good day for you, Elderon. The option I have chosen is not one I offered you. I have decided to spare you. I once gave Joseph a second chance, and he did well. Therefore, I will give you a second opportunity to become someone better."

Elderon looked stunned in disbelief. Finally, he said, "Thank you, General Valerias, for your mercy. Thank you. I shall be better. I promise to do better." Elderon bent over and kissed Valerias' ring.

"I truly hope so, Elderon. I promise anything less will not result in a third opportunity." Valerias pressed the point of his dagger into Elderon's throat to emphasize his words. The sharp point of the knife pricked Elderon's neck, a droplet of blood blooming and spilling onto the shiny metal.

"I promise. I swear to God. I swear on my parents' graves!"

Bukarma relaxed the strap around Elderon's neck, and Elderon pulled himself out of the loop.

"Now go and await Joseph's return. Show *him* how a good Christian acts."

Elderon left the house, his head hanging low, his mood somber. After he was gone, Bukarma asked Valerias, "Would you have executed him?"

"Absolutely!" Valerias answered. "His contrition saved his life. I believe he was being truthful."

Revious wondered, "Do you think he will reform, as he promised?"

"Revious, human nature is difficult to predict. For his sake, and Joseph's, I hope so. Don't tell Joseph what happened here."

Valerias looked at Bukarma and Revious, who both nodded in agreement.

***

The wind was blustery and cold as Claire and Joseph walked along a path north of the Villa's buildings. Neither seemed to notice the chill as they were deep in conversation.

"Life has not always been as good as it seems here, Joseph. Marcus is a wonderful husband and father, and the Villa . . .

sometimes I wake in the morning and can't believe I am here. It is so safe and full of life."

"I agree," answered Joseph as he looked at a clump of yellow flowers frozen in place near the path.

"Marcus has gone through dark periods. He lost interest in everything, including me, I think. He would disappear for days. I didn't know if he was alive and if he was, if he would even return."

"He always returned, Claire." Joseph stated the obvious.

Claire continued, "When he did finally return, he would go to a barn and sit for hours. He had little to do with Alena and Elsha. Then, all of a sudden, the old Marcus would reappear, and he was the strong husband and doting father. It was like spring had come. However, the darkness would return and he would disappear again."

"I can't picture Marcus like that. He has always been larger than life." Joseph remembered the Valerias he first met.

"I finally procured a dog for him. However, Marcus thinks Wolf was a stray that he found. I also reached out to Bukarma, and he and his family joined us at the Villa. Then they opened the successful training camp—the Warriors' Palace. Through the efforts of others, I even persuaded Revious to come here. I have tried . . ."

Tears welled up in Claire's eyes. Joseph put his arm around her for support.

"Did you invite the Huns, too?" Joseph casually remarked.

The comment caught Claire by surprise and she laughed. "No, they were a bonus." Claire became serious again. "I think I have failed him, Joseph."

"Nonsense, Claire!" Joseph replied forcefully. "I can promise you that if you had not entered his life, he would be dead by now.

Dead! You gave him something to live for. When he suffered the darkness, you were there to help him find his way back to here, to you."

Joseph waved his arms in a circle and pointed to Claire's heart. "Without you, there would be no Wolf, no Bukarma, no Revious, and no home—which has become his center. No, you are the strong one, Claire. I have the greatest respect for you."

Claire felt a sense of confirmation for what she had always believed. It was good to hear those words from someone else. She smiled at Joseph and gave him a hug.

"Joseph, I have another matter to discuss with you—Mary. Her death came as a shock to me. I thought she was well. We corresponded regularly, and she never gave me any indication that something was wrong. She knew I was in a trying situation with Marcus and did not want to burden me with her problems."

"Are you sure you could have helped her? Sometimes a body just gives out. Remember, she barely survived her capture by Morguard's men. And giving birth to Marian had to be difficult. That may have contributed to her early death."

Claire nodded and Joseph continued, "It took heroic measures by several people—Flavius and you, Claire, are at the top of the list of those who helped save her."

"Mary had a strong will to live, Joseph. But don't forget about you. I would say you were foremost on her list of angels."

Joseph started to shake his head, but Claire continued, "She sacrificed herself for others, including me. I want to do something for her. Having Flavius released from exile so he and Marian can live with us at the Villa is a start."

"When do you expect them to arrive?" Joseph asked.

"Any day now," Claire answered hopefully.

“Good. I want to see my old friend again. I pray he has kept the faith after Mary’s passing.”

“Do you think Mary is in the Christian heaven?”

“Oh, yes, Claire! There is no doubt in my mind that she is one of God’s angels.” Joseph looked at Claire and saw her eyes glisten again.

“Thank you. I wish you were closer to us than Britannia.”

“My mission is Britannia, Claire. That reminds me, as we discussed earlier, Drostan would like to join Father Timothy’s order. I have denied his request until you speak to him. What do you want me to do?”

“I don’t know. I think becoming a Christian brother can be honorable. To give one’s life to a just cause as you have is a good thing. I agree with Marcus, though, that many of your fellow clergymen are corrupt and act as demigods. I don’t want Drostan to be involved with or become one of those people. And now with Emperor Theodosius’ Edict, I think that will cause more corruption, should free thought and religious liberty end. Marcus is correct about that.”

“I may disagree with you,” Joseph said.

“Also, Drostan is heir to the throne, should something happen to Eustice. I would be concerned for his well-being if he became a young, inexperienced king in these wild, unpredictable times. But he is the potential future king of our people, and to me, that position weighs more than being a brother in a small religious order.”

Claire had a look of defiance when she spoke, showing a side of herself that Joseph rarely saw.

“People believe I live in a realm of tranquility, but I don’t. I worry about Marcus. I worry about Drostan. I worry about Alena and Elsha. I think of my people in Britannia. I cherish the stability in my life; it seems so hard to attain. Marcus has often spoken of achieving a sense of contentment. I agree with him—contentment does not last."

Joseph placed his hand on her shoulder and gave it a comforting squeeze. "Uncertainty is part of life. When you were on the run from Argus, did you think you would be where you are today? That your children would be alive and you would be married to an amazing man? I believe only God knows what tomorrow will bring. What comes, comes. We must embrace life and all that it offers. By not doing so, we could miss something valuable. I will pray that tomorrow brings you fulfillment in what you desire."

XXXI

Eustice

"Where is my wife, Captain Amron?" Eustice asked.

"I don't know, my king. She was supposed to attend combat training this afternoon."

"Well, did she?"

"Voltrex conducts the training. Queen Rega believes that we live in such an unsettled time that she should be able to defend herself should the need arise."

Eustice gave Amron a cold stare. "You have not answered my question. Find her and report back to me. Now!"

"Yes, my king." Amron bowed and started to leave the room, almost backing into Rega and Voltrex.

Rega crossed the room to Eustice and gave him a kiss on the cheek.

"I just finished training with Voltrex. Today we worked on using the Roman short sword. They call it the gladius. It is a good sword for a woman."

"I'm not sure why you need this training. I will protect you. And if I'm not present, my bodyguards will protect you."

"My husband, we have talked about this. I want to be able to fight. Voltrex knows weapons, and I am learning his techniques."

"If you feel that is important to you, Rega, then continue. Claire never learned how to use a sword, but she is an excellent marksman. I know her mastery of the bow saved several men's lives when the Romans fought the Huns."

"I think markswoman is a more appropriate term," offered Rega.

Eustice frowned.

Rega continued, "Have you made any progress finding Morguard? Unfortunately, I have not uncovered anything of use."

"He is no longer in the kingdom. If he was here, his enemies would have killed him by now. Although, *if* he shows his face, I will be the one who kills him."

"What about the rumors of Drostan?" Rega asked.

"I continue to hear talk, but there is nothing substantive. We don't know if he is alive, and if he is alive, where he can be found."

"You know, my king, if he does surface, he could lay a rightful claim to your throne. You would be deposed," Voltrex warned.

"I have thought of that possibility, Voltrex."

"Then you know we can't let him surface. I refuse to serve a boy who hides like a coward. I serve you, the true king and queen!" Voltrex said, his voice growing louder.

"Your loyalty is impressive, Voltrex. I shall consider what you say." Eustice's tone lacked sincerity.

"Voltrex speaks the truth," Rega joined in. "I don't want to see you thrown out just because the boy decides now is the time for him to climb out from the weeds."

"You two keep forgetting that he is my nephew, and Claire is married to a powerful Roman general. He may decide to come to Drostan's aid, should it come to that."

"They live in Italia, far from here. And I heard he is old and retired. I don't fear an old Roman. He has only one hand!" Voltrex replied sarcastically.

Eustice moved closer to Voltrex. "I have met this old Roman you derisively speak of, Voltrex. He is not someone you want to dance with. My sister and Valerias make an unusual pair. I still find it difficult to believe that a Briton queen married a Roman general. However, *never* underestimate them."

"King Eustice," Voltrex offered, "I understand what you say. Let me take a squad of cavalry and see if we can uncover Drostan. I give you my word that if I find him, I will bring him to you alive, and then you can decide what to do with him. Let's offer a larger reward to anyone who reports any sightings."

"Yes. If we find him, perhaps Claire will come to Britannia and take him back to Italia," added Rega.

"I will give it some thought," Eustice said, but he was distracted. His mind had shifted to another matter. "Now I must meet a nobleman I do not like and settle his land conflict with another nobleman I like even less. There are days I believe I could give this kingship up."

Eustice left for his meeting. Amron and two other soldiers went with him to act as bodyguards. Rega and Voltrex were left alone. Voltrex moved close to Rega.

"Not today, lover." Rega's mind was elsewhere.

"Why not?" Voltrex asked, disappointed. He still managed to rub Rega's shoulder affectionately.

"Fine." Rega immediately warmed up to Voltrex's attention, and soon they were disrobing each other in her private chamber. On this occasion, though, the interlude between the two was quick and not fulfilling.

"I do not apologize—but I was not the lover today that I can be," Rega announced as she curled Voltrex's hair between her fingers. "I thought our constant reminders of Morguard and that spawn of Claire would drive Eustice mad for revenge and mad with jealousy. Instead, he has little interest in either. Now he's hinting at giving up the throne. I can tell you that would be bad for me and for you."

"There is time, my love, for all to work out." Voltrex tried to soothe Rega. He placed his finger over her lips, reminding her to keep her voice down.

Rega nodded and spoke softly, but harshly. "Morguard is a myth, and we have no knowledge of whether Drostan is even alive. Soon Eustice will completely ignore the rumors. He is a better king than I thought possible. And one of these days, someone is going to find out about us. Do I need to explain to you what would happen if he learned of our secret?"

"I understand your worry, Rega. I will take care of our problem. Eustice will not find out about us. Will you promise to go along with me no matter what happens? Your world is going to change."

"Yes," Rega said as her eyes softened. "What will you do?"

"You do not need to know now, my love. Word will come of what you will need to do. Just be ready when it happens."

"I will. My trust is with you."

Rega embraced Voltrex and he kissed her hard on the mouth.

***

One week later, Voltrex left to visit a relative a half-day's ride from the Black Fort. Eustice watched over one meeting after another in his court chambers and secretly yearned for Rega. At the end of the final session, he and several noblemen sent everyone else away and called for ale, which they drank until most could not stand straight, Eustice among them.

Rega's attendant suddenly appeared before him.

"King Eustice, the queen awaits you in your chamber. She says it is time for spring."

Even in his haze, Eustice knew what she meant; "spring" was their code word for his wife to welcome him into her bed. Eustice wanted an heir more than anything, and he smiled broadly.

Eustice mumbled his excuses to the other men and set off to his bedchambers. Because the hall was near his bedchamber, he dismissed his bodyguards. He stumbled up several steps to an outside walkway that led to his private quarters. As he reached the middle of the walkway, he urinated over the low wall. Eustice felt good. He would free his bladder and finally impregnate his queen.

Eustice heard no sounds and barely felt the push from behind that carried him over the edge of the wall to his death on the cold ground below.

XXXII

Reckoning

Dawn arrived at the Villa. Valerias awoke and ventured outside for a walk. The air was still and cold, and he could see thick frost covering the short grass near the courtyard. To his surprise, he saw Joseph sitting on a bench reading sheets of parchment Valerias assumed were part of the Bible. He walked over to Joseph to engage in an early morning conversation on the Bible and Christianity. Valerias had read most of the Bible and enjoyed debating its contents with Joseph. He wasn't going to let this opportunity pass. When Valerias drew close, though, he saw a troubled look on Joseph's face.

"Are you disagreeing with your Bible again?" Valerias joked.

"No, Marcus." Joseph handed Valerias the sheets to read. It was a letter.

> Dearest Joseph,
>
> I hope this letter finds you well and your position as bishop is rewarding. I do not wish to trouble you, as my village is not of your diocese. However, our local bishop has declared he wants nothing to do with the problem and has gone to Rome for training. I fear he left to avoid what needs to be addressed.

The village priest, Erasmus, believes that he is God's instrument on this Earth. He and his band of zealots have taken over my village, Menze. They believe one needs to have absolute faith in the Nicene Creed as the one and only way to be a true Christian and join God in Heaven. Erasmus has stolen the goodness of the Nicene faith and is using religious piety to enforce his beliefs on the people. He and his followers use religion as a way to gain total control and obtain personal wealth in my poor village.

We have people of all faiths in Menze. We encourage discussion and acceptance of many different religious beliefs. However, Erasmus detests anyone who believes differently. He and his followers have beaten villagers, confiscated their property, and even executed people! Those persecuted by him include pagans and Arians. I fear I will be in one of his next purges, and I am a Nicene believer.

I am aware that you are coming to the Council of Bishops in Mediolanum. Menze is not far from Mediolanum, just to the northeast. I pray for you to come to Menze and put a stop to Erasmus and his followers. He must listen to you, as you are a bishop and have authority over him.

Your friend in God,
Antonio Felix, Elderman of Menze

Valerias finished reading the letter and looked at Joseph.

"You wonder why I have chosen not to accept your Christian religion, and then you show me this letter. What am I to think?"

"Erasmus is a poor example of what a Christian should strive to be. He has used his position as shepherd of the people for his own advantage."

"I think there are many more Christians like your errant priest."

Joseph ignored Valerias, and after a moment of thought said, "I must go to Menze and settle the situation."

"I will go with you. We will take a cavalry escort. Erasmus won't do anything that causes you or any of the villagers harm if I am there."

"No, that will not be necessary. Erasmus is still a man of the cloth and a follower of Jesus. He is adhering to Emperor Theodosius' Edict, but much too vigorously. He must step back for the time being."

"Do you think he will listen to you?" Valerias was skeptical.

"Yes. He must listen to his superiors." Joseph's tone prompted Valerias to pose another question.

"Do you believe solely in the Nicene Creed faith, Joseph?"

"Yes. However, as we previously discussed, there should be a phase-in period. It is the role of the church to show tolerance and patience as we persuade nonbelievers of the way of the Nicene faith—the true way."

"When will you leave?"

"Tomorrow morning. I will take Elderon with me. If we face a situation that I cannot manage, we will return to the Villa and plan our next strategy."

"I will count on your objectivity to make the right decision. You should also know that Flavius is due to arrive from Spain this week. And tomorrow the Huns are coming to the Villa to try their hand in an archery contest with Claire. You will miss an opportunity to convert the Huns," Valerias teased.

"Don't fear, Marcus. I will return and see Flavius. Then I shall travel to the Hun camp and convert lost souls—including yours, if you will let me!"

Valerias let out a hearty laugh and Joseph chuckled. "I can always try, General."

Early the next day, Joseph and Elderon left for Menze. When Joseph rode past Valerias, he was given the Roman salute and a smile while Elderon received a stern stare. Claire joined Valerias as the two men rode away from the Villa.

"You are worried about him, aren't you, Marcus?"

"Of course. He is naïve about what he is riding into."

"I'm concerned, too. I have heard about these pockets of Christian zealots. They can be violent."

"Joseph said he would return late tomorrow. If not, then *I* will visit Menze—and it won't be a friendly visit."

***

Later that day, Revious led Oxanos, Arb, and ten Hun warriors to the Villa. Oxanos dismounted and waved to one of the warriors. The man had brought a bow and gave it to Oxanos, who in turn presented it to Claire.

The bow was beautifully crafted in the classic Hun style. Claire carefully examined the recurve bow and caressed the stave. It was shorter than the bows usually carried by the Huns, and she realized it had been designed specifically for her. A quiver of Hun-made arrows accompanied the bow.

"My people want to give this bow and these arrows to you, Domina. It is for the kindness you have extended to us."

"I accept your generous gift, Oxanos. I thank your people." She looked at the Hun warriors and smiled. In unison, they returned her smile.

Oxanos turned to Valerias. "I can't wait for our contest. When do we start?"

"Now," answered Valerias. He was not surprised at Oxanos' exuberance.

Valerias had selected ten of his better archers from the Warrior's Palace, and they arrived with dozens of other curious Romans. The Huns and Romans walked to a nearby field where a temporary archery range had been set up.

During the contests, the Romans held their own with the Huns during short-range target shooting. The Huns, though, bested the Romans in both accuracy and power in hitting long-range targets.

Oxanos asked Claire to try out her new bow and she agreed. Claire was nervous, and her first arrow sailed high of the mark. Her second arrow flew wide to the right, but no one laughed. To laugh at the Domina would be disrespectful. Also, Valerias stood among them, and no one wanted to anger him.

Claire's third arrow hit the bull's-eye, followed by two more arrows in almost the same location. She stepped back and Valerias announced that his wife was a true marksman. The crowd applauded.

Once the archery contest was finished, Valerias felt comfortable enough to show the Huns the Warriors' Palace. Roman soldiers demonstrated swordplay and wrestling at the camp. In the evening, Valerias held a banquet at the Villa in honor of the day's activities. He was relieved there were no incidents involving his visitors.

Valerias invited the Huns to stay the night in the barracks, but most chose to sleep outdoors. The next day, Romans and Huns conducted more training exhibitions. By early afternoon, the Huns prepared to return to their camp, accompanied by Revious.

As the Huns mounted their horses, a rider approached the Villa from the north. Clouds of soft powdered snow followed him. A soldier caught up to the rider as he slowed down in the courtyard and Valerias felt a stab of concern when he realized the rider was Elderon. He was exhausted and appeared injured. An attendant helped him from his horse and took him to Valerias.

Elderon did not wait to be questioned.

"They have him. They took Joseph!"

"What?!" Valerias cried.

"Erasmus and his men. They are crazy! Joseph tried to reason with them. He told them that he agreed fully with the philosophy of the Nicene Trinity but he urged tolerance of other faiths. Because he did not support the ways of Erasmus, they deemed him a traitor to Christ. Erasmus called Joseph worse than a pagan and even an Arian.

"Erasmus will sentence Joseph to death. He believes that is the punishment Emperor Theodosius would pronounce. That madman is going to execute Joseph as an example of Erasmus' supposed authority. I'm scared to death, General Valerias, of what is going to happen to Joseph!"

Valerias patted Elderon on the shoulder. He gave a command to Alexander to tend to Elderon and marched over to Claire.

"I'm going to remedy this." Valerias called to Oxanos. "Will your men ride with me under my command, and be prepared to fight? I want you to arm yourself with your bows. It is time you became warriors again."

Oxanos was caught off guard, but he needed no time to respond. "Yes, General, we will do as you command."

Oxanos addressed the Huns, who were preparing to leave the Villa. In the Hunnic tongue, he translated what Valerias had said. The irony of the situation passed through Valerias' mind as he watched the mood of the Huns brighten as Oxanos finished speaking. *I won't have to say much to inspire the Huns to fight*, Valerias thought. *I hope I can keep them under control.*

Valerias called for Bukarma, who came running when he heard the commotion in the courtyard.

"Bukarma, gather as many men as you can and be ready to ride. They must be armed with swords and javelins. Leave a detachment here to protect the Villa. Who knows where that damned Garzad is."

Gulic and Alena emerged from the Grand House, holding hands. Valerias ignored their open affection toward each other and gave a curt order to Gulic.

"You are the senior officer here. Guard the Villa while I'm away. Claire will stay with you. Make sure nothing happens to anyone or anything. I am counting on you!"

Claire ran into the Grand House and returned with Valerias' sword. She helped him attach the sheath to his back and slid the blade into it.

"It is ironic, Claire. Years ago I told Joseph that I would give up the sword, and now I must use this very sword to save him."

"Be careful, my General. And bring Joseph back to us."

"I will!" Valerias kissed Claire on the cheek and mounted his horse.

"Revious, ride with Oxanos and Arb, and make sure they follow my orders! Have them form a line facing me."

Revious spoke to Arb, and soon the Huns were lined up in the requested formation. Valerias rode by each Hun and looked them in the eyes. The Huns looked back in acknowledgement that he was their commander.

Bukarma rode up to him with twenty-one seasoned Roman fighters.

"We are ready, Marcus!"

"Let's go!"

***

Soon after he and Elderon had arrived in Menze, Joseph was taken prisoner by Erasmus and his band of elders. In disguise as an Arian, one of Erasmus' followers approached Joseph as he walked through the village and complained about Erasmus's tactics. Joseph calmly explained to the man that Erasmus was wrong. He would try to persuade Erasmus to be more tolerant toward Arians and other religions until the Nicene Trinity matter had time to take effect. Erasmus had set the trap, and Joseph unsuspectingly took the bait.

Erasmus had several armed followers haul Joseph to a small building with no windows. In the confusion, Elderon fled Menze as fast as his horse would take him.

Erasmus badgered Joseph with a host of questions that were intended to implicate him.

"Do you confess your crimes, Joseph?" Erasmus glared smugly at him.

"What crimes do you speak of, Father Erasmus?"

"Heresy, cavorting with heretics, disobeying the emperor's order, and thus being a false bishop!"

"No. Those are falsehoods of your imagination."

"No, they are not. You have no support here. Even your lackey deserted you."

The interrogation continued through to the next day, and Erasmus became increasingly belligerent. Joseph grew genuinely worried for his safety. *I am dealing with an insane priest,* he thought in a panic. *How can I reason with this man?* Grim humor took over and he thought, *Marcus would enjoy pointing out to me the negatives of Christianity in this situation.*

Finally, Joseph had had enough. “Release me now, Erasmus. I am a bishop and your superior. I will tell Bishop Ambrose what has happened here and you will be removed!”

He never saw the club that hit him hard on the back of the head. Joseph lost consciousness. When he regained his senses, he heard Erasmus giving orders, then turned his attention to Joseph.

“It has been decided. You are traitor to God, Jesus Christ, and the Holy Spirit! Therefore, you are a traitor to the Christian faith. As a bishop, it was your duty to be an example and teach the flock the way of God. It is the only way and the way I believe. I *am* the true disciple of Christ! You are a false bishop and a false Christian!”

“You are a false prophet, Erasmus. The Bible warns of men like you. I will report you as soon as you release me.”

Erasmus laughed. “You are not going to be released. God and I have decided your fate. You are going to be burned at the stake tonight, just as all heretics are sent to the fires of hell. You will be an example to all the infidels left in the village.”

Erasmus left the building. At dusk, he returned wearing a white habit.

“Take him to the stake!” he commanded the elders.

Joseph could not believe what was happening. Hands reached for him and dragged him to the nearby village square, where three wooden stakes had been pounded into the ground. Joseph was taken to the middle stake surrounded by bundles of firewood and his hands were tied around the stake.

“You can’t do this!” Joseph yelled at Erasmus and the crowd.

Several men cursed at him. However, Joseph noticed most onlookers were frightened.

Slowly, the ominous figure of Erasmus came toward him. His white habit stood out in the gathering darkness. A hood covered the back of his head. Erasmus stopped in front of Joseph, eyes bright with the power he craved. To Joseph, he was a nightmare.

"False bishop, do you have any last words before your sentence is carried out?"

"This is not God's will!" Joseph made one last attempt to reason with Erasmus.

"It is God's will because I am God." Erasmus' eyes grew round and his lips formed a wicked smile.

"You're not God! You have lost the Christian way!"

Joseph was so intent on engaging Erasmus that he didn't feel the blade until it was well into his chest.

"I am the true God. I decided your fate. If you are a great bishop and God is at your side, free yourself and live. But you are finished! God stands with me!"

Erasmus withdrew the dagger and slipped it back into his habit. No one saw what happened. Erasmus stepped back and looked at two elders standing at his side with burning torches, pleased to see his disciple Marcot standing firm.

"Let this man feel the fires of hell! He does not serve our God! He serves Satan!" Erasmus shouted to the crowd with little response.

Erasmus nodded to Marcot and his fellow zealot. The two men moved forward with their torches held out toward the firewood around Joseph. As they began to light the wood, each man dropped his torch and fell on his back, grasping his chest. The two men died instantly from the arrows protruding from their bodies.

A dark man on horseback raced forward, scattering people. He dismounted and with a mighty blow of his sword, shattered the chains that held Joseph. Bukarma pulled Joseph away before he was enveloped in flames. In one motion, the big man snuffed out the burning embers on Joseph's clothing before he thought any real damage had been done.

Erasmus gave a signal and two more men, with their swords held high, moved toward Bukarma. A volley of arrows pierced the men's chests and necks, and they fell dead. The crowd was so focused on what was happening at the stake that they didn't see Valerias approach.

The Huns stormed into the village, bows ready to shoot anyone who threatened Valerias, Bukarma, or Joseph. Some of the crowd started to flee but found their paths blocked by Valerias' cavalry.

Erasmus felt the situation careening out of his control and strode briskly up to Valerias. His eyes reflected the fire in front of him.

"Who are you to interfere? We are carrying out the church's wishes—what the church demands must be done!"

"I am General Marcus Augustus Valerias. The man you tried to kill here is an exemplary Christian, and my friend." Valerias' voice boomed across the square.

"Emperor Theodosius will deal harshly with you, Valerias, for your interference today and for the deaths of my men."

"Mad priest, you are a blind fool full of imagined power. You are anything but a Christian. You are evil. The emperor will do nothing to me!"

Erasmus silently brought his dagger out and moved it toward Valerias' chest, just as he done with Joseph. Valerias never took his eyes off Erasmus' face. Erasmus moved to strike but was startled when Valerias grabbed the hand holding the dagger, and with immense strength turned it inward, and pushed it into Erasmus' belly. Valerias placed his left arm around Erasmus' shoulder and with his right hand moved the blade upward, tearing flesh. Valerias twisted the knife, pulled it out, and tossed it on the fire.

"I am the Roman General who has killed many men who are much more worthy of life than you. It is time for your journey to hell!"

The brightness in Erasmus' eyes dimmed. Valerias grabbed Erasmus by his clothing and flung him into the raging flames meant for Joseph. Erasmus never uttered a sound as his body burned.

Valerias turned his back on the priest and hurried to Joseph, who was lying on the ground, his head in Bukarma's lap. Bukarma looked at Valerias and shook his head. Valerias put his hand on Joseph's chest and felt the warmth of the blood that oozed out of his wound.

"Marcus, my friend, I am glad you are here," Joseph rasped as he recognized Valerias.

"I am here, Joseph." Valerias tried hard to keep a firm voice as he clutched Joseph's hand.

"Forgive them, Marcus. Forgive them. They need to be shown forgiveness, for that is what Christ did so we could be saved. Forgive them."

Joseph smiled weakly and closed his eyes. His chest stilled and he died quietly, his face reflecting his internal peace.

More armed Roman cavalry arrived and filled the village square. Valerias still knelt by Joseph, with his head bowed. Bukarma took Joseph's arms and folded them gently across his body.

Valerias looked up at Bukarma, his face contorted with grief and rage. Bukarma had never seen such a face on Valerias. When he spoke, his words were full of venom.

"Torch it! Burn this damned place to ground! Kill anyone who resists!"

PART II

"The long distance between marine raiders' place of origin and the areas they attacked suggests that knowledge of a short-term Roman weakness or direct Roman provocation were not likely to be motives and that raiders simply set out to plunder. Other naval raids were shorter in range, such as those of the Franks and Saxons against north Gaul and Britain.

"The plunder taken by raiders tended to be confined to easily movable items. Gold, silver, and jewelry were probably preferred, though they would rarely be available in large amounts unless towns were sacked. Cattle and sheep would be useful plunder in the short term, providing food for raiders and essential supplies for groups wandering within the Empire.

"A third type of plunder was prisoners (who could be ransomed later, but were usually kept as slaves)."

—Taken from *Warfare in Roman Europe AD 350-425*, by Hugh Elton

XXXIII

AFTERMATH

A solemn procession returned to the Villa the morning after Joseph's death. There was little chatter among the Romans, and the Huns kept quiet. Occasionally Bukarma issued an order. Valerias rode in front. His head and torso were bowed forward on his horse. Joseph's body was wrapped in a blanket and carefully placed over a second horse tethered to Valerias' saddle.

Even from a distance, Claire knew something was terribly wrong. She called for Gulic and several attendants to join her in the courtyard. She prepared for the worst.

"What happened, Marcus?"

Valerias pointed to the wrapped body tied across the horse behind him.

"They killed Joseph. He is martyred by his own kind."

Claire carefully undid the cloth around the head of the body, hoping what Valerias said wasn't true. But the body was Joseph's. His face, usually blessed with the vibrant hue of life, was now pale, matching the snow scattered about the grounds. Claire placed her hands over her mouth and took a step back. Gulic rushed forward and caught her before she fell.

"We were moments away from saving him." Valerias' eyes glistened but no tears fell. "That monster priest stabbed him and then was going to burn him. This wasted life all because of a few words."

"Where is the priest now?" Claire asked firmly.

"In hell!" Valerias spat.

He dismounted and joined Claire. "It appears to me that there are Christians who have adopted their own version of what they call the Golden Rule—do unto others until you get what you want. This is one priest who, in the end, did not get what he wanted."

Valerias called for Wolf. "I need to be alone. I will be back by dusk, I promise." Valerias and Wolf walked slowly out of sight.

With Valerias gone, Bukarma took control. The Romans were to return to the Warriors' Palace and Revious was to escort the Huns back to their camp. Before they left, Bukarma spoke to Oxanos.

"Your men did well. General Valerias would tell you that. Perhaps after time has settled this matter, we can train jointly."

Oxanos nodded affirmatively, and the Huns followed Revious back to their camp.

"Bukarma—what happened?" Claire shook with grief.

"We rode in to Menze and saw Joseph tied to a stake. He was to be burned alive by that insane priest, Erasmus. As the village men lit the fire, Marcus ordered the Huns to kill the torchbearers. We thought we had saved him, only to discover that Erasmus had already stabbed him. Erasmus tried to take Marcus' life in the same way, but the priest underestimated Marcus' response and Marcus killed him. Marcus was enraged at the villagers for allowing this to happen."

"What happened next?" Claire asked. She knew what her husband was capable of and feared the worst.

Bukarma took a deep breath and gazed at Claire. His mind returned to the events at Menze.

"Joseph asked Marcus to forgive the village and its people. We both heard him, but Marcus refused to listen. He ordered me to burn the village and kill anyone who opposed him. Our men carried torches, and I thought everything would be engulfed in fire. I asked Marcus to reconsider his command and accede to Joseph's dying words. He glared at me as if I was mad. He stood up and looked at the villagers, at Joseph's body, and then back at me.

"It was an imposing sight. Marcus stood between the villagers and the fire lit by Erasmus' men. The fire mushroomed up from behind Marcus. Combined with the loud crackles from the fire, it seemed the god of vengeance had emerged and stood with us. The Huns formed a line off to his side, their bows poised to shoot at his command. Our soldiers positioned themselves behind the villagers, carrying their torches.

"The villagers had never seen a Hun before and thought they were devils Marcus had conjured to punish them. They believed their deaths and the destruction of their village were imminent. I witnessed several villagers throw themselves on the ground, crying for mercy. They told Marcus they feared Erasmus and could not fight him. They, too, had lost loved ones to the priest's vindictive ways.

"I looked into Marcus' eyes and saw a slight flicker of mercy. He turned and gazed at the fire and then, unexpectedly, countermanded his own order; the village was spared. I cannot remember a time when Marcus countermanded a punishment. He did exact a price on the village, though.

"Marcus asked for the leader of Menze, a man named Antonio Felix. He had been held in Erasmus' custody. When released, Felix explained to Marcus about the evil Erasmus and his followers had brought to the village. He profusely begged Marcus for mercy.

"Marcus ordered Felix to produce any of Erasmus' followers who were still alive. Five men were brought forward. They begged for mercy. I thought Marcus would spare them, as he did the villagers. He did not. He had them decapitated. Their bodies and heads burned in the same fire that consumed Erasmus.

"I understand Erasmus' few remaining followers scattered into the night. Marcus put a bounty on their heads—just their heads.

"Marcus demanded that Felix provide ten men to travel to the Villa. These ten men are to do whatever Marcus orders and he promised he would not execute or enslave them. Instead, they are to be attendants at the Warriors' Palace. Felix hesitated, so Marcus gave him an alternative. Marcus would pick the ten men, but he would give them to the Huns. It would be anyone's guess if they would survive.

"The villagers looked at the Huns in disbelief, and Felix quickly relented. So, ten men were selected and they are with us today." Bukarma pointed to the men from Menze, who remained on their horses.

After a brief pause, Claire said, "Marcus and Joseph's relationship was complicated. He almost executed Joseph, yet over time, they became close friends. Why do you think that was so, Bukarma?"

"I believe Marcus regrets holding the dagger to Joseph's neck and almost killing him. But he allowed Joseph to live and watched Joseph transform into a man of the faith. That transformation gave Marcus hope that there is good in religion. I can tell you from my experience with Marcus, that was rarely the situation before."

Claire added, "Marcus has changed over the years. Joseph was a source of that change. Marcus has faith in people he trusts and respects, besides those in the army. It still amazes me that he befriended the Huns."

"I agree. Except *you* are the reason for Marcus' change, Claire. However, the spirit of the past general still has a place within him.

I saw a glimpse of that man in Menze. I hope that was only temporary; I pray that it is so."

Valerias returned at dusk, as he had promised. When he saw Claire, he embraced her tightly.

"I have decided to have Joseph buried in the churchyard of Tevgium. The priest there is a kind old man, and it is too far to transport him to Rome or Britannia. He will be close to us there."

"I agree. I want him nearby."

Valerias looked around the Villa's courtyard and saw Elderon sitting forlornly on a tree stump. Valerias called out to him.

"Come here, Elderon."

Elderon had no idea why Marcus would want to speak to him, especially after Joseph's death. He did not hesitate, though, and quickly walked over.

"You did well yesterday. I thought you would flee from us at the earliest opportunity, but you didn't. You returned to the Villa and gave us word Joseph was in trouble. You stood by him."

Claire nodded her concurrence. Elderon started to relax, but it was short-lived.

"Elderon, I want you to consider following in Joseph's footsteps and becoming a representative of his God. I see promise in you, as I saw promise in Joseph many years ago. Think about what I have said. Also, Joseph's funeral will be tomorrow. I'd like you to perform a joint ceremony with the Tevgium village priest." Valerias was not asking.

"What?" Elderon muttered meekly, confused.

"I will speak at the service. Now go and prepare."

Joseph's service was held on a brisk, raw day as winter kept hold on the land. The funeral was well attended, even though Joseph had no family and his religious jurisdiction was well to the north in Britannia. Valerias, Claire, Alena, Elsha, Bukarma,

Penelope, Revious, and Gulic were present. Alexander and most of the Villa's staff came, as did representatives of the Warrior's Palace. A delegation of Huns, led by Oxanos and Arb, also attended, which pleased Valerias.

Valerias had mixed feelings about the ceremony. The old priest spoke softly and was difficult to hear. Elderon bumbled his way through his part. Valerias was even dissatisfied with his own eulogy. He had a difficult time trying to merge the good of Joseph to his own view of the evils he saw in Joseph's faith.

Valerias ended his eulogy saying, "Joseph was a man of unbounded spirit and conviction. He was fair, kind, and generous to his people and to those not of his religion—such as myself.

"When I first met Joseph, he was lost. Joseph found his true self through his faith. He sacrificed his personal life for the betterment of his people. Joseph carried out the tenets of his religion without asking for anything in return. And his path in life was successful.

"I consider Joseph a good man and a good Christian. He was my friend, and I will deeply miss him."

Valerias was relieved when the service finally ended. He underestimated the impact it would have on those who attended, including himself. Many expressed their gratitude to Valerias, and extended appreciation to the old priest and Elderon.

"Joseph would have liked what you did for him today, Marcus," Claire said, looping her arm through his.

"I'm sure he would have offered a valid critique. I fear I was long-winded."

"Perhaps. But I think he would have asked why you were so forgiving of the people of Menze and of Elderon."

Valerias gave Claire an odd look.

"I know about Elderon's thievery."

"You are wise beyond your years, my love." Valerias pulled Claire's arm tighter against himself.

During the afternoon, Valerias, Claire, Alena, and Elsha went for a walk. Wolf plodded along behind them, sniffing the air. The cold of winter had eased slightly. They had almost returned to the Grand House when a call came out from one of the sentries that a rider was approaching. A man on a large, dark horse moved slowly into the courtyard. A small child rested in the saddle in front of him.

The man asked the attendant, "Is this the house of General Marcus Augustus Valerias and his wife, Domina Claire?"

"Yes," the attendant replied.

"Good," answered the man. "I am Flavius and this is Marian. They are expecting us."

XXXIV

FLAVIUS

"Flavius!" Valerias called from across the courtyard.

Flavius looked up from the attendant to the voice and saw four people and a large dog approaching him. Flavius dismounted and, with the aid of an attendant, lifted Marian from the horse.

"Welcome to our home," Valerias said, reaching out and grasping Flavius' hand. Wolf sniffed Flavius' leg, causing Marian to hide behind his other leg.

"Welcome, Flavius." Claire said warmly. She bent down and spoke directly to Marian. "I know who you are."

"You do?" the little girl, who was almost five years old, replied.

"You are Marian. I am Claire, and this is Marcus. These are my daughters, Alena and Elsha." Both Alena and Elsha smiled at Marian. "This is our home. You are very welcome here."

"Hello," Marian replied. "Does the big dog bite?"

"Not brave little girls," Valerias laughed. "His name is Wolf. Alena and Elsha, please show Marian our home while your mother and I talk to her father."

To Flavius' surprise, Marian let go of his leg and took Elsha's outstretched hand. Wolf continued to sniff Flavius.

"And take Wolf with you." Valerias ordered Wolf to go inside, but the dog just peered at him.

Valerias sighed, and Claire said to Flavius, "He can command an army, but the dog won't do a thing he says. I wonder who the master is."

Flavius burst out laughing while Valerias just groaned. Marian was pleased to see her father laugh. It had been a long time since he had even smiled.

While Alena and Elsha showed Marian around the Grand House, Bukarma joined Valerias, Claire, and Flavius.

"I felt gloom in the air when we approached your house. Has something happened?" Flavius asked.

"Joseph is dead," Claire said, looking down at the ground.

Flavius stood stunned. He folded his hands in prayer and waited for several moments before saying a word. "How? It cannot be! We have been corresponding, and he was looking forward to visiting with us here. He was to bless Marian. God have mercy!"

"God had something to do with his death," Valerias spoke somberly. "A priest murdered him."

Valerias retold the story. When he finished, Flavius looked like he had been punched in the gut. He sank to his knees, wiping at his face with the back of his hand.

"Praise God for the life of Joseph." Flavius repeated the phrase over and over again.

With a final sigh, Flavius stood up. "Where is this priest?" Flavius said, his voice filled with threat.

"In his hell." Valerias' words were tinged with anger.

Flavius exchanged a look with Valerias and understood they would continue their conversation later.

"Tell us of Mary," Claire said gently.

"What can I say that you don't already know?" Flavius shrugged, the weight of his grief visible.

"I want to hear it from you in person," she added.

Flavius grew intense. "Morguard and his men tortured Mary. Why they did not kill her, I do not know. Joseph and I tried to make her stronger. The move to Spain helped, too. And she did improve, for a while.

"Mary did well after the birth of Marian. But then her health began to spiral downward. She became physically weak, yet her spirit stayed strong. I could do nothing and neither could the physician. We needed Joseph!

"When she passed, she had practically withered away. I would have taken my life to be with her, if I didn't have Marian. Keeping Marian well and safe is my only priority. Thanks be to Marcus for obtaining the pardon from Emperor Theodosius, and to you two for inviting Marian and me to your Villa. I will be forever grateful."

"We thought it was best for *both* of you." Claire smiled and Valerias nodded.

"I cannot believe what happened to Joseph. He pulled me through a dark time. I thank God for him." Flavius returned to thoughts of Joseph.

"Joseph helped me through a dark time as well." Valerias did not elaborate. "Joseph had an aide named Elderon. He is here with us. I am encouraging him to follow Joseph's path. Tomorrow, after you are settled, I want you and Revious to escort Elderon to the Hun camp that has set up near here. It is time for Elderon to be introduced to the Huns as Joseph's replacement. Elderon should only be an observer."

Valerias read the shock on Flavius' face. "Yes, I did say Huns."

Later in the day, Alexander took Flavius and Marian to their quarters at the Grand House. Valerias took that time to find Elsha. She was outside in the courtyard teaching Wolf a new trick, to stay absolutely still until a call came for "release." Elsha and Wolf had become close, and when Valerias entered the courtyard, he called for Wolf to come. He was not entirely surprised when Wolf sat on the ground and did not move. Valerias shook his head.

"Your dog does not obey well, Elsha."

Elsha said "release" and Wolf immediately ran to Valerias, turned, and sat facing Elsha. "Release," she commanded, and Wolf raced to her, turned, and sat looking at Valerias.

"Good dog, Wolf." She rubbed Wolf's back. "Father doesn't understand you like I do!"

Valerias laughed as he said, "Elsha, walk with me. Wolf can come."

"Yes, Father. I promise not to ask you about suitors!"

Valerias smiled. Elsha could tease him better than Alena, who was more direct.

"You have done a fine job training Wolf. But I want to talk to you about Marian. She and her father will be our permanent guests. I want you to keep an eye on her—to become her friend and mentor—as you have done with Wolf. Only Marian is a little girl."

"I understand, Father." Elsha kicked a stone.

Valerias added, "She is a good child who has seen difficult times. She needs a friend. Alena can help you, but she also has Gulic. I want you to be the leader. I know you will do well with what I have asked of you."

"And I hope you will be as understanding when my suitors come calling."

Valerias laughed heartily. Wolf barked. Elsha giggled. *I like seeing Father laugh*, Elsha thought.

XXXV

RAIDERS

"My king! Emissaries for the Angles and Jutes have arrived from the north," the servant spoke excitedly.

"Good! I knew they would come soon. I hope they bring the news I want to hear." Staigrik looked down at the servant. "Escort them to the Great Hall. We will join them shortly."

The servant left as quickly as he came. Staigrik picked up his battleax and smiled at Borgnar.

"It is all coming together now, cousin." Staigrik seemed revived. "The end of winter is near."

"I agree, King Staigrik. The construction of the fleet is almost complete. And we are making great progress training the men to become expert seamen and warriors."

Staigrik smiled and roughly placed the handle of his ax across his massive shoulders. "Get my son. I want him present when we confer with our guests."

When Staigrik arrived at the Great Hall, he heard loud talk from inside. When he entered, the voices subsided. Staigrik's huge size and bushy red hair and beard made him stand out markedly from the other men. His great battleax was legendary. Few men could carry it as easily as he could. It was like a small wooden stave to him, but with a sharp double-sided blade. It was rumored that he had slain a thousand foes with it.

Several Saxons walked behind Staigrik; all resembled lesser versions of the new king. Six were former bodyguards of King Alfredson.

"I want a beer!" Staigrik bellowed as he took his place standing on the platform at the front of the hall. All eyes settled on him. Staigrik looked toward a group of Angles standing in front of him.

"I see my allies are present. I am pleased to welcome you, my friends. You made a wise decision to join us."

From his side, Staigrik watched Borgnar and Guenter enter the hall. A slave brought over a large horn of beer.

"I drink to our upcoming raid on Britannia. May the land prove rich in plunder and slaves! May the cowardly Britons put up a fight—I want battle! I relish the blood of our enemy on my war ax!"

Staigrik's rousing call triggered waves of cheers and toasts. Guenter mused that the exuberance was due in part to the brevity of his speech, which allowed the crowd to consume their beer without delay.

A question was shouted from the crowd. "When do we leave for Britannia?"

"I wanted to leave months ago, but we were not ready. We did not have nearly enough ships to transport our great army in one wave. I understand we are almost ready—two more months. Let me ask our allies to report on their readiness to attack Britannia. First, the Jutes."

"I, Lathrin, speak for the Jutes." Lathrin, a tall, slender man with a thin black beard, stepped forward. "We are ready now. We have well over one hundred ships. We, too, want the blood of Britons on our seaxes and their gold in our hands!"

Staigrik pounded the handle of his ax on the floor. "Excellent! You carry the spirit of our cause well!" Again, Staigrik pounded the floor. "Angles!"

A stout man with thick, long brown hair spoke. He had only one ear. His long hair covered his severed ear hole, which became exposed when he rubbed his head. "I speak for the Angles. I am Korken. You, Staigrik, need to remember that my people were told of your war late. We need two months, like you, to ready our fleet. We will have greater than one hundred warships. "

"Be ready, Korken, or we will leave the Angles behind!"

Staigrik poured the remainder of his beer down his throat and yelled for more. He once again pounded the platform with the handle of his ax.

"It is time for the Saxons! Borgnar!"

Staigrik winced at a sharp, sudden pain in his chest followed by an intense sense of weariness. He immediately sat down on his throne, pleased that Borgnar was the center of attention.

All my planning and desire to raid Britannia have caused these ill feelings, Staigrik thought. *I will be fine as soon as I have more beer!*

Borgnar was well known throughout the Saxon kingdom not only as a great warrior, but also for his intelligence. He was clean-shaven except for a recently grown thick, blond mustache that ran partly down the sides of his chin. Borgnar carried a sword he took from a Gallic nobleman during a recent raid, and had used the weapon to kill several Gauls. Guenter knew that Borgnar would be the brains behind Staigrik's rule.

"Welcome, kingdoms of the north," Borgnar began. "I must first apologize to the Angles. We did not provide you sufficient time to join us. That is my fault. You are full partners with us and the Jutes." Borgnar looked directly at Korken when he spoke. Korken seemed pleased with the apology and nodded.

Borgnar held up his muscular arm, and two Saxon warriors brought over a large sheepskin map. Several of the map's features were difficult to read, so the warriors in the hall pressed in tightly to view it.

"This is a map of the southeastern shoreline of Britannia. This is where most of our previous raiding has taken place," Borgnar explained, tapping the map with his sword. "We propose landing in this new area."

The tip of Borgnar's sword moved northward and pointed to a large estuary. "And here is the main town, Branodunum, on the southern shore. Our scouts report it is a wealthy, tranquil area. The churches contain much gold, silver, and gems, and the people will make good slaves. The Britons have plenty of cattle, sheep, and grain to sustain us while we are there. The best aspect of this large bay is it will allow us to access the center of Britannia without having to travel far. We strike here!"

The Great Hall exploded positively to Borgnar's proclamation. Borgnar smiled slightly and looked at Staigrik, who nodded expressionlessly. Borgnar continued, "We will follow this route. We will go down the coast and cross the sea to Britannia here. We will follow the coastline out of eyesight from the Britons and enter the bay. Surprise will be our ally!"

Guenter interrupted. "It is not a bay, it is an estuary. The Romans call it Metaris Aest."

"I don't give a rat's shit what it is or what it is called," Staigrik growled. "I know it is our entranceway into Britannia and where we will start feeding the Britons our steel. Guenter is busy reading his books when he should be planning our raid! Ignore him."

Staigrik's pain was diminishing and he nodded for Borgnar to continue.

"Questions?" Borgnar asked.

Korken inquired, "What about the Romans?"

Borgnar answered, "The Romans are weak. Their king, Maximus, has moved south into Gallia. The Britons and Romans will pose minimal resistance to our large force."

"More beer for everyone!" Staigrik yelled in his deep, booming voice. The pain and tiredness were gone. The assembled mass roared in response.

"Wait!" Guenter shouted. "I believe this should be more than just a raid. We should conquer Britannia and create a Saxon kingdom there."

He stepped forward on the dais. The crowd grew quiet. Borgnar sighed. Staigrik stared lightning bolts at his son.

Guenter spoke solemnly. "Our lands here are crowded and much of it is inhospitable. Britannia is much better suited for our people to prosper. We need to plant and harvest crops, and raise livestock. Britannia offers those opportunities. Our people already in Britannia agree with me. I ask each of you to consider remaining in Britannia after we conquer the land."

Guenter's remarks were met with bewilderment and derision. Questions and insults flew at the young prince.

One Saxon commented, "Who here wants to become a farmer? Britannia is a foreign land. I am a warrior, not a settler. Staigrik, your son speaks of weakness!"

After a period of disorder, Staigrik stood and banged the handle of his battleax on the platform floor. The sound reverberated throughout the hall and silence gradually descended.

"My son has had too much to drink and forgotten our purpose. We raid, not settle. To plunder Britannia is much better than sitting around watching crops grow. Settling is for the weak, not for warriors! I have heard enough!"

Guenter stared at Staigrik, knowing he would be punished for speaking out. In an instant, Staigrik pulled out his seax and chopped off the little finger on Guenter's left hand, tossing it onto the floor. He glared at Guenter. His son closed his eyes but did not make a sound.

"This is to remind you that you are the son of a king. As prince, you are a warrior, not a farmer. That is, if you want to remain my son! You will be by my side in Britannia, or I will disown you and tie you to the back of my warship for the seabirds to peck your eyes out!"

XXXVI

End of Normality

"Marian, come here," Flavius said.

"Yes, Father?" Marian replied as she played with her doll.

"Elsha is here. I want you to go with her today. I will be back after supper."

"Where are you going, Father?"

"General Valerias has asked me to go to a village of people who live on his land."

"Are they nice people?"

"I don't know, I have never met them before. But the General would not allow them on his land if they were not nice. I will tell you all about them when I return," he said with a wink.

"Marian!" Elsha called from another room.

"Go now." Flavius gave Marian a hug and they left their room.

Elsha reached for Marian's hand, and they skipped off to another part of the Grand House, Wolf charging after them. Flavius eyed Revious and walked over to him.

"Do you have ill feelings toward me, Revious?"

"If Claire and Marcus accept you, then I do as well. You will have to win over Bukarma, though. He is not as easily persuaded as I am," Revious laughed.

Flavius smiled uneasily, not sure what Revious meant.

Revious, Flavius, two Roman soldiers, and Elderon started their journey to the Hun camp on horseback. They were followed by several packhorses. Revious motioned Flavius to his side.

"Marcus likes us to take supplies to the Hun camp. If they are well fed and sheltered, they are less likely to cause trouble. And we can keep an eye on what they are doing."

"Has this arrangement worked?" Flavius asked.

"Yes, so far. It helps that their chief advisor, Arb, is my friend, and their leader, Oxanos, understands how things need to be. He speaks Latin as well as Bukarma does! They feel fortunate to be alive and are grateful for the hospitality Marcus has extended to them."

The day with the Huns proved to be a productive one for Flavius, who felt a kinship with them due to his previous exile in Spain. Flavius, like Valerias and Claire, was particularly interested in the Hun bow. He shot targets with them and demonstrated swordplay moves.

Flavius felt refreshed in mind and body as they rode away from the camp. On the ride back to the Villa, he talked excitedly with Revious about how he wanted to learn more from the Huns and how he could be a mentor to them.

Revious smiled. *This has worked out just as Marcus and I thought it would. Flavius and the Huns are a perfect match.*

***

Gulic reeked of nervousness. He paced back and forth across the room, focused only on his thoughts. Finally, he heard a knock at the door. It was Alena.

"Father is in his study reading a land title document. He agreed to mediate a land dispute, and he is bored. Now is the time, my brave tribune." Alena sounded confident, but inside she was as nervous as Gulic.

“Yes, now is our time,” Gulic said, less convincingly.

Alena gave him a hug and quick kiss. “Go, bring back good news!”

Gulic slowly wound his way to Valerias’ study. He thought back to when he was a prisoner in Valerias’ war camp. His stomach was in his throat then; now it was in his mouth. When he arrived at the study, Wolf had parked himself at the front of the room. Gulic bent down and petted the dog with a shaky hand.

“Enter, Tribune.” Valerias’ voice echoed around the room.

Gulic stepped hesitantly into the study. He was sweating profusely in marked contrast to Valerias, who appeared calm, sitting behind his desk.

“Tribune, you seem ill.” Valerias never looked up from what he was reading.

“I am fine, General.”

“What do you want? Is your bridge completed? You seem to be at the Villa more and more these days. When will Emperor Theodosius give you your next assignment?”

“The bridge construction is almost at a point where I will no longer be needed. There are final matters I need to attend to. But that is not why I am here.”

Valerias put down the document he was reading and looked up at Gulic. “Sit.”

Valerias pointed to a chair across from him. Gulic sat uneasily. He spotted a tear in his tunic. *That’s not good,* he thought. *The General does not stand for sloppy dress.* Another bloom of sweat emerged around his neck.

“Well?” Valerias demanded.

Gulic summoned up all his courage and announced in a wavering voice, “I’ve come before you to ask for Alena’s hand in marriage.”

Valerias stared at Gulic, expressionless. He turned his head toward the door and bellowed, "Claire!"

Claire hustled into the study, her long hair tied behind her head. "What is it?"

Valerias looked at Claire and then at Gulic. "Whatever you ask of me, you will ask of both of us. Repeat your question."

The presence of Claire bolstered Gulic's courage. He stood up. "I am standing before you to respectfully request Alena's hand in marriage."

"Do you love my daughter?" Claire asked sternly.

"Yes, very much."

"And does she love you?"

"Yes . . ."

Valerias cut him off. "Thank you. We will take your request into consideration. You may take your leave."

Gulic was dumbfounded. He had expected an immediate answer, but wasn't given any response. On top of that, he was asked to leave. *What has happened?* he thought.

"NOW!" Valerias boomed.

Gulic bowed slightly and left, stunned.

***

Bukarma stood outside the Grand House watching his children play. Penelope leaned on her husband.

"I never thought I would have children," Penelope said softly with an air of satisfaction.

"What about a husband?" Bukarma answered playfully.

"Oh, a husband is cheap. A child is invaluable." Penelope smiled as she pulled on Bukarma's sleeve.

"A child can grow up to be a husband or wife, you know."

"Or a mother or father," Penelope said. After a pause she added, "You are a wonderful husband and father, Bukarma. You have enriched my life."

"And you, mine. Tell me, are you happy that you and the girls came to the Villa with me?"

"Yes. It is so peaceful here. Claire opened her home to us and made us feel so welcome. And Marcus is not as formidable as you sometimes describe. He gave you a position—co-commander of the Warriors' Palacc. I have no complaints."

"Neither do I," Bukarma said, looking at his daughters.

Their privacy was disturbed by the clatter of hooves as Flavius, Revious, Elderon, and the two Romans rode into the courtyard. Flavius looked agitated and unsettled. He was off his horse and into the Grand House before the horse had come to a full halt. After a few moments, he came out. A scowl covered his face as he walked over to Bukarma.

"What is wrong, Flavius?"

"I would like to visit Joseph's grave."

"Then you should do that."

"Marcus asked that you take me there."

"Now?" Bukarma was annoyed. He looked at his family and turned back to Flavius. "Give me a few moments. It is a short ride from here."

Bukarma said a quick farewell to his family and readied his horse. The two men traveled to Tevgium where Joseph had been laid to rest. Flavius was quiet the entire journey.

Bukarma grew tired of the silence and asked, "What is wrong with you today? You have not spoken and are glum."

Flavius replied, "Marcus said you have a problem with me. I can assure you that the Flavius from long ago in Britannia is not the Flavius here today. I have changed. First Mary, then Joseph, and now Marian have influenced me greatly. I am a better man. I have something to live for!"

Bukarma laughed vigorously.

"Why do you laugh at me, Bukarma?" Flavius said, frowning.

"Marcus played a trick on you. It is Revious who has the problem with you, not me. When Joseph asked me to accept you as man of the Christian faith, I did so readily. It will take Revious longer. Give him time, and all will be fine." Bukarma winked at Flavius, who in turn shook his head.

The two men reached the cemetery. They dismounted and tied their horses to a nearby tree. Bukarma led the way to a neatly kept gravesite marked with a simple stone that read: "Joseph of Rome—Priest, Bishop, a True Christian, and a Good Man for Britannia."

"Joseph lies here." Bukarma nodded at the grave. "Marcus comes here." He pointed to a worn area off to the side of the grave. "I will give you privacy and wait at the entrance."

"Thank you." Flavius knelt by the gravesite.

Bukarma walked slowly back the way they had come, gazing at other gravesite markers. Flavius knelt in a position of prayer. Finally, after an hour had passed and dusk made its usual appearance, Bukarma yelled, "We need to leave now, Flavius."

Flavius touched his head, his heart, and finally Joseph's grave. He rose and walked back to Bukarma.

"Did you find what you were looking for?" Bukarma asked.

"Yes. He told me to continue on the path I am on and the rest will fall into place. Thank you, friend, for bringing me here."

Bukarma nodded, and they began the short ride back to the Villa.

***

"How did your visit with Father go?" Alena was pensive and curious.

Gulic's pained look told her it went poorly, but she wanted to hear it from him.

"Your father is General Marcus Augustus Valerias and your mother is a queen."

"Yes, I know who they are, but that doesn't answer my question." After a second of thought, Alena added, "Mother was there as well?"

"Yes. Your father called her in."

"And she said nothing in our favor?"

"No. She offered nothing in our favor. Your father is a very intimidating man. He has been from the first time I met him."

"Any man who is to be my husband must be able to stand up to him." Alena glared at Gulic.

"I am sorry, then." Gulic peered at his feet and mumbled, "Perhaps you would be better off with someone else."

"You won't even make love to me out of fear of him!"

"And your mother," Gulic added meekly.

"I'm not sure how you are a Roman soldier!"

Gulic was deeply hurt by Alena's sharp words.

"I will go," he quietly said. "I do not wish to tangle with your father, so I will not measure up to what you expect. It is time for you to find your true husband. But he won't love you like I love you. He won't value your relationship with your family like I do. He will not treat you as well as I will. Good fortune with your hunt!"

Gulic pivoted and quickly stalked away. He was disturbed with himself for giving up so easily.

Alena stayed angry with him until he was out of sight. Then she realized she may have made a mistake. She had been impetuous instead of considering a rational solution to their dilemma. Her mother and father had taught her better than to react in such a hasty manner. She sighed and sat heavily in a chair by the fire, and began working out how to put things right.

Supper that night was a quiet affair. Gulic had left for the bridge and Alena was silent. Elsha, sensing something wrong, stayed at Bukarma's cottage with his family and Marian. Flavius was mourning Joseph and had disappeared for the evening. Bukarma had a short meeting during supper with Valerias and Claire, and he, too, left the Grand House.

Soon after the meal ended, the sound of hoof beats came from the courtyard. Valerias heard loud rustling, and then Alexander entered the dining hall. Instead of addressing Valerias as expected, he turned to Claire.

"A man who calls himself Biglio is here to see you from Britannia, Domina."

"What does this man want?" Valerias asked, puzzled.

"He has a letter for the Domina, and he can give it only to her."

"Very well, let him in." Valerias was curious, and he glanced at Claire to see if she had any reaction to the surprise visit, but she seemed as at a loss as he was.

Biglio hustled in the room. He was tall and slender, and completely exhausted. His eyes, set deep into his head, were smudged black with weariness. Valerias asked Biglio to sit and ordered a cup of wine and a plate of food for their visitor.

"What have you brought for my wife?" Valerias demanded.

Biglio held out a parchment to Claire. She took it and read it. She was only part way through but tears fell from her eyes, alerting Valerias that something terrible had happened. Claire rarely cried.

When Claire finished reading the letter, she put her hand over her mouth and gasped. Without hesitation, Valerias wrapped his arm around his wife, grabbing the letter as it fell from her hand. It was written in Latin.

> My Dear Claire,
>
> We agreed not to correspond in this manner unless it was absolutely necessary. If this letter was to fall into the wrong hands, it would be disastrous. However, I believe now is that necessary time.
>
> I am sorry to inform you that your brother is dead. Rega said his death was an accident. She reported Eustice was drunk and fell off the battlement. Others say he committed suicide.
>
> I can tell you most emphatically that he did not take his own life. I also doubt he was so drunk that he fell. I fear those who want the throne murdered him. I would place Rega at the top of the list of suspects. The throne is rightfully yours, and it is the throne that Drostan should rightfully inherit.
>
> The second matter is only a rumor, but one with great substance. According to what I hear, the Saxon barbarians are plotting a monstrous invasion of Britannia. Estimates are that the Saxons and their allies will have more than one thousand ships and over twenty thousand warriors. They are planning to land near

> Branodunum at the estuary the Romans call Metaris Aest. As you know, that is where our hermitage is located and where your son resides.
>
> The Saxons are a brutal people. I fear for our property and, most importantly, our lives. Yet, God would not want us to flee from adversity. We will remain, but your son should not be here. You must decide what to do. I will be here to help in any way that I can.
>
> May God help guide you and be with you. May God protect all of us.
>
> Your holder of the faith,
> Father Timothy, Abbot of Branodunum

After reading the letter, Valerias read it again, more slowly. He turned his attention back to Claire, who was visibly distressed, tears still falling down her cheeks. He put the letter on the table and reached out to take her hand.

"My love, we will deal with this together." Valerias smiled, but he spoke with the fierce determination of a general.

XXXVII

THE WAY BACK

Winter gripped the Villa in early 384. In his past, Valerias did not mind the season, but he intensely disliked this harsh winter. His knees and elbows hurt, he had frequent headaches, and the pesky bump on his leg caused him more pain than usual. He admired Wolf because nothing seemed to bother the dog. *Maybe I will come back in my next life as a dog*, he mused.

Because it was the first year of operation for the Warriors' Palace, Valerias and Bukarma experimented with a winter training program. Valerias strongly believed that winter conditioning was important, so that became the focus of the hearty individuals who stayed.

Claire was deeply upset by Joseph's murder, Eustice's death, and the approaching Saxon invasion. The invasion posed a grave threat to Drostan, the Branodunum hermitage, and Britannia. She felt helpless, which drove her into melancholy.

She spent most of her time in her room. In her absence, Valerias was left to run the estate. Alena and Elsha grew increasingly concerned for their mother, although Alena had grown equally despondent about her loss of Gulic's attention.

One cold afternoon, when Valerias was in the Great Room with several soldiers warmed by the Villas' underfloor hypocaust, Elsha appeared at the door. She caught his eye and he quickly excused himself. They met in his study.

"Father, I am sorry to take you away from your meeting—I could have waited."

"Nonsense," replied Valerias.

Elsha spoke frankly. "I am becoming very worried about Mother. She once was a force around the Villa. Now she acts like a haggard old woman. She is not an old woman!"

"No, she is not," he replied. "Recent events have taken a toll on your mother's spirit. The turmoil in Britannia is especially hard on her. I ask you not to despair. She will return to the strong, vital force you know. In the meantime, I have a favor to ask of you. Talk to your sister. She, too, needs her spirits raised. These things will work out. Trust me, Elsha."

Elsha gave Valerias a tearful hug and left. Valerias stayed in his study and silently asked Joseph to help his family—not a prayer to the dead, he insisted to himself, but a mere plea to a friend.

Several weeks went by, and although Claire thought the situation was hopeless, Valerias did not see it that way. His passion for leadership was rekindled. People at the Villa and in the nearby countryside noticed the transformation. He was no longer the old man the children followed. They once more referred to Valerias strictly as the General. In that role, Valerias knew he had much to do.

During a cold winter's evening, Claire retired early. Valerias sat outside under a warm blanket talking to Bukarma. They both squinted their eyes as a rider entered the courtyard looking for Valerias. *What news could such a latecomer bring?* thought Valerias.

The rider dismounted and the three men went into the Grand House, where the messenger handed Valerias a rolled parchment. On the outside was the seal of Emperor Theodosius.

Valerias unfurled it and read the correspondence. When he finished, he smiled, excused himself, and went to his bedchambers.

"Marcus, why are you here so early?" a soft voice came from a chair by a window.

"I have something to show you."

Valerias lit two candles. He started to hand Claire the scroll but became too excited, and decided to read it to her.

> To Marcus Augustus Valerias—Magister Militum of the Armies of Emperors Valens and Valentinian,
>
> I received your letter in which you described the approaching crisis in Britannia, the source of which is the godless Saxon barbarians. I discussed your letter with my advisors. After deliberating the matter and upon prayer to God, I concur with your evaluation and your recommendations.
>
> Your reputation is impeccable and your friendship with my father remains invaluable to me. You are hereby reinstated as an active general in the army with the title Magister Militum of Britannia.
>
> I have ordered a legion of combined infantry and cavalry to serve under you. As you read this letter, the legion marches to Gallia. The commander is General Luxcinious. You are to meet him and his legion at Augusta Treverorum.

> A second legion will also serve under your command. It is stationed in Londinium, and serves the new emperor of the West, Magnus Maximus. The leader of that legion is General Divinicus. You will join him when you arrive in Londinium.
>
> By joint agreement between Emperor Maximus and myself, any limitanei you can find in Britannia shall also serve under your command. You may appoint whomever you wish as officers in your command structure.
>
> General, I give you one piece of advice: Emperor Maximus is a man full of ambition. I have heard he desires the purple of the emperor for a consolidated Roman Empire. Be as wary of his ambitions as I am.
>
> I wish you the best in your expedition. Keep Britannia safe and under Roman rule.
>
> I pray that Christ be with you.

The seal of Emperor Theodosius was affixed to the letter.

Claire looked amazed at what she heard.

"If I understand correctly, then both Emperors Theodosius and Maximus have jointly appointed you as commander of a campaign in Britannia to defeat the Saxons."

"That is correct. And they have each provided me a legion."

"Will that be enough?"

"No, but we shall have the limitanei, and I hope the Britons can provide warriors. We will need every man and every weapon. I also will employ a special weapon."

Claire didn't need an explanation—she knew what he was referring to.

Valerias moved next to Claire, put his hand over hers and gave her a look of sincerity.

"I know I have gone through dark periods, and you have suffered more than anyone. I am truly sorry for putting you through that. It was during those periods that you took over and were the general. You kept our family together. Now it is my turn. This is what I was meant to do in life—to be a soldier and your husband. I love you, Claire. We are meant to be together because as a team, we are so damned formidable."

Valerias' earnestness was so intense that Claire knew there was no doubting his resolve. Tears formed in her eyes. She saw his eyes were wet as well. Claire passionately kissed Valerias and murmured softly, "I love you, Marcus."

Valerias returned the kiss and abruptly stood.

"We can continue this later, my love. Now I must talk to my officers."

Valerias turned and strode out of the bedchambers, his held head high and his shoulders square.

My General has returned, Claire thought. She slipped out of her nightgown and back into her daily clothes. *This will be a long night.*

Valerias left the Grand House and called out, "Bukarma! Bukarma, come here! I need you."

As soon as the words left Valerias' lips, Bukarma stood in front of him. "I want you to find Revious and Flavius. Send a messenger to Gulic and tell him that I would like him to come to the Villa as soon as possible. Finally, give the men at the Warriors' Palace an order to be here tomorrow at noon."

"Who shall I say the order comes from?" Bukarma grinned as he asked the question.

"Tell them by the order of General Marcus Augustus Valerias, Magister Militum of Britannia, as commissioned by Emperors Theodosius and Maximus." Valerias smiled. "Go!"

Revious was taking a nap when Bukarma found him. He had consumed several cups of wine that evening. Within minutes, a groggy Revious walked unsteadily to Valerias.

"Revious, good thing I am here to keep track of you," Valerias said.

Revious groaned and Valerias laughed. Valerias put his hand on Revious' shoulder.

"My friend, I need you to go the Hun camp and ask Oxanos and Arb to come here to tomorrow at noon. I have something to tell them that they will be interested in."

"Yes, Marcus," Revious mumbled. Revious had no idea why he had been summoned or why Valerias required the presence of the Huns.

"Revious, Emperors Theodosius and Maximus have reappointed me as General—Magister Militum of Britannia."

Revious looked at Valerias, puzzled. "What?" he muttered.

Valerias kept his hand on Revious' shoulder. "As the newly re-designated general, I have been given the power by the emperors to appoint whomever I want to whatever position I choose. You and Bukarma are promoted to commanding legates. You will be my chief officers and will report only to me. You can keep your unruly mustache!"

"But Bukarma and I are not of Roman nobility to be assigned such a rank."

"That does not matter anymore, my friend. We are going to Britannia!"

XXXVIII

TRACTION

Flavius took Marian to Bukarma and Penelope's cottage at the Villa to play with Evaline and Lavonica. Such time was balm for both Flavius and Marian. Marian enjoyed playing with the younger girls. She became their big sister, as Elsha had become her big sister. Flavius was pleased that Marian appeared to be emerging from her shell. Her laughter warmed his heart.

As Penelope and Flavius chatted easily, Bukarma entered the house, breathing hard.

"Greetings, Flavius. The General would like to see you. Now."

Flavius was confused. "What general?"

"General Valerias! Now!"

Bukarma caught Penelope's attention. "Penelope, please watch Marian."

Penelope nodded apprehensively as both men left for the Grand House.

"I don't understand, Bukarma. What is happening?" Flavius was baffled.

"I'll let General Valerias explain."

Bukarma did not say another word as they hurried to the Grand House. When they arrived, Claire gave them a brief greeting and ushered them into a corner of the Great Room where Valerias was waiting with another man.

"Good, Bukarma. You found Flavius."

Valerias addressed Flavius directly. "This is a messenger from the emperor. He has information that will set our paths to the future and perhaps our destinies. Tomorrow at noon, we will hold a war council. You will be apprised of the details at that time. Suffice to say, we are going on campaign against the coming Saxon invasion of Britannia. I want to take this opportunity to ask you to join our effort." Valerias ignored Flavius' bewildered look and explained further.

"The emperors have granted me the power to choose who I want as officers. But there is a caveat—your past as an army deserter hangs around you like an anchor. I cannot promote you to an officer. But I can appoint you as my special emissary. You will report only to me, Bukarma, and Revious. You have tonight to decide. I need your answer in the morning before we begin preparations for war. Good night, Flavius."

Bukarma and Flavius left the Grand House. On the way out, Flavius meekly inquired, "What about Marian?"

"I have children too," Bukarma responded tartly. Then he softened, "She will be cared for."

Flavius added, "What about my history in Britannia?"

"The General has moved beyond yesterday. He is only interested in today and tomorrow."

The next morning came far too quickly for Flavius. He had spent the night deep in thought, watching Marian sleep. *She reminds me so much of Mary.*

In the morning, Flavius and Marian walked slowly to the Grand House. It was a brisk winter's day. Valerias stood in the doorway and stretched as the two approached.

"Good morning, Flavius and Marian. Marian, why don't you go inside and find Elsha and Wolf while I speak with you father."

Marian, unaware of her father's apprehension, rushed inside, calling for Elsha.

"What did you decide, Flavius?"

"If I agree, I want Marian to accompany us on the campaign." Flavius tried hard to be firm.

"She can come to Britannia—but she goes no further than Londinium. It is the same with my daughters and Bukarma's children." Valerias waited for Flavius' reply.

Flavius looked down as he spoke slowly, "I have done terrible things to many Britons. I cannot make up for that. Joseph told me to forgive myself because Christ has forgiven me. To go on a campaign to help save Britannia is one way I can make up for my past. Should anything happen to me, will Claire look after Marian?"

"Claire is going with me—just as when she fought with me against the Huns. This is her land. Alena and Elsha will care for Marian. Penelope will also travel to Londinium with Evaline and Lavonica. There should be no problem for you or Marian with this arrangement."

Flavius stared into Valerias' eyes and took a deep breath. "I agree to your request."

"Good. I anticipated as much. We will develop the logistics at the council meeting. Once in Londinium, we can set the plan to counter the Saxons. Return here at noon."

The war council assembled at noon in the Great Room. Valerias and Claire sat in the main chairs and the others spread out in front of them. Bukarma, Revious, and Flavius were present. Gulic arrived from his bridge encampment just before the meeting. Oxanos and Arb sat next to Revious. Current and former army officers, including several from the Warriors' Palace, sat among the others.

Valerias began the meeting. "My friends and colleagues, I thank you for attending today. As you may have heard, Emperors Theodosius and Maximus have commissioned me to take a campaign to Britannia and repel the Saxons. Britannia is in turmoil and ripe for such a barbarian invasion. The Domina's former kingdom has a new leader, Rega, who attained her status as ruler through questionable circumstances. We will not receive help from her.

"Emperor Magnus Maximus is in Gallia attending to other matters of the empire and cannot give Britannia the attention the Saxon invasion merits, and Emperor Theodosius is too far away. Therefore, I am going to Britannia on the emperors' behalf to defeat the Saxon barbarians and establish stability there until Emperor Maximus can address the situation himself.

"Each emperor has designated one legion to my command. Each legion consists of twenty-five hundred men. Most are infantrymen; there will be smaller units of cavalry. I understand the Saxon barbarians will be almost entirely infantry.

"Bukarma and Revious will serve as my commanding legates. I will assign other ranks later. We leave in one week to meet Emperor Theodosius' legion, under General Luxcinious' command, in Augusta Treverorum. We will then cross the Narrow Sea and join Emperor Maximus' legion, under General Divinicus' command, near Londinium. From there, we will travel northeast. I want to engage the Saxons as they arrive on Britannia's shores. I do not want them to establish any more of a foothold than they already have.

"I will take a contingent of men from the Villa and Warrior's Palace with me to Britannia. Your involvement is voluntary. I am not ordering you to join me, but I hope that many of you will. What questions do you have?"

Several men had questions.

"Where did your information about the Saxons come from?"

Valerias replied, "Traders have seen hundreds of warships in the Saxon harbors, as well as a buildup of ships in the lands of the Angles and Jutes. The traders have heard the Saxons talk of a massive raid on Britannia. Christian priests along the eastern shore of Britannia, closest to the Saxon lands, confirmed talk of the attack. The Saxons are not disguising their intentions."

"Have you ever fought the Saxons before?"

"No, but they are like most barbarians. They want to raid areas they think have value and are vulnerable, taking whatever they want. They may even try to claim land. I doubt many of them have ever fought the seasoned Roman troops that we will assemble before them."

"How many Saxons are there?"

"We are unsure of the exact count—at least several thousand. Other northern barbarian tribes will join the Saxons, such as the Angles, Jutes, and perhaps the Franks. They will be no different than the Saxons in terms of motives and fighting skills."

"How will we be paid?"

"The emperors have authorized treasury funds to be expended. I will personally augment wages for those who are not covered."

Several men asked questions to which Valerias did not have answers. He informed the men that information was being gathered and as soon as he had answers, he would pass along the information.

Valerias showed a relaxed patience that he had seldom exhibited in earlier years. When there were no more questions, Valerias raised his right arm.

"Each of you must now decide if you want to join us. It has been some time since we had such a chance as this to fight for

Rome's glory! Some of you fought at Adrianople and know what a horrific defeat that was to the empire. I came out of retirement for the opportunity to relieve that sting. I will seize this opportunity! I ask you to join me!"

The men in the crowd were excited for the possibility of action, and strongly voiced their agreement.

"Good!" Valerias shouted. "See my commanding legate Bukarma to sign up for the campaign."

As the men gathered around Bukarma, Valerias addressed Oxanos and Arb.

"Oxanos, you and your people have done everything I have asked since you moved onto my land. To be honest, I am surprised and pleased. I am now asking you and your men to join me. You would not act independently, but as a unit of the Roman army."

Arb talked excitedly with Oxanos. "This would be a great opportunity for us to show off our battle skills. Our men also need a release from the tedium of camp. We must do this, Oxanos!"

Oxanos listened intently but showed no emotion. He nodded once as Arb talked. Valerias watched the Hun leader closely.

Oxanos turned and asked Valerias one question: "Would you allow our men to bring their wives and families?"

Valerias knew that his family, Bukarma's family, and Flavius' daughter would be accompanying them part of the way. He needed to craft his answer delicately.

"No, that would not be possible, Oxanos. We will travel too fast to take women, children, and the elderly. We are taking our children, but they are going only part of the way. They will not be involved with the war. Your families will be much better off in their village here on my land."

Valerias was aware of the risk involving the Huns. He needed soldiers who would obey orders, and there was no guarantee the

Huns would do that. A small part of Valerias wondered, *At some point, will the Huns turn on me out of revenge for the Battle of Three Tongues?*

Oxanos risked the welfare of his people. His warriors would go to a strange land and many could die. The women and children would be left behind, where their safety might be in jeopardy without their men and, in particular, without Valerias and Claire at the Villa to protect them.

After a few moments of thought, Oxanos spoke. "Yes, we will fight with you, provided you protect our women and children."

Valerias smiled. "Of course, I will take care of your concern. You will see."

Oxanos appeared satisfied. "I trust you, General Valerias."

Oxanos left and Valerias crossed the floor to where Gulic was standing quietly by himself.

"What are you thinking, Tribune?"

"I cannot join you. I already made a commitment to complete construction of the bridge. There is too much to do to leave, too many loose ends to tie up."

Valerias handed Gulic a small scroll. Gulic started to unroll it, but Valerias interrupted.

"It is a letter from Emperor Theodosius. It says that you are relieved of your assignment and are to join me in the war against the Saxons. Your role in the bridge construction is almost complete, anyway."

Gulic looked shocked. "Why do you want me? I am not worthy of your daughter, so why would I be worthy of your expedition? Alena won't even speak to me."

Valerias put his arm gently around Gulic's shoulders. "You are the best engineer I know, and I want you with us. I specifically requested you when I wrote to Emperor Theodosius." After a short pause, Valerias added, "Besides, Claire and I didn't say *no*. I would use this opportunity to show Alena that you will continue to seek the Domina's and my approval of your marriage proposal."

Gulic knew Valerias spoke honestly and he therefore found his decision easy. "General, I accept the engineer's position with your campaign."

"Good," replied Valerias. "Tie up those loose ends regarding the bridge and return to the Villa as soon as possible."

After Valerias finished speaking to Gulic, he spotted Elderon walking across the Villa's courtyard. Valerias called to him, but Elderon just waved and continued walking.

Valerias rarely spoke to Elderon, and now Valerias had called his name several times. *This can't be good for me*, Elderon thought. He slowed his pace, saying a quick prayer; Valerias was on him like a hawk on a hare.

"How is your training proceeding with the priest from Tevgium?" Valerias did not even greet Elderon.

"I am learning much, but I have a long way to go." Elderon knew Valerias did not make small talk, and was anxious about what he really wanted.

"Joseph said that one can never stop adding knowledge to one's self, even as a bishop. Do you accept the path to become a Christian leader?"

"I don't know yet, General." Elderon nervously dabbed his forehead with a cloth.

"I *do* know!" Valerias' patience had worn thin. "I am drafting you into the army I am assembling. I assume you have heard about us going north to Britannia to fight the Saxons."

"Yes." Elderon wiped away more sweat.

"Since Joseph has passed on to his glory and is no longer with us, I need someone to provide spiritual comfort to those in the army who request it. I also promised Emperor Theodosius that a Christian leader would accompany our expedition. The emperor is a Christian."

"Yes, General, I know."

"The priest in the village is too old for such an assignment. You are the only other Christian—with priestly potential—in the area. I will pay you myself, if you are thinking about compensation. I will also fund your training when we return. We leave in less than a week. Prepare yourself." Leaning forward into Elderon's face, Valerias said, "You owe me this."

"But I have never been in a battle. I don't know what to expect."

"I have been in many battles and I do not always know what to expect. You will learn. Joseph learned."

Valerias got very close to Elderon and spoke sternly, "If you try to flee here, along the way, or in Britannia, I will have your eyes cut out, your tongue removed, and your ear drums pierced. You can return to the life of a beggar."

Valerias left a dazed Elderon in the courtyard. Elderon knew Valerias meant what he said.

Valerias called for Wolf. This time the dog came, and the two walked out into the open land of the Villa.

XXXIX

CONUNDRUM

"Damn!" Garzad exclaimed as he finished reading the parchment. "Damn!"

"What is wrong? Isn't that a letter from Emperor Maximus? It has his seal." Honorario was puzzled at Garzad's reaction.

"Read it yourself," Garzad said, holding the letter out to Honorario.

> Tribune Garzad,
>
> You have made a remarkable rise in rank since you joined the army almost ten years ago. You have completed every assignment beyond expectation, and have earned your rank. You have developed several allies on your ascension, including Generals Octavio, Diocles, and Tiberian. I stand as emperor in the West due in no small part to your efforts. In time, you will be fully rewarded for you efforts.
>
> I have an additional task for you. When you complete this task, the rank of general shall be yours. I am ordering you to go to Londinium in Britannia. There you will proceed to my main camp and become General Divinicus' senior

> aide, whom I tasked with confronting the Saxon invasion. You will receive your next set of orders there.
>
> Before I crossed the Narrow Sea into Gallia and assumed the purple of the emperor, I commanded the legions in Britannia. I am concerned about the stability of that land. I trust you to be General Divinicus' second in command to secure Britannia for our great empire. You are one of few men I trust with this task. I expect your usual results.

"This is wonderful news, Garzad!" Honorario's eyes were wide with excitement.

"Is it, Honorario?" Garzad was strangely subdued. He cursed Britannia under his breath.

"I do not understand. Supporting a proven general and fighting Saxons is the ideal way for you to rise to the rank of general."

"I do not want to go to Britannia, Honorario. It is a foul place. The emperor does not care about Britannia. I would much prefer to be assigned directly to Emperor Maximus' court. Anything is better than Britannia!"

Garzad's attitude disturbed Honorario. "Would you rather return to Africa?" Honorario asked.

"Yes, I would."

***

Garzad and Honorario reached the outskirts of the Roman camp near Londinium. An old messenger met them at the entrance and handed Garzad a document. Garzad unrolled the parchment and after several moments, angrily threw his arm down at his side and stared at the camp.

"This is becoming worse and worse!" Garzad cursed violently, holding out the parchment to Honorario. "There are times that I question the value of you teaching me to read!" Because of his dense beard, the only visible evidence of Garzad's emotion were the veins popping out of his thick neck.

Honorario took a few moments to read the communication. "This is a letter from Emperor Maximus' secretary, simply providing our orders."

Honorario frowned, mystified by Garzad's outburst. It was the second time Garzad had reacted harshly at correspondence from the emperor.

"Garzad, we are to march to Ratae with General Divinicus' legion and headquarter there until we receive our next orders. We are to show support for the ruler in Ratae. I see nothing unusual here."

"You do not see what I see, Honorario. Britannia, and particularly Ratae, is the sewer in the golden meadow of the empire. I do not want to go there."

"Why? A promotion to general is in your future. This is a great opportunity!"

"We are officers without soldiers. Further, I don't even know this Divinicus. He cannot trust me yet, which means his legion will not trust me. I doubt they want to be in Britannia or go to Ratae either." Garzad shook his head vigorously from side to side.

"I disagree with you," Honorario stated politely. "You are the special envoy for Emperor Maximus. That carries great weight. Divinicus and his legion are loyal to the emperor, and they will accept you. Besides, I doubt we will sit in Ratae long. As we traveled to Londinium, I talked to soldiers and there is word we will soon be marching east to fight the Saxons. The legion will want to fight the Saxons. You, as an officer, will have the opportunity to lead by word and deed."

"I have heard something similar as well." Garzad focused on Honorario's last comment. "I would love to fight, and if it is against the Saxon barbarians, so be it."

As usual, Honorario had a soothing effect on Garzad, and slowly he began to calm down.

"When do we leave for Ratae?"

Honorario glanced at the scroll. "The orders say within four weeks. We are to camp in an old Roman barracks in Ratae, previously used by a General Titus."

"Titus!" Garzad growled. The large veins in his neck began to appear again.

"You know him?" Honorario was surprised at Garzad's response.

"No, not personally. I did hear Britannia drove him crazy, just like it will do to me!"

"Have you been to Britannia before, Garzad? It sounds like you have."

"No, but soldiers have told me that Britannia is a hell hole. I think wandering about in Britannia is no way to shine a light on what we can do to help the empire *and* ourselves!"

Garzad followed his statement with another round of cursing in even uglier language. After his tirade, he looked at Honorario as if he were in severe physical pain.

Garzad snarled, "Let us go to Divinicus' headquarters and introduce ourselves. I want to coordinate our efforts in the impending march to Ratae. I don't know what is worse, this boring camp in Londinium or having to go to Ratae. Shit!"

XL

OPPORTUNITY

"It has been one month since Eustice's unfortunate death and still many of *my* noblemen will not pledge their loyalty to me." Rega's voice carried a note of disgust. "Why?"

Voltrex rubbed his hands together. "It is not because of your ravenous beauty, my queen." He laughed at his own comment.

Rega glared at him. "Be serious, Voltrex!"

"My queen, you and I are from another kingdom. The noblemen here resent having a foreigner, so to speak, as their queen. It will take time. I suggest meeting with them individually. At the meetings, we can provide them with incentives to join us."

"They think I killed Eustice. I did not! I was in my bedchamber with servants at the door. Eustice brought this on himself by drinking so much he couldn't walk around his own fort. And he dismissed his bodyguards!"

"He may have had help in his fall." Voltrex said flatly.

"What do you mean?"

"I didn't kill him, at least not directly. You may recall I was away on business. He had enemies. Maybe one of them decided it was time for a new leader."

Rega's anger rapidly melted away and her tone changed. "I am pleased Eustice is dead. All he wanted from me was an heir. Just think, over a year ago, I was a throwaway daughter to my father. I am now the queen and sole ruler. In time, my kingdom will merge with my father's. Then I will have the great kingdom I deserve!"

"Your father is still a king, my love. Do *you* have something arranged?"

"My father is old. He does not have much time left."

Voltrex frowned, confused. Suddenly he understood and smiled. *We are very much alike in our ambitions,* he thought.

Rega continued, "We have a response to the letter sent to the new Roman emperor, Magnus Maximus. The emperor is concerned about the stability in Britannia, particularly with King Eustice dead and my father in a feeble condition. Emperor Maximus is sending a legion to Ratae to support my rule. General Divinicus is the commander of the legion. He has an aide by the name of Garzad, who I understand follows orders and is as ruthless as we are. The emperor believes that I am the one who can unite kingdoms."

"Will I be at your side when the unification occurs?" Voltrex was interested in Rega's response.

"Of course, Voltrex. You are my true love. I even predict there will be more than one unification. After the kingdoms merge, we shall marry and you will become king."

"My queen, I very much look forward to that."

Voltrex rarely exhibited emotion, but he relished the prospect of becoming king.

"Perhaps we can influence this Garzad to do our bidding," Voltrex noted.

"You think like I do."

Rega kissed Voltrex and whispered, "Doesn't power feel good?"

***

"I don't understand it! I don't understand why this is still happening!" Rega's temper flared.

"Your feelings are justified, my queen." Voltrex paced the room, balancing the hilt of his dagger on the palm of his hand.

"I have properly mourned Eustice, as I should. It has been four months since his death. I have maintained his policies and still there is unrest in my kingdom. There is an insurrection occurring to the north. I do not have complete confidence in the army, so I can't just send troops out to quash the rebels; the army may revolt and join them. My weak father has his own difficulties and has sent me only a contingent of five hundred men. That is not enough! You are commander of the army, Voltrex—why can't I trust its loyalty?"

"It is complicated." Voltrex sheathed his dagger. "You know the volatile history of this land. There was Gerhard, who was killed by the Saxons. Claire was usurped by Argus, and he was killed by the Romans. Eustice took the throne and fell to his death. And now you, an outsider, are the kingdom's ruler.

"The countryside is full of bandits and outlaws, and has been forever. The dwindling Roman presence and resulting lack of governance and security are creating a vacuum. Argus' supporters continue to cause trouble even though he is long dead. Also, the whereabouts of Flavius and Morguard are unknown. It is no surprise to me to see the state of things as they are. Remember, though, you are still the queen—a young queen—and I am your faithful servant." Voltrex bowed and kissed Rega's hand.

"Don't forget, lover, Eustice has followers who are suspicious of his death," Rega said. "As long as Claire lives, she is a threat to my throne. I have heard rumors, this time rumors with merit, that her son is alive. Now I hear the Saxon's forthcoming invasion is a reality. I worry something will happen and delay my coronation of the unified kingdoms. Planning how events should transpire does not guarantee that they will."

Rega sat cold and expressionless.

"You are the queen." Voltrex played with his dagger again. "You have the power to help us. And I am always available to grant the queen whatever favor she desires."

"The favor I desire from you I cannot have at this time. How can I rectify our situation? I am beginning to feel trapped."

"Do not worry, Rega. Your situation is about to have relief."

"*Our* situation!" Rega quickly corrected. She did not know whether Voltrex was serious or not. She suddenly felt alone.

"Emperor Maximus' legion should arrive in Ratae soon. The Romans will support you and confront the Saxons. At that time, we can crush any local rebellion—and we will. Then you shall reign as queen for a long time, with me at your side."

"We work well as a team," Rega softened.

"Power is a strange thing, Rega; the weak Romans are not quite ready to give up on our little kingdom. They cling to the illusion that they have power in Britannia when it is but a ghost of its glory years, yet that ghost will be *our* source of power."

XLI

NORTHWARD

Preparations for the Britannia campaign began in earnest as soon as the war council meeting ended. Spring was tantalizingly close, which boosted spirits. Valerias granted freedom to all his slaves. Those who wanted to join the expedition could do so as freemen. About half of them chose to accompany Valerias northward to Britannia. The other half remained at the Villa to work.

In Claire and Valerias' absence, Alexander was to assume the role of Master of the Villa. Valerias had been impressed with his energy, loyalty, and ability to effectively manage the day-to-day affairs at the Villa.

Almost all of the trainers and trainees at the Warriors' Palace eagerly signed on with the campaign. So many volunteered that Valerias asked several men to remain and protect the Villa in his absence. To offset their disappointment, Valerias provided them with additional compensation.

Duvanous was given the military leadership post at the Villa. He was trusted by Valerias, and Claire agreed with his appointment. Duvanous had also made multiple visits to the Hun encampment and got along well with them. Thus, Duvanous received a second assignment from Valerias: to look after the Huns who remained behind.

After careful thought and counsel with Revious and Oxanos, Valerias made Flavius his special envoy to the Hun warriors.

Flavius and the Huns collaborated well together, as both grew to appreciate the other's fighting abilities. It was a natural fit, as far as Valerias was concerned.

Besides, Valerias wanted to keep Flavius' contacts with the Britons to a minimum. Claire advised that Flavius was despised in her former kingdom, so Valerias believed that if Flavius remained immersed with the Huns, the Britons might not notice him. Valerias also thought the assignment would take Flavius' mind off of Mary and Marian.

The day before Valerias and his contingent left, the Villa was unusually quiet. Those men who had families spent the available time with them saying goodbye. Alena and Elsha had packed for the long journey and were now at Flavius and Marian's quarters. Gulic sat with the single men, drinking wine.

Valerias asked Claire to join him for a walk. They held hands as they strolled around the buildings.

"I will miss this place," Valerias said, fondly looking around the grounds.

"We will return shortly. Then we never need to leave again," Claire replied.

"When we first acquired the Villa, it was difficult for me to stay here. I had been a mobile soldier for so long that I had never spent enough time in one place to call it a home. Now I feel content here. You made the Villa my home." Valerias smiled and squeezed Claire's hand.

"You are making a sacrifice going to Britannia and leaving the Villa behind." Claire wanted to ensure that Valerias wasn't having second thoughts.

"While it's true I don't want to leave here, part of me yearns to be a soldier again. I relish the opportunity to be the commanding general. I also look forward to meeting Drostan and bringing him here where he will be safe with his family."

"Do you really think the Saxons will invade near Branodunum, or will they target other areas?" Claire couldn't hide the concern in her voice.

"The Saxons must believe the area around Branodunum is rich with gold, silver, and jewelry tied to the religious orders and noblemen. There is also agricultural land, livestock, and people—all assets the Saxons covet. Of particular appeal to them is that they have not raided that area in force yet."

"How do you think the Huns will do in battle?" Claire asked, changing the subject.

"They will be excellent. They have been sitting idle so long at their camp; they are itching to engage in any sort of action. I am not concerned about their fighting abilities. I am more wary of the actual journey from the Villa to Branodunum. It is a long way, and I do not want the Huns to get distracted. My instincts tell me that Flavius will be a good mentor for them."

Valerias continued, "I agree it is best to keep Flavius from the people he tormented—even if he wants to help them now. People have not forgotten the infamous deeds of Argus, Morguard, and Flavius. Flavius' future in your kingdom is tenuous, at best."

"How many Huns will go with us to Britannia?" Claire asked.

"As many as Oxanos will allow. I imagine it is the same volunteer ratio that I got from the Warriors' Palace—nearly everyone. As I said, the Huns have been idle too long."

"They aren't here yet," Claire said skeptically.

"No, but they will be first thing tomorrow morning."

Valerias paused and gazed upon the setting sun as it dipped into the trees. "I want to tell you something. Last night I was reviewing war logistics in the study and I fell asleep. When I awoke, there he was again, standing off in the corner."

"Who?" Claire asked cautiously, though she already knew the answer.

"Death. Just like the figure I dreamed of in the meadow several months ago. He didn't move or talk, and I was not angry this time. I asked if he would follow us to Britannia. Death nodded and disappeared. I think Death is the foreteller of a bloody campaign. There will be souls to take, and he will be there, ready. I don't know if he is telling me my fate, or the fate I will bring upon others."

Claire leaned into Valerias' shoulder. "Next time you need to fall asleep in our bed. Then you won't have such dreams."

The next morning brought cool air that displaced the warmth from the previous day. When Claire arose, the bed was empty.

Valerias had risen before dawn to meet the Huns led by Oxanos and Arb. They had arrived very early, as Valerias had predicted. Revious rode with them. There were one hundred and one Hun warriors in total, including three women. Valerias frowned when he saw the women.

Oxanos swiftly responded to Valerias' look. "Those women are better archers than most of the men in our camp."

"I prefer women not to be involved in combat. I cannot be responsible for their well-being. And I don't want them distracting my men."

Oxanos started to speak, but Valerias cut him off. "I know what you are about to ask, so here is my response. Domina Claire will come with us because she has other matters to deal with besides the Saxons. As you know, she was the queen of a kingdom in central Britannia long ago, and has some unfinished business there. No other women or children in our party will go north of Londinium."

Valerias could see that his bluntness surprised Oxanos, who was looking at him defiantly. Valerias tried a softer approach.

"Oxanos, I am the highest general in command of the campaign. I give the orders, and I expect them to be obeyed without question. I require your Hun warriors and everyone else in the campaign to follow that primary rule. To ensure that everyone complies, I need you to lead the Huns. That is why I am appointing you the title of Tribune—Master of the Huns. Your warriors—the men *and* women—are your responsibility.

"It will be your charge to lead your warriors on and off of the battlefield, just as you have successfully done on my land. They are to take an oath of loyalty to the Roman Empire and its army. As compensation for your participation in the campaign, your people will be allowed to continue living on my land for free. Any plunder you take from the Saxons is yours. You are to report to me or Flavius. Arb shall be your aide. Am I clear? Talk to your men . . . and women. Those who agree to my terms will ride with us. Those who don't will stay here."

Valerias nodded to Arb, who translated for Oxanos to ensure there wasn't any misunderstanding. But it wasn't necessary. Oxanos answered in Latin, "I understand. I will talk to my people. Also, General, I know your language. What do you think I do at our camp all day—scratch my ass?"

Oxanos and Arb erupted with laughter, and Valerias and Revious smiled.

"Go!" Valerias said, still smiling, and Oxanos and Arb joined the Hun warriors.

"They will all follow you," Revious said. "They still think of you as a god and Claire as a goddess. I can understand their view of Claire. However, why they think that of you is anyone's guess!"

Revious tried to keep a straight face but couldn't. He added, "Besides, they can't wait to take Saxon spoils of war."

"Good. Then you shall lead them to Augusta Treverorum and instruct Flavius along the way. Congratulations, you are now the commanding general!" This time, Valerias laughed.

The expedition was ready to leave the Villa before noon. As Revious predicted, all the Huns, including the three women, accepted Valerias' offer. Eighty-nine freemen and Roman soldiers from the Warriors' Palace also joined them. The conscripted villagers from Menze added ten more to the ranks. Thirty-seven servants and former slaves volunteered for the expedition. All took an oath of loyalty to the empire.

At the end of the oath, Valerias shouted, "Honor! Loyalty! Victory! Glory!"

The throng of Romans mounted their horses and rode out of the Villa. Bukarma took the lead, seconded by Gulic. The Huns, led by Revious, followed. Elderon, Penelope and her children, Flavius and Marian, and Alena and Elsha went next. Valerias and Claire were the last to leave.

"It is my wish to see the Villa again with you and our daughters," Valerias said wistfully.

"Of course you will, Marcus. This is our home."

"What do you think Drostan will do? Will he stay in Britannia or come back here with us? I fear if he stays in Branodunum, he will die. We can temporarily fend off the Saxons, but they will return. To me, barbarians are like the water in a river: You can build a dam to temporarily stop them, but the water eventually gets through. The defeat at Adrianople is a catastrophic example.

"In Britannia, the Roman dam has almost been demolished, and the barbarians are coming. You may be hard-pressed to recognize your former kingdom in another decade, or maybe even today."

"What you speak of dispirits me, Marcus. But I know you speak the truth. I must convince Drostan to join us. We could be a family again. It has been ten years since I last saw him. That is far too long for a mother to endure without seeing her son, and for a family to be apart."

"We *will* defeat the Saxons, my love. You *will* be reunited with your son. After that, I can make no guarantees."

Valerias glanced back at the Villa one last time with silent uncertainty in his heart. Claire looked forward with apprehension. Valerias turned and slapped Claire's horse on its rear, and they both galloped off to catch up with Valerias' command. Wolf, too, had decided to travel northward.

XLII

THE FOREST

Valerias' company traveled northward without supply wagons. Instead, packhorses accompanied every Roman soldier, Hun warrior, and man from Menze. Before leaving the Villa, Valerias sent a messenger ordering General Luxcinious to take his legion from Augusta Treverorum to Caletum and cross the Narrow Sea to Britannia. From there, the legion was to march to the Roman fort at Londinium.

The first stop for Valerias and his company before Augusta Treverorum was Menze. Valerias' troop rode into the center of the village, packing the space with men and horses. Valerias wanted to provide the villagers with an impressive show of force during daylight. The Huns added to the effect. When the villagers saw the troop, they fled, terrified, into their homes, believing their village was about to be sacked. From his jet-black horse, Valerias called for Antonio Felix.

After a few moments, the diminutive man emerged from a nearby building. "I am Antonio Felix. I remember you, General Valerias."

"I remember you, too. Shall I assume you are now in charge here?"

"Yes, I am. Please spare us, great general. We have purged all remnants of the vile priest Erasmus. We are no longer plagued by his evil."

"Good. Yet that does not bring back my friend, Bishop Joseph. But I did not come here today to dwell on the past. I am here to tell you that the men you sent with me are going north to Britannia for our war against the Saxons."

"But . . ."

"Do not interrupt me. One of your men did not meet my exacting standards. I need to exchange him for another."

"What did he do?" Felix was perplexed.

"Nothing I would consider a punishable offense. He simply is not strong enough for the journey to Britannia. You have half an hour, about the time until the sun clears that tree, to provide me with a new and more able man. During that time, family members of the other nine men can take the time to say goodbye."

Felix looked at the village men Valerias had conscripted and saw they looked healthy and fit. *Valerias has kept his word*, thought Felix. The villagers began to emerge from their huts. They were used to seeing Roman soldiers, but the Huns were terrifying and intriguing. A couple of young children approached a Hun on horseback. The Hun looked back at the children, expressionless.

"Don't be concerned, Elderman. I will treat the men of Menze as I do my soldiers. If they are loyal and follow orders, they shall have the opportunity to live and thrive. The alternative is not good."

Felix excused himself and returned shortly with a man whose appearance was starkly different from Felix's. The man was easily a foot taller, and while Felix was nearly bald, this man had a full head of long, brown, curly hair and a ruddy complexion.

"General, this is my son, Gerlok. He will go with you."

Valerias looked at Gerlok and then Felix, wondering how these two men could possibly be related. *How could such a small man produce such a large man? And with all that hair! This is a strange lineage.* However, he kept his thoughts to himself.

"You are the leader of Menze; therefore, Gerlok shall be the leader of your men who ride with me." Valerias turned to Gerlok, "Get your horse and any belongings you can carry. We will provide you with weapons. We leave soon."

When enough time had elapsed, Valerias and his troop left for Augusta Treverorum. As they rode out, Valerias noticed Gerlok was about as large as his horse, and he laughed to himself. *We must get a larger horse for Gerlok. He is going to crush that animal!*

***

Between Menze and Augusta Treverorum, Valerias' column traveled on Roman-built roads. As they passed by a heavily wooded area in central Gallia, several corpses could be seen hanging from trees on both sides of the road. Valerias slowed his column and motioned to Revious to join him.

"Revious, what do you make of this?"

"It could be a number of things. My guess is they were thieves who were caught and hung. Or they were innocent travelers who met the same fate as Joseph."

"Whatever the cause, we must be vigilant. See what you can find up ahead."

Revious waved for two men to join him and they disappeared up the road. Valerias turned to speak to Bukarma and found Elderon next to him.

"What do you want, Elderon?" Valerias was curious about Elderon's unsolicited approach.

"Those men," Elderon pointed to four men hanging close to the east side of the road, "are the ones who beat and robbed Joseph."

"How do you know that?"

"I was there. I will never forget the man with the scar on his face." Elderon pointed to a corpse with a large scar above its left eye. "I see the others, too."

"Well, it seems justice has a home." Valerias turned his attention from the dead men to the road down which Revious had gone.

Valerias motioned for the group to ride forward slowly. Revious returned and with a serious face, nodded to Valerias. Valerias again halted his troops and placed his right arm behind his back. Bukarma followed Valerias' signal, and the men from the Villa quietly reached for their shields and swords. Revious rode back to the Huns and whispered a message to Oxanos. Hun bows were immediately readied.

Claire, who had experience with these actions, pulled Alena, Elsha, Marian, Penelope, and her daughters into a tight circle surrounded by soldiers. Bukarma situated himself beside the women.

Penelope quietly asked, "What?"

Claire whispered, "Ambush. Bandits."

No Roman or Hun moved for some time. Valerias spotted numerous movements in the underbrush, but there was no panic by his troops. Finally, a bush shook and a man stepped out into the open. He was of Valerias' height, but thin. He had greasy, auburn hair and an untrimmed beard. He wore decent clothes; Valerias assumed they had been stolen.

"Who are you?" Valerias asked the man through Revious' translation.

"It doesn't matter, Roman. Where are you going?"

"To Britannia, to kill Saxons."

The truth proved to be the correct response.

"I, too, would like their heads in baskets," the man replied. "We are Burgundian and are at war with the Saxons."

"I know of your war, Burgundian. Then you see our mission is important from your point of view."

"I agree. However, we would still like a small tribute from you to pass. Because you will kill Saxons, I will reduce the usual tribute. Two hundred of your Roman coins to pass."

"I will not pay you anything. Be warned, Burgundian. The bulk of my army will soon arrive. You will not want to be here then or harm us in any way."

Valerias bluffed, but his manner and speech did not provide the Burgundian with any indication he was not being truthful.

The Burgundian leader was surprised at Valerias' response. He was not sure what to do next. Most men readily agreed to pay whatever they could to stay alive, or they were killed.

Valerias, though, had assessed the situation and took command. "I'll tell you what, Burgundian. We will have an archery contest. Pick your man and I will pick mine. If my man wins, you will let us pass safely without paying a tribute. If your man wins, then I won't unleash my Huns on you." Valerias pointed to the frightening group who rode with him.

"What?" the Burgundian replied. Again, he was perplexed about what to say and how to act. "Aren't the Huns a mythical people?" he managed to ask.

"Yes, and they ride with me, Burgundian. They eat the livers of their conquered victims, dead or alive, it doesn't matter."

The Burgundian shook his head. After a long pause, he whistled into the woods and a ragged-looking Burgundian approached carrying a bow. Valerias waved, and Oxanos and another Hun rode up. The Hun carried himself with an intimidating presence that was not lost on the Burgundians.

"See that large tree," Valerias pointed to a tree about fifty yards away, "that has a knot about five feet from the ground? Whoever shoots closest to the knot wins. Your man can go first." Oxanos translated to the Hun archer and Revious translated to the Burgundians.

The Burgundian set an arrow to his bowstring and took careful aim for several moments. He let the arrow go and missed the knot by less than three inches. Normally, it would be an excellent shot. Before the Burgundian archer could look at his leader, the sound of an arrow, immediately followed by a second arrow, flew by their heads. Both arrows hit the center of the knot. The Burgundian leader turned to look at the Hun. He was stunned by the accuracy and speed of the Hun archer, shooting the bow while on horseback. The Burgundian saw all the Huns with bows at the ready. The Romans had drawn their swords and bristled with intensity.

The Burgundian was a survivor. He knew that to fight this Roman and his Huns would be a disaster for him. There would be easier prey along the road.

"You may pass, Roman," he said. "But first, who are you?"

"I am General Marcus Augustus Valerias, defender of Rome."

The Burgundian nodded, his eyes a little wider. "I have heard of you. I thought you were dead."

"I have returned from the dead, and I have a question for you—who are the men hanging from the trees?"

The Burgundian said, "Competitors, scum, and thieves. The forest isn't large enough for everyone. So, it is just us."

Valerias stared hard at the man before turning to his party and ordering, "Let's go." The group left in an orderly fashion.

***

In Augusta Treverorum, Valerias met with Emperor Maximus. They discussed the approaching Saxon invasion in Britannia and the Burgundian bandits. The emperor also expressed concern for maintaining the stability of the Briton kingdom centered in Ratae.

That night, Valerias and Claire dined with the emperor. Afterward, they walked back to their quarters, arm in arm.

"Did you notice anything during our supper with Emperor Maximus?" Valerias asked.

"Are you testing me, husband?" Claire laughed softly as she looked at him.

Valerias smiled, but his face soon lost its softness. "Emperor Maximus has great ambitions. He has set his sights on the south, on the portion of the empire controlled by the boy emperor, Valentinian. After he conquers that, he will turn on Constantinople."

"Are you going to inform Emperor Theodosius?"

"Theodosius is already aware of Maximus' cravings for ultimate power. Anyway, I do not have time to approach Theodosius with my suspicion, no matter how strong." Valerias paused and added, "However, when the campaign in Britannia is over and I do not need Maximus' legion, I will inform Theodosius of Maximus' ambitions."

"I think you would be a wise advisor to Theodosius," Claire said. "He would be well served by your counsel."

"Ha! Emperor Theodosius would take the opportunity to order me to convert to Christianity! I will take my chances to avoid that possibility."

Claire laughed as she squeezed Valerias' arm.

"Besides, my love, we have our own concerns to deal with. I first need to kill Saxons and then meet Drostan. Emperor Theodosius can take care of himself."

XLIII

Crossing Over

The narrow stretch of water separating Gallia from Britannia lay before Valerias and his company, the distant, white cliffs of the coast of Britannia visible across its width. The small port at Caletum bustled with activity. Luxcinious' legion had already crossed and was stationed at the Roman camp just outside Londinium, the same camp used by Divinicus and Garzad, who had recently departed for Ratae.

The Huns had never seen such a body of water before. They were uneasy about crossing on what they thought were nothing more than fancy rafts.

"This is not good, General!" A disturbed Oxanos walked from the edge of the shore and stood in front of Valerias. This time, Oxanos spoke in the Hun language, which Arb translated for Valerias.

"I understand, Tribune Oxanos, but this is the only way to cross over to Britannia. There is no land bridge, magic, or dragon to carry us to the other side."

Oxanos was not humored. "What is to stop a monster from picking us off from the ships? The water is vast and the ships are specks. I have heard your men talk of the kraken. It has many arms and an insatiable hunger for men and horses."

"There are no krakens, Oxanos. I have been on many ships and have never seen a kraken or any other monster." But Valerias' tone lacked confidence.

"General, I don't think you believe what you speak. You dislike the water, as we do."

Valerias knew a candid approach would be best. "You are right, Oxanos. I do not like being on the water. But, as I said, I have sailed on many ships, and here I stand before you and not inside the gullet of a kraken."

Oxanos remained unconvinced. Valerias was at a loss for words and nervously slapped the reins of his horse on the stub of his left arm. He gazed out at a ship that was being loaded. In the lead were Claire, Alena, and Elsha, who were laughing. Their horses, led by attendants, trailed behind them. They quickly boarded when they reached the ship. Valerias stood in silent awe at their lack of apprehension, but he knew he had to continue hiding his own feelings of worry from Oxanos.

"See, Tribune Oxanos, the women are not afraid. We have retained many ships to carry us across, so now we must move."

Valerias took the reins of his horse and headed over to the ship Claire and his daughters had just boarded.

"Oxanos, I want you and some of your men to go with Revious. Flavius will accompany you. Arb and other Huns will go with Bukarma." Valerias pointed to both Revious and Bukarma, who were waiting by their ships. "The rest will go with me."

"The Domina is very brave, General."

"Yes, and she bested some of your warriors in an archery contest."

"True, but we did give her the best bow." Oxanos smiled for the first time since they had arrived at the Gallian shore.

"We will be in Britannia shortly, Tribune Oxanos. Then you and I won't have to go on a ship again," Valerias said with a reassuring smile.

"But what about our return?" Oxanos began to look nervous again.

Oxanos' question caught Valerias off guard. Valerias had not thought of that possibility. He paused before answering. "I cannot predict that which is unpredictable, Oxanos. However, I believe we will have the same discussion about ships and krakens when we return from our war with the Saxons."

Oxanos was not satisfied with Valerias' remark, but he asked nothing further. Oxanos' thoughts had turned to surviving thc upcoming voyage.

Crossing between Caletum and Britannia was uneventful for some of the passengers, and a nightmare for others. For the Romans and Claire, it felt good to be at sea. The salty breeze was refreshing, and the time on board provided a rest. For the men from Menze, and particularly the Huns, the crossing proved to be a challenge. The choppy water made half of the passengers seasick. Those afflicted heaved overboard. Unfortunately, that caused particular anguish among the Huns. Staring into the dark water while retching conjured up terrifying images of monsters lurking in the depths.

Valerias fought hard to keep the contents of his stomach under control. He tried talking to Claire. He focused on the horizon. He gave orders for the sake of giving orders. But nothing worked, and he soon found himself vomiting over the railing of the ship. When he looked up, he saw Oxanos on the next ship over, peering at him. Oxanos was not sick. Valerias cursed his weakness.

"Marcus, how are you faring?" Claire touched Valerias' shoulder.

"I'll be fine as long as we reach land soon. This is embarrassing, Claire. The leader of the army—is sick. And in full view of Oxanos!"

“You are not infallible, husband.”

“That is certainly true on this voyage. When we returned from Britannia several years ago, Titus and Joseph kept me amused during the crossing. Now all I can do is look at the horizon and hope I don’t retch again! The kraken is Oxanos’ worry. I just don’t want to totally lose my insides.”

“What do you know about the Saxons?”

“Not enough. They were always north of where I was stationed. I have talked with Romans who have encountered them. The Saxons are like most barbarians—savages who desire to raid and plunder. There are some who may want land.”

“How will the Saxons organize their forces once they arrive in Britannia?”

Valerias’ thoughts switched from seasickness to the upcoming war. Claire skillfully steered him into explaining battle strategies, weapons, and the crumbling state of the empire. Before he knew it, Valerias was at the shores of Britannia.

“You fooled me, Claire!” Valerias exclaimed as the ship maneuvered into a small bay with a pebble beach. “And what a great trick it was.”

Valerias embraced Claire and kissed her cheek. “You are a better navigator of the mind than either Titus or Joseph. We must now move onto land!”

Valerias chose to disembark in the bay at Dubris with a series of small piers rather than travel by ship to Londinium. He figured most of the men would want to get off the ships and onto their horses as soon as possible. Valerias was correct, because several Huns did not wait for their ships to dock before fleeing into shallow water and then on to the beach.

Oxanos kissed the ground once he reached the shore.

Valerias yelled over to him, "Any casualties during the crossing?"

"Only our insides. But not mine!" Oxanos answered. "How are you faring?"

"Your men will be fine in time." Valerias ignored Oxanos' question. His stomach still churned, but he was determined not to let it show.

"Assemble your people over by that bluff. We need to send the ships back and pick up the rest of our forces before going to Londinium. We will camp here and leave in three days. This is a good time for you to clean your weapons and organize supplies."

Valerias observed Bukarma disembarking from his ship. He and Penelope, with their children, were the last to leave.

"Congratulations, General—you made it!"

Bukarma's grin made Valerias flinch. *I hate the water.* Valerias loathed the way seafaring made him look to others.

"Of course. Did you have doubts?" Without waiting for a response, Valerias continued, "The weather is holding. I want the ships to return to Caletum and ferry back our remaining men, horses, and supplies. There is also additional equipment that General Luxcinious wants us to bring. Since you are so seaworthy, you will bring the rest of our party across the sea. Penelope and the children will stay with Claire and me. Be off, the sea is calling you!"

When Bukarma returned to Britannia, the captains and others prepared animal sacrifices to thank the gods for their safe crossings. Bukarma watched on and shook his head.

"They should be thanking the one true God for their good fortune, not these false idols."

"Thank whatever god you want, Bukarma. I am pleased you are here with me and that our entire company made it safely."

Valerias' tone darkened. "I can't say it is good to return to Britannia."

Revious found Valerias and Bukarma together. "The Huns are becoming restless. They do not like this place. Gerlok and his men are also anxious."

"Tell them we leave tomorrow morning. I cannot wait to arrive in Londinium either. Also, order Elderon to camp with the Huns tonight. Maybe he can be of spiritual value to them. Keep Gerlok's men busy on logistical support. Idle minds are the breeding ground for dissension. I will tolerate nothing from men who deviate from my plan."

The next morning, Valerias' party began their two-day ride to Londinium. Elderon rode with the Huns. *Perhaps there is hope that Elderon will follow Joseph's path*, Valerias noted.

XLIV

To Londinium

The ride from Dubris to the Roman camp outside Londinium went quickly. As he rode, Valerias discovered that his small army had grown in numbers. Over one hundred retired Roman soldiers had joined his group between Augusta Treverorum and Caletum. A dozen more men allied themselves with Valerias after he arrived in Britannia. Valerias now had a small army.

"Many men want to soldier for you," Revious remarked at a resting point.

"I see that. They know I cannot pay them much for their efforts. The treasury pays for the legions; I have to pay for my soldiers."

"They are retired soldiers who served with you and want to serve with you again. They are bored with their lives and seek adventure. Besides, they are confident you will defeat the enemy—as you always do."

"There is not much of a mystery as to why I'm here if veteran soldiers want to join us," Valerias said.

"The men talk among themselves and with soldiers and civilians they encounter. You know rumors fly faster than the truth."

"I recognize many of the old soldiers, Revious. Are any of them scouts who served under you?"

"That would be my secret, General." Revious smiled slyly.

Valerias looked to his side and noticed Gulic sitting forlornly by himself under a tree.

"Excuse me, my secretive scout; I need to address something." Valerias walked over to Gulic. "What disturbs you, Tribune?"

"I am fine, General," Gulic said to the ground.

"No, you are not. Tell me. Soon I will be counting on you in many ways. I cannot have my chief engineer moping under a tree."

Gulic looked up at Valerias realizing he was sincere. "I have no colleagues or friends here. I feel alone."

"That is too bad, Tribune, but I do not feel sorry for you. Being alone clears your mind so you can focus on what needs to be accomplished. Now, tell me what is really upsetting you."

Gulic threw a small rock at a nearby tree. He missed his target and sighed. "Alena has rejected me. She thinks I am not man enough to stand up to you. She thinks I should have been more forceful when I asked you for her hand in marriage."

Valerias looked first at Gulic, then at the sky, and finally over at Alena, who was sitting with Claire, Elsha, and Wolf.

"Come with me," Valerias ordered.

"But . . ." Gulic started to speak and was immediately cut off.

"Now!" Valerias snapped, already walking away.

Valerias led Gulic over to where the women rested.

Valerias didn't waste time with pleasantries. "Alena, Tribune Gulic has informed me that I did not fairly consider his marriage proposal to you. I was not prepared to talk about such a subject when he approached me. But I respect Tribune Gulic. His words have had an impact on me. I will discuss the possibility of your marriage to Gulic with your mother tonight. Your mother and I will reach a resolution soon—assuming you two still want to marry."

Valerias turned to Claire and gave her a fast wink. He glanced at Alena and then Gulic, and in the stern tone of a general said, "I have spent too much time on this matter—there is a war to plan!"

As Valerias marched back to Revious, he had a grin on his face that only Revious could see. Revious tried hard to keep a straight face because Alena was looking directly at him. He said, "General, you are becoming soft in your old age."

"No, I am simply more well-rounded and flexible, Revious. You should try being more like me."

Without waiting for a response, Valerias changed the subject. "Do you think the Huns can ride through Londinium without causing problems among the locals?"

"I do not recommend such a move, Marcus. A parade of foreign barbarians through the city will cause great concern among the residents. You don't want to draw any unnecessary attention to the Huns or your mission in Britannia, or to create a panic."

"Exactly what I was thinking, Revious. Take the Huns, the men from the Villa and Menze, and those who have recently joined us to the encampment outside of Londinium and wait for us. Avoid Londinium. We will not be long. I know a place where Alena, Elsha, Marian, and Penelope and her children will be safe while we travel north. Bukarma, Gulic, and Flavius will go with Claire and me to see them off. These goodbyes can be emotional. The fewer men who are there, the better it will be for everyone."

"As you command, General."

"We will meet you tomorrow evening at the camp."

Valerias whirled around and barked orders to his officers. He told Oxanos that Revious was now in command until Valerias rejoined the company at the camp. He gently requested that Claire, Bukarma, and Flavius prepare the children for the ride into Londinium.

As they were departing, a rider from Londinium galloped up to the group.

"Greetings. I am Leo, son of Bradicus." Leo picked out Valerias from the crowd. "You are General Valerias, correct?"

"Yes."

Leo handed Valerias a letter. Valerias read it and thought of Bradicus, his former administrator.

When he finished, Valerias said to the group, "There has been a change in plans. My friend Bradicus has offered to let you stay at his country farm while we are away. The farm will provide more space and privacy from prying eyes. Bradicus is retired and spends most of his time on the farm these days. Leo runs his shop in Londinium. I agree with Bradicus—the farm is a better option. Lead the way, Leo."

The group rode the few miles to the farm mostly in silence. The approaching separation of parents and children, a husband and wife, and a tribune and his love—possibly for months—weighed heavily on everyone's minds. If things did not go in Valerias' favor, it could be even longer. There was a very real possibility that some of Valerias' party would never return to Bradicus' farm. No one mentioned that, though.

Bradicus met the group as they arrived at the farmstead.

"Marcus, my friend. You made it. And welcome, everyone, to my humble farmstead."

"Bradicus! I thought I would never see you again. Yet here we are. I—we are most appreciative of your hospitality." Valerias embraced Bradicus. "It is good to see you."

Bradicus walked over to Claire, Alena, and Elsha. "I am pleased to once again have you in my presence. It has been many years since you passed through my shop on your way to Gallia and beyond."

Bradicus focused his attention on Claire. “You look radiant, as always, Claire.” Bradicus bent and kissed her hand.

He turned to Alena and Elsha. “How you have grown! You are no longer small children. I see your mother’s beauty in you.”

Valerias introduced Bradicus to Bukarma, Penelope, and their daughters. Flavius and Marian were next, followed by Gulic. After the introductions were completed, Gulic walked firmly over to Alena and grabbed her hand.

Bradicus noticed Gulic and Alena’s affection for each other and said with a smile, “Are these two betrothed, Marcus?”

The question surprised Valerias and he looked to Claire. Claire reflexively looked back at Valerias. Valerias knew he had to say something and blurted out, “We are considering Tribune Gulic’s marriage proposal to Alena.”

“I see. It seems to me that decision should be easy.” Bradicus winked at Alena. “Now come inside for supper. I know you want to leave tomorrow morning to catch up with your legion.”

Bradicus monopolized the conversation throughout the meal, which his guests were thankful for as it took their minds off the approaching separation. After supper, everyone in Valerias’ group experienced a restless night’s sleep.

Early the next morning, Valerias gave Alena and Elsha each a gold necklace he had commissioned specifically for them. At the center of the necklace was a solidus. On one side of the coin was the image of a building that represented the Grand House of the Villa. On the other side, the likenesses of Claire and Valerias had been stamped into the surface.

“This is so we will always be with you,” Valerias said as he gave Alena and Elsha their necklaces. “I love you both.”

Both girls embraced Valerias with tears in their eyes. “We have nothing to give you, Father,” Alena sniffled.

Valerias kept his emotions in check. “Your love is all I want, and I know I have that. I am a happy man. I never thought I would have children, but life is strange. I now have two daughters that I am very proud of. Life is good—very good.”

Claire put her arm around Valerias’ shoulders. Tears streamed down her cheeks.

“Oh, I almost forgot.” Marcus reached into his pocket and pulled out a third necklace that was similar to the girls’, only the coin was slightly larger. He placed it gently around Claire’s neck.

“You know I love you more than my life,” Valerias said as he gazed into her eyes.

He looked at Alena and Elsha. “Your mother’s pendant is slightly larger because your mother is older!” He winked at his daughters.

Valerias continued, “I am leaving Wolf with you, girls. He belongs to you. Let him be your guard, as you will be for Marian. And help Penelope with Evaline and Lavonica when she needs it.”

Valerias turned to Alena. “I will ensure that Tribune Gulic returns to you,” he said, nodding at Gulic, who now stood behind her. Valerias glanced at Claire, who smiled.

“Alena and Tribune Gulic,” Valerias announced, “You have Claire’s and my consent to marry. Your proposal request is granted.”

“Thank you, Father!” Alena gushed as she threw herself into Valerias’ and Claire’s arms.

Gulic stepped forward, “General and Domina, thank you. It will be an honor to join your family.” Gulic’s expansive grin showed his happiness and relief that he finally had Valerias’ and Claire’s blessing. “I give you my word that I will be a model husband.”

“See that you are,” Valerias replied. “See that you are.”

Standing behind Gulic were Flavius and Marian. Valerias noticed Flavius was struggling to tell Marian that he was going away for an indeterminate time. Marian had just lost her mother, and she feared she was losing her father as well. She cried inconsolably. Nothing Flavius said could stop her tears.

"Elsha, take Wolf over to Marian and tell her that you, Alena, and Wolf are staying too. And you will be her big sisters and look after her. Her friends Evaline and Lavonica will also be here with her. I know she looks up to you, and she loves Wolf. Tell her that her father will return soon."

"Can you make that promise?" Elsha asked with tears in her eyes. Valerias knew she was not talking about just Flavius.

"Elsha, I promise to do my best to make sure Flavius returns to Marian. And I promise the same for your mother and me. Hopefully, fortune will smile on us all."

Elsha nodded and took Wolf over to Flavius and Marian, whose tears gradually dried. Valerias pulled Flavius aside.

"The decision is still yours, my friend. You can stay if you want. Perhaps it is not such a bad idea to have an armed guardian here."

"General, I gave you my word and I will keep it."

"Then I am counting on you. Say your farewell to Marian. We leave soon."

Valerias walked over to Bukarma and Penelope as Lavonica and Evaline ran to play with Wolf.

"Your dog has an enormous capacity for punishment," Penelope observed as Evaline and Lavonica pulled, stretched, and rubbed Wolf's fur coat.

Valerias smiled. "He is a good dog; not particularly smart, but loyal. He will watch over you. I pity anyone who tries to come between you and Wolf. Penelope, you will be in charge of the household here. Please use Alena and Elsha when you need help. And thank you."

Bradicus approached Valerias. "What do you want me to do with the volumes of your history, Marcus? I made your requested copies and stored them and the originals in my shop in Londinium."

Valerias recalled his long-ago determination to have scriveners record his history as a soldier and general, his war strategies, and his commentary on the events of the day.

At that time, the manuscripts were Valerias' prized possession. He referred to them as his history. The history was dictated nightly and carried through battle and boredom. Valerias had felt an urgency to record his place in history for the benefit of future readers.

When Valerias retired from the army, he had taken his history to Londinium. There, he retained Bradicus to make copies. Now, many years later, he was not sure that saving his history mattered. His previously important gift to posterity collected dust on a remote shelf in Bradicus' care. *Is it time, destiny, or the seasons of life that cause so much change in a man?* Valerias wondered.

"Did you find my history interesting when you worked on copying the volumes?" Valerias was curious about Bradicus' thoughts.

"To the right person, the information in your volumes would be quite valuable." Bradicus avoided directly answering the question.

"They are yours, Bradicus. Do with them as you wish. I only hope they can be of some use to those who follow."

Valerias grew anxious to leave, so he told his party to say their final farewells.

As they prepared their horses, an unexpected visitor arrived at the farm—a young man on horseback.

"Greetings. My name is Zircronic. I am a scout for General Revious."

"I see Revious has promoted himself again," Valerias chuckled. "Zircronic, the moon is pale."

"No, General, it is red. Red as Zantar's fire breath."

"Good!" Valerias exclaimed.

Bukarma looked at Valerias and frowned, confused.

"Revious and I established a code so we know true messengers from imposters and traitors. You and I should establish a similar system."

"Perhaps we will not be separated, Marcus," Bukarma said teasingly. He then glanced over at Penelope and sighed. "Do you think we will all return?"

"I hope so, Bukarma, with all my being. But, as I told Oxanos when we crossed the sea, I cannot predict that which is unpredictable."

Bukarma was startled by Valerias' response. Usually he was a buoyant optimist, always conveying enthusiasm to his soldiers.

"Mount up!" Valerias ordered. "Let us depart for Londinium and see what mischief General Revious has concocted!"

Final goodbyes were said, and Valerias, Claire, Bukarma, Flavius, and Gulic, with Zircronic in the lead, set course for the Roman camp outside Londinium. Valerias knew a new chapter in his destiny was about to begin.

XLV

War Council

The road to Londinium was soaked in sullen silence. Ten years had passed since Claire left her daughters and joined Valerias in the campaign against the Huns. She had promised herself that she would never leave Alena and Elsha again. Yet here she was, leaving them for another campaign. This time, though, it was to save her son, and perhaps her kingdom. Claire was not a Christian, although she prayed to Joseph's spirit to watch over her family in the coming days.

Bukarma and Flavius were saddened to leave their families. At the same time, both men were exhilarated by the prospect of the campaign. They believed, in their own ways, that God would protect them and they would return to Londinium.

Gulic could only think about his future bride and how wonderful life would be with Alena. He wondered how Valerias would be as a new father. *He is incredibly tough, but I see compassion in his heart.*

Valerias gave the impression that the upcoming war was the only thing on his mind, but that was not so. He was concerned for Claire's safety. She had to survive the war, and he knew there would be trouble in her former kingdom. *There are many enemies in her land who pose a threat to her, including Rega. Eustice's death troubles me—it seems too convenient. I also do not believe that Morguard is dead.*

Before the group reached the Londinium camp, Valerias had a private talk with Bukarma.

"This is the first time I have led officers I don't know—besides you, Revious, and Gulic. I am not familiar with the legions here. My list of allies is short."

"I have heard that General Luxcinious is a loyal man," Bukarma said reassuringly.

"Loyal to whom? Is his loyalty to Emperor Theodosius, Emperor Magnus Maximus, or possibly himself?"

"Probably all three; whatever is convenient at the time." Bukarma knew that his old friend was apprehensive. "It is not like you to worry, Marcus."

"Maybe I'm losing my edge in my old age. There are many things that trouble me. I also know little of the Saxons, including how many will land in Britannia or what barbarian allies will join them.

"I prefer Claire to not be on the battle lines. We were fortunate not to lose her against the Huns. I like to be knowledgeable about everything and in total control—as much as I can be. But I have little control over this situation. So much is unknown."

Bukarma noticed the deep creases on Valerias' face and tried to allay his friend's worry.

"Remember, Marcus, you are the fearsome, undefeated general. Soldiers flock to your standard. Barbarians have bowed before you. You carry the authority of both Emperors Theodosius and Maximus. The men will welcome fighting barbarians more than fellow Romans in a civil war. You underestimate yourself. I still see the powerful general in front of me. Older, but still the great general and a leader of legions!"

"You speak wisely, Legate Bukarma. Yet, I would not have undertaken this campaign without you or Revious. I hope we can find Claire's son. She can stay with him and wait for me until this is over and we have triumphed!"

"That's the General I want to see!" Bukarma cried happily.

***

When Valerias' group arrived at the Roman garrison outside of Londinium, Revious was there to meet them. The group dismounted while Zircronic rode ahead.

"Greetings, General Valerias! I am pleased you found your way here," Revious teased.

"Of course, General Revious. Any reason why we shouldn't have? I realize I did not have our brilliant scout to lead us. Perhaps we found someone better," Valerias teased back while watching Zircronic disappear from view.

Revious suddenly became serious. "I have some news you will not want to hear, Marcus."

"It is about the Huns?" In the back of his mind, Valerias wondered how the Huns would get along with others.

"No, it has nothing to do with them. Thanks be to the gods!" Revious jokingly looked to the sky.

"Did one of the emperors renege on the number of troops he will provide us?"

"No, the emperors have followed through."

Valerias grew more anxious. "Tell me!"

Revious paused and answered slowly. "The tribune who Emperor Maximus assigned to General Divinicus' legion under your command is Garzad."

"What?!" Valerias' face immediately flushed bright red with anger.

"Yes, *that* Garzad," Revious confirmed.

"The man who tried to assassinate me just a short time ago at the Villa?" Valerias fumed.

"Yes, the same man. We should have killed him when we had the chance. But you ignored my recommendation."

"I will continue to disagree with you, Revious. I don't kill Roman officers unless absolutely necessary. And Garzad is obviously a favorite of Emperor Maximus. If we had done away with him, we likely would not have the service of Maximus' legion. Tell me, where is Garzad now?"

"That is the other half of the bad news. Garzad is stationed at Ratae under the standard of General Divinicus."

"What?" Claire was nearby and heard mention of Ratae. She immediately interjected herself into the conversation. "Do you think Emperor Maximus, Garzad, and Rega have formed an alliance?"

"No," Valerias responded. "Not yet. There hasn't been enough time for the three of them to conceive such deviousness."

"I am still concerned, Marcus. Ratae is the major city center in my kingdom. If Rega had anything to do with my brother's death, she will do anything to hold onto the crown, including lying in bed with that dreadful Roman. I know I am a target now."

"I do have some good news," Revious added.

"I hoped to hear some good news from you! You are making this a long day."

"I have heard General Divinicus is jealous of Garzad. He thinks Garzad has risen too quickly through the ranks. General Divinicus is also quietly ambitious, so he might be persuaded to our way of thinking and become our ally."

"When I get the chance, I will meet with General Divinicus alone and try to determine what his intentions are. Whatever the result, I want Garzad to be in the front lines against the Saxons. That will keep him occupied."

Valerias looked around until his eyes lit upon Flavius.

"Flavius, you are not to travel with us to Ratae. The Britons will not be kind to you if you suddenly appear there."

Valerias retrieved and unfolded a map. "Flavius, take the Huns and half of the Roman volunteers. Go to the fort at Branodunum. We will meet you there." Valerias pointed to the spot on the map marked Branodunum. "You are to leave tomorrow at sunrise."

Valerias looked at Claire, who was clenching her fists.

"Claire, I don't think it is a good idea for you to go to Ratae with us either. I fear the situation there is too fluid. You should go with Flavius and the Huns."

"I am not going anywhere without you, Marcus. We are a team. We are stronger when we are together."

Valerias nodded in mild compliance and Claire continued, "I also want to see for myself what the situation is in Ratae. You forget that I still have many allies there."

Valerias replied reactively, "I hope so, because we are going to need their help fighting the Saxons." He paused. "You are right. You should come with me. This time, though, will be different than when we fought the Huns. I knew the men fighting with me. I could count on them. Now, outside of a few hundred men, I am uncertain how the legions will fight. Will they hold their ground? Will they be loyal to me? The unknown increases our risk."

Zircronic approached Valerias in a hurry. "General Luxcinious awaits you, General Valerias," he announced. "Domina Claire and your officers are also welcome to see the general in his war room. Ride with me now."

Zircronic waited patiently until Valerias, Claire, and other members of Valerias' group mounted their horses. He turned his own horse and headed straight into the Roman garrison.

Once they arrived, a swarm of servants emerged from the twilight shadows and stabled the visitors' horses. As Valerias and his group approached the building that housed the war room, a stout younger man burst through the doorway.

"General Valerias!" the man shouted. "I am General Luxcinious of Emperor Theodosius' fifth legion. I have been waiting for you for a week. I hate this camp. I want to fight Saxons!"

Valerias guessed Luxcinious' age to be about thirty-three. He had trimmed, curly black hair and blue eyes, an odd combination that Valerias seldom saw in his men. Luxcinious had a strong, clean-shaven protruding jaw. He wore an impeccable uniform and appeared to have the energy of two men. He reminded Valerias of General Cratus, a former charismatic general from Valerias' past.

Valerias instinctively sensed he would like this man. *If his legion is a reflection of his personality and appearance, I believe the Saxons will have a bad day. I just hope they can fight as well as their general dresses and acts.*

"Come inside, General. Your wife and officers are invited as well." Luxcinious bounded enthusiastically back inside the building.

Valerias and his group followed. Several officers greeted them as they entered Luxcinious' war room. Two things immediately struck Valerias: first, he did not know anyone in the room. Second, he was by far the oldest of any of the attendees. Both thoughts made him shudder.

Luxcinious introduced his officers, and Valerias followed with introductions of Claire, Bukarma, Revious, and Gulic. Flavius had remained behind to prepare the Huns for their march to Branodunum. Luxcinious and his men appeared to be genuinely appreciative of having the great General Valerias in their presence.

After pleasantries were exchanged, Valerias' personality changed abruptly.

"General Luxcinious, officers, we are here today because Emperor Theodosius has given us a charge—defeat the Saxons who threaten Britannia's eastern lands!"

The officers in attendance voiced their approval. Valerias continued, "The Roman army is the greatest force ever assembled on this Earth. I am confident we will crush the invaders and send them back to Saxony!"

More cheers erupted from the crowd. Bukarma smiled and thought, *This is the General I remember. It is good to have him back leading us again.*

"I have brought with me men who I have served with and who will be critical to our campaign. Legates Bukarma and Revious will be my aides and will coordinate my strategy with the army. Legate Bukarma is a weapons expert. Legate Revious has been my chief of scouts for several years. I strongly believe accurate intelligence will give us an advantage over our enemies. We do not have that intelligence at this time. Tribune Gulic will be in charge of all the engineering aspects we need. Flavius, who is not here, is my chief envoy."

"Didn't Flavius fight for Argus during Argus's reign of terror in Britannia?" a voice spoke from the crowd.

"Yes," Valerias answered emotionless. "Flavius reformed and Argus was set to execute him. Fortunately, General Titus intervened, killed Argus, and freed Flavius." Valerias embellished the story to protect Flavius. Valerias knew Titus would have executed Flavius if he hadn't stepped in.

Valerias added, "I trust Flavius implicitly. And he is familiar with the area in Britannia where we are going.

"Domina Claire, my wife, is the former queen of the kingdom in Britannia where Argus usurped her throne many years ago. She has allies there, and she, too, knows the country. Most of us are unfamiliar with this part of Britannia. We will need all the information and help we can get to successfully fight our enemy. I am also hoping the Domina can recruit thousands of her countrymen to join with us against the Saxons.

"As we stand here, I have ordered Flavius to lead a century of Roman cavalry and the century of Huns straight to the Roman fortress outside of Branodunum. The rest of my force will march to Ratae and join General Divinicus' legion."

Before Valerias could continuc, his audience peppered him with questions about the Huns. "Who are they? Where do they come from? What weapons do they fight with? Are they cannibals? Are they demons?"

Valerias laughed at some of the questions. He held up the stump of his left arm, which caught everyone's attention. The room became still.

"They *were* my enemy. They were Rome's enemy. They took my hand from me. But the Huns who ride with us now are not our enemy; they are our allies. They are crucial to our success in this war. They are great warriors. They fight on horseback as well as on foot. I will wager these Huns can shoot arrows from their horses farther and with more accuracy than Roman soldiers standing on the ground. I want the Huns and our legions to conduct joint training sessions when we reach eastern Britannia. We can learn much from them, and we can teach them our skills."

"How did you defeat the Huns at Three Tongues?" Luxcinious asked. "You were severely outnumbered!"

"We had the greatest army ever fielded. The power of Rome was with us. I must add that our allies in the battle, the Goths, fought for their very existence. That is how we defeated the Huns. It took all of us together. That same power is with us in this room right now, and will be with us when we fight the Saxons."

Luxcinious and his officers were in awe. Standing before them was a man undefeated in battle, the general who formed an alliance with the Goth barbarians and defeated the Huns.

Luxcinious spoke. "I believe the primary reason was your leadership, General Valerias. We stand with you as one and are ready to follow your command." Luxcinious stood shoulder to shoulder with Valerias as he spoke, providing a look of solidarity between the men.

Valerias felt good. The nervous qualms he shared earlier with Bukarma had temporarily evaporated. "Let us share wine and toast to that which lies before us. We need to remember what we salute today becomes our foundation in the days to come."

XLVI

LAUNCH

"What a grand sight, cousin!" Staigrik stared out at the crowded bay. Hundreds of warships appeared before him on the calm waters ranging in length from sixty-five feet to eighty feet. They were long, narrow, flat-bottomed, keel-plank ships with oarlocks and no sails. Each ship could transport twenty to twenty-five warriors and one trusted slave.

"Yes, King Staigrik, it is a sight which I doubt any Saxon has ever seen," Borgnar said.

"Our ships are ready. The Angles and Jutes have arrived. There have even been sightings of Frankish ships. Tomorrow we set our eyes to the shores of Britannia and the great bounty it holds!"

"There is tremendous excitement among all the clans," Borgnar added.

"Will my son be prepared to go with us?" Staigrik inquired.

"Of course, my king. That is your will."

"What will be his weapon of choice?"

"Guenter's preference is the seax and short spear," Borgnar explained.

"Good choices. He is not strong enough for the battleax." Staigrik lifted his ax over his head with one arm. "I am sure you have taught my son well in the art of war and combat."

"Guenter prefers the strategy of war to combat."

Staigrik's impatience flashed across his face. "You don't need much strategy when you raid. We will have so many men roaming throughout the Britannian countryside, who would dare stop us? I anticipate the Briton men will shrink from our might and hide behind their women. And we will take their women and kill the men anyway! Then we have the Romans, if they haven't already deserted Britannia. Ha! Why should I be concerned about strategy?" Staigrik took a deep breath and shifted his thoughts. "Is my son still droning on about establishing a damned Saxon kingdom in that pathetic land?"

"No, my king. Raiding and collecting plunder is what is important to him now," Borgnar lied. "But we already have outposts in Britannia. We could add to them. I know we could get volunteers to settle in Britannia."

"First, we raid, and then we can talk about increasing a large permanent Saxon presence there. I am not a fool, Borgnar."

Borgnar looked stunned. It was the first time he had heard Staigrik speak positively about further colonization.

A messenger approached the two men and Staigrik beckoned him forward. "They are all here and present in your Great Hall, King Staigrik," he told the king.

"Tell them I will be there shortly." Staigrik picked up his battleax, gazed once more at the flotilla of ships in the bay, and strode off to the Great Hall. When he reached the hall, he stood off to the side for several moments. The noise level inside rose.

"They grow impatient, my king," Borgnar stated.

"I want them to be. I want them to know who the real king is—me!"

Staigrik entered the hall with a powerful stride. His long, red hair bounced with each step. Behind him came Borgnar and a host of Saxons who had been waiting near the hall. Guenter brought up the rear. The crowd cheered as Staigrik walked to his throne. He oozed confidence with each step. He hopped up to the dais and placed one hand on his throne, adrenaline pulsing through his body.

Staigrik raised his battleax and thundered, "It has begun!"

The crowd responded by banging their shields, pounding their spear handles on the ground, and raising their seaxes over their heads. The moment Staigrik dreamed about for so long had arrived. His powers were at their peak. He was the undisputed master of the northern barbarian tribes.

I know now what it feels like to be a god, Staigrik thought.

After several moments of soaking in the praise that washed over him, Staigrik raised his battleax again and slowly pounded the handle three times on the floor of his dais. He raised his free arm over his head for silence. The crowd quietened down, though the shuffling of feet could be heard as the men jockeyed for the best position to see and hear him.

"Tomorrow at daybreak we say farewell to our families, our homes, and our people for what will be the greatest raiding adventure ever undertaken by the Saxons. With our allies—the Angles, the Jutes, and the Franks—we have assembled over one thousand warships. Twenty-two thousand men stand under our banners. Britannia shall quake and crumble before us!

"We will travel light with minimal supplies; we will take what we need to survive from the Britons. They have much to give us! The stores of our ships will be empty so we can return with the massive treasures we take from the Britons."

A voice cried out from the crowd. Staigrik peered down at the men directly in front of him. Korken, the powerful Angle warlord, stared at him and waved his arm back and forth. Staigrik was annoyed at the interruption but he was aware that he needed to appease the leader of his largest ally.

Staigrik knew what Korken wanted. "My warrior brothers, our allies, the Angles, have requested that we establish additional colonies in the areas of Britannia we conquer. These colonies will be the start of a vast Saxon, Angle, and Jutish kingdom. Future generations of our peoples will then have new land on which to prosper. I firmly support my brothers, the Angles, in this new mission."

Korken nodded with a faint glimmer of a smile. Staigrik felt he had addressed the matter and continued with the conclusion of his speech.

"This will be a glorious time for all our people and for you, my warriors. Your families will sing your praises for generations. Now we drink to our success, and tomorrow we begin our journey to raid Britannia!" Staigrik shouted, waving his ax in the air.

The men yelled loudly and began drinking beer from the great tuns provided for them by their king. At the back of the hall, Guenter could not believe what he had just heard. He left shortly after Staigrik finished speaking. Borgnar met him outside the hall.

"He has humiliated me time and again, Borgnar. He belittled my ideas about establishing a Saxon kingdom in Britannia. He said it was a fantasy. He even cut off my finger because I raised the idea! Now he rolls over to appease an *Angle*. I am his son, and he does not take me seriously."

Guenter took a deep breath and stared at the sky before looking back at Borgnar. "I don't know how my father's grand plan will end. Will it be a great success, or will it end in disaster? I don't know. I do know, though, that he has let the power of his position define who he is.

"He believes this giant raiding party will be easy—simply land on the shores of Britannia and the plunder shall magically be ours! What if the Britons put up greater resistance than he expects? What if the Britons invaded our homeland? Would we fight? Of course we would! We would fight to the death! The Britons will as well. Further, he grossly underestimates the potential for the Romans to mount a campaign against us. The Romans have not given up on Britannia.

"My father thinks only brute force will dominate his enemy. But he is wrong. We need both physical *and* mental powers to wage a successful war. And don't forget the spiritual aspects. I met the oracle today and asked him if tomorrow is the right time to launch our invasion. His response was that the gods are angry with Staigrik. He has not performed the proper sacrifices. He has not been humble before the gods and requested their blessing. The gods will punish us. I don't know if that means during the actual voyage, when we are in Britannia, or both."

Borgnar's brow became more furrowed the longer Guenter spoke. "Guenter, you realize that you are talking treason, speaking ill of our king. Yet there is a hint of reason in what you say. The more ships he sees and warriors he counts, the more intoxicated with power he becomes. I am also concerned about the timing of our attack. My knee has been aching the last two days, which usually portends the approach of bad weather. We should delay a few more days."

Guenter pressed his hand on Borgnar's chest. "We will be all right. I had a vision last night that we were in Britannia."

"Was King Staigrik there as well?" Borgnar asked.

"Yes," answered Guenter. "He was in Britannia with us." Guenter swallowed whatever else he was going to say. "I must go now and say farewell to my mother. I have no idea if I will be returning. I will see you in the morning, my friend. A new life will begin for all of us."

Guenter trudged back to what served as the king's palace, which in reality was a large lodge. His mother, Queen Hildegarde, was waiting for him. Guenter was sullen.

"What is troubling you, son? You know you must go with your father to Britannia. You will disgrace this house if you stay here. Your father is a difficult man, but that does not excuse you from attending to your responsibilities."

Those were not the words of comfort that Guenter expected to hear from his mother. Yet he knew she was correct. He gazed at her and sighed.

"I know my responsibilities and I will not shirk them, Mother. However, many things bother me. Father is in his full glory. He is getting drunk when he should be planning for what our warriors will do once we reach Britannia. To just jump off a ship and begin raiding will not work. He also has not paid the proper tribute to the gods for our crossing the great sea or for our time in Britannia or, finally, for our safe return home."

"Is that what is truly disturbing you?" Hildegarde knew there was another reason for Guenter's distress.

"He accepted the Angle Korken's proposition to colonize eastern Britannia! I have asked for that very consideration for over a year now. Father ignores and derides me on the subject, and gives me horseshit tasks to complete. He even cut off my finger because he thought I was insubordinate to him. I can contribute to our cause! I just have a father who won't let me."

Hildegarde quietly listened and counseled her son. "Your father is a powerful warrior. Men follow him. I was attracted to that power. There is a difference, though, between being a great warrior and a wise king. Your father is not at that point yet. It took my father, your grandfather, several years to become the great king he was. I do not know if your father is able to learn to do what it takes to follow such a path."

Hildegarde took Guenter's hand in hers. "I have asked the gods for your safe return, my son. I believe they will agree to my request. You must return, Guenter, not just for me, but for our people."

There was a loud rustling at the door. Staigrik gradually pushed it open and promptly fell down, drunk. He was disheveled and reeked of beer. He tried to get to his feet but couldn't. Hildegarde and Guenter helped him into a chair.

Staigrik looked at Guenter and mumbled, "I know, I know. It was you who persuaded that damned Angle to talk to me about colonies and the like."

He then focused on Hildegarde and slurred, "I want to get laid one more time before Britannia, and maybe I won't need any Briton whores," before passing out.

Guenter went to bed and had a restless night. One dream was of several beautiful, shape-shifting women from Britannia who wanted him. When he awoke, he found his mother and father talking. Staigrik sat dressed in his war clothing with a full pack on one side and his battleax on the other. His dark red hair with patches of gray flowed down to the middle of his back. His beard was thick and long. Guenter knew his father was an impressive man; he was particularly striking this morning, despite the previous night's drunkenness. Staigrik looked at Guenter. It was not his usual hard glare.

"Are you ready, son?" Staigrik asked.

"Yes, Father."

Guenter collected his pack and weapons, quickly embraced his mother, and walked out the door.

Staigrik shouted to Hildegarde as he left their lodge, "I shall see you again wearing the crown of Saxon glory!"

The reflection of the morning sun glistened off the water between the warships in the bay. The bright light temporarily blinded those facing east. A huge crowd gathered to celebrate the departure of the great fleet, with visions for a triumphant return. Horns blared and drums pounded in excitement as the call went out for the warriors to board their ships.

As they walked to the ship, Staigrik had the appearance and attitude of one who had been sober the night before. He kept a brisk pace and extended greetings to a multitude of men. Guenter knew only a few of them. *Remarkable,* thought Guenter. *He truly is a king.*

When they reached Staigrik's ship, a young Saxon woman approached Guenter. She gave him a bracelet and he in turn handed her a small black rock with an inscription. They briefly embraced and then Guenter boarded Staigrik's warship.

Staigrik smiled at his son's discomposure and remarked, "See, you have a reason to return home and not rot in a foreign land."

XLVII

MORASS

"General Divinicus' lackey, Tribune Garzad, is here, my love. General Divinicus is close behind. Shall we entertain them?" Voltrex seemed bored.

"You know we have to see them, and you are my commander. The power of Rome is still evident here in the kingdom. We can use the Romans to help our cause," Rega said, annoyed with Voltrex's lack of interest.

"Very well. I will arrange the meeting in your receiving room."

Voltrex started to leave when Rega grabbed him by the arm.

"Remember, Voltrex, we want the Romans to accomplish one thing—defeat the Saxons. When they do, they will defeat the enemy that poses the greatest threat to us. And while they engage the Saxons, we can focus on removing Claire as a threat to our kingdom. I suspect her son is not dead. Why else would she come back here?"

"Perhaps she wants to be queen again," Voltrex said, indifferent.

"We have heard from several people who know her that she has no interest in reclaiming her throne. Yet here she is! Actions speak louder than words. She is coming here the day after tomorrow. Then we will learn her motives. She is not here to fight the Saxons. I know she is here to fetch her son and reclaim her crown. We cannot let that happen!"

"She travels with that old Roman General Vapiderias." Voltrex laughed at his own joke.

"You know it is Valerias, Voltrex. Do not insult him. He is the commanding general of the Romans. We need that general to send the Saxons back to their lair."

"Yes, my queen. We can deal with him later if old age doesn't catch him first!"

Voltrex ordered a servant to bring Garzad into the receiving room at the Black Fort. Voltrex left Rega with a dismissive wave of his hand and took his time going to the receiving room. *I do not wait on Romans—they need to wait for me and wait on me.*

When Voltrex arrived, he found Rega already present with Tribune Garzad and Centurion Honorario. Garzad's facial hair engulfed his face, particularly when he was not talking. Both Rega and Voltrex were transfixed by Garzad's prodigious beard. Voltrex started to play a game with himself called "Where is Garzad's mouth?"

Garzad stroked his thick beard as he glared at Rega and Voltrex. "I am Tribune Garzad, commander and emissary from the great Emperor Magnus Maximus. This is my chief aide, Centurion Honorario." Garzad pointed to Honorario. "I am here to introduce General Divinicus."

Garzad was aware that he was being stared at and remarked, menacingly, "I am fortunate to be blessed with the ability to sprout a full beard. It covers all my battle scars. I have fought in many battles and survived. How many battles have you fought in, Briton?" Garzad took an immediate, strong dislike to Voltrex. *Another boorish brat of a Briton,* he thought. *He wouldn't survive one breath in a fight with me.*

Voltrex glared threateningly back at Garzad. *I hate Romans!*

Divinicus chose that moment to enter the receiving room. He was shorter than his officers and had a paunch. Divinicus did not have the appearance of a Roman general that Rega had imagined.

Garzad wasted no time in announcing General Divinicus and continued down the line, introducing Divinicus' officers. Voltrex noticed that Divinicus was frowning. He obviously was not pleased to have entered the room after Garzad and Honorario, and have Garzad introduce his officers.

"Welcome to Ratae, soldiers of Rome, the central city in my kingdom. I am Queen Rega. This is my commander and advisor, Comitem Voltrex."

Comitem. Voltrex had never heard Rega refer to him as her companion at arms before. The use of the Roman description made him chuckle.

"I understand you have come to stop the Saxon invasion of my kingdom. Is that correct, General?"

"Yes, Queen Rega. That is our primary mission. Actually, I have learned it is a kingdom to the east that is in the most danger."

"We are all in danger. The large numbers of Saxons will not stop in the east," Rega countered. "We do not want to disappoint Emperor Maximus, do we?" Rega had a parchment in her hand, which she waved in front of Divinicus.

Divinicus knew the parchment was a letter from Emperor Maximus informing her of his legion's deployment to engage the Saxons. The legion was also to provide stability to Rega's kingdom. Divinicus looked briefly at the letter and at Rega, saying nothing. He passed the letter to Garzad, who skimmed it without expression.

Rega continued, "We understand the other legion under General Valerias' command will arrive tomorrow. Then you will be at full force."

Voltrex observed Garzad wince at the mention of Valerias. He decided to see how much friction there was between Valerias and Garzad.

"Who is in charge of your war effort, General Garzad? Is it you, General Divinicus, or General Valerias?" Voltrex already knew the answer but wanted to hear it from Garzad.

Instead, his response came from an angry Divinicus.

"Comitem Voltrex, Garzad is a tribune, not a general! He is my second in command. General Valerias is the overall commanding general of the legions tasked to engage the Saxons. He is my superior."

Voltrex kept his eyes on Garzad, knowing the conversation made him uneasy.

"I see," Voltrex replied, believing he had found Garzad's sore spot. "Tribune Garzad—will Valerias have a second in command, as you are to General Divinicus?"

"Yes," Garzad snapped.

"Who will have the higher rank, Tribune, you or Valerias' second in command? It seems to me that *that* man should have the higher rank because General Valerias outranks General Divinicus."

Garzad's anger began to infect his thinking. "For a Briton, you pretend to know much about Roman military hierarchy."

Honorario saw the situation deteriorating and intervened. "The integration of our officer corps will occur when General Valerias arrives here. We are not going to speculate further. General Valerias is the commanding general."

Honorario's timing could not have been better as he defused the situation—at least temporarily.

Garzad composed himself and uttered, "Queen Rega, I apologize for my rude behavior."

Divinicus added, “We will leave now and reconvene when General Valerias arrives.”

General Divinicus was disturbed at how the meeting had transpired with Rega and Voltrex. He was supposed to be in charge; instead, Garzad and Voltrex had taken control. He was secretly looking forward to General Valerias’ arrival. Valerias would then take sole command.

The Romans returned to their temporary garrison in Ratae, set up in the old barracks. Garzad spoke quietly to Honorario, “Thank you, Honorario. If you had not stepped in, I would have removed that ass Voltrex’s head! Then the other ass, Valerias, would have removed mine!”

***

Valerias and Claire rode within sight of Ratae. Luxcinious’ legion under Valerias’ command marched behind in crisp formation, with clean, polished uniforms and weapons. It was a sight not lost on Rega, Voltrex, and Garzad.

Valerias sent Revious ahead, who informed Rega, Divinicus, and their attendants to meet him at the council room in the Roman garrison. The reason Valerias requested that Rega meet him there was apparent to all; he was *the* general of the legions in Britannia. Valerias also wanted to show Garzad his place in the Roman hierarchy. He was a tribune, not a general.

Before the meeting convened, Valerias sat with Claire in a small room adjoining the council room.

“I need to make an opening statement to all parties involved in our mission here in Britannia. I must clearly and emphatically declare that I am the general in command.” Valerias paused and carefully pondered his next statement. “Claire, there are underlying interests that may complicate the completion of a successful war against the Saxons.

"The road ahead is filled with uncertainty. I have little familiarity with the legions and their officers that I will command. I do not know General Divinicus. I like Luxcinious, but he tends to be overly obedient. He attempts to hide his ambition. I have found ambitious people, even Roman generals, sometimes are not to be trusted. They are out for themselves, everything else be damned. Still, I will give Luxcinious the benefit of the doubt."

Valerias continued, "I do not trust Garzad, and I do not trust Rega—even though I have never met her."

"I feel Rega is too ambitious," Claire added. "I will *not* give her the benefit of the doubt."

"Lastly, I have concerns about the Huns. Not that they won't be good soldiers, but whether they will follow orders. Moreover, will others let them be good soldiers?"

"I understand all your concerns, Marcus. However, good fortune comes to those who deserve it."

"I am a realist. Things have gone well so far. That includes our confrontation with the Burgundians in Gallia and our crossing of the Narrow Sea. Yet, I feel a turbulent time is coming."

"I take a slightly different view," Claire said. "We are where we are today not because of luck or fate or the gods' will, but because of who we are. It takes a lifetime of experiences and deeds to create us. You are *the General.* That is undeniable, no matter how you see it. That will win the day for us."

"I feel the same toward you, Claire. To many here in Britannia, you are still the queen of your kingdom—regardless of your current title of Domina. Rega knows that and is jealous of you. And your presence here as former queen will help us mobilize an army of Britons to join us in fighting the Saxons."

"I wish Joseph was with us. He would offer calming, reassuring words." Claire noted wistfully. "Do you think, if he were alive, he would have come with us?"

"I don't know what Joseph would have chosen," Valerias answered.

"Perhaps he would have come in order to save his hermitage and the Britons who will be attacked by the Saxons."

"Yes, my love, perhaps. Regardless, with or without Joseph, no god, pagan, or other is going to appear out of nowhere and help our cause. There will be no gods throwing lightning bolts to destroy our enemies. It is up to us to help ourselves."

Valerias looked at the room they were about to enter and said softly, "It is time for me to be the General again."

***

Valerias selected officers, Legates Bukarma and Revious, and Tribune Gulic to attend the council meeting at the garrison. Luxcinious and his officers represented the legion sent by Theodosius. Divinicus and Garzad and his men were representatives of the legion offered by Maximus. The final attendees were Rega, Voltrex, and Rega's bodyguards. Claire stood at Valerias' side.

Valerias merely nodded at the assembled group. "For those of you who don't know me, I am General Marcus Augustus Valerias, Magister Militum, servant to emperors and commanding general of the Roman army in Britannia. This is my wife, Domina Claire. She was once queen of this kingdom."

Several cries of "Hail General Valerias!" came from the Roman officers. There were even a few murmurs of "Praise be to God." Valerias noted that Rega and Garzad showed no emotion. In contrast, both Generals Luxcinious and Divinicus and their men shouted their support. The attitudes expressed by his generals and officers impressed Valerias.

"You may wonder why I am your commanding general, here in this far-off province of the empire. My answer is simple—I win battles and I win wars. I follow the orders given to me by the emperors. Over the years, even though the emperors have changed, my approach has not: bring the emperors a victory while crushing our enemies under Roman boots!"

More cheering erupted from the council.

Valerias continued. "Tomorrow we leave for the fort at Branodunum. My scouts have informed me that the Saxons will land in Metaris Aest near Branodunum, where several rivers meet and the water is shallow enough for a mass landing. They will target Branodunum and the surrounding areas first. They believe there is great wealth there. Queen Claire has informed me the Saxons' expectations will not yield reality." Valerias noticed Rega's face cringe when he referred to Claire as queen.

Valerias opened the meeting to questions.

Rega immediately asked, "Will Claire go with you to Branodunum?" She refused to address her as queen.

Valerias responded, "Yes, she will. Domina Claire has a business matter to attend to in Branodunum. After she concludes that matter and we defeat the Saxons, she will return to Italia with me."

Rega was about to ask another question, but Valerias cut her off, noting, "The Domina goes with me on campaigns. She was with me in the Battle of Three Tongues against the Huns. Her presence will not hinder the campaign. In fact, she can help me interact with the local people, as she speaks their language; I do not."

Valerias glanced at Claire and noticed she had locked eyes with Rega.

"Tell us about the Saxons, General," an officer asked.

"I know little about them," Valerias admitted.

Voltrex smirked. Valerias ignored him and continued.

"However, I know much about barbarians; I have fought them all my life. The Saxons are simply another barbarian horde. They come to Britannia to raid and plunder. Once they have what they want, they will return to their homeland, although some Saxons may desire to stay. It doesn't matter. The objective of our campaign is to halt their invasion and send their battered corpses back to their homeland."

"The Roman army has brutalized civilian populations in the past," Voltrex said, his voice dripping with disdain. "Will your legions take their own plunder from the Britons before or after the conflict with the Saxons? Or both?"

Valerias gave Voltrex a glare so icy he took a step back. Valerias stared at him, then at Rega, and finally back to him.

"You know little," Valerias said brusquely. "My legions do not harm civilians. My men know that to commit crimes against civilians, such as robbery or bribery, will result in flogging. Any soldier who commits rape will be executed. Now tell me, comitem, how have you treated the men and women who have not agreed with Rega's rule?"

"That is not your concern," Rega answered for Voltrex.

"Precisely, and you have no involvement in how I command my legions. Do not interfere with my campaign and we will not have a problem. If you interfere, I can snap two necks just as easily as one."

"Are you threatening me?" Rega was beside herself with anger, but kept her temper in check.

"Not if you keep out of my way. You do that, and once we crush the Saxons, we will leave Britannia. You will then be free to do what you want."

"I have Emperor Maximus' support," Rega said with assurance.

"I have the *emperors'* support—both Theodosius and Maximus—whom I know personally!" Valerias countered sternly.

The room fell into silence and Valerias dismissed the council. As they began to leave, he ordered the Roman generals to be ready to march in the morning. The last men to leave were Garzad and Honorario. Meanwhile, Claire signaled to Rega that she wanted to talk privately with her. Bukarma went with Claire; Revious stayed with Valerias.

"Well, Garzad, we meet again," Valerias said. "Only now I'm not the old retired fool, I am your commanding general."

"I suppose you will strip me of my title. Will that be your revenge?"

Valerias ignored him. "I have asked my colleagues, and they said your fighting skills are exceptional. Your leadership capabilities are suspect, though. You have never led a legion into battle."

"I am as qualified as either General Divinicus or General Luxcinious."

"We shall see, Tribune Garzad. Be warned—I am aware of your role in undermining Emperor Gratian. As we know from our past together, I do not want your knife sticking in my back."

Garzad was stumped. *How did Valerias know about my involvement with removing Gratian from the throne? Which general told him? Was it Emperor Maximus, himself? I must be careful to whom I talk in the future.*

"I chose Emperor Maximus over Emperor Gratian. Gratian was weak and prone to allowing barbarians inside his court. Maximus will lead Rome back to its glory," Garzad spoke forcefully.

"Perhaps," replied Valerias. "However, I never want to hear about you taking the same type of action against me as you did with Emperor Gratian. I deal harshly with traitors. Just ask anyone who knows me."

Garzad began to respond but was cut off sharply.

"You are to remain the subordinate tribune under General Divinicus. You will remain so until I find something that justifies your removal. Coordinate with your general and have your legion ready to march tomorrow with clean uniforms and polished weapons. Dismissed!"

Garzad knew he had no other course of action. He replied, "Yes, General," and left the room.

As he walked out of the building, he spoke quietly to Honorario. "No one talks to me like that. When this campaign is over, I will show that damned old man just how much death can hurt."

Back in the council room, Revious paced uneasily. "Garzad is not to be trusted, Marcus."

"I know. Have your men watch him closely. I will choose the opportune position for him when we fight the Saxons.

***

Claire and Rega met immediately after the council meeting in a small room off of the main room. Bukarma and Voltrex stood outside in the hallway, ignoring each other.

"Queen Rega," Claire began. "It is time that I finally met you. My brother spoke highly of you when he wrote to me."

"Yes, Eustice spoke well of you. Your escape from Argus is legendary. Eustice recounted your courage and desire to survive."

"I had my daughters to care for. I did it for them."

"Where are your daughters now, Claire?"

"They are in Italia, at our Villa," Claire lied.

"When the king died, I was brokenhearted. We were planning to have our first child. Eustice always wanted an heir. I wanted children, like you have."

"Are you with child?" Claire was surprised by Rega's statement.

"No, we were not so blessed. Now I fear I will be childless." Rega quickly changed the subject. "Why are you traveling with General Valerias? I thought you would want to be with your daughters."

"My husband and I agreed that I should accompany him. As he said, I have affairs to take care of in Branodunum. I want to be there before the Saxons arrive."

"What business?"

Claire tried to downplay her reasons by saying, "Property records and other business matters."

Rega was distrustful. "Will I see you again, Claire?"

"I do not think so. I would like to return to Italia as soon as possible. Do not worry Rega; I abdicated my throne to Eustice. It is yours. I have no desire to reclaim it."

"Good," Rega replied firmly. "There is only room for one true monarch in our kingdom. You had your opportunity and now it is mine. Have a safe journey. I hope you find what you are looking for in Branodunum."

With her final statement, Rega left the room and called for Voltrex. They left the garrison, accompanied by Rega's bodyguards.

Bukarma joined Claire.

"I don't trust her, Bukarma. I wager she will have spies on the way to Branodunum within the hour. I pray to the gods and Joseph's God that they protect Drostan, Father Timothy, and his order."

On the following morning, Valerias' legions departed for Branodunum.

XLVIII

BRANODUNUM

Valerias felt the urgency of time. Even though the legions were primarily infantry based, they made excellent progress after departing Ratae. Valerias kept his two ambitious generals and Garzad occupied to avoid any scheming or infighting. At Valerias' request, Revious planted spies within each legion to gauge the soldiers' mood. So far, morale was excellent. Valerias believed, though, that once they reached Branodunum, the generals and Garzad would have time for idle thoughts.

The legions advanced east and stopped at a village between Ratae and Branodunum. There, Valerias ordered his men to rest. Valerias and Claire left the group for a short ride in the surrounding country. To excuse their absence, Valerias told his officers that Claire wanted to visit a relative who might have information regarding Branodunum.

One mile south of the village, the two dismounted at a small house where several horses were tied to a post. Eight men stood as Claire and Valerias entered through the only door. The men bowed to Claire. All were Britons.

"Queen Claire, we have waited for your return," a white-bearded man said. He had a long face, creased with age and a thin, pointed nose.

"Weylyn, it is good to see you again," Claire replied, smiling. Weylyn had been a village leader when Gerhard and Claire ruled the kingdom.

"We also extend our greetings to your husband, General Marcus Augustus Valerias."

The men didn't know what to think of Valerias. He was Roman, not Briton, but he was Claire's husband, and he had come to fight for them.

"My husband and I need your help," Claire said.

"More importantly, you need our help." Valerias immediately took command of the room. He began in the Briton language and then switched to Latin, with Claire interpreting.

"I do not need to tell you that the Saxons are on their way here in staggering numbers. I don't know if they plan to plunder and return to their homeland or stay here. If they defeat us, I believe they will stay and more Saxons will come. They will gradually take over a large area of Britannia, perhaps all of Britannia.

"It *is* Britannia that is being threatened by the Saxons, not Rome or Constantinople. We must stop them on the shores. To accomplish that, we need as many men as you can muster. You will have to mobilize quickly and come to Branodunum within days. We will need to set our defenses, and you are a key part of our strategy. We need each other to be successful."

"How many Saxons are there?" one of the men asked.

"We do not know, exactly. Our estimates are between twenty and twenty-five thousand Saxons and their allies. They all want a piece of your country."

Valerias could see apprehension in the men's faces.

"Years ago, I fought a battle against one of the most fearsome enemies I have ever encountered—the Huns. They were on the verge of destroying the Goth kingdom. Together, with the Goths as our allies, we defeated the Huns. The Goths who fought with me were as brave as any man I have fought with in battle. Today, there are Huns serving in my army, and they will fight for you.

Now, it is your turn. You must fight for your women, your children, yourselves, and your country. We Romans will do what we can—but it is up to you to protect your homeland!"

Valerias' voice grew stronger with each word. At the end of his speech, the Britons were engaged and eager to fight. The group spent the next hour discussing logistics before Valerias and Claire left to rejoin the legions.

As they mounted their horses, Weylyn asked Claire, "Will you ever return to the throne, my queen?"

Claire smiled and Valerias answered for her, "We shall defeat the Saxons first before discussing other matters."

Claire and Valerias rode back to the Roman camp. On their way, Valerias pondered Weylyn having spoken of the issue that he and Claire would need to address at some time: the future of Claire and her kingdom. He decided not to broach the subject now, turning his mind instead to preparing for the Saxons.

"Tomorrow we arrive in Branodunum, and the focus of the campaign will change. It will no longer be about getting there, but about how best to set our defenses against the Saxons."

"I understand, Marcus. However, I'm concerned about your safety. I think an assassination attempt on your life is possible."

"Perhaps, but unlikely. I have become more comfortable with Generals Divinicus and Luxcinious. The generals and Garzad are more concerned with each other than with me—traits I can use in my favor.

"They know I am the commanding general for only a short while. Then, if the position opens, there will be the fight to become my successor. I'm sure all three men believe they should be commanding general. But it is up to fate and the emperors to decide.

"What's ironic is that none of them is competent to be *the* leader. Revious tells me the men in General Divinicus' legion don't care for him. He is quiet and keeps to himself. General Luxcinious has tried so hard to curry my favor that he has alienated his own men. And then there is Garzad. He is a lower rank than the generals, and does not have his own legion. The soldiers will have a hard time following him."

"I know your reputation is such that any man would have to think twice about confronting you," Claire said. "But I still worry about your well-being."

Valerias ignored Claire's worry and changed the subject. "Our second set of concerns is Rega and her lackey, Voltrex. She reeks of ambition. He has little conscience, perhaps even less than Garzad. It also doesn't take much imagination to think that Rega and Voltrex are lovers. Ambitious lovers can do horrific things to get what they want."

Claire reflected, "It is amazing to think about what has transpired within the last ten years in my kingdom. First, there was Gerhard and me. Second was the serpent, Argus, and Flavius—I thank the Christian God for Flavius' reform—then Eustice, and finally Rega and Voltrex."

"You forgot Morguard. He was worst of all." Valerias spit as he named Morguard. "Even Joseph would have had a difficult time finding his soul."

"Oh, I didn't forget him. We both came within an eyelash of being killed by him. Remember, though, he was an instrument of Argus."

"They are both in the darkest depths of Tartarus and pets of the hydra," Valerias said conclusively. He wanted to move on.

"When we arrive at Branodunum, we need to plan your meeting with Drostan. I do not trust the group of Britons Rega sent with us. You do not want them to know that Drostan is alive. You will go with a Roman escort—men who were at the Villa and scouts handpicked by Revious. I will meet Drostan later, when I have better control over our war preparations."

"I am so excited to see Drostan after all these years. How do you think he will react to seeing me?"

"I think he will be a tangled mass of emotions. You should be ready for anything. He will be resentful that you didn't come for him earlier or engage him as his mother. After you get over the initial difficulties, he will ask questions. Just be tolerant and patient. It has been ten years."

"Do you think he will leave Father Timothy's hermitage and come with us?"

"No, at least not at first. He may change his mind after his initial anger subsides. Don't hesitate to blame me for your not seeing him sooner."

"I am not going to blame you, Marcus."

"Be prepared, Claire. He may choose not to come with you. He seems to have affection for the abbot's order. If he doesn't come and wants to join the order, you should let him. He may change his mind later."

"It would be too hard for me to leave the hermitage and not bring Drostan with me."

"Drostan *is* going to leave the hermitage. We will move his religious order out of the hermitage to avoid the Saxons and relocate the brothers to a safer place. So, he will move out. It is just a question of whether he comes with you or stays with his order."

***

Valerias and his legions reached Fort Branodunum. The fort had been built around 230 AD during the reign of Emperor

Severus to guard against uninvited approaches to the estuary. The fort was rectangular with rounded corners. The solidity of the fort gave Valerias an inner satisfaction that the empire was still strong and standing.

Revious rode ahead to notify the fort's commander, General Quintus, of Valerias' arrival. Valerias did not know Quintus but heard he was a capable fort commander.

Quintus and Revious met Valerias outside the main gate.

"Greetings, General Valerias. On behalf of my officers, welcome to Fort Branodunum."

"Greetings to you as well, General Quintus. We are glad to be here." Valerias returned Quintus's salute. "I bring two legions with me, one legion provided by Emperor Theodosius, the other sent by Emperor Maximus."

Valerias watched his legions march formally toward the fort. The cavalry units for each legion followed behind the infantry, the sun gleaming off the soldiers' polished armor and weaponry. Quintus nodded, impressed.

Valerias turned back to face Quintus. "General, this is my wife, Claire, the Domina. She is the former queen of the kingdom centered in Ratae."

General Quintus was tall and was not wearing his uniform. His dark, curly hair was on display, matching his short, trimmed beard. To Valerias, he resembled his former second in command, General Braxus.

Quintus nodded at Claire and pointed to the south where there was a cluster of tents. "Your early arrivals are over there, General Valerias. There are about two hundred Romans and one hundred warriors from the Hun tribe."

"I assume they have not given you any trouble, General Quintus."

"No trouble," Quintus confirmed. "They stay to themselves. The Huns are an odd people, though. Where did you find them?"

"They found me," Valerias replied. "They are from the people I fought against at the Battle of Three Tongues. These particular Huns are exiles who fled their own people who were trying to enslave and kill them. They found their way to my estate in Italia. You should know, they are incredible fighters and amazing archers. Have you conducted any training with them?"

"No, not yet."

"You will," Valerias said with a smile.

***

Valerias gave the legions the rest of the day to set up their camps. While they arranged themselves, he counseled with Revious. Afterward, he summoned the leaders of the legions to the fort, where he had established his headquarters.

As usual, he began his staff meeting briskly. "We are obtaining more accurate intelligence from our sources about the strength of the Saxons and where they will likely attack. We know they have at least twenty-two thousand men and over one thousand warships. They have left their shores and are on their way here."

A small groan rippled through the men. Someone shouted, "They will outnumber us three to one!"

Valerias' temper flared. "We do not have time for cowards here. If you are afraid, leave now!" No one moved or made a sound.

Valerias calmed and continued. "On numerous occasions my army has been outnumbered. But that didn't matter. We outsmarted them, we were better prepared and equipped, we were stronger, and we defeated them. Ultimately, the Roman army was victorious in every battle. I have no intention of losing this war to an inferior enemy—even though they may have more men. Roman soldiers do not shrink from such a challenge. I do not shrink from this challenge. Do you accept this challenge, as I do?!"

"Hail Rome! Hail General Valerias!" rang out from the crowd.

Valerias was satisfied that his command would not be questioned again. He then said something that surprised the men.

"I will be leaving the fort for possibly two weeks to recruit more men. My goal is to form a limitanei legion that will join the comitatenses legions under Generals Luxcinious and Divinicus. I also have General Quintus's soldiers under my command. I have asked the Domina to do what she can to rally the Britons. If our efforts are fruitful, we won't be so outnumbered." Valerias spoke the last sentence with a hint of sarcasm that was not lost on the attendees.

"Who will be in charge while you are away?" Garzad asked contentiously.

Valerias had anticipated this question. "My legates, Bukarma and Revious, will remain at the fort."

"But they are not generals!" Garzad protested. The other generals nodded as well.

"I did not say they would be your superiors, did I?"

"You implied . . ."

"I implied nothing!" Valerias interrupted. "You will all maintain your positions. I have no intention of undermining your authority. I will give each of you a set of orders that I want carried out while I am away. Legates Bukarma and Revious will ensure that my orders are obeyed. I would also like to remind you that Bukarma and Revious have more battle experience than all of you combined. You should be thankful for any knowledge they share with you. Learn from them. Learn from the Huns. When you go against a formidable enemy, you will need that experience and knowledge. Now, are there any more questions?"

No more questions were asked. Valerias looked around the room and said, "Meet here tomorrow at first light for your orders. You have a long way to go to prepare for this war."

As the men filed out, Valerias called out for Gulic.

"Yes, General?" Gulic asked.

"I have a special project for you. I want you to form an artillery division. Build as many portable catapults and stone and bolt throwers as possible. They must be mobile. The Romans from the Villa will help you. I will also see to it that each legion and General Quintus contribute twenty-five men with engineering backgrounds. That should give you more than two hundred men. You have two weeks to complete the work. The Saxons may be here by then."

That night, after all the officer meetings were completed, Valerias sat with Claire in their quarters at the fort.

"I am tired, my love," Valerias confessed. "The vigor I possessed when I was younger has drained out of me. I also do not have the officer corps that I had in previous campaigns. I am too old to manage officers who need nursing. It used to be much easier. Today, I am mentally and physically spent."

"I understand, husband." Claire gently rubbed Valerias' sore shoulder. "It has been a long journey since we left the Villa."

"I will be fine. The upcoming trip to Hadrian's Wall will do me well. I am looking forward to recruiting new soldiers and visiting the wall, which is something I've always wanted to see. Imagine a wall that stretches all the way across northern Britannia . . ."

"Why Hadrian's Wall?" Claire wondered.

"Because it represents Rome's power. It was built at a time when the empire was at its pinnacle—when barbarians feared mighty Rome. Now barbarians seem to be lodged in every nook of the empire. And they no longer fear Rome. The slow deterioration of the empire makes me yearn for the old days. Adrianople set the foundation for Rome's decline."

Valerias grew quiet as he withdrew into his thoughts.

"Who are you taking with you?" Claire asked as she continued to rub his shoulder.

Her voice jolted Valerias back to the present. "I am taking Flavius, two guides Revious recommended, and a squad of eight cavalrymen I selected. We will travel fast; we don't have much time. We need more men, and I know where to find them.

"Bukarma, Revious, and the generals will have difficulty maintaining control over Garzad while I am away, but I have given Garzad several tasks to complete. Hopefully, that will keep him occupied and out of mischief until I return."

Valerias gently took ahold of Claire's hands and looked deeply into her eyes. "Tomorrow you will be reunited with Drostan. I truly hope it goes well—for both of you."

"I am nervous. I think he will reject me." Claire's brow furrowed.

"If he does, then when I return, I will introduce him to the Huns. That may change his mind!" Valerias smiled.

"Your words are odd, Marcus, but I appreciate your sentiments." Claire also smiled.

"I have arranged a Roman escort to accompany you to the Branodunum hermitage. You should remain with your escort at all times. The Britons have asked to join your escort, and I reluctantly agreed. They would come even if I did not give them permission. This way we can keep an eye on them. Beware—I repeat that I do not trust those Britons Rega sent with us. I believe they killed your brother, and they will kill you and Drostan the first chance they get. You should only be gone for one day. I will send Revious with you. His presence will keep any enemy in check. I also want Elderon to accompany you. It is time he sees what a real Christian community is like."

"I agree with all that you say, Marcus. I wish I didn't have to waste your resources."

"Nonsense. You are a queen, and a queen deserves the appropriate escort. You are also my wife, the Domina. Now let's rest. Tomorrow will come soon enough."

Valerias put his arm around Claire and gave her a kiss, which she eagerly returned.

XLIX

REUNION

Claire woke early the next morning as the sun broke through the slit of a window in their quarters. Valerias had already left, as was his custom. Claire saw something shiny on the windowsill and walked over to it. The object was Valerias' dagger, which he usually kept strapped to his leg. It was the same dagger he gave her whenever he thought she needed to protect herself. There was a note attached to it.

> My love, think of me when you hold this dagger. It will protect you. I will return in two weeks. I look forward to meeting Drostan. May the gods be with both of us.
>
> Love, Marcus

Claire turned the dagger over in her hands, admiring its beauty as she had done numerous times. She remembered the first time she held it when she was in the cave with Alena and Elsha years ago when Morguard's men had surprised her. She shuddered at the memory and placed the dagger gently on a nearby table.

Claire heard a knock at her door. She opened it and saw Revious standing impatiently.

"We must leave now, Claire. Your escort is ready. We found Elderon in the camp with the Huns. He is with us."

"I am ready."

"I question the motives of the two Britons who insisted on accompanying us," Revious remarked. "We must make sure there are trusted men between you and them. I do not want to be responsible for the assassination of a domina, a queen, *and* my friend."

"I agree, and Marcus gave me something to protect myself."

Claire pointed to the dagger on the table. She placed the blade in a sheath that she wore at her waist. Revious gave her a nod of approval.

The ride to the hermitage went without incident. Revious positioned himself with Claire, followed by the Roman guards and Elderon. The two Britons rode toward the end, followed by two Roman soldiers.

Within half an hour, they reached the hermitage at Branodunum. The main gate opened and the riders entered the courtyard and dismounted. Claire was struck by the carefully tended flowers planted around the edges of the courtyard. *I am impressed. Someone here takes great pride in keeping such a peaceful and beautiful garden. I especially like the pink roses.*

Father Timothy hurried out of the main building, followed by several frantic monks.

"My lady!" he announced as he bowed to Claire.

Claire was embarrassed. "Father Timothy, I am no longer a queen and you should not bow to me. In fact, it is I who should bow to you. Is there somewhere we can talk privately?"

Father Timothy led her to a small room off of the courtyard. Once Claire was sure they wouldn't be overheard, she opened up.

"My dear Father, you have taken such good care of my son for so many years."

Claire gave Father Timothy a heartfelt embrace that surprised him. He returned the embrace.

"I have waited for this day for what seems like forever," Father Timothy exclaimed.

"I cannot imagine the stress you have been under, Father Timothy. You had to look after and teach my son, protect him, and not let anyone know our secret. You taught him to be a man. I am in your debt."

"Nonsense. I have learned over time what it takes to be a good Christian. I pray to God that I am one." Father Timothy added, "Where is your husband? I thought he would have accompanied you."

"The General, Marcus . . ." Claire stuttered. "He went north to recruit more Roman troops. We will need them to fight the Saxons."

"That is too bad. I was looking forward to meeting him. He has been a great benefactor to our hermitage. And he is not a Christian."

"No, he is not," Claire confirmed. "In many ways he acts like a good Christian, but he will never convert. I hope you will meet him one day and have a chance to discuss Christian theology. He and Joseph were close friends, and they had many insightful conversations about religion. I assume you heard of Joseph's death. He was murdered at the hands of a mad Christian priest."

"Yes, I heard of the bishop's tragic death. I knew from the first moment I met Joseph that he was a good man. I pray every day for his soul."

"Now you can see why my husband and I will not join your faith—at least until Christians cease fighting about words and start carrying out the mission set by your Christ."

"It is not always an easy road we travel. I suppose the hermitage insulates us from some of what goes on out there."

Father Timothy swept his arm out in front of himself, gesturing to the world at large.

After a few seconds of staring wistfully, Father Timothy asked, "And what about you, Claire?"

Claire pretended she did not hear him and quickly changed the subject, "I must tell you that Marcus wants you to relocate, at least temporarily. He thinks the Saxons will target the hermitage first. They believe you hoard the treasures they desire, such as gold and jewels. They will not spare anyone. They will rob you and either kill you or enslave you. It will be a tragic ending for your order. Be ready to depart when you receive word. Marcus will send an escort for you and your men. Pack all your necessary belongings—you may not be returning."

"It will be difficult to convince all my brothers to come with me. They think God will protect them against their enemies."

"I can promise you that your God will not protect them. Make sure it is done. Anyone who stays behind does so at their own risk. They will become a martyr to no one."

"I understand," Father Timothy said with a quick nod. "I will do my best. I believe you would like to see your son now."

"Yes, I would. But first, tell me—how does he feel toward me?"

Father Timothy's face creased in consternation, but he tried to soften it. "Conflicted. He has very mixed feelings about you and his situation. He repeatedly says he wants to become a brother of our order, and I have repeatedly refused his requests. I told him to wait until you talk to him. I do not know what is best for him. God has given me no answers."

"Take me to him, please." There was a touch of uncertainty in Claire's eyes.

Father Timothy led the way to the room where Drostan awaited his mother's arrival. He was gazing out the window at the sea.

"Drostan, your mother is here. I will leave you two alone. My study is just down the corridor on the right, should you need anything." Father Timothy bowed slightly to Claire.

"Thank you, Father Timothy," Claire said as he closed the door behind him.

Claire was left alone with her son, whom she had not laid eyes on since he was a child. *So much time, so many years.*

"You look well, my son," she began, thinking it a safe way to open. "Father Timothy . . ."

"How would you know how I look? Would you know if I looked sick? Perhaps I am sick now and you just can't tell."

"You . . ." Claire was startled by Drostan's harsh interruption.

"Why don't you allow me to become one of the brothers here? It is what I want! I am a man now. You have no say in what I do! I have no desire to become a king over this vermin-infested land. Look at you, *Mother.* You were a queen once, now you are the wife of a Roman butcher."

"That butcher, as you call him, saved my life and your sisters' lives. He is a wonderful husband and man, and a good father to Alena and Elsha!"

"You insult my father. He is your real husband and my sisters' real father. He is my father, not some Roman dog!"

Claire drew in a deep breath, "I loved your father, but he died on a foolish expedition orchestrated by Argus. You remember Argus? He was going to murder you. And he was also going to kill me and your sisters. Is that what you would have wanted? It is only by the grace of the gods, a few kind people, and Marcus that we are all alive today."

"Yes, it was the gods," Drostan spat. "You live under Roman rule in a Roman land with a Roman killer. The Romans are occupiers of our land."

"I live where I choose to live, and that is with Marcus. Do you know that he is here in Britannia *voluntarily* to try to stop the Saxons from taking our land? He is risking his life to save Britannia. And he is here to escort me to you."

"I would rather live with the Saxons than any Roman, Mother."

"You insult me, Son!" Tears of anger formed in Claire' eyes. "You can stay here and see what the Saxons bring for you. You said Marcus is a butcher—I assure you he is not. You will be praying for him when the Saxons come. You will learn what butchery really is!"

Claire could not take the pain anymore. She turned and hurried out of the room before she became even more emotional. Father Timothy waited in the hallway and led her gently into his study.

"Forgive him, Claire. He will think about what he has said and will apologize. That was ten years of pain he has kept inside. That pain just exploded, and he took it out on you. I will work with him. I know Drostan to be a receptive and understanding young man. Just give him time."

"Thank you, Father. You are a good man." She embraced him.

A knock at the door heralded Revious' arrival. He entered and saw Claire's tears. He knew things had not gone well.

"Father Timothy, as I'm sure Claire told you, you will need to abandon the hermitage—at least until the Saxon threat is gone."

Revious said no more but turned and walked down the corridor to Drostan's room and stood in the open doorway.

"I am Revious, Roman Legate and friend of General Marcus Augustus Valerias and your mother. Begin collecting whatever belongings you want to take with you. We are pulling out of here shortly. I will take a personal interest in making sure that you depart from here safely." He glared coldly at Drostan as he spoke.

Drostan looked at Revious without saying a word. He noticed that Revious did not have the common characteristics of Romans that he imagined, particularly his long, curvy mustache.

Revious left Drostan's room and strode down the corridor issuing the same command to the other brothers in the order, only not as harshly.

Claire did not say a word as her group returned to the fort from the hermitage. Claire's long anticipated reunion with her son had been a heart-wrenching failure.

L

HADRIAN'S WALL

Valerias, Flavius, and their escort left Fort Branodunum at first light. Following their guides, the group maneuvered through the Fens to the south of the estuary. Once the Fens were cleared, Valerias turned north to Hadrian's Wall.

The countryside grew bleaker the further north they traveled. The guides told Valerias that there were many reasons for the desolation. The region was still recovering from a recent invasion by the Picts and Scoti tribes. Roman military presence was also much scarcer than in previous times. The people who remained in the area feared that additional attacks by the northern and western barbarians were imminent, and that the Romans would not be able to stop them.

Then there were the widespread rumors of the coming great Saxon invasion. Many locals believed the Saxons would take over the entire country, including northernmost Britannia. They also heard that not only were the Saxons seeking plunder, but they practiced cannibalistic rituals.

Valerias laughed when he heard that rumor. "I have seen more barbarians than you could ever imagine," he told the guides, "but I have never seen a barbarian cannibal."

The guides were not comforted by Valerias' words.

Valerias crossed the river Tyne and arrived at the small Roman military compound at Corstopitum, south of Hadrian's Wall. There, he and his men spent a quiet night. Early the next morning, they set off for the wall. On the outskirts of a nearby village, Valerias spied a small cemetery just off the road. He stopped there, dismounted quietly, and walked through the unkempt grounds. Weeds sprouted around every gravestone; no one had visited the cemetery in years.

Flavius joined Valerias while the rest of the escort remained mounted.

"Why did we stop here, General?"

"Because I want to pay my respects to those interred here."

"But you don't know anyone who has been buried here, do you?"

"No."

"I do not understand, then."

"Look at the graves, Flavius. Many are Romans. They have been neglected for a long time. Some have the Christian cross, others have pagan signs I don't recognize. This one over here has no legible marker. At least, I assume it is a burial plot. Do you think anyone remembers the people buried here?"

"I don't know," Flavius replied. "Perhaps."

"Why does this matter, you are undoubtedly asking yourself. Is the old general losing his mind? Let me tell you. In a few short years, this will be us: dead and forgotten. Maybe not right away—our children will remember us—but that is about the limit of time that will be allotted to our remembrances. Then we will be forgotten."

"Marcus, you are a famous general. Your name will be remembered forever."

Valerias smiled with an air of resignation. "No, it won't. Maybe a generation or two, but surely no more than that." Valerias waved his hand in the air to indicate the passing of time. "And after we leave this earth, how will we be remembered? Will I be written about as a cruel and inhuman killer or a brilliant Roman general? Who will write these words? I have my own written history, but I doubt anyone will read it. And if they do, will they believe it? What will people think when they read about me?"

"It will be better for you than for me." Flavius spoke quietly as he looked at the funeral monuments around him.

"I disagree—I don't think it will be any better for me." Valerias pulled a tall stalk of grass and tucked it in the corner of his mouth. He continued to focus on the neglected cemetery.

"It may not even matter in the end. Anyway, I plan on having a funeral pyre. I don't want a marker covered in weeds!"

Valerias snapped back to his old self. "Take to your horse, Flavius. I want to reach the fort at Onnum within the hour."

***

Hadrian's Wall at Onnum was decaying slowly. Stones that formed the wall were cracked in numerous places, and some were missing. Valerias noticed that the same weeds from the cemetery were also prevalent at the foot of the wall. A few had grown to his height. The walkway on top of the wall appeared unstable.

The attitude of the Roman soldiers at the fort mimicked the state of the wall. Valerias summoned the commander. When he appeared, Valerias realized the man was drunk. Valerias was disturbed by the condition of the wall and the state of the soldiers supposedly on guard.

Valerias pointedly asked the commander the location of the nearest fort. The commander gestured to the east and slurred, "Vindovala."

Valerias had seen enough. He lacked the authority to discipline the soldiers at Onnum. He also did not want to waste precious time exacting a remedy for the sorry condition of the fort. Valerias mounted his horse and led his group eastward to Vindovala.

At a Roman milecastle about halfway between the two forts, he stopped to rest the horses. Immediately, the captain of the milecastle emerged. Valerias grinned broadly.

"Tentrides!" he shouted.

"General!"

The two men embraced. Valerias studied Tentrides and observed a gaunt, white-haired man with a sword sheathed on his back in the same manner Valerias wore his. A dark red patch covered Tentrides' right eye; he had lost it at the Battle of Three Tongues. Valerias stepped back and stared.

"You look in a poor condition, my old friend. The weeds growing at Hadrian's Wall look to be better tended. Your appearance troubles me."

Valerias remembered Tribune Tentrides as his trustworthy master of engineers for his legions several years earlier. During those years, he was a confident man and competent engineer. Tentrides had been instrumental in constructing the temporary bridge across the Danube that allowed Valerias' legions to cross the river and fight the Huns. Tentrides had also been a mentor to Gulic, teaching him Roman engineering.

"I made a poor choice, General, I supported Emperor Gratian instead of Emperor Maximus. So, I was exiled here. It is half a step better than being executed, although some days I'm not so sure. Now, let me ask you a question. What are you doing here?"

"And why are you in this particular place, Tentrides?" Valerias ignored Tentrides' question. "This is a pitiful place. You are one of the best engineers in the empire. To be stationed here is clearly a waste of your talents."

Tentrides spoke slowly. "One of Emperor Maximus' generals placed me here. I'm in charge of this rat hole, and this rat hole is part of a larger rat hole, which is this wall. I hate Britannia!"

Tentrides' voice grew louder the more he talked. Valerias put his hand over his own mouth as a signal. Tentrides quickly stopped his rant and composed himself. "And once again—why are you here, General?"

"Two reasons. First, I wanted to see the wall. This great bulwark formed the edge of our empire."

"Now that you have seen it, what do you think of it?" Tentrides asked.

"I am disappointed. Its condition reflects the condition of the empire as a whole." Valerias turned to Flavius. "Flavius, have you ever seen Hadrian's Wall?"

"No, General," Flavius spoke as he gazed upon the wall.

"Is this the Flavius who served Argus the tyrant?" Tentrides was surprised to hear Flavius' name. He spoke directly to Valerias without even glancing at Flavius.

"One and the same, Tentrides," Valerias replied. "Flavius is a different man now. He seeks salvation for his past life. He rides with us to help us."

"I hope so. Though, I am not sure what you mean by salvation," Tentrides said. Looking directly at Flavius, he added, "You are legendary in areas of Britannia, but not in a good way."

Valerias interceded, "I said he is on a different path! He is my trusted aide. That is all I will say on the matter."

Valerias was no longer involved in the conversation. Instead, he stared intently at the wall in front of him. He reached for his dagger and, finding the sheath empty, remembered he had given it to Claire.

"Do you have a stone chisel, Tentrides?" Valerias asked.

"Yes, of course. Better yet, I have stonecutters within shouting distance. What do you want, General?"

"Call your stone cutters. I have a small task I would like completed."

Tentrides called his aide, who received his instructions and then disappeared behind a building attached to the milecastle. Within moments, two rough-looking men appeared before them. Word had spread throughout the milecastle and beyond that the famous General Valerias was in their presence. A crowd of soldiers gathered.

Valerias took out a piece of parchment and drew on it. He handed it to the nearest stonecutter.

"Can you carve these symbols into that stone?" Valerias inquired, pointing to a nearby stone in the wall.

"Yes, General Valerias," responded the stonecutters.

The section of wall in front of them stood about twelve feet high. The gray stones were roughly the same size except that one in the center was a large, rectangular block several times larger than the others. It was pristine compared to the surrounding ones.

The stonecutters set to work. Only one at a time could do the actual carving, so they took turns. The etching of Valerias' diagram into the stone took less than an hour to complete.

When the stonecutters finished, they stood back so Valerias could see what they had done. He took his right hand and gently brushed away the dust. He stepped back to admire the work. He did not speak for some time.

Valerias finally said, "Good work, men. You captured what I wanted."

"We just copied what you drew on the parchment, General."

"You did well. I am pleased." Valerias spoke to the men without taking his eyes off of the carving. "Are you soldiers?"

"Yes, we were soldiers and then, like Captain Tentrides, we were sent here to exile. All these men here have similar stories."

Valerias turned and faced the group of soldiers and Tentrides. "Your exile has ended! I am reinstating you to the legions!"

"You can't do that, General!" several of the men cried out. "It goes against what Emperor Maximus has decreed. We have gone against him before; we cannot do it again. It would mean our death!"

Valerias nodded to Flavius, who promptly gave Valerias a scroll, which he paraphrased out loud.

"The reason I stand before you is contained in this parchment. The document is from Emperors Maximus and Theodosius. It allows me to do what I must to stop the impending Saxon invasion, which I am sure you have heard about. I will establish a legion of limitanei and incorporate any man into that legion who will fight the Saxons. If you agree to do that, I am in the position to grant you a pardon. I know this is unexpected and you know little of what I ask, but it is a chance for a new life. Who here wants to join my legion of limitanei?"

The entire group of men standing with Valerias shouted, "We do!"

"I thought you might," Valerias responded as he returned the scroll to Flavius. "Flavius and my escort will document your reentrance back into the army."

The men moved with Flavius away from the wall. Valerias turned back to scrutinize the carving. Tentrides joined him. In the right center portion of the block, the carved initials "MAV" slightly touched each other. To the left of those letters was a notably larger letter "R." An etching of a sword was placed between "MAV" and "R."

"I understand the meaning, General, but why here?" Tentrides asked.

"I want to leave a sign at this location, at the very limits of the empire, that Rome is not dead, and I was here when it was alive."

Valerias gazed at the carving for another long moment before turning his attention to another subject.

"What happened to your tribune ranking?" Valerias asked.

"I was demoted and . . ."

Valerias abruptly interrupted him. "That demotion is rescinded. As my tribune, you are now tasked with forming the limitanei legion that I need. You are to recruit as many volunteers as you can, as quickly as you can. I want to reemphasize that time is of the utmost essence. I predict that you will not have difficulty recruiting men. They can sit here and rot or fight in the legion with me. How do you suppose they will choose?"

"But what shall I tell the officers in charge here at the wall? Who will guard the wall?"

Valerias motioned to Flavius, who had returned and was standing quietly nearby. Flavius again handed Valerias the scroll.

"This scroll essentially gives me the power to do what I want. It is from both emperors, and no general or anyone else will stand in your way. If someone does, let me know. The drunk soldiers at Onnum can be left to guard the wall."

Valerias handed Tentrides the scroll, but Tentrides was reluctant to take it. "Don't worry, Tribune, I have a duplicate," Valerias said.

Tentrides took the scroll from Valerias. "Yes, General. Where and when shall we meet?"

"You are to proceed in less than eight days' time to the fort at Branodunum. Bring as many men as you can recruit. I have also contacted other officers on my way here. I have sent members of my escort to forts along the wall at Condercum, Vindovala, Brocolitia, and Cilurnum with similar instructions. My goal is to form a legion of limitanei numbering at least two thousand men. I want you at Branodunum quickly so the men can undergo minimal fundamental training before the Saxons arrive. There will be many thousands of Saxons to fight. You shall be the core of the limitanei."

"Yes, General!" Tentrides had difficulty restraining his excitement at his future away from the wall. "You have defeated so many enemies—the Huns and soon the Saxons! You are indispensable to the empire."

"Ha!" Valerias scoffed. "You are mistaken."

Valerias looked around and pointed to a bucket of water located just outside a small shed. The bucket was almost filled to the top.

"Flavius, bring me that bucket without spilling."

Flavius retrieved the bucket and set it in front of Valerias. Tentrides seemed curiously amused. Flavius stood back and furrowed his brow.

Valerias squatted by the bucket of water. "Years ago, an old, wise man gave me a lesson about indispensability."

Valerias let the surface of the water become completely calm. He slowly placed his closed fist into the bucket and gently pulled it out. Small ripples in the water spread out to the rim of the bucket. Quickly, the surface of the bucket was placid again.

"What did you see?" he asked Tentrides and Flavius.

"Your fist went into the bucket, and when it was removed, there were tiny waves. Then the water became still again. What should I have seen?" Tentrides remarked, not sure where the lesson was headed.

"There was much to see, my friend. The water was still before I put my hand in the bucket. After I removed my hand, the water's calm surface returned."

Tentrides looked confused, but Flavius understood and nodded.

Valerias explained, "No one is indispensable—not me, not you, and not Flavius. My hand represented me and the water was life, which is all around us. The water did not change after I removed my hand compared to before I inserted my hand.

"We come into this life, produce a few ripples, and then we are gone. Others may try to carry on what we start, but the result is the same—they are not indispensable either. What you need to remember, Tentrides, is that no one is indispensable—not even the emperors."

Valerias stood up with the sun at his back. "Get your legion ready, Tribune Tentrides. The Saxons will not wait for you!"

"One more thing, General," pondered Tentrides. "Did you know I was here at this milecastle, or was it a coincidence that you found me?"

Valerias smiled and said, "Whatever you want to believe, Tribune. Now prepare yourself for something other than sitting on your ass! I feel a storm coming, and I want to be in Branodunum before it hits."

LI

USURPATION

While Valerias was at Hadrian's Wall, Garzad's ambitions flared. He and Honorario spent several days trying to convince the generals and officers that a change was needed in the command position for the campaign. Garzad justified his position based on Valerias' age. Personally, he craved revenge. *He is too old; the other officers must see this. He is not vigorous enough to oversee war preparations here at the fort. He deserted us.*

Ten days after Valerias left for Hadrian's Wall, Garzad decided to call an impromptu council meeting of select officers. Generals Luxcinious, Divinicus, and Quintus, along with their aides, attended. Bukarma, Revious, and Claire were not invited.

Garzad addressed the group. "Generals and fellow officers, I have called this assembly to discuss the lack of leadership here at Branodunum."

Quintus immediately responded. "What do you mean lack of leadership? Who are you to say there is a lack of leadership?"

"I do not mean you, I meant General Valerias. He is off somewhere while you spend time here at the fort taking naps like old men."

"We are following his orders," Luxcinious spoke up.

"He is not here to lead the training, is he? We don't even know if he is alive or will even return. A local man saw a Roman with his appearance riding hard for Londinium. He is an old man and wants to return to Italia. Valerias no longer has the stomach to fight. We need a real leader!"

"And who would that be?" Luxcinious asked skeptically.

"We will vote." Garzad tried to disguise his ambitions.

Luxcinious again questioned Garzad. "I do not see this old man you refer to. I see General Marcus Augustus Valerias, commander of our legions. He wears the insignias of two emperors! He is no old fool. His reputation in battle is impeccable—he is undefeated. His victory at Three Tongues is legendary. How many battles have *you* led and won?"

Quintus was skeptical as well. "His wife is at my fort. He is not going to leave her to go to Londinium. If I didn't know better, I'd think I am hearing talk of treason."

Garzad was indignant at facing such unanticipated questioning when he was trying to be subtle. He believed many of the younger officers stood with him, but the generals were obviously and openly against any change in leadership. *They are jealous of my righteousness and my ambition*, Garzad justified their opposition to himself. *I might have to rid myself of them as well.*

"General Divinicus, what do think?" Garzad asked disingenuously.

Garzad found Divinicus' silence difficult to read. Divinicus was short and portly, not athletic. Those traits indicated weakness to Garzad. He had also learned that the general was more of a nobleman than a soldier—another perceived weakness. He spoke little except to give orders.

Because everything about Divinicus was questionable, Garzad thought he would work with the man's aides to first usurp him and then Valerias. He was surprised by the fat general's response.

"This is a serious subject you bring up, Tribune Garzad. I want to be sure I understand you. You want to replace General Valerias with someone else, perhaps yourself, when you are not even a general. What would be General Valerias' fate should he be removed from his command position?"

"If he indeed returns, he will be forced to retire permanently and stay here at the fort with his wife under house arrest until the Saxons are gone. I will then send them back to Italia where they can enjoy retirement again. I would not harm General Valerias or his wife. That is my word to you." Garzad attempted to be sincere.

"I understand, Tribune Garzad." Divinicus showed no emotion. "As I said, this is a serious matter. I will consult with my officers. You will have my answer tomorrow at midday."

Garzad started to protest the delay, but Divinicus waved him off. "Tomorrow, midday," he repeated.

Before leaving the meeting, Divinicus issued a warning to Garzad. "Make no move on this matter until tomorrow!"

Luxcinious and Quintus nodded in agreement. Garzad was frustrated but decided not to contest the matter. He could not attempt to dislodge Valerias unless he convinced one of the generals to join him. Luxcinious and Quintus were skeptical, and Divinicus appeared thoughtful. Divinicus, then, was his best hope, and now he had to wait for the night to pass. *The delay gives me and Honorario more time to foment unrest in the lower ranks.*

"We will reconvene tomorrow, as you have requested, General Divinicus."

As the officers left, Honorario said under his breath, "The fat general has balls."

***

Valerias, Flavius, and their remaining escort left Tentrides' milecastle before the sun rose on the following morning. They stopped at several small forts on the way to Branodunum, where Valerias was able to recruit another two hundred soldiers for his limitanei legion. When Valerias was within thirty miles of Branodunum, Zircronic approached the party at speed. He was as exhausted as his mount.

"General, you need to return to Branodunum as soon as possible," Zircronic said, disregarding customary greetings.

"Why?"

"Tribune Garzad and a few other officers are talking about replacing you."

Flavius grew red in the face. "Traitors!" he shouted, venting his anger.

Valerias, however, remained calm. "I expected something like this. Garzad has great ambitions. I can use that ambition against the Saxons."

Flavius and Zircronic stared at Valerias, confused by his lack of concern. Valerias should have been irate, but was not.

He simply asked, "Are Bukarma and Revious aware of Garzad's intentions?"

"Yes, General, they are aware," Zircronic said.

"Good. Lead the way to the fort."

***

Shortly after noon the following day, Garzad anxiously held the council meeting. When he took stock of the attendees, he was alarmed to see Revious. *He is either a surrogate for Valerias or agrees with my assessment of the old General,* Garzad assumed to explain away his presence.

He conferred quietly with Honorario. "What do you make of Valerias' uninvited lap dog being here?"

"That it is not good for our cause," Honorario replied. "The man is no traitor to Valerias. He is here as his eyes and ears. It is time to reconsider our plan."

Garzad turned to look toward where Revious sat and was dismayed to see Revious staring intently at him. It was a trap and he needed to escape. He could make Honorario the scapegoat by saying Honorario was the instigator, but no one would believe that. He also could not turn on his friend. Then a mad idea hit him.

"Legate Revious, I am glad you are here. Is there any news from the General?" Garzad asked.

"He will arrive shortly, Tribune Garzad."

"Good. I can report back to him on the results of my review of our officer corps, to see if there are traitors in our midst."

"That is appreciated, Tribune," Revious replied coolly. "As you know, General Valerias demands complete loyalty from his subordinates. He deals very harshly with traitors and deserters. You are his subordinate, are you not, Tribune Garzad?"

Before Garzad could respond, Revious addressed the room. "Do any of you here dispute General Valerias' standing as the overall commander on this campaign?"

Not a word was spoken.

"Good," Revious said. "Tribune Garzad, you may continue. I am just an observer for General Valerias."

Garzad was in a bind of his own making. The only purpose of the council was to form a majority of officers who wanted Valerias ousted. That would not happen now. This was the second time Valerias had bested him. Inside, Garzad was furious and humiliated. He was also speechless.

"Tribune Garzad, give us an update on the training." Revious' intervention temporarily removed the pressure from Garzad's inner turmoil.

"As you wish, Legate Revious," Garzad said, finally finding his voice.

Garzad started to speak but was interrupted as several men entered the council room. Bukarma led, carrying a large spear and shield. Behind him followed Valerias and eight burly, heavily armed soldiers. It was a show of force intended to curb any officer's ambitious plans, and it worked. "Hail General Valerias!" erupted from the gathered officers.

Valerias walked straight to the front of the room and motioned for Garzad to move aside.

"My fellow generals and officers, I have returned from my mission to northern Britannia. It was a success. You soon will see two thousand Roman soldiers joining us. They will form the limitanei legion. They will be known as the Valiant Legion because it takes supreme courage to do what these men are about to do: form a diverse but unified legion in a very short time to fight a difficult battle.

"Tribune Garzad, since you seem to have unbridled energy, I am installing you as the officer in charge of the Valiant Legion. I, of course, will be monitoring your progress. Are you up to the task of organizing a large group of disparate men into a coordinated fighting force in a few days' time?"

Garzad had to swallow before he could reply. "Of course, General," he managed without stuttering. "Thank you for the opportunity." So many emotions coursed through his head that he could not think of another answer.

"You are dismissed. Tomorrow at noon we will have another council meeting. I want a briefing from each general and you, Tribune Garzad, regarding our readiness for the Saxons, who will arrive on Britannia's shores."

As the men began to leave the room in two and threes, Valerias held Garzad back. "When this campaign is concluded, Tribune," he said, his voice low and threatening, "I will give you a chance to settle our issues. Now go!"

Garzad showed no outward emotion but seethed inside. Once he left, Bukarma spoke softly in Valerias' ear.

"He is a traitor—I expected you to execute him."

Valerias stared at the door. "I considered it, but I need Garzad's brashness in battle."

"What will we do with the younger officers who have fallen under Garzad's influence?" Revious asked.

Valerias' face changed to a sly smile. "Be sure they are placed in the front lines when we face the Saxons. Most of them have likely not fought in a battle of significance. They will gain that experience."

Bukarma and Revious nodded and left the room. Valerias and General Divinicus remained.

"I want to thank you for the information you provided me, General Divinicus. I appreciate your loyalty to me and to the campaign. Go now and join your legion. You will be rewarded."

Valerias made his way to the set of rooms that he and Claire shared at the fort. After seeing Claire, Valerias was on his horse and riding fast to the hermitage.

***

Drostan angrily packed his belongings, as instructed by Father Timothy. When he finished, he left the room briefly to talk to the cleric. Drostan looked in Father Timothy's study, the dormitory, and the church but could not find him, so he returned to his room, his mood not improved. There he found a man sitting in the chair, staring at him.

Drostan stared back in shock. "Who are you? What are you doing in my room? Is Father Timothy aware you are here?"

"I am Marcus Augustus Valerias, your mother's husband. Father Timothy showed me to your quarters," Valerias answered.

Valerias crossed his left arm over his right, revealing his stump. Drostan glanced down and knew he was being truthful.

"Did my mother send you to try and talk me into coming with her, or are you going to force me? I would expect nothing less from a Roman. I don't have to obey you. I answer only to God and Father Timothy. Now leave!"

Valerias listened intently to Drostan. He thought back to his first encounter with Joseph and what he had learned from that confrontation. His delay in responding made Drostan even edgier.

"Sit down," he said firmly.

Drostan hesitated. When Valerias pointed to a chair, his movement revealed the hilt of his sword sheathed on his back.

"Are you sure that you are a man of God, Drostan? I thought a Christian offered hospitality to a guest. Father Timothy offered me the hospitality of your order. I know the Father is a Christian. But you don't even offer me a drink of water."

"How do you know Father Timothy?" Drostan asked, fighting against the intimidation he felt.

"I have corresponded with the abbot on several occasions. His most recent letter provided me with comfort after my good friend was murdered. I think you knew him—Bishop Joseph."

"Who killed him? Why?" A stunned look crossed Drostan's face.

"A wicked priest named Erasmus who claimed to be a Christian, but he worshipped other gods. And now he is dead."

Drostan gazed down at his feet, hit by grief.

"The world can be a cruel place, Drostan. You have much to learn. You have thought of me as a Roman killer who somehow enticed your mother into marrying him. That is not the case at all.

She fell in love with me, and I with her. She changed my life for the better."

Drostan lifted his eyes.

"You have no idea what your mother went through to save you and your sisters," Valerias continued. "She sacrificed everything for you three, and she would have given her life to keep you safe. I know, because I was there.

"It pained her greatly to have you here in Britannia while she was in Italia. But, as I said, the world can be cruel. You are heir to her throne. The current occupants of your mother's kingdom would kill you in a heartbeat if they knew you were alive. Also, the remnants of Argus' butchers would readily take your life. That includes Morguard, whom Argus retained to hunt your mother—should he still be alive.

"She could not risk moving you out of the country. I did not have the resources either. However, the campaign against the pending Saxon invasion provides me with the forces I need to secure your safety. I have vowed to provide security to your Christian order as well. Father Timothy understands the threat.

"The Saxons will come. You will not want to be here when they do. I cannot protect you here—it is logistically impractical. The Saxons will either kill or enslave you, which may be worse than death.

"Once we defeat the Saxons, you may choose to come back here. But I think you will choose to be with your mother."

Valerias rose from his chair. "Father Timothy and the brothers are waiting for you. Get your things. Let's go!"

Drostan could not remember anyone speaking to him as Valerias just had. His mind swirled around everything he had said; so much to take in so suddenly. Numbly, he gathered his pack and walked with the General to where Father Timothy waited.

LII

WINDSWEPT

Spindrift blooming on the peaks of the wind-whipped waves stung Staigrik's eyes. He was used to sea travel, but this storm was not normal. *Why are the gods subjecting me to such a trial? I am doing this for them, and the glory of the Saxon nation.*

The storm had been unexpected. The sea was pleasant when they began their voyage westward. But then, as if a host of sea monsters in the deep decided to simultaneously shake their tails, the turbulence was swiftly upon them. Staigrik found it difficult to tell the direction of the waves. They rolled here and there, with the swells topping out at almost fifteen feet. The sky was black except for occasional blinding bolts of lightning.

The warships were not constructed to travel in such a large body of open water through treacherous weather. None of the boats in the fleet had sails, so rowing was the only source of propulsion that would take them from their homes to Britannia. The men became terrified of the conditions and stopped rowing. They believed the gods were angry with them. Without sufficient manpower to row, they were hopelessly in peril.

Staigrik thought about the condition of his ships. He initially believed it was a good thing they were lightweight. He only allowed essential supplies, food, weapons, and the men themselves on board. Staigrik figured there was much plunder to be taken in Britannia; that plunder would fill his currently empty ships on their return to the homeland. The lack of weight was good when traveling in fine weather. But the combination of turbulent seas, gale-force winds, and the slight weight of the ships created an untenable situation.

Staigrik despaired, with grim thoughts that his invasion was doomed. He wasn't easily frightened, but he now felt a sense of despair. He didn't mind dying and his body sinking to the bottom of the sea. His greatest concern was the thought of failing in his long-held dream.

Staigrik wiped the seawater and rain from his eyes and surveyed his warship. What he saw astonished him.

Guenter stood up straight at the front of the command ship as if the wind and waves had no effect on him. He was dressed in white, his blond hair flowing over the back of his shirt. He carried a covered lantern in his left hand. Staigrik believed he was witnessing a vision from the gods.

Guenter turned and walked back to the rear of the ship. Again, he resumed his straight posture and shouted at the men.

"You must turn the oar as hard as you can for us to survive!"

Guenter began a slow, rhythmic chant that reverberated down to the oarsmen. The men responded and began rowing in time with Guenter's chant.

Once the oarsmen resumed plowing through the seas, Guenter took turns facing off the starboard, port, and stern sides of his ship, flashing his lantern, repeating his movements. Within moments, lanterns in ships all around the command vessel were visible through the storm.

The storm rapidly wore itself out. The sea calmed, and tranquility spread through the ship.

"That was foolish, son, but brave." Staigrik had regained his sea legs. "By the gods!" Staigrik exclaimed. "I cannot believe that was you!"

"I would like to claim that I have a magical power to stop the storm or the gods intervened, but I cannot make that claim," Guenter replied calmly.

"I don't understand," Staigrik said.

"While you sharpened your weapons, drank beer, and plotted this adventure, I studied the weather. I knew the storm would be brief and not terribly violent. It blew itself out before becoming the tempest you feared. A few months from now, I would not make such a prediction."

Staigrik listened to Guenter and was pleased to be alive with his war machine intact. However, he did not care for Guenter's arrogance.

Before Staigrik could respond, Guenter continued. "I have reviewed the maps prepared by our brothers in Britannia. I suggest we head to the north shore of the estuary and make any necessary repairs to our fleet. I am sure we lost ships and men during the storm, as you and I were in one of the better-constructed ships. Lesser craft will have taken on water and others may have sunk. Once we have readied ourselves, we can cross to the southern shore. You can launch your attack there. Branodunum is located just beyond the southern shore."

Staigrik was again stunned. He had assumed his son was not inclined to a warrior's ways. *Now Guenter is almost at the point of giving orders to me, Staigrik the Great!*

"Is there anything else I should know?" Staigrik growled.

"Of course, there is always something new to learn, Father."

Staigrik's annoyance was clearly apparent. Still, he wanted to learn what Guenter knew. "Go ahead."

"My contacts have told me the Romans are fielding a large army to confront us."

"So it is true, then!" It was news Staigrik himself had been unable to verify. "How many men?"

"I do not know yet. I have heard several thousand. They are led by a famous general from Rome."

"This just makes our invasion more interesting." Staigrik's confidence and authoritarian tone returned. He was determined to regain the dominant position over his son.

"I will take your information and adjust my plan, which I will reveal to the chiefs when we land."

Then, with a subtle jab at Guenter, Staigrik asked, "Since you have emerged as a warrior, do you want to lead one of my divisions when we face the Romans?"

Staigrik knew the answer before Guenter spoke. The hierarchy had returned.

"You know I am not a warrior. To place me, an inexperienced leader, in charge of one of our fighting groups is foolish. You know what the outcome would be."

"You proved to be useful today, maybe for the first time." Staigrik had made his point. "When we attack, I will place you with the other noncombatants. You can organize our plunder. Perhaps your knowledge of weather will aid you with these tasks."

"Some things never change, do they, Father?"

"Not until you pick up a seax and slay an enemy, whether it is a Briton or a Roman. A Saxon warrior kills and does not hesitate to do so."

Staigrik called for Borgnar. Borgnar's nearby vessel moved close to Staigrik's, and the two ships were lashed together. Borgnar crossed to the command vessel so Staigrik would not have to howl to him across the waves.

Staigrik summarized his revised plans.

Borgnar was impressed. "Wise choice, King Staigrik, to move to the other side of the estuary. We must take stock of the storm damage to the fleet and reorganize before we start raiding. I will inform the other ships."

Borgnar crossed back to his ship and gave orders for the ships to be uncoupled. His ship rowed to the next closest vessel to inform those men of the change in plans.

The entire fleet was soon aware of the new destination and headed for the north shore of the estuary. Guenter returned to his written notes, he being one of the few Saxons on the raiding expedition who was able to read and write. Staigrik glared at his son and resisted the urge to throw him overboard. *I should have had a daughter*, he thought.

Once the Saxons arrived on the north shore, they took two days to assess the damage from the crossing. On the second evening, Staigrik ordered an assembly of his chiefs. Borgnar sat with Staigrik while Guenter stood off to the side. Representatives of Saxon settlements already in Britannia had come to the landing point and were also present.

The meeting commenced with a drumbeat. The assembly became quiet.

"My fellow warriors—welcome to Britannia!" Staigrik shouted.

The crowd roared in response.

"We fared well from the storm. We lost only eight ships and a few dozen men. But here we are. We have sat here for two days to heal and regroup. During that time, we plotted how we want to advance and attack the areas around Branodunum and beyond. I have asked our Saxon brothers from the existing settlements in the area to share their knowledge of the land."

Staigrik nodded, and a brawny man emerged from the crowd and took a position at Staigrik's side. To many, Staigrik and this man looked like brothers—both were massive, had full, long red beards, and carried battleaxes. The resemblance was so strong that Guenter thought Staigrik's father must have had more than one wife.

"Saxons, Angles, Jutes, and friends of the Saxons! Prepare for our greatest victory as we feed on the bones of the Britons!" the man cried.

The crowd shouted again with much foot stomping. *Yes, they are brothers,* Guenter thought with amusement.

"I am Kindrof, leader of the Saxons who came to Britannia many years ago. I will tell you what you will face.

"First, we must cross the estuary. We will land on the southern shore at high tide. From there, we will carry the ships up on land. If we land at low tide, we will not be able to save them. The mud is too treacherous to negotiate, and the tide comes in rapidly here. The ships will be lost to the sea.

"Second, we have constructed paths for you take once we are on land. The area has large stretches of marsh where we do not want to become entangled. Once we reach this point, we will be on solid ground."

Kindrof had two men hold up a large map. He proceeded to identify the features he had just discussed.

"Third, the Romans have sent their army to meet us when we reach flat ground. They camp at the fort near Branodunum. We know these Romans are tough and battle seasoned. I prefer not to fight them head on. We will lose many men in a pitched battle.

"I suggest we split our forces in two. One half of our warriors will land here." Kindrof pointed to an area west of Branodunum. "The other half will travel east by warship under cover of darkness to the estuary's entrance. From there, they will land at this area east of Branodunum." Kindrof directed the tip of his knife south from the mouth of the estuary. "There is a beach here where we can land our ships. At this point, we march west. The Romans will not expect an attack from behind. We will pinch them. They will not know what hit them. Victory shall be ours!"

"How much longer will it take to send half of our fleet to this spot you pointed out?" Staigrik was clearly impatient and did not want to waste any more time. He had waited years for this moment. Branodunum and the rich countryside were so close he could taste the Britons' gold.

"Two extra days is all you will need, my king," Kindrof replied.

Staigrik cursed and looked at Guenter, who was sketching. Guenter's apparent lack of attention set Staigrik off, and he cursed at his son.

"Tell me, my son, what would *you* do? Draw pictures to scare the Romans away?" Staigrik mocked.

Guenter lowered his parchment and said casually, "I would do what our brother Kindrof has recommended. He lives here and knows the terrain and the sea. You and I have no such knowledge. I have heard the Romans prefer a straight-on battle in a situation such as this. A second attack at their rear may turn the battle in our favor. But that is just my opinion."

Staigrik was shocked. His son had been paying attention. Staigrik looked out at the assembly and realized most of the men were nodding. He had no choice but to support Kindrof.

"Then that is what we will do. Tomorrow we assemble here and organize our forces. I want the fleet that will attack from the rear to leave tomorrow evening on the ebb tide once the sun sets.

We will wait one night and launch our attack at first light on the following day.

"May the gods be with us! We shall grab Britannia by the neck and squeeze its life out! It is our time to bleed the Britons and their Roman dogs into the soil. We shall triumph. Victory! Victory! Victory! Victory for our people! Death to the Britons; death to the Romans!"

The throng of warriors exploded in such a raucous response that the shouting could be heard for miles.

LIII

PRELUDE

Valerias escorted the members of Father Timothy's order, including Drostan, to the fort. They were to stay there until the conclusion of the conflict with the Saxons. Drostan was confused by Valerias, having imagined him as an ogre who would eagerly slay all those he perceived as an enemy. But in their meeting, he did not seem to be a cold-blooded killer. Valerias also spoke as if he and his mother were equals. The relationship between his mother and Valerias frustrated him.

Word of the Saxons' landing swept through the countryside as a rolling wave of terror. A large group of desperate civilians joined Valerias and the members of the order on their way to the fort. Valerias ordered Gerlok and the men from Menze to assist the locals. *They can be useful and be kept out of harm's way*, Valerias told himself. *I promised their leader they would return, and I will keep my promise. That is, unless we are defeated. Then we will all be dead.*

Once they were reasonably settled by the fort, Valerias hustled to his quarters, where Claire waited for him.

"I can feel the presence of the Saxons," Valerias announced. "You can see it in the eyes of the Britons. If I was them, I, too, would be afraid. I fear Britannia will go up in flames. The Saxons will come from the east, the Picts and Scoti from the north and west. Rome has always been the bulwark to stop the barbarians. Previously, Britons complained of Rome's occupation of

Britannia. Now they complain that Rome has neglected them. Once again, though, it will be Rome that protects them."

Valerias looked at Claire. She had heard little of what he said. There was worry in her eyes, but not for Britannia. Valerias wanted to avoid talking about the news she wanted to hear most.

"And Drostan?" she asked.

"Drostan feels we abandoned him. He thinks we should have made more of an effort to take him from the hermitage and bring him to Italia and the Villa. I told him it would have been too dangerous for him to leave. I doubt he believed me. He will come around and let you into his life. But it will take time. I would not force the issue. Time and your continued presence will heal the wound."

"I can't help but to think I let him down. It is a terrible feeling to have as a mother, Marcus. It continuously gnaws at my heart."

Valerias sat next to her on the bed. He put his arm around her. She wept softly on his shoulder. He noticed her hair had notably grayed in the past few months, and wrinkles had appeared on her brow. He knew she had carried a great burden for a long time.

"We will work this out, my darling," he said softly. "We *will* send the Saxons back across the sea. Then we can focus our attention on those vultures, Rega and Voltrex. The more I think about them, the more I am convinced they murdered your brother."

Claire stopped weeping and put both arms around Valerias. He held her tight until she was asleep. Valerias himself could not sleep and peered into a darkened corner of the room. The hooded being stood straight, not moving or speaking.

"You will soon have all the death you crave," Valerias spoke quietly to the image. "Tell me, stranger, what is your relationship to Joseph's God?" The shadow nodded but did not reply.

Valerias blinked and saw that the image had disappeared. *I don't know if I dreamed it or if that apparition was real. It doesn't matter anymore.*

Valerias shrugged off the encounter and walked out into the night. Bukarma, Revious, and Flavius were waiting for him at the fort's gate.

"How is the boy?" Revious asked.

"Confused and angry, but I think he is trying to forgive. He does not care for me, though," Valerias replied. "If I was in his skin, I probably wouldn't feel any differently." Valerias changed the subject. "Tell me about our war preparations."

Bukarma spoke. "We will not have trouble with Generals Luxcinious, Divinicus, or Quintus. You have clearly established yourself as the overall commander. They will curry your favor to power their own ambitions. Use them as you choose.

"Garzad, however, is a different story. He has not accepted you. We have kept him and his aide busy integrating the many soldiers who have come to Branodunum to form a cohesive Valiant Legion. Still, do not turn your back on him."

"How many limitanei have arrived?" Valerias asked.

"We have counted over two hundred and fifty men," Bukarma answered. "We have heard that our old friend Tentrides will arrive tomorrow with perhaps two thousand more."

"How about the Britons? Will they provide men in defense of their land? This is *their* land!"

"We really don't know." Revious spoke this time. "The chieftains who swore loyalty to Claire pledged thousands of warriors. We have not seen a response anywhere near that magnitude yet."

"What about the Saxons? Where are they?"

Revious continued, "My scouts tell me they are still on the north shore of Metaris Aest. There are many thousands of them, as predicted. They will cross and attack very soon."

"We also know the Saxons already have settlements here," Bukarma added. "They have told their newly arrived brothers from across the sea that we are here to repel their invasion. General, does that affect our planning?"

"Perhaps," Valerias answered. "I will speak to the generals about strategy and timing. Revious, inform Tribune Gulic that I want him to ride with me at first light. You are to come, too. Tell Oxanos to prepare his men for battle as an auxiliary cavalry force to the legions. Flavius, you will be my aide to Oxanos and the Huns. Let Elderon know he needs to stay with the comitatenses legions. Bukarma, you are to organize Claire's protection. I do not trust the Britons Rega sent with us. Killing Claire is at the top of that damned Rega's list—dealing with the Saxons is a lower priority for her. Bukarma, also coordinate with General Quintus to form a detail of Roman troops that will provide security to Father Timothy's order, particularly Drostan."

Valerias looked at the three men. "Do all of you understand what I want you to do?"

"Yes, General!" the men responded in unison.

As they started to break up, Flavius asked Valerias, "You seem bothered, General, and I think it is more than concerns about the Saxons and Drostan."

"You are perceptive, Flavius. I am not a superstitious man, but that storm we just experienced may be an omen that fortunes are changing." Valerias thought back to the specter of Death he had just seen in his bedchamber.

"General, the fortunes changed for the Saxons, not us. They were hit much harder by the storm than we were."

"I suppose you are correct, Flavius. Then let the gods—or God, in your case—be with us."

***

The next morning, Valerias rose at dawn. Claire was finally sleeping soundly. He kissed her on the forehead and quietly left the room. Revious and Gulic were outside, along with Zircronic and a squad of Roman cavalry. The wind blew from the east. Valerias thought he could taste the brine of the ocean.

"You must be getting old, General. You sleep late, just like an old man." Revious laughed.

"A legate should show more obedience to his commander than what I see from you. Maybe I should demote you to horse follower—you know what they do! Take me to the shore."

Valerias' group rode east and then turned south from the mouth of Metaris Aest, where Valerias gazed at the sea stretching east to the home of the Saxons. The water glistened from the rising sun. Valerias rode up and down the shore at least one mile each way, staring hard at the shoreline. He turned and retraced his steps twice. Finally, he returned to his original location and called Gulic to his side.

"What do you see, Tribune?"

"I see water and a beach. It is what we have been looking at for the past hour."

"You are correct, of course. But you are missing something."

"General, I do not know what you mean. It appears clear to me—a beach and the sea. There are no people."

"Revious, explain to our young tribune what I mean," Valerias said.

"They will come here," Revious said assuredly as he casually tossed a stone toward the water.

"Who?" Gulic asked, perplexed.

"The Saxons, of course." Valerias spoke. "Tribune, the Saxons will think we are congregating all our forces west of here in anticipation of their invasion. They know we have fewer men than they do, but they are not confident they can defeat us with an all-out frontal assault. Therefore, they will think the best way to defeat us is to split their forces into two. One will attack us from Metaris Aest, to the west. While we are occupied with that force, they will land here and attack us from behind. This maneuver is a classic pincher assault. I would even consider enacting their plan."

"But you don't know whether they will attack this point of land, or even split their forces." Gulic was skeptical. He was an engineer, a man of reality, and not inclined to such assumptions.

"They will." Valerias was firm in his belief. "Move all your ballistae to this location. Set up your artillery along the top of the slope above the beach and camouflage the weapons so they cannot be seen from the sea."

"If you are wrong, General, we will have positioned our artillery and men in the wrong place and will be susceptible to a massacre."

"I am not wrong, Tribune. The beach is long and flat here—perfect for ships to land. The banks are not high and can be scaled readily. And we are not far from Branodunum, where the Saxons believe there is much to plunder. Revious, do you agree?"

"Your assessment is sound, General. I hope you are right." Revious smiled and winked at Valerias.

"It also doesn't hurt that we captured a Saxon spy, who we persuaded to confirm my assumption," Valerias said nonchalantly.

Gulic was curious about which came first: Valerias' assumption or the information from the helpful spy—but he kept his curiosity to himself.

Valerias turned to Gulic. "You had better start moving; I don't want you to be out of position when the Saxons come. When Tentrides arrives, I will send him your way, along with the Valiant Legion. Tribune Tentrides will work with you. Garzad will command the limitanei."

Valerias returned to the fort. Tentrides had arrived from the north along with over eighteen hundred men. Valerias calculated that he now had over two thousand men to form his Valiant Legion. He summoned Garzad and Tentrides to his council room.

"Tribune Garzad, the Valiant Legion is here and needs a leader. As I promised, I appoint you as their commander. You are to organize that mass of men into a cohesive fighting unit."

Valerias continued, "Your task is to stop any Saxon advance at the beach and provide protection for the ballistae regiment commanded by Tribunes Gulic and Tentrides. And you are to coordinate with the Britons when they arrive. You are not their commander, but cooperating with them will help your cause. Any questions?"

Garzad felt a burst of excitement. *If I do well here, I could become a high ranking general for Emperor Maximus*, he envisioned. "How long do I have to prepare, General?" Garzad asked.

"Until the Saxons arrive, and that may be tomorrow, but most likely the day after. You'd better hurry."

Garzad felt his heart sink a little as his dreams of glory vanished. How he hated Valerias for setting him up for certain failure. He could lose and be killed. If his position was overrun and his legion defeated, he would be held responsible for the defeat. Still, Garzad relished the challenge. "I will get started immediately," he said.

"Good," Valerias said. "Do what I expect and I'm sure Emperor Maximus will reward you."

Valerias turned to Tentrides. "You did well, bringing so many men here. We will need them all. Go now, and join Tribune Gulic on the beach. He will want to see his mentor."

"I look forward to seeing him again."

Garzad and Tentrides left Valerias. Shortly thereafter, Zircronic entered the room.

"General, Queen Claire wants to meet you half a mile south of the fort. The Britons are here," Zircronic announced.

"Did you see them?"

"Yes, General, I did."

"How many are there?"

"More than I could count."

"Take me there. I want to speak to them and see my wife."

***

Valerias and Zircronic left to meet Claire and the Britons. The number of men Valerias found there impressed him. Flags of Claire's former kingdom flew everywhere.

A sea of tents circled the Briton command quarters where Valerias headed. Claire, Weylyn, and a number of Briton chiefs were waiting for him. Claire smiled broadly when she saw her husband. He wore his full Roman battle uniform, and his sword was sheathed on his back. He brought with him a dozen heavily armed bodyguards whose purpose was mainly ornamental.

"General Valerias, it is a great honor to welcome you and your legions. We are most appreciative of you being here to provide a barrier between Britannia and the Saxons," Weylyn said.

He had positioned himself as leader of the Britons, but he accepted Claire as their ultimate leader.

"That is true, Weylyn. I fight for Britannia. However, I also fight for the glory of Rome. I am well aware that Rome's star has dimmed considerably in Britannia as of late, and may burn out altogether in the future. But for one more day, Romans and Britons will fight as one and defeat our common enemy, sending them back across the sea. Are you and your men with me?"

Claire translated Valerias' words, which were followed by a lusty cheer.

"What do you want us to do, General?" Weylyn asked earnestly.

"You can do much." Valerias looked at the assembled Britons, most of whom appeared to be farmers. Women were scattered among the men. Their weapons were crude: rust-pitted swords, wooden spears, pitchforks, hammers, and clubs. *They could not stand up to my army,* Valerias thought. *How can they even stand up to heavily armed Saxon warriors? Yet I have no choice.*

"I can tell you what you are not," Valerias said. "You are not an organized fighting force. Your weapons are lacking or of poor quality. I am sure most of you have no fighting skills. But what you *do* have is spirit, an intense spirit to defend your country, your land, and your families. Regardless of your weapons and fighting ability, that spirit is worth much more than the Saxons' desire for riches. Let your spirit crush the Saxons' desire so that victory is yours! I relish having you fight by my side!"

The crowd seemed inspired by Valerias' words, although apprehension could be detected in their eyes. Valerias sensed that he needed to be more persuasive.

"As I told your leaders earlier, years ago, a mighty army of Huns descended on the Goth kingdom. The Goths would have been destroyed and its people enslaved. But the Goths fought hand in hand with us Romans and we prevailed. It is the same opportunity you have now. The Goths had the will to defend their people and land. Do you have that will, that spirit, to defeat the Saxons?"

The Britons cheered louder, and Valerias began to feel more assured. He turned to Weylyn.

"I will send one of my best officers to spend the short time that is left helping your forces prepare. He will be here within the hour. You should do exactly as he tells you. His name is Bukarma, and you can trust him with your lives. I do."

Valerias, Claire, Weylyn, and the Briton chiefs continued discussing battle strategies until Bukarma arrived with a Briton interpreter. Bukarma's size and booming voice instantly commanded respect from the Britons. Valerias and Claire left and returned to the fort. As they rode, Claire confessed that she still worried about Drostan. She knew, though, that any further contact with him would have to wait until after the war with the Saxons.

***

Two days later, Revious woke Valerias before dawn.

"Come with me, Marcus." Revious spoke softly so as not to wake Claire.

Valerias dressed and rode with Revious to a spot overlooking Metaris Aest.

"It has been some time since I have seen a sight such as this," Revious stated, staring straight ahead as first light crept over the eastern horizon.

Before them in the distance were hundreds of Saxon warships. Some had landed and others were in the process of being beached. Thousands of lanterns on the warships and shore highlighted the huge Saxon presence. A large group of heavily armed men amassed at the base of the slope.

The arrival of the Saxons reminded Valerias of ants clustered around their anthill. The men all looked alike—shaggy beards and thick hair covered their heads. They were armed with war hammers, spears, seaxes, and axes. Several warriors carried bows. Half did not have shields. They were all infantry. It was an impressive sight.

"They're here," remarked Revious, staring straight ahead at the mass of men.

"Let it begin," Valerias answered without emotion. "Let it begin."

LIV

MOBILIZATION

Valerias and Revious returned swiftly to the fort. With dawn on their heels, they passed through the gates. Valerias signaled to the gatekeeper who in turn waved to a soldier, and a bell rang. Quickly, bells in the neighboring village of Branodunum began carrying their ominous message—the Saxons had arrived.

Generals Luxcinious, Divinicus, and Quintus, and their primary officers met with Valerias, Revious, and Flavius. Valerias ordered the generals to immediately assemble their comitatenses legions. In a suitably quick time, they were set to march north to meet the Saxons. But before the legions departed, Valerias repeated his orders so there would be no misunderstandings.

"We have seen the Saxon fleet and their men. There are at least ten thousand of them. They know we are here and expect a battle. And they shall have one.

"Legate Revious, you will stay with me. Flavius, join the Huns. I don't want you on the same battlefield as the Britons. They would just as soon kill you as a Saxon.

"General Divinicus and General Luxcinious, your legions are twenty-five hundred men each. General Quintus, your legion is two thousand men strong and consists of your force stationed at the fort and several limitanei centuries that were located south and west of Branodunum. In total, our troop strength is seven thousand men. We have six thousand infantrymen and one thousand cavalrymen.

"General Quintus, one hundred and fifty of your soldiers are to remain at the fort. If our lines are breached, all civilians are to be barricaded inside. Use as many locals as necessary to help defend the fort. I have found barbarians do poorly at conducting sieges. Your men will just have to wait out the Saxons. Do not try to flee. The Saxons will run down anyone in flight, and the results will be brutal. Tell your men that they and all civilians must stay in the fort! Father Timothy and his brothers will aid the civilians.

"We have trained and prepared for this fight. To review: General Divinicus, you will take your legion and be our right flank. General Luxcinious, your legion will form the center. General Quintus, your men will take the left flank. Your infantries will form three lines. Our best archers are to be positioned in the second line. I want the lines rotated as needed to keep the soldiers fresh. The cavalry will be separated into two units and stationed on both the far left and far right under my command. I want a squad of cavalrymen set behind the lines. I don't know your men well enough yet, but any deserters are to be struck down by the rearguard cavalry. I despise deserters.

"The Saxon barbarians will outnumber us, but we have faced much worse odds before and triumphed. This battle will be no different. Our enemy has no cavalry except for an occasional local chief. They wear only light armor for protection and are not disciplined. I saw very few Roman weapons in the hands of the Saxons, which means they have had few encounters with us and don't know what to expect.

"They are savages and would like nothing more than to have the blood of a Roman on their weapons and Roman plunder in their hands. The Saxons fight primarily with battleaxes, war hammers, short spears, and the seax, a curved blade. They will attack as a mob without formations.

"The Saxons will not take prisoners unless they have need for them. You do not want to be their prisoner. Don't be fooled by the lack of armor and training; they are fearsome. If we give them an opening, we will be crippled and likely perish. We have faced this type of barbarian before, and there is no doubt in my mind that we will crush them as we have crushed others. Show me you have the heart for this battle!

"Now go—the day is ours! For the glory of Rome! Honor! Loyalty! Victory! Glory!"

The officers exploded into cheers, and the legions marched rapidly in disciplined order toward the Saxons.

Valerias took Revious aside and told him that he needed a short time to visit with Claire. Valerias found her outside the fort. Bukarma had returned from the beach and was at her side. Valerias felt a stab of concern.

"I could try again to talk you into staying at the fort, away from combat, but I know you won't."

"Marcus, you know I must join my fellow Britons on the beach. They look to me as their leader. If I am there, they will fight that much harder."

"If you stay at the fort, you could inspire your people to hold a siege, should the Saxons defeat us."

"You will not be defeated—you are Marcus Augustus Valerias. And I am needed at the beach."

"But Drostan is at the fort," Valerias said in a last effort to convince her to remain behind.

"Marcus, he is one person. I must do what I can for my people. That is what takes priority."

"At least promise me you will not fight and will just let your presence be an inspiration to your people," Valerias pleaded.

"I will not fight unless necessary, my brave husband. But I have my Hun bow, my arrows, and, most importantly, the dagger you gave me. I do not want to die. I want to defeat our enemy and return to the Villa with you, our daughters, and Drostan, if he agrees. That is all I want. Promise me you will be careful as well, my love."

"The Villa seems so far away," Valerias said as he looked southward. "Of course, I will be careful. You are my true love. Returning to our home is my utmost desire."

The two kissed briefly and Valerias held Claire's hand.

"Marcus, do you think Joseph is watching us?"

"Of course. He wants to see if I will pray to his God for victory."

"Will you?" Claire asked, curious.

"I already did!" Valerias smiled broadly.

He kissed Claire again. "Watch out for Rega's Britons, my love. May the gods smile on us!"

"Are you ready for war, General?" Revious shouted as he rode up to Valerias. He wanted to turn Valerias' attention away from Claire and to the upcoming battle.

Valerias' steely glare told Revious what he needed to know. The two rode off to catch up with the legions.

Claire watched Valerias ride away with tears in her eyes. *Joseph, look after him,* she pleaded.

A Roman from the Villa approached Claire and Bukarma.

"We must go now, Domina!"

Claire nodded, and the squad of heavily armed Roman cavalry, personally selected by Valerias and Bukarma, rode hard to the beach where Valerias theorized the Saxons would land.

LV

War I

"They arrive just beyond the slope to the water." Revious squinted to the north.

"Our plan must be carried out precisely. We have little room for error." Valerias looked straight ahead at the enlarged throng of Saxons.

"It shall be, General. The men are prepared. They want this fight." Shifting topics, Revious asked, "Do you still think the Saxons will land at the beach east of us, on the other side of Branodunum?"

"You saw the Saxon fleet in the estuary, Revious. Did that look like a thousand ships to you? I know they split their forces and will attack the beach to the east at the location I have marked. Now go and conduct your task. Return here when you are finished. A legate should remain with his general!"

Revious disappeared behind a formation of small ragged hills. In front of Valerias, a loud roar crescendoed from the Saxons followed by several more roars. After the final cry, a huge man carrying a battleax appeared on the top of a large, flat rock.

The man, with his long, flowing red hair and beard, reminded Valerias of a lion and its mane. With one arm, the man raised the battleax three times over his head. The Saxons responded with a war call that started as a chant and gradually grew louder. The war cry was meant to frighten their enemy, but all the bellowing managed to do was amuse Valerias.

Hundreds of Saxons joined Staigrik near the rock as thousands more swarmed behind him. Staigrik turned to face the Romans. On the plain before him was one man on a black horse. He sat for several moments, motionless. It was clear to Staigrik the lone man on the impressive mount was the Roman leader.

Guenter looked up at him. "Father, I have studied Roman battle strategies, battle formations, the use of skirmishers in battle . . ."

Staigrik held out his arm to silence Guenter. "Your books are worthless to me. My scouts tell me that we already outnumber the Romans—without including Borgnar's forces. The use of skirmishers to draw us into battle is a lie. Look, there is one Roman out in front of us. He is no skirmisher. I do not need to be drawn into this fight—I am already committed to killing Romans. You have more to learn than I ever could teach you. Go back and help finish unloading our warships. I must now do what I was born to do—take my warriors into battle and to victory! Leave me!"

To Valerias, the large, red-headed Saxon was just another barbarian leader. He thought back to Three Tongues and of Uldric, the Hun. *That Hun was impressive.*

Valerias raised his arm. Within heartbeats, thousands of Roman swords and spears pounded against Roman shields, followed by the Roman war cry. The cry began as a low groaning and rose to a howl.

Staigrik cocked his head as if he were trying to understand its meaning. *I want that Roman's head*, he thought. *His helmet must be my prize.*

The Romans marched forward and appeared on top of an upraised slope behind Valerias. The legions' perfect formations, with the early morning sunlight reflecting off the polished metal armor and the shields, created a sight most Saxons had never witnessed before.

Staigrik stood mesmerized by the sight of the legions. Most of the conflicts he had been involved in were hit and run, not pitched battles. This time, though, he relished what lay before him. *I cannot wait to taste the blood of a Roman. My battleax will sever countless Roman heads and limbs.*

Staigrik suddenly clutched his chest as he felt the same stinging pain he had endured once before in the Great Hall. This time, it grew steadily worse and he squatted; standing had become too difficult. Kindrof appeared at his side, his concern evident.

"King Staigrik—what is wrong?!"

Staigrik swore. "All of these pre-battle postponements have weighed on me, when all I want to do is fight. Years of preparation have led to this moment, and now I feel this pain! Shit!" He gritted his teeth against the stab of agony that gripped him. He took several steadying breaths before he spoke again. "I just need to rest for a moment. I want you to begin the charge against the Romans. I will join you shortly. Kill a Roman for me!"

"As you wish, my king."

Kindrof left Staigrik and moved to the front of the Saxons. His dark red hair was pulled back and tied behind his head. In one hand was a seax and in the other a war hammer. He screamed, "NOW!"

The Saxon mass hurtled across the open land in anticipation of their victory and the spoils they were about to seize. Staigrik pulled himself to his feet again to watch the charge. He felt dizzy and lost his perception of where he was, and he started to teeter backward. Several Saxons stopped his fall and sat him on the ground. The Saxons nearest Staigrik no longer were intent on charging the Romans and were occupied instead with their king.

“What does this mean?” they asked each other. “Are the gods angry?” Confusion surrounded the stricken Staigrik.

Staigrik thought of nothing except the pressure in his chest and why it was happening now—on the cusp of his great victory. He felt an excruciating pain, like a hot knife had been plunged into his heart. He clutched his chest with his right hand and slowly stretched out on the ground. His eyes were open, but he could not see or speak.

Staigrik’s guards watched his collapse and yelled for Guenter. The call passed down the slope. Guenter appeared and ran to his father. He placed his ear close to his father’s mouth but felt no breath. He looked at Staigrik’s face but saw no spark of life. Guenter stood without taking his eyes off his father. The great Saxon warrior had succumbed to death without a fight. Time had robbed Staigrik of his long-awaited plans for plunder and glory.

Several thoughts raced through Guenter’s head as he looked at his father’s body. *My father tormented me for as long as I can remember. I’m not sure if he even thought I was a man. Maybe treating me as he did, he was trying to make me into a man like him. Now, at the height of his greatest battle and victory, he dies. What am I to do? I cannot be the man he was. I am my own man. The gods foretold I would become a king. Now today, I am the king of the Saxons.*

Saxons circled Staigrik’s lifeless body, uncertainty taking hold of them about what they should do. Finally, one Saxon spoke hesitantly to Guenter.

“You are now king. Long live King Guenter!” The other men responded with the same call, first quietly, then more robustly.

“What is it that you would like us to do, King Guenter?” one of the soldiers asked, urgency coloring his voice. “The battle has started and our forces are divided. Borgnar should be at the beach, where he will attack the Romans from behind. It is too late to tell him what has happened here."

Guenter looked at his father's body again. *The foretellers were right. I became a man and a king, Father. Just sooner than you or I imagined.*

Guenter looked across the flats where a large force of Saxons was hard charging the Romans. He realized he could do nothing except let the battle play out, hopefully ending with a Saxon victory. *I cannot stop what has already begun.*

He called for his friends Torberg and Wulfric, who were nearby.

"Yes, Guenter—I mean, *King* Guenter?" Torberg asked hesitantly.

"I want you two to organize a party of men and take my father's body back to the boats. I don't want him here to be trampled by our men or violated by the Romans or scavengers. We will bury him at sea, properly."

"But we want to fight," Wulfric spoke.

"This is my command. See that it is obeyed!"

"Yes, King." The two men grumbled and walked away to find men and materials to make a stretcher strong enough to haul Staigrik's heavy body back to the boats.

I may have just saved their lives, Guenter told himself. *And they will not appreciate what I did. They may hate me. I understand now that to be a king is to be alone.* Guenter stepped up on the rock where his father had recently stood. Saxons to his left, right, and behind him waited for the command of their new king. Guenter waved his seax in the air and moved it down to point at the Romans.

"My father, King Staigrik, would want us to fulfill his dream, and we must do that. Join our brothers, who already attack the Romans. Use all your power and kill the bastards! Go!"

The Saxons around Guenter regained their battle fervor. With renewed energy, they hurried to engage the Romans.

After appearing alone to the Saxons, Valerias turned and rode his horse slowly through an opening in the legions that closed as he passed. He ordered his men to stand as a solid wall behind their shields against the oncoming horde. When the Saxons were within one hundred yards of the Roman phalanx, he sliced his arm downward. The first line of infantry immediately dropped down to one knee with their oval shields up.

Behind them stood a line of infantry armed with bows. Valerias gave the command, "Launch!" and hundreds of arrows darkened the sky over the Saxons. Saxons with shields were able to block most arrows. Many of those without shields were cut down. The Saxon charge, though, was undeterred.

Valerias ordered a second round, and this arrow volley slowed the Saxon advance. A third round of arrows filled the sky and found more targets. In turn, the Saxons began hurling spears and shooting arrows at the exposed Roman bowmen. Several Roman archers were hit.

Even under the Roman arrow barrage, the Saxons maneuvered to within twenty yards of the Roman line. Valerias called out another order. The men in the three rows pulled the javelins that had been tied to the back of their shields and hurled them at the Saxons, bringing down men in the front of the Saxon charge. Still they did not back down. They pushed forward, throwing their own spears, axes, and heavy war hammers at the Romans. The weapons crashed into Roman shields, disrupting the Roman lines.

The Romans tried to re-form the wall of shields just as the Saxons reached their first line. Metal, leather, and flesh crushed together as the two armies merged. Roman spatha and short spears clashed with Saxon axes and seaxes. The Romans' utmost priority was to keep their formations together, while the Saxons furiously attempted to break that order. Roman legs exposed under shields were cut. When one Roman infantryman fell, his spot was filled by a soldier behind him. Several Saxons attempted to hurdle over the Roman shield wall, with little success. Men who fell were trampled. Bodies on the ground were pierced by swords and spears. War hammers cracked shields and skulls. The ground turned slippery from the blood of both Romans and Saxons. Men on both sides grunted, cursed, and groaned in the universal language of war and death.

As the two sides merged into one mass, Valerias raised his left stump above his head. An arrow drenched in fire was shot high into the sky. Even in daylight, the arrow was visible to the men who looked for it.

The sighting of the arrow resulted in the sound of hoofbeats that, at first, were difficult to hear. Its meaning soon became clear to the combatants. The Saxons and even the Romans turned in the direction of the thunder from the ground. The Saxons closest to the rumbling were pincushioned by arrows loosed from a group of men riding straight at them. The Huns rode up through a drainage ditch that bisected the western edge of the battlefield near the Romans' formations. There they joined the battle under the leadership of Tribune Oxanos and Flavius.

The Huns had lived for this day since they moved onto Valerias' land. They were fierce warriors who had become pacifists, but now it was time for them to unleash their repressed desire to fight. They also needed to prove their worth to their friend and benefactor, General Valerias.

The Huns' arrival sent a wave of dismay through the Saxons. As much as more combatants were unwelcome, they had never seen such strange looking people. A murmur quickly spread throughout the Saxon army that the Huns were demons. While the Saxons tried to grasp the mystery of the Huns, the Huns rode among the Saxons, shooting arrows and using their sabers to attack from horseback, with great effect. Flavius, riding with the Huns, brought blow upon blow down on the Saxons with his sword.

After losing well over one hundred warriors to the Huns, the Saxons regrouped.

A call went out: "Cut their horses!"

The Saxons used their seaxes to slash the legs of the Hun horses. Several Hun horses tumbled to the ground, throwing their riders. The Saxons also formed groups around Hun riders to drag them out of their saddles. They tried to mount the riderless horses but were cut down by carefully aimed arrows.

Valerias motioned to his left and the cavalry on that flank charged hard through the mass of Saxons in an effort to join the Huns. The cavalry's advance was halted by the sheer number of Saxon warriors, and the horsemen became engulfed. Valerias watched the development with frustration.

"I cannot lose the Huns and my cavalry regiment," Valerias growled to Revious. "The fortune of this battle may hang on my next decision." He looked to his right at the other half of his cavalry. While the infantry under his generals was fully engaged, the right flank of the cavalry was not. Valerias called General Luxcinious over to this side.

"Take the right cavalry regiment, join the left cavalry regiment, and advance to unite with the Huns."

"But General, that will expose Divinicus' right infantry flank, which is under fierce assault!"

"I am well aware of the risk, General Luxcinious. Our infantry must and will hold. If you are successful, we can push the Saxons in two directions."

A Saxon arrow flew within inches of Valerias' head. Because of the different helmet plumage worn by Roman officers, it did not take long for the Saxons to distinguish the soldiers from the officers, and killing officers became a priority. They also knew that Valerias was the "king" general, and that victory for the Saxons would follow his death.

A second Saxon arrow strayed slightly away from Valerias' neck. He did not flinch from either arrow. Luxcinious was impressed by Valerias' steadfastness when he himself had shifted in his saddle. *Most commanders I know would have ducked or winced when death came so close,* thought Luxcinious. *He is the legendary general I have heard about.*

"Now!" Valerias ordered Luxcinious, "It is time to show your mettle!"

Luxcinious saluted Valerias and rode off to command the cavalry as ordered.

Valerias turned to Revious. "Go to General Divinicus and tell him that he and General Quintus are in charge of the infantry until General Luxcinious returns. They must hold their lines until the cavalry prevails! They must hold, Revious! No retreat!"

Revious replied, "Yes, General." He added, "Those arrows were very close."

"Legate, I am alive until I'm not. And I am very much alive. Death has not claimed me yet. Now go!" Valerias smiled reassuringly as he spoke.

"General, I believe you are invincible!" Revious shouted and promptly rode off in Divinicus' direction.

Valerias refocused on the cavalry charge. He spotted something that was difficult to comprehend. Instead of serving as a behind-the-lines chaplain to the Romans, Elderon was in the midst of the cavalry brawl. He was on horseback, carrying a sword in his right hand. He had no shield.

Why is Elderon acting this foolish way? He will be dead in moments, and there is nothing I can do, worried Valerias. *Joseph would not be happy.* Valerias recalled Joseph's reluctance to use a sword to stop the Huns from killing the physicians during Three Tongues.

Valerias' fear was confirmed by a Saxon who roughly tugged Elderon from his horse. Elderon dropped his sword and rolled furiously on the ground to avoid becoming a target. The Saxon moved in and was about to behead him with a seax when the quick action of two Romans saved him. One Roman threw a javelin into the chest of the Saxon as the other rode in and hoisted Elderon up on his own horse, taking him to safety.

The battle between the Saxon and Roman infantries reached a stalemate. Neither force could advance. Roman discipline was a deciding factor in generating more Saxon casualties than Roman. However, there were many more Saxons than Romans.

The Roman cavalry under Luxcinious fought through the Saxons and reached the Huns. Oxanos stood by his dead horse, his left arm bloodied by an attack from an ax-wielding Saxon. He appeared dazed and would likely be killed. Flavius suddenly rode by and sliced the head of a Saxon as he advanced on Oxanos. As Flavius turned to aid the Hun, he was jerked off his horse. Flavius fell to the ground and was about to receive a Saxon ax to his head when a Hun arrow pierced the Saxon's neck. Oxanos and Flavius looked at each other with relief. They were alive, if only for another moment.

Guenter watched the battle from the top of the rock. He felt helpless to provide any kind of leadership. He prayed for guidance from Alfredson. *Grandfather, this is Father's fight. If we succeed, I will give him the credit. If we don't . . . hopefully we will live and be given another opportunity. I pray to you that I become the leader that you foretold.* Guenter picked up his seax and headed toward the heart of the battle.

Valerias had not yet pulled his sword from its sheath. He had not needed it. The fighting grew more chaotic and he finally unsheathed it. He realized the battle was at the turning point—victory for the Romans or victory for the Saxons would soon be decided. Valerias knew it was time to press his forces forward or be defeated.

Well, Death, you have taken so many souls today. Shall my soul become your captive as well? Perhaps Joseph's God will protect me a little while longer. I have no fear of you. Ha!

Valerias rode back and forth along the Roman lines urging his legions forward. An occasional spear or arrow whizzed by his body. A lone Saxon passed unseen through the Roman lines and rushed Valerias. Valerias, occupied with the battle, did not see the Saxon until it was too late to react. As the Saxon drew back his axe to strike, a spear slammed into his body, the entire blade penetrating through the Saxon's back. Valerias nodded to his cavalryman and immediately turned his attention back to the battle.

The Romans witnessed Valerias' resolve and rallied, pushing forward against their enemy. Meanwhile, the Saxons had been essentially leaderless since Staigrik's death. Guenter was too far removed from the fighting. Kindrof lay dead with a javelin through his chest.

Finally, the Saxon charge wilted under the relentless Roman push. The Saxons began a slow retreat, which was hampered by the bodies of their own dead as well as Romans, Huns, and the great corpses of horses. Roman spathas quickly ended the lives of any stragglers. Valerias felt the turn in the battle and urged his infantry forward.

Luxcinious reached the Hun leader. Oxanos had regained his senses as Flavius helped him remount. Luxcinious' boundless energy inspired the surrounding Romans as well as the Huns.

"General, what are our orders?" Oxanos shouted at Luxcinious.

"Together let's push the Saxons into the sea. That will free up the infantry."

"I am ready," Oxanos responded as he nodded to Flavius and Arb.

Oxanos and Luxcinious regrouped their forces. The combined Roman and Hun cavalry pushed deep into the Saxon forces. Luxcinious decided to split the Roman cavalry in two. He would take one part and press groups of Saxons back toward the Roman lines, which would cause the Saxons to be pinched from multiple sides.

The Saxons became desperate and resorted to near-suicide tactics. A Saxon war hammer thrown at Luxcinious hit him directly in the head, the tall plume on his helmet making him an easy target.

Luxcinious valiantly attempted to stay on his horse, but to no avail. He became disoriented and slid to the ground. Flavius tried to reach him, but he was too late. The general was bludgeoned and trampled by retreating Saxons.

After Luxcinious' death, Flavius took the Roman standard of his cavalry unit and led a furious Roman-Hun assault on the Saxons who stood to fight. The Saxons were savagely cut down.

The Roman infantry advanced as Roman and Hun cavalry carved out a significant area previously occupied by the Saxons. As a result, the Saxons' morale faded fast. They were being attacked on several sides by a determined, disciplined force. The Saxons' long-held visions of plunder were replaced by those of survival. The rout was on as the Saxons ran toward the marshes and eventually the shore of the estuary, where their warships waited.

Guenter stood still as the panicked Saxons rushed by him. He was fascinated by how the Romans organized their defense and how they attacked. The Roman forces advanced to within a hundred yards of him when two men appeared at his side.

"Guenter, you must go! To stay here is certain death," shouted Torberg.

"We need you as our king, especially now that Staigrik is dead," seconded Wulfric.

Guenter stood still for a few more moments as the remainder of the Saxon force rushed by him. Finally, he said, "I understand now," and the three men hurried to the shore.

As the Romans pursued the Saxons, Valerias issued orders to his officers. "Kill the severely wounded men. Capture any Saxons if they are in good condition! I don't want any potential prisoner killed. Stop the pursuit at the beginning of the marsh. I do not wish to become entangled in that quagmire."

Divinicus rode up to Valerias. "General, why are we not killing as many Saxons as we can? Why take prisoners?"

"You will see soon enough, General Divinicus. Follow my orders!" As Divinicus prepared to leave, Valerias stopped him, saying, "Are you aware General Luxcinious is dead?"

"I have just been informed," Divinicus replied. "He was a good general."

"Yes, he was," answered Valerias. "He had a spirit that I value in my officers. It was his initiative with the cavalry that turned the battle in our favor."

Divinicus, though, secretly had no remorse for Luxcinious' death. He desired a high command position, and Luxcinious' death would hasten such an opportunity. *General Quintus is a fort commander, and he will not provide opposition to my ambitions.*

Before Divinicus had time to fully mull over the implications of his rival's death, Valerias announced, "General Divinicus, you are now in temporary command of both comitatenses legions. See that my orders are carried out! A final thought: I know you are not sorry to see a rival die. You have ambition, as good Roman officers should. Just don't allow your ambition to overcome your honor."

Divinicus looked into Valerias' face and found a sincerity he seldom saw in Roman officers.

"Yes, General!" Divinicus rushed away, shouting to his officers.

Flavius and Revious joined Valerias as they watched the battle end. Valerias started to place his sword back into its sheath and found both men assisting him.

"You both excelled today. I am grateful that I can serve with you," Valerias said warmly.

Both Flavius and Revious were struck by Valerias' sentiment. "Thank you, General," they replied humbly.

After an hour, Divinicus with Quintus returned to Valerias.

"We have captured over four hundred and fifty Saxons, General," Divinicus offered.

"General Quintus, construct a stockade and place them in there. Treat them well. Give them food and water."

Valerias' order drew odd glances from the officers, but Valerias did not explain himself.

"Must I repeat myself?" Valerias asked, his impatience showing.

"No, General—you are our commander," Divinicus and Quintus nodded and replied in unison. Both generals left hurriedly to carry out their orders.

With a broad smile, Oxanos rode alongside Valerias holding a Saxon seax and a gold necklace.

"Do you want any of the plunder we took from the Saxons?" the Hun asked.

"No, Tribune, I do not want it. I collect victories, not spoils."

LVI

WAR II

The shoreline during the early morning felt serene to Claire. The dense, low-lying clouds blocked the light from the early dawn. She took in a deep breath and exhaled slowly as she gazed upon the dark sea in front of her. She thought of her husband and how he would fare against the Saxon horde. *If anyone can defeat those barbarians, it is he*. Her mind drifted back to the Battle of Three Tongues and all those who had died, and more importantly to her, those who had lived. *I imagine this battle will have the same result—much blood and death, and hopefully victory*.

"Domina." Gulic's voice snapped Claire's attention back to reality.

"Yes, Tribune?"

"We have positioned the artillery units where General Valerias requested. I hope the Saxons land here."

"They can be moved at a moment's notice, can't they?"

"It depends, Domina. We designed the machines to be mobile. It will take time to reposition them, though. We constructed three dozen dart-throwing scorpions, ten bolt-and-stone-throwing ballistae, and five onager catapults. We can move the scorpions easily. The ballistae are larger and will take more manpower to relocate. The onagers will likely have to stay in place during the battle. The farther away the Saxons land from this location, the more difficult it will be to move our artillery."

“I understand, Tribune. Is the artillery camouflaged, as General Valerias ordered? Is Tribune Tentrides assisting you in your preparation?”

“Yes, and yes, Domina. It is good to have Tribune Tentrides here. I have much to learn from him.”

“Good. Now, have Tribune Garzad and Commander Weylyn join me here. I would like to speak with them.”

Bukarma stood by Claire the entire time, not saying a word. Valerias was concerned that some of Rega’s Britons, and even Garzad, might attempt to assassinate her. Thus, Bukarma’s role changed to that of a bodyguard, a legate bodyguard. Several Roman soldiers provided reinforcements for Bukarma.

Within moments, Garzad, Weylyn, and Gulic appeared before Claire and Bukarma. Honorario accompanied Garzad.

“Tribune Garzad, is the Valiant Legion in position?” Bukarma spoke this time. Claire and Bukarma had decided that Bukarma would address Garzad and she would talk directly with the Britons.

“Yes, Legate. We will protect the artillery as well as be in position to stop the Saxons from advancing up from the beach—as General Valerias ordered.”

“I know we have had our difficulties, Tribune, but at this time, we have only one goal. Is that understood?”

Garzad did not say a word, but Honorario answered in his place, “Yes, Legate Bukarma, we know our orders from General Valerias.”

Claire focused her attention on Weylyn. “How many men are under your command?”

“We count almost four thousand.”

Claire was pleased. “You will need every one of them, Commander. As you all know, surprise and stealth are our allies.

Keep your forces out of sight and be quiet; no fires. The Saxon scout we captured told us that he is to set a small fire on the beach as a signal to show the Saxons where to land. We replaced that scout with our own man. He will act as the Saxon sentry and keep the signal fire lit to lure them in. Once they land, we will attack. Any questions?"

Garzad looked angry, but said nothing.

Honorario nodded and replied, "No questions, Legate and Domina."

I wish Honorario were the tribune and Garzad his aide, thought Claire. *Honorario will keep volatile Garzad focused on defeating the Saxons.*

Weylyn appeared nervous to Claire, and his gaunt face looked even thinner. Gulic, though, had the appearance of a veteran. *After all, he fought at Three Tongues. I thank the gods for Gulic.*

Claire offered a parting thought: "I do not need to tell any of you that we cannot let the Saxons advance past this beach. We must push them back into the sea. Let the sea devour them!"

After the men left, Claire turned to Bukarma.

"I am sorry you have to be my guard instead of joining in the fight, my friend."

"I understand the reasons for Marcus' concerns," Bukarma replied. "I cannot afford to lose either of you. I know Revious has Marcus' back, and I have yours. I predict I will fight at some point. You know I don't trust Garzad any more than those foul Britons sent by Rega. He hates any semblance of taking orders from me and a Briton, particularly a Briton woman."

"Yes, I know. We need to keep him occupied as much as possible. I will let Marcus deal with him after the battle. Garzad is a Roman, after all."

"Here's to victory, then!" Bukarma's face beamed a broad smile.

"Yes, to victory! I will be so happy for all of us to return to the Villa."

Later, Garzad orchestrated a short time alone with Honorario, out of earshot of the rest of the army—Claire and Bukarma in particular.

"You are the friend I can count on to keep me centered on what is important. I don't need to waste time listening to that bitch, Claire, and her henchman, when all I want to do is fight in this battle. You are the only person I trust."

***

Staigrik had wanted a strong Saxon presence in the attack on the eastern shore, so he gave Borgnar command. To appease the Angles and Jutes, he named Korken of the Angles and Lathrin of the Jutes as co-commanders. The entire Angle and Jutish fleets, and the few Frankish ships joined with about one-quarter of the Saxon force in the assault.

They planned to travel at night without lamps or torches, and at dawn reach the point on the shore where the Saxon sentry had lit a fire. From the shore, they would move inland and attack the Romans from the rear. By then, the Romans would be fully engaged with Staigrik's army in front of them, and the Romans would be crushed between the two Saxon armies.

At dawn, Borgnar's scout on a lead ship spotted the small signal fire on the beach. Puffs of smoke rose and swiftly dissipated into the wind. Word was passed to Borgnar, who ordered the Saxon ships to row quietly in the direction of the signal. The Angle and Jutish ships followed Borgnar's fleet. The only sound was the occasional clunk of an oar and the lapping of waves on the beach.

The ships landed on the shore and the men quietly disembarked. A Saxon moved stealthily across the sand to the fire, but there was no sentry. When Borgnar received word that the sentry could not be found, he became wary and passed word to his chiefs that something was not right.

He decided to send his scouts up the shallow, grass-tufted dunes beyond the beach to seek out possible threats to the landing. One scout discovered a small scorpion artillery piece covered with branches. He also found the sharp end of a Roman spatha as it penetrated his chest, his final cry before he died alerting his companions.

A dim light crept over the eastern horizon through the dense clouds as the battle began.

Claire looked to Tentrides, who waved to Gulic. Gulic shouted a command and his specialists removed the camouflage covers from the artillery pieces. In short order, the scorpions, onagers, and other ballistae hurled their missiles of death—stones, bolts, and darts—at the Saxons and their allies on the beach.

The artillery pummeled the invaders and their ships, caught between the sea and the dunes. Claire again turned to Tentrides. He waved his arm, and this time Garzad called out the order. The Roman Valiant Legion immediately ran over to the edge of the dunes above the beach and began loosing arrows and hurling javelins at the Saxons. Hundreds of the enemy lay dead or wounded from the barrage from the Roman artillery and archers. The Saxons' expectations of an easy beaching had been thwarted.

The problem for Claire and the Romans was that the Saxons and their allies sharply outnumbered them.

Borgnar and several Saxons overturned a ship and used it as a giant shield to stop the Roman missiles from inflicting any more damage. Borgnar believed the Romans were outnumbered and concentrated in the area just in front of him. He turned to a Saxon chief sitting near him.

"They were expecting us. I'm not sure how, but we still have many more men than they do. We can turn the battle around."

He faced the sea and motioned to several ships that had not yet landed to disembark further up the shoreline. The Angle chief, Korken, saw the signal and, having watched events develop on the beach in front of him, understood what it meant.

Korken commanded his men and the Frankish ships to row to a spot about half a mile north of the Romans' location. The Angles, finding no resistance when they landed, quickly ascended the slope from the small beach to the flats above. From there, they would attack the Romans from the side.

Claire was alerted to the new enemy strategy. She had Bukarma order Garzad and the Valiant Legion to withdraw from the artillery and face the Angles on the flats. Garzad needed no persuasion to fight; he, Honorario, and the Valiant Legion marched with grim determination to face the Angles.

Borgnar watched the Valiant Legion's withdrawal as it headed north to meet the Angles. He knew that the small force of Romans left could be overpowered even with their "magic" weapons, as some of the Saxons called the Roman artillery pieces.

"Attack!" he screamed, and the Saxons began a full assault on the Roman position. They hurled spears and shot arrows in unison toward the Romans manning the artillery, striking several men.

Claire felt disaster was imminent if the Saxons gained control of the high ground and captured the Romans' artillery. She raised her hand and a great roar came from behind her. Weylyn appeared at her side. Claire had her bow and quiver on her back. She held Valerias' dagger tightly in her hand, the blade gleaming from the rays of the now emerging sun that reflected off the water.

"We are ready, my queen!" Weylyn shouted above the noise of the battle.

"This is a fight to the death, Commander. There is no retreat. We either triumph here or we fall and die! No retreat!" Claire shouted as the Saxons and Jutes ran from the beach and were within yards of the Roman artillery. "We cannot lose! For Britannia!"

Weylyn turned and let out his own war cry. "For Britannia!"

The Britons started flowing over the crest above the shoreline down to the beach where they met the Saxons head on like charging rams. The war cries of both sides devolved into individual personal battles. Death descended on the beach.

Gulic saw that he could no longer fire his artillery indiscriminately at the Saxons for fear of hitting Britons.

"Tentrides, we cannot aim our weapons at the beach. What should we do?" Gulic shouted, confused, not wanting to accept that his war machines could no longer be of use.

"Target the ships, Tribune. Target the ships!"

Gulic smiled, *So obvious!* After readjusting the artillery, the Romans' ballistae and onagers launched their projectiles at the ships drawn up on the beach and still bobbing in the water.

The Jutes, stunned by the damage inflicted by the discharge from the Roman artillery, turned their focus from the battle to the plight of their ships.

Borgnar continued to urge his Saxon forces to press the fight into the Britons. He found the poorly armed Britons easy prey and slaughtered a dozen with his sword as he advanced up the slope. A wall of Saxons followed him.

In the ascent to the top of the slope, the Saxons overran several Roman artillery pieces. Gulic was attempting to repair a broken ballista when the Saxons set upon him. Gulic pounded one Saxon in the head with a pole he had in his hands. Another Saxon slashed at the pole with his seax and intended to do the same to Gulic's head. The two men wrestled against the ballista. The soil underneath the artillery piece gave way, and Gulic, the Saxon, and the machine crumbled down the bank.

Gulic fell into a narrow ditch as the ballista fell on top of him, pinning him while the arm of the ballista hit him in the head, knocking him unconscious. The Saxon was not as fortunate. The defective bolt that caused the artillery piece to malfunction was released during the fall and pierced the Saxon through the throat.

Borgnar reached the top of the slope, knowing victory was in his grasp. Only a squad of Romans stood between him and Branodunum. He raised his sword above his head to show his men they could gain control of the flats and win the battle.

An arrow stung him in the shoulder and a second hit him in the thigh. Borgnar hunched over in pain as blood pulsed from both wounds. He straightened and tried to encourage his men forward. As Borgnar refocused on the enemy lines, he was shocked at what he saw. A woman on a horse held a bow less than twenty-five yards from him. She took aim and an arrow splintered the chest of the Saxon warrior who had advanced beyond Borgnar's position. Pain gripped Borgnar, more intense than he had ever experienced. He tumbled to the ground, losing consciousness.

The Angles ran into the solid wall that was Garzad and the Valiant Legion. Both forces had roughly equal numbers, yet the Valiant Legion was not as disciplined as the legions led by Generals Luxcinious, Divinicus, and Quintus, and cracks appeared in the Roman lines. A number of Romans dropped their weapons and ran. Garzad, though, held his ground. He urged his troops not to yield as he raced back and forth among his men, an obvious target. Garzad had no fear of dying; he led his men by example.

No wonder Valerias didn't execute me, Garzad thought. *He wanted me to win this battle. I shall succeed!*

Garzad turned to give Honorario a change in battle tactics just in time to see an Angle spear puncture Honorario's side. The tip of the spear protruded out of his friend's back, blood gushing from the wound. Honorario grabbed the spear as his face contorted. It was to no avail. Garzad rushed to assist, but there was nothing he could do.

Honorario managed to gasp, "It has been good, my friend," before he succumbed and became still.

Garzad lost all control. He was no longer the tribune, the leader; he was simply a fighter possessed by thoughts of avenging his friend. He grabbed a short-handled spear with a long blade in his right hand and held his sword in his left, and rode straight into a group of Angles. They did not react quickly enough, and in short order they were dead or retreating.

Garzad's actions triggered a powerful rejuvenated reaction from the Valiant Legion, and they retook the offensive. The Angles retreated under the assault with Korken in the lead. Garzad continued to pursue them out in front of his men. He fought through several Angles and was close to Korken when his horse abruptly stopped and he was thrown into a small grassy dune. An Angle had thrown a bolo around his horse's front legs, causing its legs to buckle and toss Garzad forward. The impact on his head made him pass out for a few moments.

When he came to, several Romans surrounded him and fought off the Angles who had returned to finish him off. The Angles were repelled, and he was helped to his feet. Garzad looked at his dead horse and back in the direction of Honorario. In between, he saw all the carnage. His swagger was momentarily gone. *Honorario is dead,* thought Garzad. *Was this all worth it?*

"Follow them!" The order came from another officer of the Valiant Legion. The Romans continued to give chase after the Angles. Several wounded Angles, including Korken, who could not flee readily succumbed to Roman spathas. The surviving Angles and Franks managed to reach the beach, where they jumped in the boats and rowed furiously away from the shore. The victorious Romans let out a cheer.

Garzad arrived at the beach. His militaristic attitude returned, and he shouted in an angry outburst.

"Why do you stop when the main battle is still ongoing and we could be defeated?" Garzad pointed to the beach where the Saxons first landed. "Return to the main fight! Kill our enemies! We must have victory!"

The mood of the Valiant Legion went from the exhilaration of victory to a sobering possibility that the Saxons had defeated the Britons at the beach and were marching westward. Garzad and the Valiant Legion hastened to the east and joined the melee between the Saxons and the Britons.

As the Valiant Legion entered the fray, Garzad removed his officer's uniform. He knew that the more a soldier looked like an officer, the sooner he became a target. He did not wish to die that easily when there were plenty of enemies to kill.

The return of the Valiant Legion turned the battle in favor of the Romans and Britons. The wounded Borgnar was carried to a ship. Lathrin was dead, decapitated by a stone from a Roman ballista. Several Saxon chiefs were killed when a large stone fired by an onager hit the center of the warship carrying them, causing the ship to shatter. Someone gave the order to retreat, or perhaps the Saxons simultaneously realized that was the prudent course of action. The surviving Saxons and Jutes rushed to their ships in a panic. Tentrides maintained the Roman artillery assault and continued to punish the enemy's ships until they were out of range.

Garzad seemed to have endless energy and did not want the battle to end. He waded out into the sea until the water was up to his chest, holding his sword over his head. He cursed the Saxons loudly for their cowardice. In return, they shot arrows at his head. All missed their mark, the motion of the waves beneath them throwing off their aim. When Garzad returned to land, he threw his sword aside and sat among the dead. The sand was soaked in blood, continually blooming and foaming with the waves of red seawater.

Gulic was found and pulled out from underneath the damaged ballista. He sat, confused, until well after the battle had been won, able only to look on the field of victory but not yet celebrate his part in it.

Claire watched the enemies' ships retreat until they were specks on the horizon. She was ecstatic. She congratulated the Britons and Romans, and offered a special gratitude to Tentrides, Garzad, and Weylyn for their bravery and leadership. In a quiet moment, she thanked Bukarma for providing her with security instead of fighting in the battle. Later, she told Gulic that he would be a welcome addition to Valerias' and her family. Claire also gave silent thanks to Joseph for watching over her and her friends.

Claire followed Valerias' order that all dying Saxons and their allies be put to the sword. Healthy Saxons or those with only minor wounds were spared and organized into an encampment.

Garzad returned to Honorario's body. He received congratulations for his part in the victory, yet he did not speak or respond to anyone. The Romans and Britons celebrated as Garzad sat alone with his dead friend. He was alive, but Honorario was dead and the battle he had yearned for was finished. There was no victory for him.

LVII

CAUSATUM

The battle on the flats above Metaris Aest ended and Valerias was pleased with the result—a complete triumph for his army. Outnumbered by a savage force, his legions had mauled the Saxons, forcing them into an all-out retreat. What was left of the Saxon forces was a beaten army centered around the southern shoreline. Valerias stared down on the Saxons from a hillock above the water.

He asked Revious, "Why are they still on the beach and not in their ships heading out to sea? I cannot believe they will try to mount another attack."

Valerias thought of Claire and wondered how her combined army of Roman artillery, the Valiant Legion, and the Britons were faring. Through frequent messengers, he was aware the Saxons had indeed split their forces and landed east of Branodunum. Questions rolled over in his mind. *Did the Saxons land at the exact location where I ordered the artillery to be placed? Or was I wrong and my artillery rendered ineffective? Are the Britons fighting for their land like the Goths did at Three Tongues? Or did they desert their cause, leaving the undermanned Romans to fight on their own?*

He shuddered at the second possibility. In that scenario, his wife, future son, and friends would be dead. *If my army succeeded, is Claire safe, considering the threats from the Britons sent by*

Rega and from Garzad? I hope Bukarma has remained an effective protector.

As Valerias contemplated his concerns, Divinicus and a squad of officers rode up.

"General Valerias," exclaimed Divinicus, "*Sapor est victoria! Adhuc esurient!*" Divinicus smiled, and his officers repeated the phrase emphatically.

Valerias responded in kind to Divinicus and the officers. *Even up here in Britannia, they know my battle cry.* He felt good. He had shown the younger officers that he, General Marcus Augustus Valerias, was still capable of organizing and carrying out a successful campaign. He had done so under adverse conditions, with little time to prepare, new legions, and in an unfamiliar country with unproven allies.

Personally important to him, Death had not taken him. *I barely had to draw my sword, let alone kill anyone. That has never happened to me in any battle. Perhaps Joseph would be pleased.*

"General Divinicus, have the cavalry under your first officer be ready to ride at a moment's notice to the beach where the Valiant Legion and Britons are fighting."

"Yes, General," Divinicus replied enthusiastically. "You should also know that General Quintus was wounded. He was hit in the shoulder by a Saxon war club. We are taking him to the fort."

"Keep me updated on his condition. I would like a casualty report by tomorrow morning."

Divinicus nodded and he and his men departed, leaving Revious alone with Valerias. As they watched the Saxons on the shores of the estuary, Valerias felt a tap on his shoulder. He turned back and faced Oxanos, whose arm was in a sling. Valerias smiled.

“Tribune Oxanos, again I am pleased you survived the battle. What do you think of the Roman military today?”

“General, you remember I was at Three Tongues. I fought in the center attack force against your infantry. Today I fought with your cavalry, and that was better for us.” Oxanos spoke in Latin.

“Do you mean the fighting or the outcome, Tribune?” Valerias inquired.

“Both, of course.” Oxanos smiled wryly.

“Of course,” Valerias responded with a relaxed smile. “What is your casualty report?”

“We lost seventeen warriors, one of whom was a woman. We also lost my trusted advisor, Arb. Although he was an Alan, he was my friend and a friend of the Huns. I will miss him.” Oxanos paused and muttered something like a prayer to himself.

Valerias, knowing full well what Arb had meant to others, glanced at Revious, who sat expressionless on his horse. He turned to Oxanos.

“I am sorry for the loss of a brave warrior and your friend. How did he die?”

“Saxon ax to his chest. He stepped in to protect a fallen warrior and did not see the ax until it was too late.” Oxanos’ tone was measured and calm. “Most of the rest of my men have various injuries, ranging from slight cuts to severe wounds. I am afraid we could lose at least two more men.”

“Be sure they see our surgical staff.” Valerias nodded at Oxanos to make the point. “Tell me what you know about Elderon. He was supposed to be providing spiritual support to our legions. Instead, he was in the middle of the cavalry fight!”

Oxanos shook his head. “Elderon thought he would be more valuable in the center of the battle. From our previous talks, you indicated Christian priests do not carry weapons or fight, but he tried to do both. He is not a warrior and was almost killed. He should be dead. His God must look after him."

"No, I think it was our soldiers who saved him. Should you see him, send him to me. I would like to speak to him."

Oxanos left for the Hun group as a Roman messenger approached.

"*Sapor est victoria! Adhuc esurient!*" the messenger announced excitedly.

"Yes," Valerias responded and waited patiently while the man caught his breath.

"General Valerias, great news from the shore battle. We are victorious! The Saxons and their outlaw kin have been beaten; they have retreated to the sea. Domina Claire learned of your victory here and extends her congratulations. You have saved Britannia!"

Valerias debated various responses before finally saying, "*We* saved Britannia." He then thought, *for now*.

Valerias said to the messenger, "Obtain a fresh horse and return to Domina Claire and her forces. Tell her to return with the Roman army. However, I want a company of Roman soldiers and Britons to remain along the shore in case the Saxons have the urge to return. Have Tribune Gulic bring me his most mobile artillery pieces. Go!"

Later in the day, Claire arrived at the main camp with Bukarma. Valerias was secretly more pleased that she was alive than with the results of the battle.

In a quiet moment, he asked Bukarma, "Did you feel there were any internal threats to Claire?"

"No," Bukarma answered. "Garzad was busy fighting the Angles, and I always maintained a tight security detail around her that only Weylyn and a few Roman officers could enter. I kept anyone associated with Rega away. The Saxons did come close to her, though. She had to use her bow, and that helped turn back the Saxon charge."

"Just like with the Huns," Valerias remarked. "I am so pleased that you are with me, Bukarma. Bringing you to the Villa was one of the best things Claire has done. Of course, her marrying me was her best decision!"

Valerias gently slapped Bukarma on the back and smiled warmly at his friend.

"I would now like to have some private time with my wife. I will meet with my officers later. I want full battle reports from both theatres."

A command tent had been erected between the battlefields. Valerias chose not to return to the fort because of the large number of refugees who had accumulated there. His multi-room tent was located roughly in the center of the tents. Claire waited for him there. She appeared both relieved and unsettled.

"Marcus, I cannot express how pleased I am that the Saxons suffered defeat and you are with me." Claire embraced him warmly. "Your strategic planning on the beach was perfect. Not only did the Saxons split their forces, as you predicted, they also landed precisely where you thought they would. Your battle strategy could not have been planned better."

"I wasn't there on the beach to lead the fight. Credit for the victory goes to many people: you, Tribunes Gulic and Tentrides, the Villa volunteers, the Valiant Legion, and even Garzad. And, of course, your Britons, who held their ground. The victory would have morphed into defeat if there had been a breakdown in any one of those units. I didn't even have to send reserve forces to the beach."

"I agree with you, Marcus. This was a great victory that depended on such disparate allies." Claire's mood became downcast. "I am disturbed about something else, though. Drostan will not acknowledge me or allow me to even visit him at the fort. Father Timothy cannot reason with him. What have I done to deserve such treatment from a son whom I love very much?"

Claire clutched Valerias tightly as she wept softly.

"There are many reasons. You married me, a Roman. You also just participated in a barbaric, bloody battle where thousands perished. However, I think there is another reason for Drostan's behavior, the true reason—he is frightened of the future."

"What do you mean?" Claire gazed at Marcus, her eyes wet with tears.

"Drostan has come to a crossroads in his young life, Claire. He has three options for his future. The first is the church. He has existed in the warm womb of the church for much of his life, where Father Timothy has been his surrogate father. That cozy life is over. The order is no longer safe in its current location. Even though the Saxons were defeated, they will be back. I will not be here to protect them or him the next time.

"Second, you returned to his life and he now knows that he is the true heir to your throne. He is completely unprepared for that role. As heir, he will have a target on his back. And Rega will not cede the throne without a fight. That fight includes attempting to kill him and you as well.

"The third option is that he could travel to the Villa with us. I don't know how he would react to living at the Villa. He would be reunited with his sisters, but I'm not sure what he would do there.

"Even I would be intimidated by those choices—so I imagine Drostan is terrified of his dilemma. His life has changed forever, and the future holds no right answers. I will not tolerate his being rude to you, but in this case, I recommend giving him time to sort out his thoughts."

Valerias turned the topic of their conversation. "I have heard many of your countrymen express a desire for you to return to your kingdom as queen. Of course, you would have to dethrone Rega to do so. I must ask you—do you want to follow that path?" His eyes were serious and inquisitive.

Claire's tears had dried and she looked firmly at Valerias. "My place is with you and our place is at the Villa. I have no desire to return to the throne."

"Yes!" Valerias enthusiastically replied. "That would be my choice. It is our choice."

Valerias and Claire, exhausted, collapsed into bed. They embraced and fell asleep. A call from outside the tent awakened them when dawn opened the door to the morning. Valerias answered the call. It was Revious.

"General, I would like you to see what is happening at Metaris Aest with the Saxons."

"What?" Valerias mumbled, surprised, not knowing what Revious meant. He dressed in haste, kissed Claire, and went outside where Revious waited.

"I don't think it is an ominous sign, but it is odd," Revious noted.

"We will see about that," Valerias interjected. "Have a century of cavalry meet me there." Valerias pointed to a grassy area outside the tented area.

A stablehand brought Valerias his horse. Before he mounted, Valerias noticed Elderon leaving a tent.

"Elderon!" Valerias yelled angrily. "Come here!"

Elderon scurried over. He carried a spatha on his waist, held in a poorly rigged sheath. He was surprised at Valerias' tone.

"General, I am Brother Philip now." His tone was colored with a hint of arrogance.

"Elderon—no, you are not!"

Elderon immediately lost his arrogance.

"If you want to be a soldier, then I shall place you in the legions. You shall train as a soldier. For one thing, you will learn to properly sheath your sword. If you want to be a priest, then lose the sword. Joseph never carried one. You will also need the proper training, which I will arrange. The choice is yours. Let me know your decision!"

Valerias mounted his horse, shot a final glare at Elderon, and rode out to meet Revious and the century of cavalry. They would join the several thousand soldiers camped near the top of the dunes above the estuary.

Divinicus and a squad of his cavalry met Valerias and Revious before they reached the army camp.

"I have the casualty report, General Valerias," Divinicus reported.

"Go ahead."

"From both battles we lost three hundred and forty-seven Roman soldiers. That includes the limitanei and your Villa volunteers. More than five hundred men were wounded, although most are expected to survive. Several officers perished, including General Luxcinious, as you are aware. We do not have an accurate number of Saxon casualties, but it appears to be in the thousands. Likewise, we have no number on Briton casualties.

"This is a great day for us, General. It offsets Adrianople! *Sapor est victoria! Adhuc esurient!*" Divinicus exclaimed proudly.

Valerias smiled and returned Divinicus' salute. He noted, *Perhaps Divinicus is correct regarding Adrianople—at least to a minor degree.*

When Valerias and Revious arrived at the camp, they found a solitary figure sitting on a rug at the edge of the ridge of dunes before the water. He had a long, thin wooden pole stuck in the ground. Attached to the top was a white flag.

"Revious, see what that man wants." Valerias narrowed his eyes as he stared at the lone man, suspecting a trick. "I will wait for you here. If there is any trouble, signal to me and we will come quickly." *If anyone can decipher the situation and stay alive, it is Revious.*

Revious rode to the man and spoke to him for some time before returning to Valerias.

"He wants to meet with the king of the Romans. He wants to meet with you, Marcus."

"How does he know I am the leader?" Valerias wondered.

"He watched you in battle." Revious paused and noted, "And I told him you were the king. Aren't you king?"

"Maybe to you I am," Valerias responded, watching the solitary man.

"He wants you to come unarmed, as he is unarmed."

"I don't speak the Saxon language. I will need an interpreter."

"Actually, he speaks Latin—perhaps better than you!" Revious joked.

"Your value to me decreases by the moment, old scout." Valerias removed his spatha and gave it to Revious. "This will be interesting. You know my signal." Valerias became serious.

Valerias spurred his horse into a relaxed trot and rode over to the sitting figure. As Valerias dismounted, the figure rose to greet him.

"Thank you for agreeing to meet me, King Valerias. I am Guenter, the new and reluctant king of the Saxons."

Valerias studied Guenter. He looked too young to be a king; he was only a couple of years older than Drostan. He had long, blond hair streaked with brown. Guenter's pale complexion matched his flowing hair. His eyes were a striking blue. He was of slender build and clean shaven. Guenter did not fit the pattern of Saxons that Valerias had encountered on the battlefield.

"I am General Marcus Augustus Valerias, a Roman general, not a king."

"Perhaps you should be one." Guenter paused and the two men stared prudently at each other. Guenter motioned for Valerias to sit.

"General, you are wondering how I could possibly be a king. I am young and do not have the same appearance of so many of my brethren. I am not a typical warrior."

"You speak the language of the Romans well."

"My mother insisted I learn about the cultures of other people. She is particularly fond of Romans. My grandfather, King Alfredson, also supported me. The Roman culture has always fascinated me. I have talked to many travelers who have dealt with Romans, and I have compiled a set of writings in Latin. My father was a brute who only understood violence as the means to an end. I believe using one's intelligence is a better way to attain one's goals. Don't you agree, General Valerias?"

"I have found that utilizing both the mental and physical qualities together achieves victories," Valerias responded warily.

"Yes, I can see that in your approach against us. It was quite effective."

"How long have you been king?"

"Just one day, General. My father, King Staigrik, died just as the battle began. You may have seen him, standing on the rock before the battle began. He was an immense man who always carried his battleax. He spent the last several years dominated by thoughts of coming to Britannia to plunder. And then he just died. We were utterly defeated in battle because we were unprepared. Your command is to be emulated, General."

"I witnessed you in battle, King Guenter. You showed no fighting skills, but you never backed down. Several missiles were sent your way, and you never flinched. You were one of the last men to leave the battlefield alive. You have the traits of a good leader. Just do not put yourself out there too often, or an arrow or spear or a sword will find its mark."

"I was following your lead, General Valerias. I watched you as well, and you were in total command of the battle the entire time. My chief, Borgnar, who led the attack on the beach, told me that he recognized your leadership in that battle even though you were not present."

"So, what is it that you want, King Guenter? I am aware that the remnants of your fleet that fought at the beach returned to the sea and rejoined you."

"I am here to strike a bargain with you, General Valerias."

"You realize we are the victors." Valerias gave Guenter a hard stare.

"I am well aware of the results of the battles, General."

"Normally, I would have ordered my soldiers down to the shore to wipe out any of your army that could not flee in a ship. There would be no survivors, no prisoners, except those needed as slaves in the mines." Valerias paused and his firm tone relaxed. "Today, though, I will listen to your terms."

"What I ask for is simple, General. It has come to my attention that you have Saxon, Angle, and Jute prisoners, even a few Franks."

"Yes, that is true. We have captured seven hundred and fifty-five men. They were taken during both battles. Again, King Guenter, it is only my mercy that allows these prisoners to live."

"I am grateful for your mercy, General. I respectfully request that they be delivered to me."

"Now, what do you offer me?"

"I will give you my word that we will leave Britannia for our homelands."

"Never to return, King Guenter?"

"I cannot promise that, General Valerias. I will promise we will not return while Rome occupies Britannia. Once Rome leaves Britannia, it is not for you to decide what happens here. I know Rome will abandon Britannia while I am alive."

"I want two thousand of your seaxes, five hundred axes, five hundred spears, one hundred war hammers, and five of your ships. I want these items in fine quality. None is to be damaged or broken, or have Roman or Briton blood left on them."

"Can I ask why, General?"

"If Rome withdraws from Britannia, as you seem to know will happen, I want the Britons to be better prepared when you return." Valerias paused for a moment to let Guenter consider his offer. "Do you agree to my terms, King Guenter?"

"I accept your terms, General," Guenter acknowledged without a pause. "When can you deliver my men to me? I would also like to collect the bodies of our dead."

"As soon as we have what I asked for, I will release the prisoners. You can send unarmed men to pick up your dead. After our arrangement is complete, you and your men are to be out of my sight by midday the day after tomorrow."

"I trust that you will provide me with live prisoners after you take our weapons from us."

"As I will have to trust that you will not return to Britannia until after Rome leaves Britannia—whenever that is."

"Then we must trust each other, General."

The two men stood and shook hands.

"I would like to know you better, General Valerias. There is much I can learn from you. I have one more question: Who were the people fighting with you? I have never seen anyone like them—totally fearless, excellent archers and swordsmen."

"They are the Hun people from the east. They are my allies."

"Will they stay in Britannia?" Guenter looked to the south where a group of Huns watched him and Valerias.

"They may," Valerias answered. "The Huns are protectors; perhaps they will protect Britannia after we *abandon* it."

Valerias and Guenter discussed aspects of Roman culture for an additional half hour before going their separate ways.

Valerias returned to Revious.

"What did you think?" Revious was curious.

Valerias stared at the Saxon as he slowly descended from the dunes. "He is their new king, King Guenter. He is young, intelligent, fearless, and a planner. And he is very dangerous. If I was a Briton and failed to prepare properly, I would be wary of the future."

Guenter arrived on the beach where the Saxon, Angle, and Jutish survivors quickly surrounded him. Guenter described the conditions he and Valerias had agreed on. Several in the crowd were dismayed. Instead, they wanted to attack the Romans after the prisoners were returned. Guenter brusquely disagreed.

"My word is my word, and it is good. We are also in no position to attack. I can promise you, their general will be prepared for any such action, and next time he will slaughter us all. Look, he has already set their artillery at the top of the dunes. If we attack, we will be fortunate to have any survivors. He has the upper hand for now. Be patient, my warriors, we will return. The Roman bear will not stay in Britannia much longer."

The crowd of warriors gradually accepted Guenter's rationale. They knew he was right. They promptly set about to carry out his commands.

Staigrik's body was wrapped in a cloth and placed in his warship. Guenter checked on Borgnar and found he was improving. Wulfric and Torberg sat with Borgnar. *I am pleased my friends survived. There will be another day*, Guenter thought.

"What do you think of their king?" Borgnar inquired about Valerias.

"He is a general, not a king. From what I have seen, he is a man I respect. If he had been my father . . ." Guenter's voice trailed off into silence.

LVIII

COMES THE TIME

The following day, Valerias ordered the Saxon prisoners be brought before him. Their hands were bound in front and a series of long ropes were tied around their ankles. The prisoners looked like a defeated group awaiting a violent death. Rumors, spread by soldiers who could speak Saxon, told of General Valerias' harsh treatment of prisoners. The Saxons' belief that they were to be executed wafted through the air like a highly acrid aroma and added to their uneasiness.

Valerias spoke to the prisoners through a translator. "I have reached an agreement with your King Guenter: your lives will be spared and you will be exchanged for certain materials. Once those materials are brought to me and I find them to my liking, I will release you. You will return to your king and sail off to your homeland, never to return."

The prisoners were noticeably relieved. The thought of an imminent release buoyed their spirits. But their relief was short lived.

Valerias continued, "I am allowing you to leave with your lives; however, you are to be marked. If you are ever caught in Britannia again, you will be executed immediately. There will be no mercy."

Valerias pointed in the direction of several pits where hot fires curled around thin metal bars. "March forward in five single lines. You will have a brand placed on the back of your left hand. If you resist, you will be executed. It will hurt, but you are warriors and this should not bother you much. If you think I don't know what pain is . . ." Valerias held up the stump of his left arm. "At least you will have your hand. Move!"

The branding took about an hour. No one resisted, though there was significant screaming from some of the prisoners. While Valerias waited for the branding to be completed, he summoned Weylyn and his Briton captains.

"We," Valerias pointed to his legions, "will escort the Saxons to their ships. I do not want your people around to harass them as they pass by."

"I don't know why we can't attack and destroy them now," Weylyn pleaded.

"For two reasons, Commander. First, I gave my word for their safe passage from Britannia. There have been instances in the past when Romans gave their word but did not keep it. I will not be a part of such treachery.

"Second, the Saxons and their friends are a defeated, wounded animal. And yet they still outnumber us. A wounded wolf can still bite. Why provoke an attack and more death when we do not need to? We will let them sail away, and their last views of Britannia will be silent Roman soldiers stationed above them. Jeering Britons will only serve to create a resolve for your enemy to return for revenge. If that time comes, Rome may not be able to help. Besides, as part of our arrangement, you and your men will receive a substantial addition to your armory. You will need it."

Weylyn did not argue. He viewed Valerias as a wise older brother. "As you have ordered, General, we will obey."

Weylyn rode back to the Britons and they relocated their position one thousand feet away from the dunes.

Once the branding was completed, Valerias ordered the combined legions under Divinicus' command to accompany the Saxon, Angle, and Jutish prisoners in the march to the edge of the dunes. The legions wore full battle gear, as Valerias wanted to make a lasting impression on the Saxons and their allies—both the prisoners and those men standing by the ships on the shore. Roman artillerymen stood at the ready by their war machines.

During the march to the slope, Valerias observed Garzad whipping several stragglers. He rode over to Garzad, with Bukarma at his side.

"Tribune Garzad, do not whip these men. They are damaged enough."

"You have gone soft, General," Garzad sneered. He continued to beat a limping prisoner.

"Stop!" Valerias was no longer calm. "When I give an order, Tribune, I expect it to be obeyed, whether that person is a stablehand or a general. One more whip and you will join the Saxons as my prisoner!"

Garzad wrapped his whip around his arm and turned his horse so he was face to face with Valerias.

"We are almost at that point where we will have our reckoning, General. Then we shall see who is superior to whom!" Garzad's face contorted in anger.

Valerias and Garzad glared at each other for several tense moments. Finally, Garzad rode off in the direction of the Briton camp. Valerias turned back to Bukarma, who cradled his long-bladed spear in both arms.

"He has very familiar mannerisms to me, Bukarma. I just can't place him."

"I have never seen him before he came to the Villa," Bukarma offered. "He has no conscience, Marcus."

"Oh, he has a conscience, my friend. It is just different from ours."

The Saxon prisoners reached the top of the slope and were ordered to sit. Roman soldiers armed with spears ringed the prisoners. Valerias and Bukarma rode through the center of the mass. From the edge of the dunes, Valerias gazed at the Saxons below him and raised his right arm.

The Saxons immediately began transferring the weaponry Valerias had requested. It was a backbreaking, tedious effort conducted by the Saxons. The last items to be moved were the five ships. The Saxons lifted one ship at a time to the top of the slope through the use of a system of ropes and pulleys.

The next morning, the ships and the weaponry sat on the edge of the dunes. Valerias inspected the weapons and warships. The quantity of weapons was correct. The quality, though, was no better than average. Valerias decided not to push the issue.

These weapons are an improvement over what the Britons have, he mused. *Further, they can study the ships and see how they were constructed. Perhaps the Britons can build their own fleet.*

Once Valerias was satisfied with the items, the swap was completed. The Saxons boarded their ships and sailed out to the mouth of Metaris Aest into the open sea.

Guenter stood in front of his warship as it passed by General Valerias. The Romans stood in a line along the slope—each man wearing his helmet and holding a shield and spear. Not a sound emanated from the Romans.

Guenter was at first surprised that he did not see or hear the Britons. After he pondered it, he knew General Valerias had instructed it to be so. *That General is a clever man*, Guenter noted. He turned to Borgnar.

"The Roman army and their general will leave Britannia. We must have patience. We will return!"

The Saxons vanished from sight. Valerias ordered sentry squads to be stationed at half-mile intervals across the top of the dunes for twenty miles around Branodunum. The sentries were to stay at their posts for at least one month as a safeguard to monitor for a possible surprise Saxon return.

After the Saxon's departure, Valerias and Bukarma rode over to the Huns. Revious had previously joined them. The Huns saluted Valerias, "*Sapor est victoria! Adhuc esurient!*"

"Revious, did you teach our legion battle cry to the Huns?" Valerias acknowledged the salute.

Oxanos joined in excitedly, "Yes he did! A great victory, General! After our defeat at Three Tongues, and then exile from our own people, this is a particularly great victory for us."

"Tribune Oxanos, you and your men were essential to our victory. And it was our victory—Roman, Briton, and Hun. Your fighting ability is superlative. You should give thought to joining the legions permanently as an auxiliary cavalry unit. You could teach our troops many skills."

Valerias saw Elderon standing in the shadows by a bush. Valerias rode over to him and dismounted.

"What did you decide, Elderon?" Valerias asked curtly.

Elderon stepped out into the bright daylight. "As you can see, General, I am not carrying a weapon."

"Yes, I can see that; however, that does not answer my question about your future."

"You have told me that Joseph was once like me. He became an honest priest and bishop. I hope that I can follow his lead."

"Pray that you change and maintain what you change into. Joseph left large footprints for you to fill. Anyone can say they are a Christian, but, in my experience, few act as true Christians. It takes an even rarer person to be a good and true Christian leader. I will do anything I can to help you on your journey."

"Thank you, General."

"Good, Brother Philip!" Valerias stared searchingly into Elderon's eyes. He appeared humble, which pleased Valerias.

Valerias mounted his horse. "Revious and Bukarma, come with me back to the fort. Oxanos, you come as well. Where is Flavius?"

"I sent him to the fort to organize Claire's security guard," Bukarma answered. "These are uncertain times, Marcus."

"Well thought, Bukarma. Maybe I should appoint you as legate protector!"

Both men laughed.

As Valerias and his riders started to ride back to the fort, they came across Gulic, Tentrides, and Weylyn huddled around the piles of Saxon weapons. The weapons were in worse condition than Weylyn had desired.

"We have been fooled," cried Weylyn. "They gave us their poorest quality weapons. The ships are unusable! We have been taken!"

"Have you, Commander?" Valerias mildly scolded Weylyn. "You miss the point. You have taken well over three thousand weapons from your enemy. The quality of most of these weapons is what I consider good or can be made good.

"Most importantly, you should study what you have here. I have seen your people's weapons, and they are much worse. It is the same with their ships. Craft your own weapons and ships based on these models. Think forward, Weylyn. A leader creates, and you need to be that leader!"

Valerias turned to Gulic and Tentrides and grinned. "I am proud of you both. I understand your artillery was a deciding factor in turning the battle at the beach in our favor. The Valiant Legion did well, too, even with that volatile Garzad in charge. Let's go to the fort, I want to celebrate. But I must see Claire first." *She is still trying to establish a connection with her son, and it is not going well. We need to repair that relationship before we return to the Villa.*

As they began riding to the fort, Valerias looked at Gulic and smiled. "Tribune Gulic, you will be a fine son."

Gulic felt an exuberance that he had never felt before. The great General Valerias, who was to be his future father, had paid him a compliment.

Valerias and his escort returned to the fort. Claire watched as they arrived. Roars of appreciation greeted Valerias' men as they entered the gates. "We are heroes today," Valerias commented. "Enjoy it!"

Claire, though, was upset and wanted to speak to Valerias. The fleeting moments of exhilaration that came with the defeat of the Saxons evaporated. She again tried talking to Drostan, only to be rebuffed. Claire was worn out from her efforts. She found that when she and Valerias worked together, problems were solved. He might have an answer that she had not considered.

She left word with a trusted Briton to tell Valerias that he was to meet her in a reception room at the fort. The Briton found Valerias in the courtyard and gave him Claire's message. Valerias excused himself and climbed the stairs to the room where he thought Claire was waiting for him. He did not see her and walked to the balcony for a better look of the courtyard below. The victorious celebration had begun, and Valerias smiled.

"General, Domina Claire is here to see you," the Briton spoke calmly.

Valerias pivoted, anxious to see Claire. The long blade penetrated his belly. Valerias looked down in disbelief and tried to grab the sword. The Briton gave the blade an extra push and the tip protruded out of Valerias' back. He looked at the Briton, his eyes asking, "Why?"

The man put his mouth to Valerias' ear. "Hail Queen Rega, you old fool! I am Amron, and I killed Eustice as well. I have assassinated a king and now a great general!"

Amron released the hilt of the sword and stepped back to admire his work. He did not feel the presence of the large figure move stealthily behind him. In one motion, the figure put the Briton's head between his hands and snapped his neck as if it were a small piece of kindling. Bukarma threw the man down in disgust.

Valerias started to sway from dizziness, and his vision became hazy. Bukarma caught him before he hit the floor. Glancing quickly at the sword, Bukarma decided not to pull it out. He looked at the pained expression on Valerias' face and felt ill. Bukarma forced the shock from his mind. He was a soldier, and he had to act like one.

"Guards! Revious! I need you now!" Bukarma's booming voice rang through the fort's hallways. Bukarma repeated himself, louder. In response, several footsteps were heard running down the hallway.

Revious was the first to arrive. He could not believe what was before him. He yelled in a primal voice, "No!" and drew his sword to unleash his anger on any more assassins. More soldiers arrived as the entire fort erupted.

Bukarma shouted to Revious, "Protect Claire and Drostan! They are next!"

Revious shouted back, "Flavius was supposed to guard Claire!"

At that moment, Claire emerged from the group of soldiers who surrounded Valerias. They had drawn their swords or had spears at the ready. She took one look at Valerias and swiftly knelt beside him. Her immediate desire was to collapse and cry, but she held those feelings back. *What good would that do?* Her focus turned solely to her husband.

"Marcus, what happened?" she asked quietly.

"We should not trust any of Rega's Britons. They are the Trojan horse."

Claire looked at Bukarma. "That is Rega's man. Amron, he called himself." Bukarma pointed at the dead Briton.

Claire turned back to Valerias. "You will get through this, just like all your other wounds. Remember the Huns?"

Valerias coughed up blood that ran in rivulets down both sides of his mouth. Claire took a piece of clean cloth offered by a hand from the crowd and wiped his face.

"Not this time, my love." Valerias coughed more blood as he spoke.

He looked at Claire, his face peaceful, and his body stopped moving. "Drostan will be fine." Valerias' voice was growing weak. "Tell Alena and Elsha that I love them."

"You shouldn't have to die in Britannia, Marcus. You should be in Italia, tending to your Villa and the Warriors' Palace. You did this for me."

"Claire, don't worry about me. I am a happy man." Valerias' voice was barely audible, and Claire leaned close to hear him. He stopped coughing.

"I have the two things that I wanted most. The first is to die in battle and not in bed as an old man. But most important, I am with you. Claire, you are my life. You saved me more than once. I love you more than anything."

Valerias stopped talking and gazed straight ahead at something no one else could see. Claire grasped Valerias' hand tightly.

"You are my love! I *will* see you in paradise!"

Valerias gently squeezed Claire's hand. A shadow of a smile appeared on his face. He very softly murmured, "J . . ." It was the last sound he made.

General Marcus Augustus Valerias, Magister Militum and Commander for Roman emperors, died.

Claire, who had remained calm since she first saw Valerias lying on the floor, stared at her dead love and screamed.

LIX

FURY

Claire gripped Valerias' body tightly as she sobbed. Bukarma ordered a circle of Roman security be placcd around her.

"Let her mourn." He spoke loudly but calmly. Many of the soldiers were grieving as well. These were men from the Villa. Bukarma shook his head; he could not believe what had just occurred. Revious' eyes were red as he wiped away tears.

Footsteps could be heard running down the hallway. General Quintus poked his head through the wall of men. He looked in disbelief at Valerias' body and at Claire.

"General, be sure Drostan is well guarded. Rega's Britons will try to kill him," Bukarma said urgently.

"A century of my guards already surrounds the rooms where he and the Christian brothers are billeted. No one will get through them!"

Bukarma saw Quintus's arm in a sling, a wound from the battle. Quintus, however, was still very much in charge, which allowed Bukarma to collect himself.

At the other side of the fort, two men poured wine for Father Timothy and the rest of his order. Outside they could hear dozens of soldiers taking solid positions around their quarters.

"What is all the fuss?" one of the brothers asked. "Have the Saxons launched a surprise attack on the fort?"

"No, I am afraid it may be worse than that." Father Timothy took a drink of his wine. He looked very apprehensive. "I think there has been a murder of a very prominent person. There are assassins in the fort."

"Certainly, they don't want us," another brother spoke. "We are just servants of God."

Father Timothy placed his cup down. "I must tell all of you this now. We are brothers in Christ, and we must protect our own."

Timothy paused and looked somberly around the room. He walked over and placed his arm around Drostan's shoulder, like a father would to a son.

"My brothers, Drostan is the son of Claire, who, as you know, is the wife of Roman General Valerias. General Valerias is the Roman commander who just defeated the Saxons and saved our lives. Claire is the former queen of a kingdom west of here. She is the rightful queen of that kingdom. Drostan is the heir."

The brothers registered a variety of reactions, from anger to prayer to the desire to comfort one another.

"Silence!" Father Timothy exclaimed. He was not to be interrupted.

"Drostan is like a son to me and he is your brother! We will do whatever we can to protect him and help him on his journey to wherever that takes him." Father Timothy's jaw jutted out from his red face.

The brothers stood motionless, stunned. The two servants who poured the wine nodded to each other. They moved slowly, making their way over to Drostan without drawing any attention to their actions. As they wedged themselves within a couple feet of Drostan, both men pulled daggers from their sleeves.

Father Timothy noticed the glint from one of the daggers and understood immediately what was about to occur. He stepped between the two men and Drostan, shouting, “NO!”

The closest man with a dagger responded, “Today, old fool, you die as well as the son of a bitch! Long live Queen Rega!”

The man pulled back his dagger to strike and suddenly stopped just as he was about to thrust it into Father Timothy’s chest. Blood spurted from the man’s throat as he dropped his dagger and reached for his neck. He fell to the floor, writhing in death throes like a snake whose head had been cut off.

Several Roman soldiers burst open the door and rushed in with swords drawn. The Roman captain surveyed the scene. His eyes swiftly focused on the second man who was standing with a bloody dagger clutched in his hand. The Roman officer raced over and was about to plunge his sword into the man when Father Timothy intervened.

“Stop! This man is innocent of any attempt on Drostan’s life! He saved us!”

The Roman captain did not believe Father Timothy at first. However, several brothers excitedly explained to the captain that Father Timothy was correct, the man with the knife was innocent. It was he who had killed the assassin.

The captain announced to the brothers, “I believe you, but I must take this Briton for interrogation. General Valerias has just been assassinated and Drostan was almost killed.” The captain pointed at Drostan. “We have vipers in our midst, and things must be sorted out.”

Father Timothy was shocked at the news of Valerias’ death. Drostan showed no expression; his mind tried to wade through everything that had just happened.

The captain nodded to two soldiers who advanced and took the Briton away. As they left, the captain spoke softly to Father Timothy, "I promise you, Father Timothy, I will not harm this Briton."

The captain ordered a squad of heavily armed Roman soldiers to guard the brothers of the order inside their room.

***

Claire slowly let go of Valerias' hand and stood up. She looked at Bukarma with wet, mournful eyes.

"I would like to be alone and undisturbed for the rest of the day," she announced. "Tomorrow morning, I would like to meet with Drostan, Weylyn, and Flavius. Be sure they are present."

Claire left and walked down the hallway to her quarters. A large contingent of soldiers flanked her on all sides. When she entered her room, Revious was present.

"There is no one here, Claire." Revious spoke softly.

"The one who should be here is not," Claire responded, tears again forming in her eyes. "I would like my husband cremated on a pyre suitable for a man of his position. He performed such a cremation for his friend, Titus, and I want the same treatment for him. Will you see that his funeral is set for two days from now?"

"Of course, Claire. I miss him too."

"I know, Revious."

Revious left Claire alone in her room. He ordered the guards not to disturb her.

The next morning came clear and bright. Claire did not sleep that night and instead wrestled with many memories. She recalled her life with Gerhard and Argus, and how things had changed so much for the better when she met Marcus Augustus Valerias. She thought of her life at the Villa and her daughters. They had matured in a safe environment, for which she was grateful. She wished she was back at the Villa with Marcus. And now that was no longer possible.

Her thoughts faded from the past and turned to what she must do. As the sun crept over the horizon, she called for Bukarma and Revious. She trusted the two men as Valerias had trusted them. Both had stayed outside her room all night and quickly responded to her call.

Claire opened the door to the men. She was dressed in a combination of Roman and Briton clothes. Her gray hair was marked by thin streaks of black that ran down the back of her head and past her shoulders. Valerias' dagger was visibly sheathed in a belt tied around her waist. As she left the room, she asked briskly, "Are Drostan, Weylyn, and Flavius present?"

"We have Drostan and Weylyn in the reception hall. We could not find Flavius."

"That is odd," Claire remarked as she entered the hall.

As they spoke, a rider whipped in through the gates of the fort. Flavius dismounted before the horse even stopped. Recognizing him, the sentries did not try to stop him. In the large courtyard, he saw Valerias' body being prepared for cremation.

A loud "It can't be!" echoed throughout the fort. Flavius' footsteps were heard as he rushed to where Claire waited. Roman guards prevented him from entering the hall until Claire gave her approval.

Flavius ran to Claire, who was flanked by Bukarma and Revious, throwing his body on the floor in front of her. He had removed his sword, which now lay by his side.

"I'm sorry. I'm so sorry!" Flavius sobbed uncontrollably.

Claire let Flavius spill out his emotions. Here was a man she previously thought was as cold as anyone she knew, and now he wept genuinely in front of her and dozens of other men. She grew concerned about the state of the man whom she and Valerias had befriended.

After a few moments she softly, but firmly, asked him, "Where were you, Flavius? Your position was to provide protection for me and you failed. You weren't here and Marcus is dead. I do not blame you, though. Rega planned this assassination well. She also almost killed my son."

Flavius raised his head and looked directly at Claire, his face moist with tears and sweat. "A Briton told me that Morguard was seen close to the fort. I left after the battles to kill that beast. It was a ploy to get me out of the castrum and away from you and Marcus. And I fell for it. Yes, I failed. Besides Marian and you, Claire, the people I am closest to are dead—Mary, my wife; Joseph, my spiritual leader; and Marcus, my friend. I let my emotions consume me, and I did not think. That is something I should never let happen!"

"And yet it did happen." Claire spoke without emotion.

Claire stood up and asked Bukarma for a sword. He handed it to her gently.

"Rise Flavius, I forgive you. Many years ago, when you sided with Argus against me, I would have killed you. But you changed for the better. You saved my life. You fought for us. This sword was my husband's, and your friend's. He would want you to have it. So do I. Do right with this sword, as my husband did."

Flavius was stunned. He had expected to be executed when he entered the room. Now he was being given the sword of the great general. He bowed deeply before Claire.

"Domina, your kindness is unforgettable. I swear to you and to all who are present that I will serve you from this day forward with my life!"

"That is all well and good, Flavius, but remember you have a daughter who needs a father—that is your foremost priority."

Claire presented the sword to Flavius. He took it with an expression of a child receiving a favorite gift. He gazed at Claire and she smiled.

Not wasting time, her attention turned to another subject. She summoned Weylyn.

"How did Rega infiltrate so many spies and assassins here at the fort?" Claire asked, puzzled.

"It is not so much her as it is her ruthless henchman, Voltrex. He planted more evil in the group that accompanied you from Ratae than I thought possible."

"I know that. Have you captured or killed all those who would do us harm, Commander?"

"Yes, my queen. We had to use certain techniques to obtain the information we needed."

"What about the man who saved my son and Father Timothy?"

"We have our spies as well, my queen. The man who saved their lives was one of mine. He provided us with information regarding Rega's spies. With this knowledge, combined with the confessions of her men, we put together a thorough understanding of Rega's spy network in our camp."

"How, then, did Amron escape detection as a spy?"

"We don't know, Queen Claire. Amron fooled us all."

"Something turned him from being a loyal captain for my brother to an assassin for Rega. We will likely never know what turned him."

Claire moved on to another subject, much to Weylyn's relief. "Weylyn, how many of Rega's confederates did you capture?"

"My queen, we captured five men, who are now our prisoners. Seven were killed, including Amron and the assassin who tried to kill Drostan. We believe four more disappeared into the countryside, likely headed for the Black Fort."

"Sixteen vile spies," noted Claire, "including Amron, who we all presumed was an ally. Rega and Voltrex are not to be underestimated."

Claire paused for a moment and then announced in a vibrant voice, "Weylyn, it is time we take back what rightfully belongs to me! To us! It is time for the people to take back their kingdom! We leave to assault my fort, the Black Fort, in two days' time. Have all Britons who want to fight under my banner ready to go."

"Yes, my queen!" Weylyn stepped back, his pleasure at this command obvious.

Claire surveyed the room and saw Drostan and Father Timothy standing off to the side. She motioned for the two men to come forward.

"Good morning, Son and Father Timothy."

Both men acknowledged Claire by nodding. Drostan was apprehensive. Over the past several days, he had seen his mother try hard to win him back. He had rebuffed her. Now the situation had drastically changed. Claire was now recognized as the legitimate queen of her kingdom. Drostan was not only her son and heir, he was her subject.

Claire addressed Father Timothy first.

"Father Timothy, I can never repay you for caring for my son. You risked much, and I am in your debt. Just yesterday you stepped in to take a death blow for Drostan. My husband respected you, which means much to me. As you know, he had his reservations about Christianity, but not you. You were a good example to him."

"Yes Claire, I mean, my lady." Father Timothy was pleased that Claire had returned to her role as queen.

"Drostan." Claire turned her attention to her son. The look she gave him was hard and not that of a mother to her son. It was a cold, piercing stare.

"Yes?" Drostan was nervous. He sensed their relationship had changed.

Claire proceeded directly to her objective. "You are the heir to your father's and my throne. I realize that is not what you want in life, but that is the way reality works. You will accompany me and whatever army I can muster, and take back our kingdom from the witch usurper Rega."

"But . . ." Drostan started to respond.

Claire cut him off sharply. "You will address me as Mother or as queen, because that is who I am."

Drostan fidgeted and looked around. He found he was alone. Father Timothy had moved off to the side.

"You have no idea what our kingdom has gone through," Claire continued bluntly. "Argus had your father murdered. Rega and her vultures murdered your uncle, King Eustice, and my husband, Marcus. They will turn the kingdom into a despotic, bloody pit of horrors. It is time to take our kingdom back. The people deserve the best we can give them: stability, prosperity, and justice. And I will damn well do whatever it takes to see that happen. You *will* be at my side when that day comes!"

Claire was fully engaged, and her eyes had changed from cold to blazing with determination. Her next words were meant for the entire room, not just Drostan.

"My husband, the great General Marcus Augustus Valerias, gave his life for Britannia, including our kingdom. If he hadn't defeated the Saxons, they would be a plague over this part of the country. We would be dead or running for our lives. More of their ilk would see their success and invade from the east. Soon we would be awash in Saxon vermin."

Claire looked at Bukarma and then Revious. "What truly dismays me is that I cannot bring my husband's body back to his home at the Villa for burial."

Claire returned her focus to Drostan. "You will be under the guidance of Tribune Gulic. He will be part of the group planning our assault to retake the Black Fort. He will also become your brother by marriage."

She stepped back and her tone changed slightly and became warmer. "When this is concluded, we will talk about your future. It does not necessarily end with you being a prince or a king."

Drostan's head whirled in many directions, and he was unsure of what everything meant. He had little time to contemplate. He turned and found himself sandwiched between Tribune Gulic and Father Timothy, who motioned for him to follow them.

Once Drostan left the room, Claire turned the discussion toward the strategy to take back her kingdom.

"Commander Weylyn informed me that Rega has consolidated her forces inside the Black Fort. Only small remnants of her army patrol outside the walls. They will retreat into the fort when we approach. We will lay siege, and then we will crush them!"

Claire paused and asked those in the room, "Where is Tribune Garzad?"

Weylyn responded, "He was last seen riding west. For whatever reason, he abandoned his post. It makes no sense."

"He was a fast-rising officer under Emperor Maximus. We must consider him a deserter." Divinicus spoke authoritatively.

Revious joined in, "I have heard a rumor that he now stands with Rega in the Black Fort. If so, he is also a traitor."

"I questioned his loyalty. He appeared to have more interest in killing Saxons and fighting Marcus than serving his legion," Claire interjected. "We will deal with him in time."

A period of silence followed until Divinicus said, "Queen Claire, I command Emperor Maximus' legion. We are under orders not to engage in a civil war between Britons. We cannot help you in this fight. Those were orders from Emperor Maximus himself before we began our campaign."

Claire looked disappointed, but Divinicus quickly countered. "However, we can assist you indirectly. We know Rega's father, Maxwellium, is king of the adjoining kingdom. I will position my legion between his kingdom and yours. He will be unable to advance any reinforcements to aid his daughter. I will justify my action with Emperor Maximus by noting that we needed to rest after the war with the Saxons. This is our way of honoring the memory of General Valerias. I gained great respect for the General in the short time I knew him."

"Thank you, General Divinicus," Claire nodded.

Tentrides announced boldly, "Queen Claire, the legion of deceased General Luxcinious, to honor the memory of General Valerias, has selected me as commander until Emperor Theodosius sends a replacement. Until then, we have no orders to avoid a fight. With the legion's consent, I have decided that we will follow you and provide aid to you in retaking your kingdom! My legion wants revenge!"

Claire smiled at the good news. "What about the Valiant Legion, Commander Tentrides?"

"Half will go back to their posts in the north country to provide security there, and the other half volunteered to fight for you. I must say that we fight to honor General Valerias and not to liberate your kingdom. That effort must come from your Britons. I hope they are up to the task."

"We are!" shouted Weylyn. "We have over three thousand men, and more are joining our ranks daily."

"That gives us over three thousand Roman legion soldiers, three thousand Britons, and the men from the Villa to lay siege to the Black Fort," a pleased Claire announced.

"The Huns are with you, Domina!" Oxanos stepped forward proudly.

Claire nodded to Oxanos. "I am grateful that you will join us. Marcus would be proud of you as well. He had great respect for your people—even as enemies years ago."

Claire gazed at her crowd of allies. "We leave for the Black Fort in two days. It will take five days to travel there and then we will set our siege. If the gods are willing, we shall take our fort from Rega within one month's time. I salute the continued Roman, Briton, and Hun alliance!"

The room rang with cheers as Claire had servants pour ale. The attendees toasted the past and future victories, and the life of Marcus Augustus Valerias. Just as quickly as the celebration began, Claire signaled for it to stop.

"I will leave you now. I must prepare for my husband's funeral tomorrow morning."

The next morning, Claire stood before Valerias' pyre. The sun dominated the sky and the wind was still, almost as if by command. Thousands of Roman soldiers stood in rigid formation. Revious and Bukarma gave short speeches that were toasts to their fallen friend. The newly titled Brother Philip blessed the cremation. Claire allowed it not because of any spiritual Christianity meaning, but as a way to alert those in the afterlife that Marcus Augustus Valerias would be joining them.

Dozens of Roman officers filed by and paid their last respects to Valerias. He was dressed in his finest battle uniform. His eyes were closed as if he were simply asleep. Claire was the final person to say goodbye. She bent over and gently kissed Valerias' forehead, placing her hand on his heart.

How is paradise, my love? Have they been welcoming to you? Is Joseph present? I truly hope so. It has only been two days and I miss you so. I don't know if I can go on without you, but I must. There is much to do. I know you would want to be here with me in what is to come. I only ask that you wait for me. Soon I will join you, and we shall see paradise together.

Claire did not move for some time; she showed no expression. She had shed all the tears that she would. Finally, she took several steps back. Roman soldiers moved in front of her and placed the body in its final resting place on the pyre. Two men carrying torches flanked her. After one more pause, she nodded and they lit the pyre.

It did not take long for the flames to reach high in the sky as if they wanted to touch their father, the sun. As the flames reached their pinnacle, the Roman soldiers spontaneously shouted in unison, several times, the battle cry of General Marcus Augustus Valerias: "*Sapor est victoria! Adhuc esurient!*"

The soldiers beat their shields with their spathas in a pulsating rhythm. The Huns watched the funeral ceremony quietly; the Britons were in awe. They had seen so much adversity in the last decade; it was inspiring to them to see such a service.

Drostan watched the funeral with Gulic, Father Timothy, and the rest of the order. He watched his mother intently throughout the ceremony. His views of her were changing. For all that had transpired between them, she was his mother, and he felt proud.

When the fire burned itself out, Claire requested the ashes from Valerias' remains be collected and placed in an urn. She would take the urn back to the Villa and bury it near Joseph. *I believe they will have endless conversations about religion in the afterlife. And someday I will join them.*

Claire took a small portion of the ash and added it to an ampule. She had the ampule strung on a gold chain that hung around her neck along with the pendent Valerias gave her in Londinium. Claire desired to keep Marcus near her heart for as long as she lived.

LX

QUICKSAND

"That was for me to do! I was to kill Valerias. I left that old crone and her spawn for you to kill! My fight with Valerias was to be soldier versus soldier and not by a cowardly act! You broke our arrangement!" Garzad spat furiously.

"Calm yourself, Roman." Voltrex slouched in a chair trying not to pay too much attention to Garzad. "We took care of their general. They won't blame you for the assassination."

"That means nothing to me, Briton. He was mine. His rank was to be my rank. I should have been the commanding general against the Saxons. Instead, I was given a legion of vagrants to command. Then, with Valerias' lackey, Luxcinious, dead, his legion chose an old engineer as the replacement instead of a warrior of my stature."

"Life doesn't always work out the way we think it should, Roman. It worked out better for us to kill that general. He would not have fought you in combat anyway. His bodyguards would have detained you and then executed you. You should be grateful that we saved your life."

"So I can sit in this old fort and be executed when that Briton witch comes here? I'm reminded of one thing, Voltrex: You paid so much attention to killing Valerias that his wife and her son escaped harm. And now they are coming for you. You failed to eliminate your biggest threat. I would call that an epic failure!"

In a split second, Voltrex flew out of his chair and pointed his knife within a hairsbreadth of Garzad's throat. Garzad's reaction was equally swift as he pointed his sword at Voltrex's chest.

"Enough!" Rega shouted. The two men slowly backed off. "We have bigger problems besides the petty conflicts of your personalities. The bitch usurper and her army of trolls will soon be within sight of my fort. My scouts tell me they have at least six thousand Roman soldiers, over three thousand Britons, and a number of those strange people we know nothing about."

"You mean the Huns?" Garzad volunteered.

"If that is what they are!" Rega snapped.

"Be glad that there are not five thousand of them. The Huns make the Saxons look like old women," Garzad said.

Voltrex sneered at Garzad's analogy. Garzad glared back in response.

"We have two thousand loyalists with us in the fort," said Rega. "We have supplies that will provide comfort to us for months. We can outlast any siege. They will not be able to scale the walls of the fort without great effort. And if they do, we will repel them.

"Further, Claire's Roman allies will disappear when Emperor Maximus learns that Roman troops are involved in a Briton matter. I imagine many Britons will lose interest once their Roman protectors leave. They will then be out in the elements alone, which will sap their morale. At that moment, we can strike and kill the bitch and end this problem once and for all. I want Claire and her son impaled alive on the longest spears we have! I will walk by them as they writhe in agony before dying. That will be my greatest pleasure."

Rega clapped her hands. "I have asked my father for aid, and he will send reinforcements. I did not tell him that Romans may be involved because he would balk at taking on such a fight. So, while you two argue over nothing but pride, I seek solutions for our real issues! I predict that in one month's time, we will be traveling the countryside, extolling the virtues of my leadership in the kingdom!"

"My queen speaks of what shall be," Voltrex said earnestly. "And we will do what is necessary to secure her dream!"

"You remind me of lovesick fools," countered Garzad. "Yes, I know all about your illicit relationship. But I don't care. I will help you in your fight."

"How many Romans did you bring with you, Garzad?" Voltrex's sarcasm returned.

"In this fight, Romans are not going to fight Romans," Garzad spoke firmly. "I have eleven men with me. It will be up to them to remain or go. I forfeited my officer title when I deserted and came here. I can no longer command those Romans."

"Where is your aide, Honorario? I believe that was his name," Rega questioned.

"He died in battle. He died a warrior's death, just as I intend to die."

"I am sincerely sorry to hear that, General Garzad. Yes, you will serve as my general in this fight." Rega appeared honest when she offered her condolences. "Tomorrow at first light, we and my captains will meet and discuss last-minute strategies."

It was late when Garzad walked to his quarters. He immediately fell asleep, but it was a fitful sleep. He awoke, startled by a bad dream. Honorario stood in front of him.

"Honorario, you are dead. How can you be here?" Garzad shook his head, trying to understand the image before him.

"You must get the Romans out of the castrum tonight. If they stay, they will die. You don't want their deaths on your conscience."

"I don't care about those men, Honorario."

"Do it for me."

Honorario stopped talking and stood straight as a fine Roman spear. His lifeless eyes looked through Garzad.

"What is it like, Honorario? What is death like?"

"Many things . . . one thing. It is for you to find out," Honorario answered.

Garzad blinked and Honorario vanished into the dark of the night.

Garzad sat up and placed his head down into his hands, thinking about what had just happened. He closed his eyes for what he thought was a moment. When he opened them, he peered out the window and saw the first hint of dawn. Without wasting a second, he rushed out the door to where the Romans were sleeping.

He quietly woke them.

"You must leave this place now! If you wait any longer, the Romans and Britons will have the castrum encircled. If you are captured, your countrymen will execute you as deserters and traitors. If you go now, turn yourselves in. Tell the Romans that Rega's forces captured you and you escaped. I wager nothing will happen to you. Follow me, you must go now!"

"What are you going to do? Are you coming with us?" The men peppered Garzad with questions. He waved them off.

"My destiny is here. Whether I live or die is of no consequence to you. Now move!"

The eleven Romans did not possess bonds of loyalty to Garzad that were worth their lives. Also, none of them wanted to die for the cause of a Briton, so they followed Garzad.

Garzad led them to a small gate. The guard was sound asleep, snoring loudly. Garzad silently opened the gate and the eleven men slipped out into the beginnings of a new day.

The last man patted Garzad on his back. "God be with you, Tribune Garzad," the man whispered, and then he was gone.

Garzad returned to his room and sat in a chair, wide awake. *Helping those men leave may have been the most humane thing I have ever done. I did it for you, Honorario. Rest in peace, my friend.*

Garzad remained motionless for almost an hour, contemplating his life. What he had done and what he had not done coursed through his mind. Honorario had softened his views of life. With Honorario gone, he would return to his old role—that of a cold-blooded killer.

A knock on his door shook Garzad out of his thoughts. He answered the door and looked at several of Rega's guards.

"Queen Rega would like to see you."

Garzad nodded and walked to Rega's chambers.

"I know you let the Romans out this morning, Garzad," Rega began as soon as Garzad entered her sight.

"Yes, I did. They have no reason to fight here."

"I will decide who stays and who goes." Rega's voice began to rise.

"They are Romans, Queen Rega. You have no say over them!"

"Oh, but I do. Voltrex captured them, and they will be executed for desertion, or being spies, or whatever reason I can think of!"

"That would be very foolish. If you want the Romans out of this fight, you will not kill those men. Otherwise, the Romans will participate in storming this fort. You and your dreams will be crushed."

"The Romans would view the men's very presence here as an act of treason."

"How would they know that, Rega? The men could be viewed by the Romans as your prisoners who escaped."

Rega frowned. She knew the Romans outside the Black Fort would not know whether the eleven Romans were traitors or captives.

Garzad continued, "Let the Romans handle whatever punishment they deem appropriate for their own. A Briton inflicting punishment on a Roman will be viewed as a serious affront to Rome. Don't forget, the Romans know it was you who planned the assassination of their general. Emperor or not, they will want their revenge."

"How do you suggest we resolve this issue?" Rega asked.

"Free the Romans, and I give you my word that I will stay and fight for you to the very end of this conflict. I will oversee defense strategies for the fort and train your men."

"Will you take an oath of loyalty to me and to the crown of this kingdom?"

"I will. I promise I will fight to my death on your behalf. I *will not* do so under the command of Voltrex."

Rega did not hesitate in responding. "Then it is agreed. You are General Garzad, the commander in defense of the Black Fort during the siege. You will report only to me."

"I agree. Now free the Romans. If Voltrex harms any of them, my bargain with you is off, and you can just kill me now."

"I give you my word, General Garzad."

Rega whispered to an aide, who quickly disappeared. "Now let's go to the southern wall. You will see for yourself that I let the Romans live. I even provided them with horses."

The two walked to the wall. As they did, Garzad thought of Honorario and smiled to himself. He looked over the walls and watched the eleven Romans riding south without a Briton escort. Surprisingly, Rega had kept her word.

He turned to Rega, "Queen Rega, my initial recommendation is to identify and mark all entrances into the fort. We will develop a security plan for these gateways. I would also publicly execute the guard who was asleep when I let out my fellow Romans. You fall asleep with the enemy outside and you will wake up with the enemy on the inside and a sword at your throat. You want to demonstrate to your soldiers what happens when they do not sufficiently perform their duties."

"Agreed. That is a matter for Comitem Voltrex." Rega spoke to another aide, who, like the earlier aide, disappeared into the caverns of the Black Fort.

They continued walking as Rega said, "My spies tell me that the hag Claire rides with a man who is well known but hated in this kingdom."

"Who?" Garzad's curiosity surged.

"His name is Flavius. Do you know him?"

"I have heard of him," growled Garzad. His thoughts went elsewhere as he responded to Rega. "You no longer need to be concerned about my loyalty to you, my queen. I want this fight!"

LXI

Siege

The combined force of Romans, Britons, and Huns arrived in front of the Black Fort's main gate. Immediately they surrounded the fortress, focusing on controlling all gates. Checkpoints were established near each gate. No one was allowed to enter or leave without first going through a checkpoint. Few people ventured through.

Britons manned the advance units and the checkpoints. The Romans provided support and advisory functions. The eighty-one surviving Huns took a position near the main gate to the Black Fort, forming an independent unit that reported only to Claire and Flavius. Claire established her headquarters in close proximity to the Huns. After Arb's death, she requested that Oxanos name a successor in the event he became incapacitated or killed.

Claire and Drostan were guarded by the Romans who came from the Villa and Britons personally selected by Weylyn. Bukarma and Revious took residence in Claire's headquarters. Bukarma was appointed Claire's chief bodyguard, the same position he held in the army for Valerias. Revious returned to managing the scouts and spies, a task he excelled at.

To an outsider, it was an odd mix of diverse Roman units, Briton villagers, and Huns. Together they formed the force that would lay siege to the fort. No one person was in total command, but all groups looked to Claire as the de facto leader.

Within two days of arriving, the two Roman comitatenses legions split into their natural parts: The legion led by Divinicus under Emperor Maximus marched west and disappeared from view; Tentrides and his united legion of Luxcinious' units and the remaining limitanei from the Valiant Legion took positions outside the walls with the Britons and Huns.

Rega and Voltrex watched Divinicus' legion march away and cheered. Garzad watched, emotionless.

"Come on, you sour Roman! Look, the Romans are disbanding, just like we thought." Voltrex conveyed his annoying, sneer-like attitude to Garzad.

Rega agreed with Voltrex and added arrogantly, "Soon the rest of the Romans will desert her, then the Britons. Claire's forces will be a pittance of what they are now. At that time, we shall ride out and destroy them! I cannot wait for that day!"

"You two are fools if you think that is what is happening," Garzad said. "First, they want you to think that Claire and her allies are disintegrating. They are not. Second, where is your father's kingdom, Queen Rega?"

Garzad did not wait for an answer. "They are marching west, where they will position themselves between you and your father. Your father will not want to fight a seasoned Roman legion. Thus, you will not be receiving any reinforcements. They will tighten the noose around this castrum. Day by day, they will squeeze it tighter."

"You are wrong, Roman!" Voltrex answered confidently. "We can hold out for a long, long time. We will outlast that mosaic of an army before us."

"Don't underestimate the Romans," Garzad countered. "You will see what they can do. Do not underestimate Claire, either. She knows it was you who killed her brother, her husband, and almost her son. She hates you as much as you hate her. Hate and revenge are powerful driving forces. I know."

Garzad's eyes narrowed as he stared hard at Rega and Voltrex. "I will prepare your men as much as I can. It will be fortunate, though, if we do not have the enemy within these walls within one month's time. Prepare yourselves for a short siege. They want to find your weakest point. Then they will strike."

"The great Roman is worried!" Voltrex spewed more scorn at Garzad.

This time Garzad remained calm. When he glanced at Rega, he could see traces of worry. *I must deal with children,* Garzad thought. *These two couldn't manage a fight against an army of mice. It is ironic that I have now become the general over a motley bunch of Britons. I should have settled for being leader of the Valiant Legion after all.*

***

Claire sat on the floor at the same level as the officers who were to take part in the siege. To her left were Bukarma, Revious, Flavius, Oxanos, and a Hun she did not know. She assumed the unnamed Hun was Oxanos' successor. To her right sat Tentrides, Gulic, Drostan, and Weylyn. Other Roman and Briton officers sat across from her.

A Roman officer spoke, "Domina, General Divinicus is in position along the border. There will be no reinforcements from the west for Rega."

"As I hoped," Claire responded. "It is now us versus them."

"I would like to counsel against engaging in a long siege," Tentrides offered. "I don't know how long it will be until I am relieved from my command by Emperor Theodosius. The new commander may have orders to not become involved with a native

Briton conflict. As much as I do not want to, we would have to withdraw under those orders."

Claire smiled, "I am planning on a short siege, Tribune Tentrides. I am asking for you and Tribune Gulic to construct two large assault towers. In the lower belly of the towers will be battering rams. We will move one tower in front of the main gate and the other will be stationed at the gate on the east side. Britons will man the towers and push them to the walls. How long would it take to build them?"

"With two hundred men, perhaps we could finish the towers in one to two weeks," Tentrides responded.

Gulic added, "Of course, the more men we have working on the towers, the faster they can be built."

"And we need protection by the legion for our tower builders," noted Tentrides.

"There is a mature forest nearby from which we can obtain wood." Gulic appeared to be talking to himself as he thought through the plan.

"The Britons and Huns will keep Rega and her forces inside her walls. If they venture out, we will swarm them," Claire declared.

Claire turned to Oxanos. "You are the best archers in our camp. I want you to pick off as many of their sentries as you can. If you see a body or a head at the walls, take a shot. I want to make being Rega's sentry a hazardous endeavor."

Claire's voice hardened as she continued, "I want Rega and her parasites to focus on the towers and the Hun assassins. In the meantime, I have a surprise for them."

"What surprise?" Drostan asked meekly.

"I will let the officer group know when it is time. This meeting is over. Tribunes Gulic and Tentrides, the sooner you construct the towers, the quicker we can take the Black Fort."

Tentrides and Gulic left the tent. Drostan followed beside them.

"Two hastily constructed towers are not going to win the day," Gulic said to his colleagues.

"The Domina has something in mind; what that is, I do not know," answered Tentrides. "It is best we start building. Drostan, you can help by being my apprentice."

Back at Claire's tent, all officers had left except Bukarma, Revious, and Flavius, who remained at Claire's request.

"My friends, I have something I must tell you, and this is for your ears only. On the day the towers are completed, I want you to assemble two hundred men. They should include the Huns and men from the Villa and Valiant Legion. I want to avoid having Britons or comitatenses legionnaires with us in this task."

The men nodded.

Claire lowered her voice to a whisper. "Flavius, do you remember the secret passageway out of the fort?"

"Of course—Mary told me about it. I was with Argus when we searched your room after your disappearance. While Argus pouted and had his temper tantrum, I waited as long as I could and then 'discovered' the passageway. It was all Mary's plan." Flavius' recollection of Mary saddened him momentarily.

"Mary had great faith in you, Flavius. And I was completely unaware of the tie between you two."

Flavius did not say a word as he gazed at the tent wall in front of him.

"I have faith in you, too, my friend," Claire added. "Are there any remaining people you know who have knowledge of the passageway?"

"None that I know of. Argus is dead, and the soldiers who were with us are either dead or scattered to who knows where. I do not know about any of the current servants. Rega likely purged any holdovers and installed her people in their place."

"Excellent," Claire nodded. "I agree."

"One thing, Claire," Flavius continued. "The passageway now has multiple killing traps in case anyone ever tries to leave or enter."

Claire was immediately concerned. She thought back to Valerias, who was excellent at rigging traps. "Who set the traps?"

"I did, on Argus' orders," Flavius announced in an animated voice. "I can also disarm them. You will have to let me go in the tunnel first."

"Thank the gods you are with us!"

"No, Claire. Thank God."

Claire looked at Flavius. His intenseness had taken over. She knew she had to be careful providing Flavius with one last piece of information. Still, she knew she had to be honest with him.

"Flavius, there is one final item to discuss. There is a rumor that Morguard is in the castrum. He may be in Rega's employ. I don't know if I believe that. I want you to swear an oath on Marcus' sword that you will ignore the rumors and do what is necessary to help us capture my fort. Pull your sword and kneel!"

Flavius swiftly complied.

Claire took Flavius' sword and placed it on his right shoulder. "Do you swear upon the sword of General Marcus Augustus Valerias and to me that you will follow all commands that are necessary to defeat the usurper, Rega? And you will not stray from your task to hunt Morguard?"

Flavius answered immediately, "I swear on the sword of the great General Valerias and to you that I will obey what you command!"

"I am counting on you, Flavius, as Mary did." Flavius bowed to Claire as she returned his sword. Flavius took his leave with Bukarma and Revious. Claire was alone. She said a brief prayer to Marcus asking for his guidance and strength in the upcoming fight.

The siege towers were constructed in ten days, although Tentrides and Gulic were displeased with the quality of the work. They doubted either tower could stand up to the defenses that would be employed against them. Claire, though, was grateful for them. She congratulated the engineers for their work. They did not understand her positivity.

During the construction, Tentrides and Gulic took time to teach Drostan engineering fundamentals. Bukarma stopped by daily to conduct a fight training course he had developed for Drostan. Drostan was at first reluctant to engage in the training, but over the course of the siege tower construction, his skills improved greatly. He found he enjoyed his time with the massive warrior, and he became adept at swordplay.

At night, he offered a prayer to God asking for forgiveness in wielding a sword. *I pray I never have to use a weapon of violence.*

LXII

Death's Portal

Once the two siege towers were constructed, Claire had Tentrides and Gulic move them within two hundred feet of the Black Fort's walls. That day was the pinnacle of gloom. Water seeped out from the fog and covered everything with a wet cloak. The open land between the towers and the fort became a muddy quagmire.

Initial concern rose among the Britons about how the towers could be transported through the mud. Tentrides, though, was a veteran of siege warfare. He had addressed this concern by setting the base of the tower platforms on a series of three axles and six wheels. Three chest-high poles were inserted across the platform parallel to the axles, which allowed up to twenty-one men to push the tower forward. Tentrides installed small battering rams near the bottoms of the towers whose only purpose was to frighten the defenders inside the fortress. As a result of the pounding at the gate by the battering ram, defenders would be drawn to protect the gate and away from the top of the siege towers.

Another Briton concern was that the fort defenders would unleash fire arrows on the towers in hopes they would burn and crumble before reaching the walls. Tentrides had a solution to that concern as well. On the front-facing sides of the towers, he placed metal shields and animal skins. The thick dampness of the day also would limit fire damage.

Tentrides ordered the towers to advance slowly. As soon as they were within range, Rega's men launched a steady stream of fire arrows at them. From the ground, Tentrides used the opportunity for his archers to pick off several of the Black Fort's bowmen.

The Britons pushed the towers forward under Roman leadership and were soon caked in thick mud. The Romans' charge was to make sure no marauders emerged from the stronghold to inhibit the progress of the towers.

For Claire, the towers were more ornamental than functional. However, to those inside the walls, the twin towers portrayed a menacing sense of doom. Garzad tried pointing out flaws in the towers' design, but Rega's defenders became mesmerized by the towers' creeping, steady advance.

As the towers continued forward, Rega's men became more apprehensive. They had never seen monsters such as these towers. In response to her troops' anxiety, Rega commanded Garzad to appear before her.

"What are you doing to stop the cursed Romans from setting their damned towers up next to our walls?" Voltrex inquired.

"More than you!" Garzad replied forcefully.

Voltrex leaped from his seat, sword in hand. Garzad pulled his own sword and wanted to end Voltrex's life in that instant. The soldiers in the room knew a final confrontation between Voltrex and Garzad was imminent. The question was who would triumph.

"Stand down, you two. NOW!" Rega shouted. "We cannot defeat Claire if we are killing each other here!"

The two men did not move and stared at each other. Voltrex was the first to step back.

"As you wish, my queen." Calm instantly returned to Voltrex.

“I will take care of the towers and any outside threat,” Garzad growled. “The towers are a mirage. You make sure we are strong inside.” Garzad pivoted on his heel and left the room with a company of soldiers.

***

At twilight, it was difficult to differentiate between night and day. Claire assembled over two hundred men in a forest clearing out of sight of the Black Fort. From her inner circle, Bukarma, Revious, Flavius, Gulic, and Oxanos were present. Drostan volunteered to join the group as Gulic’s aide. Claire grimaced as she thought about the danger her son, future son by marriage, and trusted friends would face.

Claire spoke to the men. “What we do tonight will determine whether we will be victorious and can once again raise the colors of my kingdom over the fortress.

“I must remind you that there is a very good chance that many, if not all, of us will die in our attempt. Rega and her lapdog, Voltrex, are not good leaders, but they have over two thousand soldiers at their command. Also, we have confirmed that Garzad has joined Rega. He is clever and utterly fearless; he is not to be underestimated. Yet if we follow our plan and fortune smiles upon us, we will be victorious.

“Revious will take us in the dark to the entrance of a passageway familiar to Flavius and me. There, Flavius will take the lead and disarm the traps he set.”

A question emerged from the assembled mass. “Does he remember what kind of traps and where they were set? What if they were changed?”

“Flavius set the traps when he served under Argus to dissuade anyone from using the passageway. Now he will disable them, as they are a threat to us. They have not been changed. Only Flavius and I know of this tunnel."

Claire spoke so matter-of-factly that there were no further questions. She looked at the crowd and could see barely half the assembled men.

"Before we begin our mission, I have asked Brother Philip to lead those who believe in the Christian God in prayer. For those of us who do not believe, it will still be good to hear his words of comfort."

Brother Philip cleared his throat and softly spoke in his tenor voice, "Dearest Lord, we are about to be tested mentally and physically by difficult conditions and a ruthless enemy. Give us the strength to carry out what must be done. Forgive those who must kill to survive. For those who perish, grant them access to your heavenly reward—believer and non-believer. We are in your hands, Lord. Amen."

Brother Philip stepped back, almost into Claire. He saw she had tears in her eyes. At that moment, she was not the queen but a woman who knew she was leading those who supported her cause into a battle where many would not survive.

"Marcus and Joseph would be proud of you, Brother Philip. It is my hope that you continue on the righteous path and become what they would have wanted you to become."

She patted Brother Philip on the shoulder. "Now return to Tentrides. You will hear from us soon enough."

Claire found Gulic and Drostan standing in front of her and addressed them quietly. "I do not want you to take part in this mission. I would prefer you go with Brother Philip. I don't want to explain to Alena and Elsha what happened to you two."

"I must go!" Gulic replied. "I served with General Valerias, and I want to be with you. I could not face Alena if I didn't go."

Drostan also answered, "It is my decision, Mother. I want to see where my father and you ruled. I want to see my heritage. I want to see what is worth so many lives. I will stay by Tribune Gulic's side so you need not worry about me."

"I will worry, Son." Claire thought back to Valerias and his attempts to dissuade her from joining him in the war against the Huns. He had relented, and she accompanied him from the beginning to the end of the savage campaign.

Claire shuddered. "I cannot stop either of you two from joining us. All I can ask is for you to be careful!" She looked softly into Drostan's and Gulic's eyes when she spoke.

Claire turned to Revious. "Take us to the entrance. It is time."

The walk to the passageway went quickly considering it was a black night; the moon was shuttered behind low clouds and the group used no torches. Claire thought about her band of volunteers. They included the Huns, men she knew from the Villa, and selected volunteers from the Valiant Legion. One trusted Briton who knew the Black Fort also volunteered. She was comforted knowing Tentrides commanded the Roman legion outside the walls and Weylyn was in charge of the Britons.

When they reached the entrance to the passageway, Revious lit a small torch and by that dim light, Flavius peeled back the covering to the entrance. He moved carefully as it became clear a trap had been set there. After a few long moments of working with the slightest light, Flavius laughed. Claire poked her head into the opening and gazed upon what was left of a skeleton. The bones were devoid of any flesh. A large spike protruded out of the rib cage in a grim warning for what lay ahead.

"It worked," Flavius remarked and continued up the tunnel. *I will wager that my traps stopped all other intruders.*

Claire thought back on her harrowing escape years earlier with her daughters and Mary through the same passageway. She shivered at the thought of reentering the very same tunnel to reclaim her kingdom. In doing so, she was fully aware that she could easily die.

A few additional small torches were lit as the group slowly walked through the tunnel. The floor was dry. Claire remembered it being wet when they fled Argus. However, the thick spider webs were everywhere, just as before. She remembered Alena's and Elsha's fear of the webs and the potentially giant spiders that patiently waited for prey. Claire could sense others in the group were as uneasy as she was, except Flavius.

Flavius moved deliberately up the tunnel, disarming the traps. He was a master at the task, and completed his work in less than an hour. He then stood at the secret doorway to the fortress.

"I fixed this wall so nobody could come or go," he whispered to Claire. "Fortunately, I am not nobody. I can reopen it."

Flavius proceeded to work on something that was near the floor and too dark to see. When he finished, he released a lever and motioned for Claire to come near him.

He whispered in her ear. "Have Oxanos come up here. When I open the entrance, the Huns must kill anyone who is in this room as quietly as possible so we can maintain our surprise."

Oxanos selected two Huns for the task.

On the count of three, Flavius pulled another lever and the door slowly opened. As soon as the opening was large enough, the two Huns rushed quietly through, bows and knives at the ready. The room was without light except a small candle that had almost burned out. Formless shadows flickered about on the walls and ceiling from the last breaths of the candle. No one was present.

Claire emerged through the entranceway. *Someone has been in the room recently, as evidenced by the candle. We must be careful.*

It had been her room many years ago. Now it was used solely for storing old furniture. Dust covered everything. Spider webs were suspended in the upper corners of the room. It was apparent to Claire that the room had hardly been used since she escaped. She noted the same mural was still in place that covered the opening to the tunnel years ago.

“I left it because Mary favored it,” Flavius said softly when he saw Claire looking at the image.

Claire motioned to Revious, and he and the Briton opened the door and stepped into the corridor beyond. The two sleeping guards in the corridor quickly had their throats slit. Revious waved to Claire, and quietly all of her men left the room.

“We will be spotted soon,” she remarked to those closest to her. “I am counting on the element of surprise to give us the advantage in getting to that gate.” She paused and in a reverent tone said to no one in particular, “I can feel Marcus’ presence beside me. I know we shall succeed.”

Claire removed the Hun bow she had slung over her shoulder and set an arrow at the ready. She looked at the men in the corridor and nodded to them. Then they were off.

As soon as Claire left for the tunnel, Tentrides ordered the siege towers to advance up to the walls. As they moved forward, a furious barrage of arrows and spears rained on the towers from the Black Fort’s walls. Many of the arrows had been lit and were intended to set the towers ablaze. Small pockets for fire sprouted on the siege towers.

Garzad has prepared his forces well to repel the siege towers, Tentrides thought.

Tentrides had previously transported several mobile scorpion and ballistae artillery units used against the Saxons to positions in reach of the fortress's walls. He also employed one onager. He maneuvered the artillery units so they launched bolts and stones at the walls. At first, Tentrides was reluctant to do harm inside the fort. However, he realized that to be victorious, he would need to unleash a massive artillery barrage into the guts of the place.

Tentrides began launching loads of burning shot over the walls. Soon he could see fires blazing inside the walls. At the same time, Garzad kept up his missile barrage. Any Roman or Briton unlucky enough to be within range of an archer was pierced by an arrow.

Weylyn approached Tentrides as parts of the castrum became engulfed in fire. Without looking at Weylyn, he said, "There may not be much of your Black Fort left when this is over."

"We can rebuild," Weylyn answered. "I would rather purge the stench of Argus and Rega anyway."

"I just hope Claire and her men are faring well and I'm not responsible for any deaths on our side from the artillery. Are your men ready, Commander Weylyn? When the signal is given, you will need to move quickly!"

"We are ready, Roman! Our destiny is in front of us. I await the signal!" Weylyn disappeared into the dark.

Claire's group had made it to an outer hallway when they were discovered. A cry went out that invaders were inside. The sound of dozens of footsteps could be heard running down the hallway toward them.

"We don't have much time." Claire no longer tried to keep her voice down. "This way!" she shouted.

They turned and ran down a narrow corridor. As the last man entered the corridor, Rega's soldiers arrived.

Someone on Claire's side shouted, "Go, we will hold them off."

"We must move with urgency," Claire brusquely declared. "We must reach the gate on the east side of the fort and open it for our warriors."

Flavius led the way, followed by Revious, the Briton scout, and the Huns. Bukarma was in the middle, staying close to Claire, Gulic, and Drostan. The Romans formed the rear guard.

When they reached the end of the corridor, a large door stood in their way. There appeared to be no way to open or close it. Even Flavius was perplexed. Without wasting time, Claire knew what to do. She slid two panels on the doorframe inward. With Flavius' assistance, she pushed hard on the door and it opened to the outside air. The smoke that rushed in was so thick that Claire and her men shielded their faces and coughed as they breathed.

A sudden breeze temporarily cleared the air of smoke, allowing Claire to look at the surroundings. She pointed to the outer wall and a gate to the left.

"There!" she yelled.

Men filed past her in the direction where she pointed. In her peripheral vision, she saw Gulic pull Drostan away from the retreating smoke and help him sit down. She started to say something until she saw Brother Philip emerge through the smoke.

"Why are you here?!" Claire demanded.

Brother Philip gave no evidence of being bothered by the smoke. "I want to see what hell is like."

"It is all around you, Brother Philip! Can't you sense it? And it will get worse. Watch yourself. Rega's men will show no mercy, whether you are a man of God or not!"

The first of Tentrides' siege towers rammed into the wall above the main gate. The drawbridge on the tower was lowered and several Britons spilled out onto the wall. Garzad was prepared and had his own mobile bolt-thrower placed opposite the siege tower.

He waited for the count of ten after the drawbridge was lowered and shouted, "NOW!"

The machine launched its charge into the tower with devastating results. The top exploded, killing and wounding tens of Britons. The siege tower crumbled to the ground into a heap.

"Beautiful!" Garzad exclaimed as he watched the tower collapse. The second tower slowly approached the wall near the east gate.

"Get that son of a bitch!" Garzad shouted to the men around him.

Before Garzad could move, he heard screaming coming from inside the walls. He turned and saw the first wave of Claire's men emerge from the smoke. He didn't stop to think how they came to be there before he yelled, "Kill them!" as he pointed toward the eastern gate.

As Claire's men advanced, a wall of soldiers moved into position between Claire and the gate. In the middle of the formation was a savage-looking figure.

"I am Voltrex!" he screamed. "You will have to come through me to get to this gate." Claire looked behind and saw the smoke had largely cleared. Her rear guard was disintegrating under the onslaught of Rega's soldiers. Now a large force led by the menacing Voltrex stood between them and the gate. It was determination time between victory and defeat.

Claire said a silent prayer, *Marcus, please help us!*

At that moment, Revious rushed past her, giving a Hun war cry, and singlehandedly assaulted Voltrex's men. He managed to kill two fighters with thrusts from his sword. Revious then focused on Voltrex. He lunged at him and missed. As he did so, he was hit by a blunt object from the side. Revious fell to the ground, stunned. His vision turned to Voltrex standing over him. Voltrex plunged his sword through Revious' gut as an arrow from Claire's bow whizzed by the left side of Voltrex's head.

Claire coughed and cursed her miss. Hun archers, however, were finding their marks with wicked regularity. Bukarma now led the attack. He drove his spear through the chest of an enemy while piercing another with his sword. He was in a rage, and he slayed any of Rega's men within reach. Under Bukarma's onslaught, Voltrex's force began to melt away, and the gate was in sight. Voltrex disappeared.

Bukarma dodged arrows shot from the walls and reached the gate. He was joined by several Huns and Romans who worked feverishly to remove the debris Garzad had placed to block its opening.

Garzad moved several archers to the wall by the gate, and they inflicted a heavy toll on Claire's group. Bukarma was first hit in the arm. Another arrow cut through the flesh of his leg.

Gulic held Claire back from going near the gate, and a group of Huns formed a circle around the wounded Revious. Arrows from the wall continued to fell the men around her. The casualty rate was nearing fifty percent dead or wounded. Claire felt all was lost and that the battle inside the walls would be over. She took bitter consolation knowing she would soon be joining her husband in death.

Garzad's attention had shifted from the wall to the gate to prevent Claire's men from reaching it. He was successful, as the gate remained secure. Garzad was troubled, though, at the ease with which Claire and her men had gained access inside the fortress.

A crash reverberated through the wall—the second siege tower had breached the top of the wall. Britons swarmed from the tower. Garzad had no artillery and not enough soldiers there to halt the Britons' advance. He swore at the gods, followed by curses directed at Rega and Voltrex.

When Garzad looked down, he winced at the now-open eastern gate as the Britons poured in. His men began to desert, and the defenses crumbled. Worse, the Roman legion had not even entered combat yet. Garzad knew the battle was finished.

The melee inside the fort gradually tapered off as fighting became more centered in pockets between die-hard remnants of Rega's forces and Claire's Britons.

Revious remained barely alive. He was conscious and in great pain. Several surviving Huns surrounded their friend with Claire, Bukarma, and Oxanos hunched beside him. Through blood-stained eyes, Revious saw Brother Philip off to the side and called for him. Philip came and squatted next to him.

"I am about to leave this world," Revious muttered through bursts of pain. "Bless me, Brother Philip, as I make my journey to the next world."

Brother Philip was shocked at the carnage and violence he had witnessed. It was indeed hell on Earth. He needed a moment to compose himself and respond to Revious.

"Revious, you are a good man fighting for a just cause. May our Lord bless you and take your spirit to the throne of God. I will pray for your soul."

Revious coughed from deep in his chest, and blood oozed out of his mouth. He looked at Bukarma and then at Claire.

"Take care of my Huns. Do you promise?"

"I promise, my friend," Claire responded. In a quiet, determined voice, she repeated, "I promise."

Revious weakly grasped Bukarma's forearm.

"I am going to tell Marcus I came first!" Revious smiled, coughed for the last time, and died.

Claire gently closed Revious' eyes with a heavy sigh. She sat on the ground with her eyes closed.

The battle had been fought over several hours, and the first light of dawn could be seen in the east. Bodies were strewn about the courtyard and on the walls of the Black Fort. Small pitched battles were still occurring. All the fires had been contained.

Claire had had enough. She stood up and bitterness took control. She faced Bukarma. A fierce resolve was etched on her face. Her look reminded Bukarma of Valerias when he faced adversity.

"They," Claire pointed to upper levels of the castrum, "have killed my husband, my brother, and now my friend and all these men. Once and for all, it is time to end this!"

Claire took her bow with the two arrows she had left and began climbing the stairway to the upper rooms of the fort. Bukarma was close behind, swearing revenge for Revious.

Off to the side, Flavius watched Garzad's profile as he walked between openings in the wall one floor above him. With Valerias' sword in hand, Flavius pursued him.

"We must support your mother, Drostan! You must be a warrior now!" Gulic shouted.

Gulic pointed to Drostan's sword, which was still sheathed. Gulic himself carried a crossbow. Without thinking, Drostan followed Gulic up the nearby stairs after his mother.

Rega and Voltrex retreated to a room adjacent to her bedchamber.

"I think things have gone badly," Voltrex said, stating the obvious.

"That Roman Garzad was worthless!" Rega said angrily. "My visions for this kingdom and my rule are gone. That hag Claire will triumph, and I cannot stand the thought!"

Voltrex responded calmly, "I have men waiting for us by the west entrance. We can leave now and flee, and start a rebellion in the countryside. Or we can just go back to your father. You can return to your life as a princess and I your valiant aide."

"My father is not going to appreciate what has happened here. I was to be queen, and gradually our kingdoms would merge. Life would be good. Perhaps killing Eustice was not a wise choice."

"You are too ambitious for the life he planned for you. And where would I be?" Voltrex smiled, but it was a smile of resignation.

Footsteps could be heard on the stairway.

"Gather your things quickly, and I will get mine. We will meet back here and then go to the west wall and gate." Voltrex's voice was abrupt.

"Yes, I will be ready, my love." Rega glanced at Voltrex, who had disappeared from sight.

Rega had no intention of leaving. She drew her sword and waited.

Bukarma sprinted past Claire on the stairway, ignoring the pain from the arrow wounds. He entered a series of rooms that appeared to be recently used by someone of high status. It was dark except for the soft glow of light from almost-spent candles. The sword he held in his right hand was the one Valerias had given him years ago. In his left hand, he grasped a double-edged dagger.

Bukarma heard a muffled sound in the room to his right. As he moved to the doorway, he felt a heavy weight slam into his chest.

He sprawled onto the floor; his sword and dagger flew out of his hands. He sensed what was coming and rolled sharply to his right. Voltrex's sword missed his left ear by less than an inch as it slammed into the floor.

"Ignorant Roman," Voltrex snarled. "You are a big man who just took a bigger fall. Now you shall feel my steel!"

Voltrex raised his sword again to stab Bukarma. This time, Bukarma blocked the blow with his left forearm. With his right hand, he pushed up on Voltrex's sword-bearing arm, preventing another strike. Voltrex punched Bukarma in the face with his free hand, hitting him again and again. Bukarma's injured arm was not strong enough to stop him. Yet with his good arm, Bukarma kept a tight grip on Voltrex so Voltrex could not use his sword.

Gradually, the pressure exerted by Bukarma caused Voltrex to loosen his hold on the sword. Bukarma gave a mighty flick of his wrist, and Voltrex's sword crashed on the floor. The Briton focused on retrieving it, and as he did so, Bukarma grabbed his neck and tightly squeezed his throat with his good hand. Voltrex tried to reach for his knife, but relieving the pressure on his throat took all his energy.

With renewed power, Bukarma surged to his feet, still holding Voltrex by the neck. He carried the struggling Briton over to a window.

"You killed my friends, and now it is time for you to die!" Bukarma shouted.

"Oh, you will join me!" Voltrex grunted as Bukarma choked him. Voltrex finally managed to grasp his dagger and dug it into Bukarma's side.

Bukarma groaned with the pain and slammed Voltrex against the wall. Voltrex went limp. With the last of his energy, Bukarma gripped Voltrex again by the neck, dragged him onto the ledge, and pushed him out the window. Voltrex fell in silence to his death.

Bukarma peered out the window and saw nothing. He felt shafts of pain from his new injury and from the others. He dropped down hard on the floor next to the window and slipped into unconsciousness.

***

Further down the corridor, Claire stalked her unseen prey. She held her bow, a shaft nocked onto the sinew string. She heard a noise coming from one of the rooms. She stepped inside, heard the noise again, and shot her arrow toward the sound. It struck a wood cabinet. Claire cursed herself for recklessly wasting an arrow. She had only one left.

She swiftly nocked her last arrow to her bow. This time, a shadowy target moved in front of her and Claire loosed the arrow, striking the figure. Claire rushed over and saw the body was one of Rega's men, not Rega. The man was dead on impact, with the arrow through the center of his chest.

Claire was furious and frustrated. *Perhaps Rega is not here,* she pondered.

She was out of arrows. At that moment, two hands came down, grabbed her bow, and pulled so the string was around her neck. Rega pulled back on the stave as hard as she could. Claire was stunned; she was being garroted.

Claire knew she had only moments before she passed out and died. She found her dagger in its sheath and drew it, careful not to drop it, and plunged it into whatever flesh she could hit behind her. Rega howled in pain, clutching her thigh, and released her hold on the bow. Claire coughed violently and lifted the bow from around her neck. As she freed herself, she dropped the dagger.

Claire stood up to catch her breath and felt the weight of Rega land on her back. Instinctively, she reached behind her and in one movement tossed Rega on the ground in front of her. The two wrestled and hit each other with fists, knees, and heads. Rega tried to use her knife, but Claire grabbed her forearm and stopped her. The women rolled over the dead man, and as they did, the arrow in his chest broke off.

Rega pulled free from Claire and straddled her, pinning her back against the ground. Rega took her knife and thrust it blindly at Claire. The blade caught Claire's right shoulder. She groaned in pain. Rega could taste the blood of her enemy.

"Look, false queen, you will never rule your land again. You were finished by the real queen!"

Rega raised her dagger to plunge it down once more. As she reached up, she felt a stabbing pain in her neck. Blood squirted out. Rega reached for the source of the pain and felt a wooden stick covered in her own blood. Claire had driven the broken half of the arrow into Rega's neck.

"I am the true queen and you are dead. You will not be missed!" Claire shouted, and with the last of her energy, she shoved Rega's body from her onto the floor.

Rega died in a wide pool of her own blood. Claire slumped down beside her, exhausted.

***

A room at the top of the fort beckoned Flavius. He could sense Garzad waited for him there. The door was open and Flavius walked in, with Valerias' sword at the ready. Flavius blinked. Garzad was sitting calmly in a chair. A blazing fire burned in the hearth to his left.

"Flavius, you found me. I suppose you have come to kill me."

"That I have. I know you from somewhere, Garzad. I just can't remember where."

"Oh, I know you, Flavius. You betrayed your master, Argus, and joined forces with that Roman dog, Valerias."

"You are the traitor, Garzad. You are a Roman officer who deserted and joined a failed usurper."

"Rega is queen of this land, fool. You fight for the usurper."

"Wrong, traitor. Claire is the lawful queen. She was queen before Rega. How could you betray the empire for a false queen?"

"It doesn't matter now, does it? You are a weak man, Flavius. I want to show you how weak you are."

Garzad reached down and gave a strong tug on a line. Flavius had been so involved in talking to Garzad that he had unwittingly walked into a trap. Garzad had set a rope in the form of a noose on the floor, and when he jerked the rope, it quickly tightened around Flavius' ankles. The pull from the rope caused Flavius to fall backward, and he hit his head hard on the floor. Everything went black.

Flavius awoke moments later when Garzad threw a bucket of cold water on his face. He lay with his back to the floor. Both hands were tied tightly in leather straps. Garzad was watching him intently.

"You still don't who I am, do you?"

Garzad reached up and pulled his dagger out of the fire. The tip was red hot. He put his face within inches of Flavius'. His left hand held down Flavius' head to avoid being struck.

Garzad's closeness and his voice stirred Flavius' memory and he suddenly knew who the man was. His physique had changed and the beard covered much of his face, but underneath the physical features, Flavius knew him.

"I see you know now, Flavius. Yes, it is me, Morguard. After that Roman bastard Titus killed Argus, I traveled to Africa as a Roman citizen and enlisted in the army. It was easy to rise through the ranks, particularly when you do the dirty work for the generals. I didn't want to return to this shit place, but I follow orders. My mission was to provide guidance to Rega, and that is what I have done. But that is enough about me. What I want you to know is that the last thing you will see is me."

Morguard placed the glowing dagger close to Flavius' eye. "I want you to know that your woman, Mary, was passed around to my men who enjoyed her company. She didn't seem to enjoy ours, though. I let her live only so the memories of our time together could haunt you both forever!"

Flavius struggled to free himself from Morguard's tight grip. He cursed him. He violently shifted his weight to the left and then to the right, but it was no use. Morguard was in too strong of a position.

Morguard slowly inserted the tip of the red-hot dagger just inside Flavius' left eye. Flavius screamed as the pain overwhelmed him. He lost consciousness for a moment and was sharply brought back to reality as Morguard slapped his face. His tormentor adjusted his position slightly as he prepared to make the same incision into Flavius' right eye.

Flavius was now limp. Morguard twisted the still glowing knife with one hand as he pushed Flavius' head back with the other. He was about to plunge the knife into Flavius' right eye when Gulic and Drostan burst into the room. They had been searching for Claire but had found Flavius instead.

"Well, it is the toy officer and the whore's spawn." Morguard glowered at Gulic and Drostan. "I may not kill her, but I will kill her son!"

Morguard stood and started to advance. Gulic raised his crossbow and loosed a bolt at Morguard, but he was too quick and jumped out of the way as the missile shot by his shoulder. Morguard watched the bolt strike the wall behind him and turned back to Gulic.

"You just lost your only chance to live, Roman!"

Gulic fired another missile from his crossbow. This time he caught Morguard inside his right shoulder.

"What?" Morguard was surprised by the strike of the second bolt.

"This is a double crossbow, traitor, something I have been perfecting for years."

Gulic reached back and pulled two more bolts from his pack to reload. However, as Gulic glanced up, he saw Morguard hurl himself at him. The force of their clash knocked Gulic to the floor, and his crossbow skidded out of reach. Morguard dropped his dagger from the impact. He drew his sword instead.

"I will cut off your head first, and then attend to the boy. I will cut him into small pieces. You will just be missing your head."

Morguard pulled Gulic's head up by his hair to make a clean slice across his neck. Gulic struggled to free his own dagger but could not because Morguard had forced him into an immovable position. He knew death was inevitable.

Before Morguard could strike, Drostan grabbed a large piece of wood from the hearth and delivered a blow to Morguard's head. Morguard was shaken but recovered enough to strike Gulic with the hilt of his sword. Gulic fell back in a daze.

"I will deal with the bastard and then I will come back for you," Morguard snarled.

Morguard rose to his feet and rubbed the back of his head where Drostan had hit him. He advanced, raising his sword at the boy. Drostan froze as Morguard faced him. His sword remained in its sheath.

"I will start by removing your hands, then your feet. It will not take long until you are in small pieces. That is how your mother will find you."

Morguard thrust his sword toward Drostan's waist, but Drostan found a quickness he did not know he had and evaded the thrust.

Morguard kept coming, bellowing, "It is only a matter of time before my head clears and you and my steel become one!"

Drostan threw a heavy metal bowl at Morguard's shoulder where Gulic's arrow still protruded. Morguard yelped in pain and his face distorted.

He swore violently and shouted, "It is the pain that drives me, you little shit, and makes me stronger. You are about to feel pain you cannot imagine!"

Drostan stepped back and tripped on a stool. At that same moment, Morguard swung his sword, ripping a long tear across Drostan's chest. Morguard stood over Drostan, glowering. Drostan closed his eyes and waited for the deathblow.

Suddenly, Morguard lurched forward; his attention was no longer on Drostan. He began spitting blood.

Flavius had managed to free himself from Morguard's restraints. He took the dagger that Morguard had dropped and stuck it forcefully into Morguard's back. Morguard turned and pushed against Flavius, who fell back onto the ground. Morguard tried to reach around to pull the knife out of his back, but Gulic's dagger plunged into his chest.

Morguard stumbled around the room without uttering a sound. He finally stopped moving, raised his arms, and cried out, "I am free, Honorario!"

Morguard crashed to the ground, face first. He was dead before he landed.

LXIII

Calm Uncertainty

Flavius struggled to return to reality, slipping in and out of consciousness. He heard voices, then silence, then voices again. He could see nothing and at first believed he was dead. A voice talking to him sounded familiar. *Perhaps I am hearing the voice of Jesus or a saint*, he thought in his stupor. Gradually, intense pain took over and he reached for the source of the pain, his left eye. A warm hand gently took his.

"Flavius, do not touch your eye. Do not touch either of your eyes."

Flavius tried to identify the speaker. His senses focused on the voice. Flavius then recalled a person from his past. The event was Valerias and Claire's wedding.

"Olivertos?" Flavius's hand trembled as he reached up to touch Olivertos' face.

"Yes, Flavius, it is me. Claire summoned me. I will do everything in my power to help you and my friends heal."

The gifted physician in Valerias' legions from years ago had come to Ratae from Bergen to face the carnage of war one more time.

"Thank God," Flavius answered, reassured.

Flavius closed his right eye and sighed. A female voice spoke to him in a soothing tone. It was Claire; she was alive.

"Flavius, you kept your promise to me and you saved Gulic's and Drostan's lives. You honor Marcus' sword."

For a moment, Flavius shook the pain from his mind. He tried to remember the fight with Morguard.

"Claire, that is wrong, they saved me. I would be blind or dead if Gulic and Drostan hadn't found me. They are the true heroes."

"What I see is that you are all heroes. Together you killed one of the most frightful beings who ever walked on this earth. To this day, I cannot believe that Garzad was Morguard in disguise. His presence as Garzad fooled all of us.

"If you hadn't managed to pull yourself from those straps, he would have killed my son and my future son by marriage. I still don't know how you freed yourself, but you did. When we found you, there were strips of your skin wrapped on the straps. You had to have suffered incredible pain. Olivertos tells me it will be weeks before you can use your hands properly, and you have lost the sight in your left eye. I am so sorry."

"I can thank God; one eye is all I need."

"You will need your eye. I have sent for Marian and she will be here before years' end. You will need to be a dutiful father. After your reunion with her, I want you to return to the Villa. A lingering presence in Britannia would not be favorable to you or Marian."

"Tell me what happened." Flavius wanted to know about the siege.

"We were victorious, Flavius. Rega and her demon, Voltrex, are dead. And, of course, you already know that Garzad, or rather Morguard, has joined the devils. We killed more than seven hundred of Rega's men. Over five hundred men surrendered and are our prisoners. Many others escaped into the crowd or fled over the western wall. They are no longer a threat. Some have denounced Rega and pledged loyalty to me."

Claire lowered her voice. "Our casualties were also great. Four hundred of our Britons lost their lives. Between the battle with the Saxons and here, the Huns lost forty-one men and women. That is almost half of those who came to Britannia. The men from the Villa and the Valiant Legion suffered about thirty percent casualties. Tentrides' legion lost eight men. However, they didn't enter the fort until the battle was nearly over."

"What about . . .?" Flavius started to ask another question.

Claire interrupted. She knew what he was going to ask. "Gulic, Drostan, Bukarma, and I are improving. We all have various wounds. Bukarma has it the worst. Time will be our ultimate healer."

Claire touched the red scar on her neck left over from her fight with Rega. "Rest now, my friend. Olivertos is the finest physician I have ever known."

Flavius immediately fell asleep. Olivertos had given him a plant extract to reduce the pain and allow him to sleep. Claire walked outside with Olivertos.

"How is he progressing, Olivertos?"

"I think he is doing better than expected. The defeat of Rega's forces is a notable morale booster. The loss of his left eye will make it more difficult for him to function as he once did. He is fortunate, though, to still have his right eye. His hands will be sensitive to touch for a long time, perhaps forever. It is possible his days of effectively handling a sword are over."

"How are Ruth and the children?" Claire could not remember the number of children in Olivertos' family.

"The family is doing quite well. Our sons, Joseph and Jacob, are healthy. Our physician clinic is no longer in the church that Joseph built. A wealthy villager gave us money to construct a new building. Life is good, Claire."

"I agree, Olivertos. I am pleased my son and future son by marriage are on the mend. Bukarma also, gods willing, should fully recover in time." Claire paused for a moment. "I miss Marcus terribly."

Claire paused and gently caressed the ampule containing Valerias' ashes held by the chain around her neck. "He can't recover from his wound."

"He was quite the man," Olivertos added. "He had such an impact on my life. Even though he never became a Christian, he grew spiritually—particularly after he met you. You changed his life, Claire."

"And he changed mine. I will always love him, always!"

Claire began to cry softly as the good memories she had with Valerias flowed back into her thoughts. She embraced Olivertos and thanked him for coming to tend to the wounded.

A Roman cavalryman rode up to Claire.

"Queen Claire," the man began, "General Divinicus will arrive shortly and would like a counsel with you."

"Have the general come to my lower receiving room in the fort."

The man rode off, and Claire hugged Olivertos again. "I must attend to the queen's business. I will see you again."

Claire walked to the receiving room. On the way, she saw Tentrides with a company of Roman soldiers. She waved to him and he walked over to her.

After the battle had largely ended, Tentrides' legion entered and secured the castrum. He had done his duty by not directly entering the fray, but contributed enough to have the battle finish in Claire's favor.

"Tribune Tentrides," Claire said, "please join me in the receiving room. General Divinicus is meeting me there."

“As you wish,” he responded. The two, with a small company of Tentrides’ soldiers, walked in.

Claire had her servants prepare a quick assortment of food and drink for the visitors. Within moments, Divinicus strode into the room, also with a cadre of soldiers.

“Queen Claire, congratulations on your victory over the murderer and tyrant, Rega. I trust you will rebuild your Black Fort and your bodies in time.”

“Thank you, General. Won’t you and your men have something to eat and drink?”

Divinicus took a cup of ale and motioned for his men to join him. Each person in the room fetched something to drink.

Claire raised her cup. “A toast to our Roman allies who helped us defeat the Saxon horde and the usurper to my throne. Long may our relationship last!”

Divinicus took a drink. He also offered a toast. “Normally, Britons and Romans do not get along well. But we have put our differences aside and defeated common enemies—at least common enemies from my viewpoint. We salute the memory of General Marcus Augustus Valerias. I served with him only a short time, but he taught me much. He taught us all much! *Sapor est victoria! Adhuc esurient!*”

The crowd of men shouted in approval. Divinicus looked over to Tentrides and motioned for him to come forward. Tentrides was unsure of what it meant.

“I ran into a messenger from Emperor Theodosius on my way here. He had this letter for you. Even though we serve different emperors, we are all Roman soldiers.”

Divinicus handed the scroll to Tentrides, who carefully opened the parchment and quietly read its contents. He smiled broadly when he finished.

"Thank you, General Divinicus. Emperor Theodosius, with the approval of Emperor Maximus, has promoted me to the rank of general. I must have done favorable things to receive such a promotion. I toast the memory of General Luxcinious!"

The soldiers cheered again and took another drink.

Afterward, Divinicus spoke to Claire privately.

"You will not have an issue with the kingdom to your west; King Maxwellium was pleased you spared the lives of so many of his soldiers. He acknowledged that his daughter overstepped her bounds. He wanted a good marriage and future between Rega and Eustice. Instead, she turned into a power-hungry adulteress.

"He gave me his word he would leave your kingdom alone, and I believe him. If he does not, General Tentrides or I will pay him a visit. Besides, he is more afraid of the Saxons returning. He wants to forge an agreement with you to become allies against future Saxon attacks. General Valerias said the Saxons would return, and I agree."

Divinicus gazed at the war-ravaged fort grounds and the wounded who hugged the walls. He visited with Oxanos and inquired about the Hun bow. Oxanos gave him one as a gift. In return, he presented Oxanos' warriors with Roman spathas.

Divinicus' last stop before leaving was a conference with Tentrides. Both served different emperors, and each knew at some point they may be enemies. But today they were colleagues and friends. Divinicus wished Claire well and left with a squad of Roman cavalrymen.

Outside the walls, the prisoners who fought with Rega waited. Divinicus would deliver them to Maxwellium as a gesture from Claire that she wished to have harmony between the two kingdoms.

As Divinicus rode away into the distance, Tentrides remarked to Claire, "He is ambitious but a good soldier. I have no doubt what he told you is true about the kingdom to the west."

Claire nodded in agreement. "We have much to do here. The burials are completed. We cremated Revious' body, as he requested. His ashes were placed in an urn that will accompany Marcus' ashes when I return to the Villa. Marcus would be proud of him."

She added a final note. "Marcus would be pleased that you were promoted to the rank of general, Tentrides. He admired your intelligence and perseverance."

***

Five months passed after the battle at the Black Fort. Repairs were slowly made to the structure and to the people. The return of Queen Claire stabilized the countryside. Rebellions evaporated and farmers returned to their fields. A relief that the turmoil was no longer a constant companion of the people spread throughout the land—even if the feeling was tenuous.

Under orders of Emperor Maximus, General Divinicus moved his legion south to Londinium and then across the Narrow Sea. Maximus had grand ambitions, and Divinicus was included in those ambitions.

General Tentrides took his legion and the remaining limitanei to fortify Hadrian's Wall. Once the limitanei were reestablished, he was subsequently commanded by Emperor Theodosius to take his comitatenses legion south near Valerias' old command center west of the Danube.

Olivertos returned to Ruth and their children in Bergen. Brother Philip traveled with him, as he decided to become the priest for the village after undergoing the proper training. Brother Philip wanted to follow in Joseph's path; starting in Bergen seemed appropriate to him. Olivertos readily concurred with Brother Philip's plan.

Claire learned that Father Timothy and his order had returned to the hermitage buildings at Branodunum. Father Timothy was aware the move would likely be temporary, but he was grateful to return home. Father Timothy also volunteered to serve as Brother Philip's sponsor.

Even though Flavius was heralded as Morguard's killer and a warrior for the Britons, his presence in the region was not well received. He would return to the Villa with Oxanos and the Huns. Claire had pardoned Gerlok and the men from Menze. They, too, would accompany Flavius back to Italia.

Before he was murdered, Valerias, through his lawyer in Rome, deeded certain lands to Alena and Elsha under the condition that the Huns could remain in Valerias' valley for as long as they desired to do so. Valerias wanted to repay the Huns for their loyal service.

The land became safe for travel, and Claire arranged for Alena, Elsha, Marian, and Bukarma's wife and children to venture north to Claire's kingdom. When they arrived at the Black Fort, Drostan was reunited with his sisters. They had all been small children the last time they saw each other. Now they were adults, or nearly adults.

Wolf was initially shy around Drostan. Within a short time, though, he was rambunctiously seeking attention from the eldest sibling.

Gulic's first words to Alena were, "I want to marry you tomorrow."

Alena wore the necklaces given to her by her betrothed and her father.

When they were reunited, Flavius wept in Marian's arms. She couldn't help but notice that his left eye was covered by a patch, and his hands were wrapped in bandages.

"Father, what happened to your eye? And your hands?"

"It is a test of life and faith, my sweet child. My vision is now concentrated into one eye, and that is all I need to look at you. I can still hold you in my arms. I promise we will never be apart again."

After their first, long embrace, Bukarma and his family knelt and gave thanks to God that they were alive and together again.

Claire tried hard to maintain a regal presence but failed miserably. The sight of Drostan, Alena, and Elsha together again was too much for her. It had been ten years since they were last together as a family. The four entered into a long embrace, and for a moment the past was forgotten.

Alena and Elsha had learned of Valerias' death well before they arrived at the Black Fort. They knew true love existed between Marcus and their mother and his love for them. He had been a good, wise man—the only father the girls remembered. They loved him, and his death caused them a searing feeling of loss.

Previously at the Villa, Bukarma and Revious had told Alena and Elsha stories of what Valerias was like before he met their mother and how she had influenced him. They knew what a good and powerful influence he had been in their own lives. When they looked at their mother, they thought of their father.

Revious' death also saddened the girls. He was the jokester who knew how to tease their parents. And he was their stalwart friend to the end.

"That is a consequence of war," Drostan explained to them later. "I am sorry I had to see his death. I pray for war to be banished from this Earth. But after what I have seen, I doubt that will happen."

That night, Claire held an early supper for her family and close friends. It was a beautiful day in late autumn. After supper, everyone took a walk just outside the fortress walls. Claire sat on a bench carved from a felled tree. Bukarma and Flavius, each carrying a sword, joined her. She called for Drostan, who came and stood in front of her. She looked like a queen but spoke as a mother.

"Drostan, you are my only son. You are heir to the throne. However, *you* must decide what it is that you will do with the rest of your life. You can return to Father Timothy's order and become a brother. You can choose to assume the crown after I leave. Or you can return to the Villa with me. I made a promise to Marcus that I would bury his ashes there. I will do the same for Revious. That is something I must do. The choice is yours. I put no hold on you."

Drostan looked intently at his mother and knew she meant what she said. He started to say something, but Claire waved her hand, indicating that she wasn't finished.

"No matter what you decide, I want you to have this." She motioned to Bukarma.

Bukarma held out a sword for Drostan. He took it, but was unsure of what to do with it. He looked to his mother.

"The sword was a gift from my Marcus to Revious. Now I am giving it to you. You never have to use it, but I want you to keep it. When you look at it, I want you to think of Marcus, know he was a good man, and live by his integrity."

Drostan stepped back. Alena and Gulic joined him, admiring the sword.

"How long will Tribune Gulic be with us?" Bukarma asked Claire.

"As a gift in remembrance of Marcus, Emperor Theodosius said Gulic can stay here as long as I need him to repair our stronghold. I foresee a wedding taking place in the very near future. After all, it is time for the next generation."

"What will you do, Claire? Will you remain as queen or return to the Villa for good? What do you think Drostan will do?" Bukarma was full of questions.

"Weylyn is a capable leader and might be a good regent. Drostan is not ready to take the throne. I am not going anywhere yet. But those are decisions for a later time, my friend. I want to embrace what I see before me. That is all I want for now."

Evening approached as the sun tried to squeeze out the last bit of light on the land. The air held a tinge of warmth to close out the day. Flavius moved the sword he was carrying and placed it by Claire. It was Marcus' old sword that she had given to Flavius.

Claire smiled as Flavius leaned the sword next to her. In front of them were Bukarma's, Flavius', and her children with Penelope. Drostan, Alena, and Gulic were laughing. Elsha and Marian played a game with Penelope, Evaline, and Lavonica. Giggles filled the air. Wolf couldn't decide who to play with next.

Off in the distance, a sunset haze formed on the horizon. In a final effort, a last ray of sun broke through and briefly brightened the party. Claire reached out her hands for Bukarma and Flavius. Each took a hand as the sunlight faded into twilight. They were silent in their thoughts.

The past is spent and cannot be changed, Claire mused. *The future is unpredictable and out of my control. It is now that is important to me, and it is now that I treasure.* Her thoughts turned to Marcus Augustus Valerias.

Claire gazed at the dark horizon, knowing that time would bring daylight to the land once again.

CLOSING

"Reflect upon the rapidity with which all that exists and coming to be is swept past us and disappears from sight. For substance is like a river in perpetual flow . . . and ever at our side is the immeasurable span of the past and the yawning gulf of the future, in which all things vanish away. Then how is he not a fool who in the midst of all this is puffed up with pride, or tormented, or bewails his lot as though his troubles would endure for any great while?"

—Roman Emperor Marcus Aurelius, taken from *How Rome Fell*, by Adrian Goldsworthy

LXIV

Distant Shadows

The day's weather was maddeningly unsettled. One moment the sun took control and warmed the land, and the next moment clouds and a cold wind carried spits of rain that dominated the air.

The Land Rover didn't care about the weather as it navigated the rough road. After an hour of bouncing around like a carnival ride, the vehicle stopped at a farmer's cottage. The driver immediately popped out and walked briskly to the front door of the house. The man didn't care about the weather. He wore a bright blue, short-sleeved polo shirt. He was clean shaven with a quickly spreading bald spot. His wire-rim glasses looked like they would fall off his face at any instant.

After a series of knocks, the door opened and an older man stepped out. White whiskers from his beard curled down on his upper chest. The driver talked excitedly for a minute, and finally the older man pointed in one direction, followed by another direction. The two men shook hands, and the driver walked to the Land Rover and jumped back in.

"Meg, we are almost there. I can literally taste it."

"Charlie, how far do we need to go?" Meg asked.

"Not far," Charlie answered. "We go this way for four hundred yards," Charlie pointed in the same direction the old man had indicated, "and then we go there for less than three hundred yards. The old man was kind, and we can go on his land."

Charlie adjusted the rearview mirror, which kept jostling out of place due to the rough road. He glanced in the mirror and announced, “Kids, we are almost there.”

Charlie and Meg had three children—two boys, ages twelve and nine, and a girl, age six. None of the children cared to be on the car trip.

Charlie zoomed down the road and almost missed the turn.

“Relax, honey,” Meg said. “It has been there for two thousand years and isn’t going anywhere.”

“Okay.” Charlie slowed down and took a deep breath.

“This is boring!” one of the boys said. “I want to go swimming.”

“I know. We are doing this now because it is something I want to do. After I’m done here, we can go back to the hotel and you can go swimming, but only when I have seen what I want to see,” Charlie explained patiently.

“We are here for your father—no more moaning!” Meg supported her husband.

Charles Pierce was a professor at a large university in the Midwestern United States. He specialized in ancient civilizations, focusing on late ancient Roman history. He brought his wife and three children to northern England on a vacation adventure. However, as part of his work, he desperately wanted to visit Hadrian’s Wall. Charlie wasn’t sure why he felt the need for this quest, but the feeling was unrelenting. His children would just have to grin and bear it.

Charlie knew he had European heritage, but was unsure of the basis for that heritage. Were his forefathers Saxon, Norman, Briton, Celtic, or maybe even Roman? He doubted he would ever have the definite answer. *I know too much time has gone by to uncover the truth.*

Charlie reached a curve in the road, which was little more than a pathway. He jumped out of the vehicle just after it came to a complete stop. He had his backpack and camera in hand, and marched up the hill. In front of him were the remnants of the great wall. Charlie ignored Meg yelling at the children to behave, or at him to take a jacket. He was singularly focused.

Although that particular section of Hadrian's Wall was gradually deteriorating, it still showed evidence of being the great wall. Charlie walked slowly along the wall, touching as many of the blocks of stone as he could. His mind left the present and drifted back to consider what it was like to live during the time when Hadrian's Wall was the divide between Roman civilization and the barbarian worlds.

He moved to a large stone embedded into roughly the center of the wall. It was slightly recessed from the others. It stood out not only because of its size compared to the others, but because it was a slightly different shade of gray.

Charlie gazed intently at the surface of the stone; it was covered in markings. He pulled out a brush, magnifying glass, and cloth from his backpack. He poured water onto the cloth and began rubbing the stone's surface. It was hard to distinguish, but gradually the markings emerged.

Charlie carefully brushed and cleaned the stone using the wet cloth for several minutes. He stepped back and waited for the surface to dry. Meg joined him.

"You seem to have found something," she observed.

"I don't know yet. Perhaps it is nothing. But I'm curious."

The children quit throwing rocks at non-imaginary and imaginary objects and walked up to their mother and father. They had all learned that when their father was serious about work, it was a time for them to be serious as well.

"What is it, Dad?" the girl asked.

"Not sure yet, honey."

Charlie removed a large, thin sheet of paper from his pack and an odd-looking pencil. He held the paper over the inscription and began to shade in the indentations. The first and second times failed when he tried to decipher the markings. On the third try, he was confident that he had captured the essence of the markings. Charlie laid the paper on the ground and studied what was in front of him.

"I don't see anything on this paper, Dad," one of the boys remarked.

"I see it!" Meg said enthusiastically. She was familiar with her husband's work.

Charlie pulled his notebook from the pack and sketched what he saw on the paper in front of him. When he finished, he looked at his family.

"I believe the letter on the left is Latin, the Roman letter 'R.' To its right are the Roman letters 'M' and 'V.' In the center, I think that is an 'A.' A broken line runs between the 'R' and the 'MAV.' I don't know what that line means."

"Do you think vandals carved their initials in the stone?" Meg asked.

"No, the markings are too old. They are Roman. But I don't have the faintest idea who placed them there. Perhaps a builder of the wall left his mark. Perhaps the signer was a guard, maybe even a general."

The children took turns touching the large stone and the letters imbedded into it.

Charlie took over fifty photos of the stone, the wall, and the countryside. He carefully rolled the paper with the imprint and gave it to Meg. Charlie would later place the rolled paper in a tube when they returned to the car. He marked on a map the location of the stone and carefully placed all his tools in his backpack. He looked at his kids.

"You guys have been good. Get in the car and we can go find a place for an early supper. Maybe that old farmer knows of a place. I'm hungry, and we can go swimming later."

The children bounded down to the car. Charlie turned back and touched the stone one last time. He reached for Meg's hand.

"I have this feeling, Meg," he said softly, "that the writing was done by a Roman officer. He may have been famous, or perhaps not. It is a mystery to me; one about which we will never learn the truth."

Charlie looked at his children playing near the Land Rover. He smiled warmly at Meg and thought, *The Land Rover is not even two years old and it rattles. This magnificent Hadrian's Wall is nearly two thousand years old and it still stands. How many generations have come and gone between construction of the Wall and the Land Rover? Now it is my time to stand with this great Wall. Life is a perpetual river on which we have the brief privilege to travel. It is a privilege that I embrace.*

Charlie turned back to the stone as he spoke to Meg. "I would like to meet the signer of this carving and listen to him talk. I believe he would have a great story to tell."

THE END

"The people that walked in darkness have seen a great light; they that dwell in the land of the shadow of death, upon them hath the light shined."

—Isaiah Chapter 9, verse 2

Made in the USA
Middletown, DE
17 November 2021